PRAISE FOR MAD[...]
THE MAGIC OF FO[...]

"Readers may have the impression that they're enjoying a typical rom-com, but unexpected decisions open the way for a welcome twist we didn't even know we needed."

—*Booklist*

"*The Magic of Found Objects* is wonderful fun! Maddie Dawson is such an engaging and charming writer."

—Robyn Carr, #1 *New York Times* bestselling author

"With humor, tenderness, and some of the strongest female characters to ever grace a page, Maddie Dawson delivers with *The Magic of Found Objects*."

—Karen Hawkins, *New York Times* and *USA Today* bestselling author of *The Book Charmer*

"Written with loads of humor and heart, *The Magic of Found Objects* is a delightful, feel-good tale of friendship and marriage, motherhood and sacrifice, disillusionment and hope. Dawson takes the reader on a quest for the perfect life partner. Is it the kind, comfortable friend right in front of you, or does the universe have something more exciting in store? Maddie Dawson at her finest!"

—Amy Poeppel, author of *Musical Chairs*

"*The Magic of Found Objects* by Maddie Dawson is a lovingly crafted and heartwarming story of friendship, family, and being true to oneself. The charming and quirky characters burrow into your heart and make you laugh, cry, and cheer. A thoughtful and joyful read, perfect for book clubs. Dawson wrote another winner!"

—Amy Sue Nathan, author of *The Last Bathing Beauty*

"Dawson delivers her signature charm in *The Magic of Found Objects*. As Phronsie makes the decision of a lifetime, her free-spirited mother and practical, loving stepmother shape her ideas of life and love. Readers will long to slip inside the pages with these lovable characters written with flawless depth and a touch of sparkle. Dawson delivers a heartfelt read that stays with you long after the last page."

—Rochelle Weinstein, *USA Today* bestselling author

"Thirtysomething public relations professional Phronsie Linnelle is ready for a family—so she just might marry her platonic, lifelong best friend. A witty and wonderful romp through the mind of an entertaining woman who wants it all and has the guts to go out and get it. Bestselling author Maddie Dawson at her absolute best. You will love this hilarious, heartwarming book."

—Marilyn Simon Rothstein,
author of *Husbands and Other Sharp Objects*

"Maddie Dawson has a unique talent for telling a story that goes deep yet maintains a certain lightness throughout, at once giving readers an authentic human experience while making them still feel good about being human. *The Magic of Found Objects* is a warm, engaging novel that utterly charmed me. Don't miss it."

—Marybeth Mayhew Whalen, author of *This Secret Thing*

"Maddie Dawson has hit another one out of the park with this charming tale about what happens when your head tells you to settle but your heart keeps whispering something else. Funny, poignant, and beautifully clear-eyed, *The Magic of Found Objects* is a delightfully grown-up coming of age story, peopled with quirky, real-life characters who remind us that sometimes before we can open the door to the future, we must first open our hearts to the past."

—Barbara Davis, bestselling author of *The Last of the Moon Girls*

A HAPPY CATASTROPHE

"Dawson has created a truly quirky story, filled with a little bit of magic (think unicorn glitter and sparkles) and a lot of love . . . An optimistic, feel-good story that celebrates love, community, goodness, and the creation of family, however it might appear."

—*Kirkus Reviews*

"Alive with action, compelling and evolving characters, and screwball comedy, Dawson's latest will appeal to readers looking for a story that is both pleasurable and substantial. Personal growth is achieved by overcoming obstacles, and the ending is honest and satisfying."

—*Booklist*

"An inherently engaging and entertaining novel from cover to cover, *A Happy Catastrophe* by Maddie Dawson will prove to be an immediate and enduringly popular addition to community library Contemporary General Fiction collections."

—*Midwest Book Review*

MATCHMAKING FOR BEGINNERS

"A charming read . . . For fans of Liane Moriarty's *What Alice Forgot* or Aimee Bender's *The Particular Sadness of Lemon Cake*."

—*Library Journal*

"A delightful, light-as-air romance that successfully straddles the line between sweet and smart without ever being silly . . . The novel is simply captivating from beginning to end."

—Associated Press

Snap Out of It

ALSO BY MADDIE DAWSON

Snap Out of It

A Novel

MADDIE DAWSON

LAKE UNION
PUBLISHING

Text copyright © 2023 by Maddie Dawson
All rights reserved.

No part of this book may be reproduced, or stored in a retrieval system, or transmitted in any form or by any means, electronic, mechanical, photocopying, recording, or otherwise, without express written permission of the publisher.

Published by Lake Union Publishing, Seattle

www.apub.com

Amazon, the Amazon logo, and Lake Union Publishing are trademarks of Amazon.com, Inc., or its affiliates.

ISBN-13: 9781542039352 (paperback)
ISBN-13: 9781542039369 (digital)

Cover design and illustration by David Drummond

Printed in the United States of America

To Jim, who makes everything possible

CHAPTER ONE

Not that I'm bitter or anything—because I'm most certainly not—but thirty-five years later, the thing that still irks me is that my first husband left me for a woman who had him convinced she was a witch.

"I've been bewitched!" he said, as though this was a medical diagnosis that could not be disputed. "I have to be honest with you. I'm helpless. Helpless!" He was grinning, and even his black hair looked like it was standing up in little peaks of happiness. I was afraid he was going to break out in a soft-shoe.

It was a freezing-cold December morning, which is supposed to be a really wonderful time of the year—holiday cheer and all that—and ohhh, he was so smug in his guilty, proud way, giddy over the fact that his life was about to become fascinating, while I knew mine was going to get so much worse.

I knew who had bewitched him. His poetry instructor at the city college. Her name was Juliette Pierrot. The kind of woman who fluttered her closed eyelids when she spoke and who wore almost cartoonishly low-cut blouses and a bunch of silver necklaces that she called talismans. She thought Shakespeare and Robert Frost would show up if you simply chanted a few words to channel them.

Big deal, I remember telling him, all false bravado. I had a grandmother in backwater Florida who knew how to get rid of people's warts just by wishing them away, and who once actually transferred warts from one person to another simply by concentrating. Not exactly a world-class witch perhaps, but still, someone you wouldn't want to get on the wrong side of.

"I can't let you go off with a woman who imagines she's a witch just because she's got you all hot for her," I said, though it killed me having to even say those words. "You bring her around here, and *I'll* show her what's what."

Victor threw back his head and laughed, showing white, even teeth. "She'd never come here," he said. "I can't even think of how weird that would be."

"Too much reality for her, huh?" I said. "Well, some can take it, and some can't."

"Too much something," he said. And when he looked around the messy kitchen, at the spilled everything, and at our reflections in the gray windowpane that showed my curly, disheveled hair, it was clear that he saw none of it for the glorious mess that it was. We were no longer *us*.

I was twenty-five years old, and I had been up since four fifteen with the baby and had nursed her and sung her songs that made her laugh and had baked the cinnamon muffins that Victor had just wolfed down. And the heartbreaking thing was, I'd been so *happy* there in the middle of the night, so pleased and contented in our messy, unconventional life, thinking of what to get at the grocery store later and did Victor's mother need me to get her some seltzer water again, and oh yes, I needed to take the garbage cans down to the curb because it was garbage day, and also I had to remember that my mother had wanted me to come upstairs and bring her my recipe for lemon bars, and where was that recipe card—was it in the junk drawer? My mother lived on the third floor of our house, and his mother lived beneath us on the first floor, and I had my hands full, balancing these two mothers, one up and one down, both full of opinions and unhappiness and needs. I was the mistress of it all: juggling the moms, the baby, and—why not be honest here?—all the sex my husband insisted he needed just so he could live through each day. I did like that part.

I was a freaking domestic sorceress, presiding over a magical chaotic mess.

And then just like that, he casually crushed me like a paper cup.

I stood there looking at him, aware that certain circuits were already flicking off in my brain's central control panel. The trust was the first to leave, followed by all the pockets of love I held hidden inside, and then the hope trudged out, turning off the lights. It hurt a lot when the hope left.

Minutes ticked by and he was still talking and talking, not even noticing that I had gone dark. I looked toward the refrigerator, and I saw the little amber mound on the linoleum, dried now and hardened. It was a symbol of us, that hard little place. A whole year before, he'd dropped the bottle of maple syrup, and I'd asked him to clean it up, and he said I should clean it up, and I said I wouldn't, I was done with cleaning up after him and why was I the one who always had to clean up everything, and he said, well that was certainly tough toenails, because he wasn't going to, and then nobody ever did it, and it dried into something three-dimensional and smooth. Something your foot knocked against when you stood in front of the fridge.

It had become a funny story, a symbol of our relaxed, bohemian household. We pointed it out to friends, with a little jiggle of pride. *This is who we are. Aren't we amusing and fun and clever with the way we don't let stupid stuff bother us?*

But right then I knew that it didn't say that at all. That little hard mound of maple syrup really said we were hopeless idiots who couldn't even clean up a spill on the floor. Idiots who wouldn't ever agree.

What if you just let her have him? I heard myself think.

Give up? said my witchy grandmother in my head. *Are you talking about . . . giving him up . . . to a woman who can't even talk with her eyes open? Get your head on straight, child.*

"Victor," I said, taking a deep breath that started my heart beating again. "You are not leaving me for some wannabe witch, and that is that. I refuse to hear any more about the idea." I wiped up a pool of milk on the floor so that it wouldn't come to the same fate as the syrup, but I really did that only so I didn't have to look at his rosy, lovesick face.

"Well, *Billie*," he said in a voice strained from the need to explain the obvious, "we can't very well stay together if I'm in love with someone else. What kind of life would that be?"

I said, "I tell you what. You can leave in ten years, when Louise, whom I named for your sainted mother under great duress, is in middle school. Until then, you have to do your part."

He blanched and looked over at Louise, who was busy mashing up butter and cinnamon bits and rubbing them into her hair. I knew he was thinking that she would *never* be in middle school, and that even if she did ever get there, this sexy witch-who-wasn't-really-a-witch wouldn't still be waiting for him with her beguiling cleavage and silk scarves and her silver necklaces and the poetry.

"Also, you bastard, in case it has slipped your mind," I said, pulling myself up to my full height and letting my eyes go wild enough to match my spiky-ass hair, "I myself have probably inherited my grandmother's freaky witch genes, and I don't think you want to get tangled up with two witches, especially when I would bet that only one of us has legit genetic credentials, and that one happens to be the one you're married to."

Boom.

4

Six months later, he was gone.

I'd like to report that I vaporized him with my steely blue eyes or planted warts all over his body, but the simple truth is that one day he finished restoring the antique car he'd been working on since time immemorial, and he got in it and drove off—a Romeo heading to his bewitching Juliette. The two of them eventually moved to the coast of France to write poetry and make love by the sea and observe life as he thought it was meant to be lived: a wild, magical, childless adventure, so he said in his poems. *life at the bone.* Yep, that was the name of his book, written in all lower-case letters like he was some avant-garde darling. Critics hailed him as a "modern Walt Whitman, but with a female muse."

In case you were wondering if karma is a thing, I think this proves once and for all that it's *not*.

～

I turn over in bed. The sun is shining in my eyes, and the clock says it's nine o'clock. Tomorrow is my sixtieth birthday, and I am not happy to discover that I'm closing out my fifties by waking up to think about Victor Steidley, the man whom I got over thirty-five years ago. What the hell is he doing showing up in my head now?

Then I remember. He sent me a text that came in at midnight. First text ever from him. The last time I'd heard from him was seventeen years ago when he'd sent the last child support payment and had written me to congratulate himself on doing his fatherly duty. So what that he'd only bothered to see his daughter three times since the divorce? He was the hero. Father-of-the-Year material in his own mind.

I roll over and get my phone off the bedside table and click it back to life, find my reading glasses, and read it again, just in case I misremembered something about it.

But no. I remembered it perfectly.

juliette is dead

That's all. No explanation. No emotion. No punctuation or capital letters even. Just this one sentence. You'd think a poet could do a little better than that. But maybe, as usual, he was saving his best stuff for other people. Why even tell me, though? Why now?

I lie back on the pillows, rub my eyes. We used to sleep together in this very room. In fact, I stood right in that doorway over there watching him pack up all his shirts and pants and notebooks, dumping everything into the taupe, glossy, wheeled suitcases we received for a wedding present. Watched him walk down those stairs and out the front door, after he slammed it so hard that the glass rattled.

And after he left—when I heard his car roar off down the street—I gave myself exactly fifteen minutes of wallowing. It was all I had time for, because Louisa, his rickety mother who had already lost a husband and two children, was sobbing, and the baby was cutting some teeth so she was running a fever and wanted to be held all the time, and my mother was wringing her hands and wondering what was to become of me—and so after indulging in a fifteen-minute personal meltdown out on the back stairs, I got busy and threw out all the stuff he left behind, his golf clubs and his cuff links and his stupid tuxedo.

So there, I said. Good riddance to you, Victor Worst Husband Ever Steidley.

Anything he'd touched, anything that had meant anything to him at all—went right into the dumpster behind our house. I stomped back up the walk, squared my shoulders, and I told the moms we'd all be fine. That first night, my grandmother told me in a dream that I should put some salt in the corners, so I did. A week later, I tore down the stained beige curtains and put up new ones with magnolias on them, and then I repainted the living room a bright daffodil yellow, a color Victor never would have allowed.

I set up a new life, learning how to change the oil in the car and how to reason with repairmen. Then I went to work at a variety of crazy-ass, part-time, work-from-home jobs so I didn't have to be away from Louise. No full-time job for me. I took care of everyone, until Victor's mom passed away a few years later, and my own mom, who was younger and still had possibilities, moved away to one of the Virgin Islands, where she married a ship's captain and worked on her lifelong tan.

One night, after both moms were gone, I looked at my daughter's face, and a truth dawned on me: two people were not enough for a family. Two people weren't enough even to play a decent game of Go Fish. So I filled the house with new people, waifs and strays and nice folks I met at the bus stop. I started a little freelance taxi service and invited people home, if they were nice. I started cooking and baking for real. The kitchen table got bigger and bigger, with people crowded around it, and I lit candles and strung up fairy lights, and somehow I perfected a pie crust recipe that won some prizes, and I laughed and danced and cried and threw things sometimes, practiced yoga and meditation, got married two more times, was divorced once and widowed once, survived a bout of breast cancer and two rounds of pneumonia. I drew Louise close to me and raised her to be a lovely human being, yada yada yada, and that pretty much brings us to today, the day I am waking up to a text from Victor—and yes, I'll admit that there *is* a ridiculous, residual pang of regret, of course there is, but it's so minuscule a pang that it merely serves to remind me that I'm fine. Better than fine without him. Without *all* my husbands, really.

So there. I win.

I win because I am still living in the same lovely worn-out, comfortable house, with its wide wooden porch with the swing, its plain, workmanlike clapboard exterior, its oak tree in the front and the little patch of garden in the back.

And I win because I get to share this house with Calvin, who is ninety and has been here for eight years, and also Marisol and Edwin, both of whom are just the latest people to show up and move in while they wait to find out what life has in store for them.

I win because Louise—she of the cinnamon muffin in the hair experiments—is still the most inquisitive creature I know, and she is married now to a photographer named Leo, and even though they don't seem to be quite aware that if they're going to have children they should get on with it, they still have a fabulous life, busy being famous on Instagram as the duo @lulu&leo. She is intent on perfection, which can keep a person plenty busy—and if that's what she wants to do with her one wild, untamable life, then fine for her.

As for me, I won't even try anymore to be perfect, or to look good for men or chase love or romance or any of that stuff. I don't believe falling in love is good for people. That's the true fact of it.

My main win—and the reason I decide to shift my thoughts from Victor's message and now smile and bound out of bed—is because three months ago I learned something truly life changing. And that is this: you have to follow your impulses, even if one of them showed up on a night you got drunk with your best friend, and the two of you thought up a business that involves you dressing up in a stuffed bunny costume and helping strangers cure their heartbreak by carting away all their sad, lonely mementos. That is *exactly* the kind of unlikely impulse you should follow. Because life is too short to let it be uninteresting, and anyway, you never know whose life you might save as the Heartbreak Bunny. Maybe even your own.

So, take *that*, Victor. You, with your pretentious, unpunctuated text messages. I am going to forget that your little bulletin ever came in. And I am certainly *not* going to tell Louise.

CHAPTER TWO

The cop is young, looks like he's twelve or thirteen, but then they all do these days, don't they? I watch him through the rearview mirror as he approaches my car, squaring his jaw and touching his hat with its shiny brim glinting in the sunlight. Damn it. I have total confidence in my ability to charm an old cop—but a young one? He's so not going to be open to my particular brand of delightfulness.

The red and blue lights are wheeling around on top of his car. Other drivers slow down so they can more properly take in the spectacle of us.

And by us, I mean me.

I'm wearing the bunny head, you see. I make one more desperate attempt to remove it before he gets to my window, although of course he's already seen it, and it won't come off anyway.

This was not on my agenda for the morning. I'm on my way to a Heartbreak Bunny client, already in a hurry—and now this. I roll down the window. I still drive my 1971 yellow VW bug, the kind of car that makes a statement. One statement it makes is that it doesn't go in for those newfangled, push-button, electric windows. You have to *earn* your fresh air in this car.

"Good morning, Officer," I say, smiling even though he can't see my face through the bunny head.

"Uh. Ma'am, do you know why I pulled you over?"

"Well, it certainly couldn't be because I was speeding, not in this traffic," I say lightheartedly. "And last time I looked, my license plate was still on the back of the car, right?"

He blinks and clears his throat. I see his Adam's apple move up and down. He has the pointy kind. "Ma'am, I pulled you over because you have an object on your head, which I believe might be obstructing your vision."

"Why, thank you, Officer, for your concern," I say. "But it's not obstructing my vision. It's see-through."

He hesitates, then clears his throat manfully. "I'm going to need to see your license and registration, and, ma'am, would you please remove that . . . bunny head?"

"Well, here's the funny thing." I lean my head toward him and lower my voice, confidingly. "You're not going to believe this, but I can't."

"You can't?"

"No. It's gotten stuck. See?" I tug at it. "Stuck, stuck, stuck! In fact, if you have a pair of scissors handy . . ."

I had put the bunny head on two blocks back—is that what he saw? He probably saw the moment when I jammed the thing on my head and my car wobbled briefly—okay, it even drifted over into the other lane. But only briefly. Two seconds. Okay, *maybe* five. No one was ever in danger, even though the pickup truck next to me honked, and I righted my car and waved an apology to the other driver, who actually smiled and saluted me, and when I tried to straighten the bunny head, I could tell that it had gotten crunched up somehow. Damaged. I'd actually been fighting with it when I looked up and saw the lights flashing in my rearview mirror.

Officer Oliver Porter Jr. peers inside my car as if he's now looking for the things they warned him about at the academy—your various hypodermic needles and loaded weapons. But there's just the usual crap that always seems to follow me around: a stained coffee mug that says LOVE HURTS, my basket purse that's overflowing with paperwork, a pair of crummy winter boots, my down jacket, a pillow that says I AM THE WALRUS. Bunches of Starbucks napkins. A hair scrunchie. One bedroom slipper that fell out of my suitcase a month ago when I stayed overnight at Louise's house.

We look at each other. I twitch my bunny nose.

He shifts his weight to the other foot. "Ma'am, why *are* you wearing a bunny head?" he says.

"Oh! That. Well, I'm known as the Heartbreak Bunny. I'm on my way to see a client."

"The Heartbreak Bunny." He takes out a pad from his pocket and writes this down. "And what do you do as a . . . a . . . Heartbreak Bunny?"

"I help people get unstuck from love gone wrong. It's my job. Taking the heartbreak out of a breakup! That's the motto of the company. We might change it, but so far it works."

"Uh, and who is your client?"

"Well, Officer, now that is confidential. I don't go broadcasting the names of heartbroken people. Their lives are tough enough, wouldn't you say? What with all the memories crowding in and all."

He looks over his shoulder and then back at me. He has moisture forming on his upper lip, even though it's January and freaking cold outside. "Ma'am, you need to tell me what this is all about, or I'm going to have to bring you in."

"Well, Oliver, I'll be happy to tell you. It's about heartbreak obviously. Surely you've noticed that romantic love is a kind of poison," I say. "Not *poison* poison," I add quickly, because he is now blinking rapidly. I reach over and touch his arm. "Obviously not that."

11

He backs away. I should not have touched him.

I start speaking in my most cheerful, comforting voice. "Anyway, I help people get rid of the sadness from love gone wrong. By removing objects that they're using to torture themselves."

His brows form one straight line of fear. "Ma'am, what does the bunny suit have to do with torture?"

"Oh my goodness. Did I say 'torture'? Not torture. *Torture* was the wrong word. Misery! That's what I meant. You know how we humans all just so willingly *ingest* the message that love is all there is, and how we can't possibly live without it, blah blah blah. All those love songs! *Sooo* many love songs, playing in our heads for our whole lives! On the radio, on TV, in the movies. Love, love, love. Love is all there is! And what happens? We all buy into the dangerous idea that life isn't worth living if we don't have true love. And really, think about it. How often does love work out? Hardly ever. People are suffering. They're holding on to objects that they stare at and cry over, and so I come hopping in as the Heartbreak Bunny and remove all the things they're using to make themselves miserable."

He looks dazed. "You remove things? What, exactly, do you remove?" Ha! Of course, as a cop, he would fasten on to that part once we cleared up the torture thing.

"Oh, Oliver! *You* know. Like old photographs and limp old corsages and sometimes items of clothing. I don't believe in wallowing. I say, get over it. Get rid of the damn poison. In fact, the name of the company I invented is Snap Out of It, LLC."

He frowns, looks down at the ground as if he's searching for answers there on the pavement, and then he remembers that we didn't even accomplish Job One yet, the turning over of my documentation. "Ma'am, I asked you for your license and registration."

Oh dear. Maybe I shouldn't have used the word *poison.* Twice. And said the part about removing things. And torture.

I unfasten my seat belt so I can lean over and paw through the papers in my glove compartment. "My friend and I thought the business up," I tell him over my shoulder while I sift through various oil change receipts, junk mail, *more* napkins. What is it with me and napkins?

I finally hand him the documents. A stray Starbucks napkin has attached itself to my registration form, and I have to tug on it. "And just so you know, I wear the bunny suit so it doesn't seem like I'm an official *therapist* or anything," I tell him. "It's performance art, really. That's what my friend Kat and I thought would be the best way. We thought this business up about three months ago. You know how sometimes you just get a great inspiration, and you have to run with it?"

I omit the fact that we were really quite laughingly drunk when we thought it up, sitting around her living room after Bob, her rather stodgy, disappointing husband, went to bed, and we were gossiping about a friend of ours who was immolating herself on the altar of love for a much younger man. And we were shaking our heads and remembering our own romantic misadventures—my three marriages and her two—and how she and I had taken on so many fixer-upper men and loved them so good that we fixed them up, and then watched, baffled, as they took all that love and marched out the door to new partners, leaving us with heartbreak and children.

We got so excited that we stayed up until three in the morning, screaming with laughter, writing out the bylaws of Snap Out of It LLC, shrieking as we thought up newer and more outrageous ways we could combat wallowing. When we came up with the idea of the bunny suit, we just about lost our minds. Kat said *she*, for one, was far too shy to go to clients' homes, so she took the job of scheduler and coordinator, but I said I was happy to dress up in a bunny costume and go off to save the heartbroken. I'd be anonymous. A performer. I hadn't acted since high school. I was delighted.

When we got up the next morning, it still seemed like the most wonderful idea ever. We started designing posters and a brochure to hang up in coffee shops and on grocery store bulletin boards. I bought a bunny suit. By the end of the week, I'd made five bunny calls, and I'd loved every one of them.

He takes my paperwork back to the police car.

When he returns, I can tell by his face that things have taken a bad turn. He asks me to step out of the vehicle. There's the matter of some unpaid parking tickets.

And after *that* happens—with people passing by and waving and staring and shouting at me from their cars, and me waving back, doing my parade-float wave, still happy and confident that all would be well—things take *another* bad turn, and . . . well, it seems we have to go down to the police station.

And then, after *that*, we have to call Louise.

෧

I'll admit it. I first tried to reach Calvin to see if he could come to the station and rescue me. But he didn't pick up—probably out at the senior center, entertaining all the eager ladies there. And my other housemates, Marisol and Edwin, were both at work and I knew better than to disturb them. Then I tried Kat, but her phone went right to voice mail.

So, it has to be Louise.

I sigh. Right now, it being ten o'clock in the morning, Louise and Leo are probably sipping their artisanal coffee out of their hand-thrown mugs. They've posted their "woke up this way" photo, which is *de rigueur*, and now they're scrolling through their feeds to calculate how many followers they've lost or gained overnight, and planning what they'll showcase on the blog today to attract even more followers. Fashion? Minimalism? The beach in winter? Perhaps a post about their enviable romance?

They live in Branford, two towns away from me, in a modern, complicated, trapezoidal house on the beach, the kind of house perfect for somebody who wants to take photos of themselves in cavernous, cold rooms with slanted ceilings . . . or perhaps standing on the rocks gazing out to the windswept sea. It is not a place that you'd want to, you know, *live*.

I find this whole Instagram life to be mystifying, even horrifying. Being an influencer, the way I understand it, means that your hair always has to look good. Every minute of the day. That alone would be a dealbreaker for me. Also, you're pretty much required to take a million photographs of yourself, posing for them in different outfits and moving around klieg lights like they do at big magazine photo shoots—only there's no full-time staff: it's just you. And then *after* that, you need to write clever posts and edit the pictures and post them on the internets—on *all* the internets—and then after *that*, you need to respond to the followers who write you to say how gorgeous you looked in that flowy peach-colored gown thing, and they need to know where they could buy such a thing (which is, after all, the point), and they tell you oh, how lucky you are to have such a handsome husband, and how the two of you look so much in love. And also, they tell you that post you wrote was so, so inspiring. Those quotes! The way you made that magnificent latte with that incredible machine! And how clean and minimalist everything is in your perfect, curated little life!

Bah. I would frankly rather live in a tent in the woods and use an outhouse every day than have Louise's existence. I prefer in-person conversations you make with real flesh-and-blood people in line at the grocery store, which don't involve any Wi-Fi. But Louise contends that the blog has brought so many people to her life, people who care about beauty and serenity, people who are her true friends. And that *this* is connecting at its best.

But—well, which one of us is currently sitting in the back room of the police station in need of a ride home? So maybe she wins this round.

❦

"Good morning, honey," I say when she answers her phone. I talk fast, knowing it's probably best to just get to the facts as quickly and simply as possible. "I know you're very busy, but would you mind terribly coming to the police station and picking me up and then taking me over to the impound place to pick up my car?"

There's a silence. "Did you say you're at the police station?"

"Yes."

"Mom! Are you okay? What happened to your car?"

"Oh, it's nothing, really. I got pulled over, and the car was towed away to the car jail, and all I need from you is a ride to go get it."

"What in the *world* is going on? Isn't it rather early in the morning for you to be in all this trouble?" she says.

"It was all a misunderstanding, really. Are you coming or not?"

"Please don't tell me this has anything to do with you being the Heartbreak Bunny. *Does* it?"

I stay quiet.

"You got pulled over because you were dressed like a stuffed bunny, didn't you?"

"The head got stuck. The cop thought I couldn't see out of it. And then there were some unpaid parking tickets. It's not a big deal."

"It sounds like a big deal, if you ask me."

"Look, did I judge you that time you ran out of gas three days in a row and had to be rescued?"

"Mom! That was when I was sixteen and new to driving."

"You know what? I'll just call an Uber."

"No, I'll come. Meet me outside? Or do I have to sign something that says I'll be responsible for you and not let you drive with a bunny head anymore? Because—"

"I'll meet you outside."

Fifteen minutes later, she pulls up in her Tesla, and I can see her shaking her head and laughing long before she even reaches me. I'm standing there on the sidewalk dressed in my bunny suit with the head now tucked safely under my arm—thanks to a pair of scissors that the dispatcher allowed me to use.

"Look at you!" Louise says. "Oh my God, Mom! Have you *seen* yourself? Do you really go out in public this way?"

I slide into the passenger seat and put the bunny head on the floor. "I was on my way to a bunny call. What else was I going to wear?"

"I don't know," she says, squinting at me. "Your regular clothing, maybe? Who goes around dressed like a stuffed animal? Do you realize I can't tell anyone what your new project is? I haven't even told *Leo* what you're doing! He'd think you'd lost your mind."

"That's fine with me. Don't tell him. He doesn't need to know."

She looks at me and sighs. Then she pats me on the leg. "I'm sorry. I'm not being helpful, am I? Tell me what happened this morning."

"The bunny head just somehow got stuck while I was driving, and when I was trying to fix it, the car swerved a mere *two inches* into the other lane, and wouldn't you know, a cop was right there. Then it turned out he was brand new on the force and didn't understand that two unpaid tickets and a stuck bunny head does not a criminal make. So it eventually all worked out, and I think I've even convinced him that romantic love is rubbish, so it was all good, except for my car getting towed, *and* I've got to reschedule all of today's clients and fix the bunny head. So could you just drive, please?"

"Mamakins," Louise says.

"What, honey?"

"How long are you planning to keep doing this?"

"Getting picked up by the police? I'm hoping this is going to be the last of it."

"No. The bunny thing. Whatever this is you're doing."

"Oh, I don't know. Until it's not fun anymore? Could we go?"

She looks in the rearview mirror and puts her car in reverse. It rolls backward with a barely audible purr. I can see stress in her beautiful blue eyes. She's all made up, of course, even though it is very early in the day, and her glossy brown hair is piled up on top of her head in a glorious bun, and she looks perfect, because she has to: people recognize her. I've seen it happen. People come up to her and say, "Ahhhh, you're Lulu!" And by the way their eyes shine, you can just tell they think they're in the presence of royalty. They scrutinize her outfit, her makeup, her hairstyle—and possibly her mother, unless her mother has had the good sense to duck out of the way.

"Well, may I ask you this?" she says, turning left out of the police station. "Are you doing this bunny thing for the money? Are you strapped for cash? Because if you are, I was thinking—"

"First of all, you know I don't do anything just for the money," I say. "I do what makes me happy."

I watch her face, but she shows no sign of knowing any such thing. She says, "I was only thinking that *if* you need money, you could stop doing this, and I'd hire you to work with us on the blog. Join our team. You know?"

"Darling," I say. "No, no, no! God, no. Thank you, but I love my life just like it is."

"What is it exactly that you like about what you're doing? If you can put it into words, that is. This *feeling* you get dressing up like a bunny rabbit and hopping into people's houses."

"Well. If you must know, there's something delightful about letting people open up their broken hearts to me, and then helping them take action. Okay? I'm getting more clients every day, and people are appreciative, and I love doing it. This is some little magic thing I manifested, and I'm proud of it."

"I wish," she says, "that everybody in the world would call a moratorium on the word *manifesting*. My whole Instagram feed is about people manifesting this and that. The world is not made of magic. You're not manifesting anything. With all due respect, you're dressing up in a freaking *costume*, and—"

"Which gives people a kind of freedom and anonymity," I say.

"—which gives *you* some freedom and anonymity," she says. "Not them. You can see who *they* are."

"Well, point taken," I say. "But whatever. It works for them. That's all I can say. I like it. It's my own brand of everyday magic." I look out the window, start humming to myself. Why *didn't* I call an Uber?

"If you want to help people get over their bad love affairs, why don't you go back to school and get a degree in social work or psychology or something? Why do you have to do it the crazy way—taking stuff out of their homes!"

"That is such a good question," I say sarcastically. "I'll give it my full consideration just as soon as I get back from my happy time hopping around people's houses and removing their bad memorabilia. Which will be tomorrow since I've already wasted today's sessions."

"Also, I frankly don't see why you want to warn people away from love. Just because you've had three husbands doesn't mean that other people can't make a go of marriage! I don't get why you think this is your job, being anti-love."

I make a mental note again to *never* ever tell her that her father texted me this morning. Really, she would make things so much more complicated than they need to be.

"I'm not anti-love. I'm helping people move on."

"Oh, Mama. I wish—listen, please think about my offer. I make enough money to support you. You could help us with the blog, and you wouldn't have to do any of this bunny stuff—"

"*Thank* you, honey. You are just *the best*, coming to pick me up! And to hardly give me any lecture at all, whatsoever!"

"Mamakins."

"Ah, ah, ah!" I hold up my hand. "Don't spoil it now. You kept the lecturing down to under two minutes, and we don't want to break the record now."

Three silent minutes later, as she's pulling into the impound lot, she says, "By the way—we'll see you tomorrow night for your birthday dinner, right? Aaaand"—she smiles—"I have a surprise for you."

Wait. Was I coming to her house tomorrow night? Thursday is known as Martini Thursday at my house—the night Calvin and Marisol and Edwin and I cook recipes from the original 1931 *Joy of Cooking* cookbook, the more outrageous the better, and Calvin makes cocktails reminiscent of the 1940s, which he says is when men and women really knew how to live. We all get dressed up and bring out the crystal and the good silver, and we turn on big band music, and it's my favorite night of the week.

"You forgot, didn't you?" she says, seeing my dismayed expression. "But you *always* come to our house on your birthday. We always blog about it. The fans love you!"

"Honey, I—I tell you what: Why don't you and Leo come to us? We're making a mushroom soufflé with sweetbreads for dinner, whatever the hell that is. And the cocktail is called purple passion, which you have to admit sounds fun."

She frowns. "But didn't you hear me say there's a surprise?"

"A surprise? Is it—? Wait. You're not . . . are you . . . *pregnant?*"

Her eyes flash, but she tries to make her voice light and singsongy, like a kindergarten teacher talking to a recalcitrant child. "Of course not. No baby for at least two more years, remember! We've got too much work to do."

"Oh, okay. Sorry." I'm pretty sure I know the real reason: Leo isn't a baby guy. I bite my tongue and suppress my impulse to remind her of the realities of fertility and how you can't control it as much as you might like. Why start an argument on a day when we're already tackling so many touchy subjects? Anyway, it's none of my business.

It's simply that I was once the expert on this particular human, and she always said she wanted children. There's something so fragile about her this morning, some little shadow behind her eyes. Like she's trying so hard to push something down. Maybe—I'm not sure—but maybe life is asserting itself, showing her that you can't ever *really* manage everything to the *n*th degree, as she believes.

"Stop it," she says. "You're doing that worry thing again. I'm fine, Mom. You're the one we have to be concerned about."

She gives me her Instagram smile, and I smile back and lean over and kiss her on the cheek.

⌒

The house is quiet when I get home, so I go upstairs and sit down on my yoga mat and breathe. Call back to my body all my energy particles that feel like they've been flung about. Deeeeep yoga breaths.

The truth is, I probably deserve all of Louise's concern. Life might have been the slightest bit haphazard when she was growing up, what with all the people coming in and out of our house. After Victor left us, I was determined not to take a nine-to-five job that would mean full-time daycare for her while I was gone. Instead, I rented out rooms and gave classes in our living room: yoga and memoir writing and calligraphy and—oh, anything, whatever anybody wanted to learn. Our house was always filled to the brim.

That's why a whole bunch of people were on hand to help me raise my sweet daughter over the years—always folks moving in and out, coming and going, with their zigzagging lives, their tears, and their laughter—mostly laughter, in my memory, but perhaps Louise remembers it differently. Sometimes I'd catch her eye across the table during some spirited debate about politics or women's rights or who left the top off the ketchup bottle, and I'd have to blink three times to reassure her. That was our secret signal, the thing that meant: *Mama says every-thing's okay.*

I wanted to raise her to be brave, to have adventures. I had been raised by absentee parents who seemed too busy for me and left me with my grandmother. Maybe that's why I was in love with taking care of Louise. Some days I'd let her skip school just for the fun of it, and we'd hang out together. One summer, on an impulse, we packed our tent and sleeping bags and drove across the whole United States because Louise didn't know such a thing was possible. We sang songs in the car and camped out in parks and ate in diners and made friends with truck drivers and waitresses. Another summer, we drove to Cape Cod, and because I had forgotten to make reservations at a hotel and they were all booked up, we slept on the beach, listening to the waves crashing while we counted the shooting stars. We set out on hikes with wild abandon, until the time we were climbing a mountain and talking so much that we lost the trail and had to be rescued after dark by a battalion of friendly park rangers.

Despite the need for rescue, everything turned out perfectly. Didn't she see it that way, too?

Maybe not. When she was nine, I noticed that she started alpha-betizing the spices in the kitchen cabinets and ironing the pillowcases. Next, she scrubbed all the old pots and pans until they shone and then painted the porch railing white. When she was eleven, she mended my patchwork skirt, sewed new curtains for the kitchen, and scraped up the famously hardened pool of syrup on the floor. All without making a big deal of it.

She was just getting ready to be perfect, that was all. You don't need a degree in psychology to know that she was creating her own little line of defense against the chaos that swirled around me.

Then there was romance. Yes, I tried to keep the men to a mini-mum, but I like men, and so there *were* occasional guys who came for dinner and then stayed on afterward, too. They danced the jitterbug with us in the kitchen, told jokes, helped Louise with her homework, cooked breakfast. Nice guys who kissed what needed kissing on me. They didn't stick around, though.

Then, the year Louise turned thirteen, loneliness and longing swept into my heart like a monsoon, flattening every wall I'd carefully constructed. Suddenly I realized I couldn't stop thinking about the swimming instructor at the Y. I was obsessed with his little orange bathing suit and his deep brown eyes. Hell, let me just be honest here: I lusted over everything about him, including the curve of his ear and the way he helped kids in and out of the pool. One day he happened to brush against my arm, and an electric current rattled me all the way down to my fillings.

Peter Gagney.

We got married that summer in a ceremony that Louise designed—with baskets of bluebells and tulips and garlands of lights and lace, and white tablecloths that people wrote their wishes for us on.

My wish—I see it so clearly now—was that I could have a husband without all the complications of true love. I envisioned a kind of marriage of convenience, one that would allow us to live side by side, while I stayed just the same.

I expected Peter would want to move into our lovely three-story row house and assume a place with us and all our crazy tenants. I figured he'd be willing to fill the position of "husband and father" in our already intact little household, as though he was somebody we hired. But he was looking for a little more than that from marriage. He thought we should buy a new house together, in the suburbs, a place with an attached garage and maybe an aboveground swimming pool. Failing to convince me of that, he thought that at least I could kick out the tenants and we could have my house all to ourselves—like "normal married people," he said. But I couldn't even do that much.

So, although I wanted all the stability and sex he offered—and oh my God, he was brilliant in bed—in the end, the force field of The

Louise-and-Billie Team was more than Peter Gagney's sexy handsomeness could penetrate, and we drifted apart. So meaningless, those words *drifted apart*, when it was really a kind of a crash landing.

I could see that I wasn't going to be loved, one on one, for who I was. But I had my daughter. I had a big life. I let him drift off. I'd find somebody else later on, maybe. Or not.

And I did. Ten years ago, I got married for the third time. Desmond Harrison. "Third time's the charm!" everyone said. "It'll be great!"

I square my shoulders now. Get up off the yoga mat. Rub my aching knees.

Desmond was going to be my companion through old age. He'd stay with me and tell me jokes and never ask more of me than I could give.

My phone dings from my purse, and I fish it out.

she died in her sleep fifty-seven years old

CHAPTER THREE

The next day, after I've managed to repair the bunny head and freshen up the costume, I go off happily to do my Heartbreak Bunny calls. No better way to spend a birthday than doing what you love, right? Before I leave, though, I make Calvin, who turned ninety last June, promise to stay home and let in the plumber, and to please swear, by all that is good and holy in the world, *not* to try to do the work himself, which is his habit. The basement floor has a perpetual puddle over by the washing machine, and I caught him heading down with a toilet plunger and a sledgehammer yesterday, wearing his high-water pants and his usual starched white dress shirt tucked in. I had to waylay him, bribe him with brownies not to go any farther. He was offended, I could tell, and now he looks at me reproachfully.

"Why do you always have Reggie here? You know I could do this work," he says. "I could save us a bundle of money, you know." Calvin worked as a Yale professor of literature, it should be noted. Specializing in Chaucer. He was not a plumber.

I tell him the truth: "You're too talented for us to waste on these little projects. We have to save you for the good stuff." And then the other truth: "Besides, Reggie needs us."

"Before you know it, you'll be giving him a room," Calvin says. "I don't know why you don't just go ahead and adopt him or something. He eats lunch here half the time. He shouldn't even be charging you for fixing leaks at this point."

"He doesn't charge much," I say.

"You should charge *him* for lunch," he says.

Then, before I leave, he says, "Show me your bunny hop procedure, please."

"Calvin . . ."

"I need to see how you're progressing. Three months of Heartbreak Bunnying and I want to see how the hopping is going. Are you authentic, or are you playacting?"

So, I hop for him, which makes him laugh.

"Playacting," he pronounces. "For heaven's sake, put your hands up under your chin. That's how the real bunnies do it."

"But real bunnies," I point out, "don't have bags of stuff they're carrying."

"Maybe you should be a Heartbreak Kangaroo," he says. "Then you'd have a pouch."

I'm in the driveway getting into my car when he runs out onto the porch waving his arms. "I can't believe I forgot to wish you a happy birthday!" he calls. "You're sixty years old today, and I didn't say a thing!"

"Do we have to tell the whole neighborhood?" I call back.

"We do! You're sixty and proud! You're a proud sixty-year-old bunny who only needs a little extra help with the hopping!"

I'm shaking my head as I pull away from the house.

❧

My first client is Amanda Pearson, and I can tell right away that this is going to be my very favorite kind of Snap Out of It call. For one thing, she's got a girlfriend with her—always good to have moral support—and they have already drunk two cups of apparently *very* high-caffeine coffee and have already packed up a box of the ex-boyfriend's stuff. They brush aside the consent form I hand Amanda; she signs it without even giving it a glance.

"I know what you do," she says breezily. "You were at my friend Elaine's house last month."

She tells me what I already know from her requisition form: she got ghosted by a guy she'd been seeing for eight months. Without any explanation, he quit responding to texts and didn't answer his phone, and when she drove over to his apartment just to make sure that he wasn't dead and being eaten by his cats, she saw him leaving with another woman. He didn't even look over in her direction. Not until she roared out of the parking lot, leaving a trail of rubber, she says. *That* he noticed.

Sometimes the victims of ghosters seem shell-shocked and unsure, with a look in their eyes of someone who's been in a hit-and-run. But Amanda Pearson appears energized by the prospect of ceremonially tossing this guy out on his ass.

And her friend Beth is *very* into it. "Take tweezers if necessary, and let's get every last bit of him out of here!" she says. "I only flew in last night, and already I've discovered a comb with his hair in it. On her *dresser*, by the way, where she sees it every day."

Amanda ducks her head. She has short black hair in a bob with a curtain of bangs, and she's wearing leggings and a Cornell sweatshirt and carrying around a big mug of coffee. "That happens to be *my* comb," she says to me. "But Beth noticed that it had four of his red hairs in it, so it's now considered an enemy device."

"Damn right it is," says Beth. "Dude spent enough nights here to pollute the place with his body hairs. I've been getting weeping phone calls from this poor woman here for weeks. And now she's arguing over the right to keep this comb." She looks over at me. "Is it normal for people to be so resistant?"

"I'm not resistant," says Amanda, laughing. "I want him gone! I just overlooked the four hairs is all. Look—" She points to the box she's packed, the stuff all stacked neatly in piles. In fact, her entire apartment looks as though it was decorated by an emotionally healthy person—shiny oak floors with floral throw rugs, bookshelves filled with books and ivy plants, furniture color coordinated and clear of clutter. "I've gone through the whole place and gotten rid of everything I could think of. Even his garlic press."

"Well, the garlic press," says Beth. "Does it really have to go? I mean, that does not scream romance to me."

"Well, it does to me," says Amanda. "He always waved it around and said it was proof that he was a better cook than me, because *he* had this expensive, la-di-da garlic press while I was content to use a *knife*." She looks at both of us. "It's a thing, believe me."

I put it in the box. "Any object that reminds you of the relationship should be expunged. And by the way, *expunge* should be your favorite word now, just like it is mine."

"Oooh, do you mind if I make a little video of this?" says Beth. "I want to show our friends back home, because they are not going to *believe* a bunny came over."

Amanda and I shrug and say it's okay, and I have a moment of feeling relieved that my face won't be in the actual video. Who will ever know it's even me?

We fill the box with a couple of photographs, a card with hearts on it, a bulky men's sweater, his razor, a pair of aviator sunglasses, a crew sock. (Stunning, really, how many crew socks show up in Get the Hell Out piles. I think men must shed them, leave them under beds, like little spies.)

Beth films while I hop around Amanda's very neat apartment, looking for things that might have escaped notice. Things that she might be secretly clinging to. A scrap of paper with his number on it. A note from him on the bulletin board over her desk. I can usually ferret these things out immediately.

"Anything you've hung on the walls? Any of these pictures his?"

"Nope, all of them are mine," she says. "Pre-Matthew."

"Okay, then, can we look at your electronics?"

"My electronics?"

"Yes. Facebook, Instagram, Netflix accounts? We don't want you making the mistake of tuning in to see his new life. He's got to be unfollowed. Any of your passwords he knows need to be changed."

At this she turns a little pale, but she sits down and opens her laptop and shows us she's already unfriended him and unfollowed him on Facebook, Twitter, Instagram.

"Netflix?" I say.

She hesitates and then looks up at us with a stricken expression.

"Oh, *honey*," I say. "I thought so. You share the same account, don't you? And I bet you've been checking to see what movies he watches."

"It's just that—well, I showed him some of my favorite romantic comedies, and now I want to know if—"

"If he's watching them with someone else. Very common," I say in my most comforting Heartbreak Bunny voice.

Amanda takes a deep breath and closes her eyes for a moment. "Okay. Yeah. I did do that. He watched *When Harry Met Sally* and *You've Got Mail.* Which he didn't even like when we watched them together."

"Okay then. If this is your account, change the password. And if it's his, cancel it and get your own Netflix account. Case closed. Expunge. Expunge. Expunge."

She changes the password.

I leave her the copy of the contract and I take the box of stuff with me when I go. She's going to be fine.

Kat calls me when I'm on the way to my next client.

"Well, girl, we have a new twist on our hands," she says. "Have you looked at the requisition sheet for your second call today?"

"Briefly. Guy named Joey Davis. Twenty-three. Girlfriend left him four months ago?"

"Yeah, routine. Except that I just found out he isn't the one who called for our services. His friend Zach did, impersonating him."

"Well, this *is* a new wrinkle," I say.

"I know," Kat says. "I just got off the phone with Zach. I think his conscience was bothering him. Apparently, Joey Davis knows something's up, but he doesn't know the whole deal. So, I don't know how you're going to manage. If it doesn't look like it's working, I think you should just bail."

"I'll manage," I say.

As soon as I get to the apartment building, I read the sheet more closely. Joey Davis is said to work from home fixing computers, and he hasn't gone on a date since his girlfriend left him. Mostly doesn't leave the house. Hygiene issues. "I am stuck, stuck, stuck, and I need help. I may even be hoarding her underwear. And oh yeah, I stink to high heaven." I can almost picture his friend laughing to himself as he wrote that last part.

Okayyy. I put on the bunny head and straighten it in the rearview mirror, grab one of the bags emblazoned with our Snap Out of It logo, and march myself up the cracked sidewalk, past the boxwood hedges that crowd the windows, to the main entrance. The steps are crumbly, and last fall's leaves litter the sidewalk. In a row of mailboxes with black buzzers, I find the one that says **J. DAVIS**, and I close my eyes for a moment and say a little blessing.

There's a silence after I press the buzzer, but then a male voice says listlessly, "Yo. Whaddya want?"

I put on my most cheerful voice. "Hellooo? I'm Billie the Heartbreak Bunny. Here to see Joey Davis."

"You're . . . what now?"

"The Heartbreak Bunny."

"No thank you. I'm not in the market for heartbreak."

"Actually, I'm here to take heartbreak away," I say.

He gives a low laugh. "Wait. Are you the bunny that Zach sent over? I thought that was a joke."

"I believe I am, yes."

"He didn't say anything about *heartbreak*. He just said there was a bunny coming over."

"Yeah. Well, he left that part out, I guess."

Long silence while he apparently thinks this over. I stand on one foot and then the other. "All right," he says with a sigh, and the buzzer honks at me.

I straighten my bunny head and then go inside. There in the entrance hall, waiting for me, is a skinny, disheveled, dark-haired guy wearing a blue hoodie that says BITE ME on it and baggy sweatpants that once may have been gray.

He looks at me like I'm merely disappointment number four hundred today.

"*You're* the bunny Zach sent? Is this some kind of joke?"

"Hi. Not a joke. I'm Billie the Heartbreak Bunny," I say, reaching into my bag and handing him the paperwork I give clients. "If you could read this and sign it, please, before we get started."

He takes the paper and frowns at me as he steps back into his apartment. "I thought Zach was sending somebody to cheer me up. You know what I mean? No offense, but you're an old lady in a bunny suit. A stuffed animal."

"Were you expecting an actual talking rabbit then?"

"No. *You* know," he says.

Uh-huh. I get this sometimes; people thinking I'm going to be a representative of the Playboy franchise, which as far as I know, does not send out bunnies to people's homes, but it's amazing how many young guys think this could be a thing.

"Also: How do you know I'm an old lady? I'm completely covered up."

"Your voice."

"Are you trying to tell me I have an old-lady voice?"

"No offense but yes."

"Well, anyway. The service I'm offering to you is going to do you more good than . . . that other kind of bunny."

"You're sure of that, huh?"

"Not positive, but I'm the bunny you've got. So, there's that. Please. Read the paper," I say. "It'll tell you everything you need to know."

The paper explains that I'm there as a representative of the Snap Out of It Company LLC, and that I will only address the client in the persona of Billie the Heartbreak Bunny, not as my real self. I am there to assist the client in ridding the premises of unwelcome reminders of a love gone wrong, and that I will collect items to be removed. These items may include but are not limited to photographs, memorabilia, items of clothing, jewelry, letters, wall hangings, appliances, sex toys, books, records, CDs, DVDs, and anything else that may be preventing the client from rejoining life. Items will be stored for at least thirty (30) days at the headquarters of the Snap Out of It Company (aka my basement), after which they will be disposed of or donated, at the discretion of the company. The client will be informed as to the disposition of such items and at that time may request that they be returned to the client or sent to the offending party. We, however, recommend discarding them and not having them returned for a second, often tragic, look.

Unlike Amanda, who merely signed and pushed this piece of paper aside, Joey Davis examines it very closely, brows knitted together, and then he says I might as well come in. Looking around, I can tell that he is clearly what Kat and I have labeled a Level Three case, which is the next to the most severe. I usually deal with Level Twos at the most. This whole place has the acrid smell of lack of effort, and the papers and books scattered everywhere practically scream their neglect. At a glance I see coffee cups (three) with mold floating in brown liquid; a vintage, half-eaten bologna sandwich on a paper plate; and a torn green cushion that has left the couch and decided to rest against the wall, next to a tower of Bud Light beer cans, threatening to crash to the ground should there be any sudden movements.

I look at him reading and frowning. He obviously hasn't bathed lately, and that sweatshirt looks like it may have melded to his skinny, concave chest. His big brown eyes, sunken and red-rimmed, scan the page, and then he looks up at me with suspicion. "You're going to take stuff? Her stuff?"

"That is the purpose, yes."

"I thought I was supposed to be getting cheered up."

"You'll have to talk with Zach about that, why he thought this would be good for you," I say. "But I think he's concerned about you and wants to help you move on. Now, if you agree and if you're ready to get started, I'm going to hop around and look things over. You can talk to me, but I will speak to you only as the Heartbreak Bunny. If there are objects that you wish to have removed, put them over here. If not, I'll look around and discern what I think might help you most by their removal."

He looks shocked.

"Okay?" I say.

"Whatever."

Oh, there are objects all right. I hop over to the bookcase and immediately collect the two framed photos, one of a ski trip—Joey with his arm around a slight and squinting blonde girl in a powder-blue snowsuit—and another in which the same girl, in an evening gown, is grinning into the camera and holding up some kind of certificate. Apparently, he had himself an *award-winning* woman.

Hopping back to the couch, I pick up a pink satin slipper peeking out from a cushion. On the coffee table there's an ashtray with cigarette butts with lipstick on them. A black lace thong, right out there in the open. He winces.

I scoop up the thong without comment and put it in the bag while he leans against the wall, with his arms folded, looking listless.

"Where's this stuff going?"

"Did you read the paper I gave you?"

"Yeah."

"Then you know."

"Could I—you know—ever get it all back?"

"That's explained in the paper, too."

"This is bananas!" he says. "What if I can't sleep without this stuff here?"

I put down the bag and look at him. He may actually be a Level Four, now that I see him up close. I've never had a Level Four until now.

"May I go into the bedroom?" I say.

He lets out a big, defeated exhale. "Knock yourself out. I don't care."

He follows me down the little hallway into a tiny bedroom, dark and musky smelling, like unwashed hair. I turn on the overhead light, a fluorescent ring that immediately starts buzzing, so I flip it off and hop over and open the blinds. The sunlight streams in. A mattress with jumbled-up brown plaid sheets sits in the center of the room, littered with papers and books and a laptop computer with Megadeth decals all over it. Next to the window is an exercise bike tipped over and draped with laundry. A woman's black cardigan sweater hangs off one of the handlebars, dragging on the floor, shedding sequins. On the bed is a teddy bear. I give him a look.

"Hers?"

He nods, bites his lip.

I tiptoe through a bunch of wadded-up T-shirts and some Starbucks cups and open the closet. A red kimono hangs there alone, and on the floor, next to some thoroughly worn male sneakers, is the mate to the pink slipper and a dangling chandelier earring.

Into the box.

He clears his throat. "She left me for her boss. Did Zach tell you that part?"

I shake my head. Kat and I decided at the outset that, beyond discussing objects, I wouldn't engage in discussions about the breakup. I am not a therapist. That's why, when we thought up this gig, we decided I'd dress in an animal costume to make that delineation clear. *I am not here as your friend or as a licensed professional. I am a performance artist.*

"So, bunny. Do you want to know her name?" he says.

I manage to stay silent.

"Well, I want to tell you. It's Saucy."

I give a brief, neutral nod, but I can feel my eyes widen underneath the bunny head.

"She was hooking up with her boss for a whole six months before I found out about it. And you know what I hate the most, besides everything?"

I put the sweater in my bag. A shower of sequins falls to the bottom.

He takes a deep, shaky breath. "What I hate the most is that he's a really terrible person, one of those people who rips off other people and thinks he's so smart for doing it. And he gets rewarded for it, so he'll never learn. He gets whatever he wants. And one day he decided he wanted her, and so he stole her."

I look over at him and shrug. Now if we were friends—or if he were sitting in my kitchen, for instance—I would tell him an important fact of life, that outside of kidnapping situations, people don't get stolen.

But I'm a Heartbreak Bunny, not a friend, so I just tug open a sticky bureau drawer. Inside I find a jumble of men's underwear and T-shirts, and curled on top is a neon-green bra with a python print—ugh! I pick it up between two fingers and put it in the bag.

"Hey, stop!" he says. "That bra. Don't put that in! In fact, all this stuff . . . wait a second. What if she comes back? What if she realizes that guy is a jerk and she's sorry?"

I shake my head at him, open the next drawer.

"No! Take that bra back out of the bag. I mean it!" he says.

I turn and look at him, tilt my head. He's pointing at the bra, so I shrug and put it back in the drawer. I'm picking through the next drawer, a jumble of mismatched socks and T-shirts, when I hear something.

When I turn around, I see him on the floor with his head on his knees. I open drawer number four, which seems to be empty except for a heating pad and a knee brace. It's possible this was her knee brace, I suppose. But I leave it and glance over at him. He's crying like a five-year-old who just found out his mom isn't coming home again, and that ice cream has been discontinued worldwide.

I stand perfectly still. Perhaps I have crossed some sort of line here. "Listen," I say. "I'm not supposed to discuss your relationship, but I want you to know that you really are going to be fine."

"How do you know that? What if I'm not? What if she never comes back?"

I put down the bag and sigh. "Honey, she *isn't* ever coming back, and you still are going to be fine. You will. These things—they get better. You'll be stronger for it. In fact, you'll look back on this one day and be so glad you didn't end up with this one. Trust me."

He sniffles, which is sort of mucous-y and disgusting, so I walk over to the bedside table and get him a tissue. There are a million balled-up tissues on the table, as well as three pictures of Saucy—which, I'm sorry, sounds like the stage name for an exotic dancer.

"And another thing, have you ever thought to be concerned about what kind of parents would name their human child Saucy? I mean, what is up with that? What did they name their son—Trouble?"

He makes a sound.

"Growing up with those parents, she may have been deprived of a moral compass and sense of reality, and so of course she would let you believe she got *stolen* by someone else, and leave you here in a heap, believing it." He's quiet, so I say, "Well? You should at least consider that."

"I want you to put everything back like it was," he says flatly. He blows his nose.

Something gets to me about the way he blows his nose, like a child does, squinching his eyes closed. And then I see his pale little knobby wrists sticking out of the sleeves of his sweatshirt, and my heart bends a little bit toward him, and I sigh. "I wish that was the answer, putting it all back," I tell him. "But I think, with all due respect, that maybe it's time for you to rejoin regular life again. You've put in enough time suffering, and now you need to get over it. Let's think of other things that might be more important in your life than this."

"This is supposed to be *helping* me?" he says. He looks up at me with a tearstained face.

"Look, sweet pea. Love *isn't* always the kind that's supposed to last. Sometimes the heart fastens on to something and then—poof!—it ends. Just like that. Happens to everybody. But you learn stuff about yourself and you move on. And, trust me, you end up way better off than you ever dreamed possible. You'll find someone else. Someone who doesn't perhaps wear a bra with a python print, it's true, but—"

"NO! NO! NO!" he yells, and his voice reverberates around the room. He bangs on his knee with his fist. "Listen to me! She and I were supposed to get *married*. I was her soul mate, and this guy just stole her away. We had everything all set. I had—I had *paid* for everything. Even the stupid ice sculpture she insisted on. Paid in full. By *me*."

"An ice sculpture?" I say sarcastically. "She wanted an ice sculpture? Oh, *well* then. I had no idea who we were dealing with. Next you're going to tell me she wanted doves released from a cage, too."

He glares at me. "How did you know?" He obviously doesn't speak sarcasm.

"I'm afraid I know the type." I pick up a rhinestone necklace I see on the floor, the kind that weighs half a pound, and flick it into the bag. "That couldn't have been cheap, either, all those stupid add-ons."

"No shit. Neither was the honeymoon trip to Cancún, that I also paid for, and which, by the way, I found out she took with that douche-bag boss of hers."

I straighten up and look over at him. "Wait. *They* took the trip you paid for?"

"Yep. They did. They certainly did." His face crumples.

"And you want her *back*?"

"It wasn't her idea to do that. It was him!"

"Nope. *She* did this to you. You had an arrangement with *her*, not with him. He was just an opportunistic bastard who took advantage—but *she's* the one who did you wrong."

He doesn't answer, just starts crying again. Great big booming sobs. I shift my weight to my other foot, think about how much my nose itches underneath the bunny head. He's on the floor, keening and wailing his heart out. I close my eyes and see stupid Saucy with her bright blonde hair and bright blonde smile, and I see her and her boss frolicking in the waves of Cancún, flinging Joey Davis's broken heart between them like a Frisbee, and then—well, there is nothing else to do if you consider yourself a decent human being but to take off your bunny head and sit down next to this heartsick boy and try to think of something to say to him that would help. So that is what I do.

My knees ache from all the hopping, so I stretch my legs out in front of me, give them a little massage.

"So how long ago was this wedding supposed to be?" I say.

He doesn't look up, but he does stop weeping. After an endless moment he says, "Four months, two weeks, five days."

"Yeah, and how many hours and minutes?" I say. Sarcasm again. I can't help myself.

"I—I don't know."

"Well, *that's* good at least."

"Why is that good?"

"Because if you knew the hours and minutes, then we'd have to be seriously worried about your level of pathology here. But now I think there's hope for you. We just gotta get you back on your feet, is all."

He sniffles loudly and wetly.

"And no offense, but also you need to blow your nose. Don't sniff that stuff back into your system. It's bad for you."

"Who are you? My mother?"

"Apparently, yes. And now that I'm your mother, I need you to stand up and let's get to cleaning this place up. I have a high tolerance for disorganization, but this is disgusting, the way you're living. It's holding you back." I get to my feet. "Also, hard facts here: what I find disturbing is that you'd even *consider* taking her back. Because that, my friend, just says you're a glutton for punishment. If there was ever a person who doesn't deserve a second chance at bashing your heart in, it's got to be this idiot woman. How would you ever trust her again, even if she did come back? Think about *that*."

He doesn't move, and I close my eyes, not even wanting to think of what Kat will say about this. The Heartbreak Bunny going all mom-ish on a guy. After a long moment, Joey blows his nose without looking at me, and then he puts his head back down on his knees. I look at his dirty long hair and again at the pale skinny arms poking out from his sleeves. Those wrists. My heart turns over. His fingernails look like bloody stumps.

I say, "Boy, those nails must hurt. I remember when my first husband left me. I bit my fingernails down to the quick every single day, like it was my job."

"My nails hurting are the *least* of my problems," he says without looking up. "Also, no offense, but did your first husband go off to Cancún on a honeymoon trip *you* paid for? And I hate to tell you, Bunny Lady, but even that wasn't the worst part!"

"Well, then, let's get to the bottom of this whole story. What else happened?" I say.

"After the whole breakup scene, she promised me that she'd get the deposit back for the wedding, but you know what she did?"

"I'm going to guess that she didn't get the deposit back."

He drops his voice even lower, to a place that sounds like a gravel road has formed in his larynx. "No. She didn't." He starts picking at some fluff on his sock and says in a voice so low I almost don't hear him, "She freaking *married* him instead. At the wedding I paid for."

"Good God, Joey. Did you say . . . *you* ended up paying for their wedding?"

"Yeah. How's that for life kicking you in the ass?"

"That—now that is truly, truly the worst."

"Right?" He looks up at me with his wet eyes and his creased, red cheeks and his wobbly chin. "And the way I found *that* out is that I called the place and asked for the money back myself, and the lady on the phone told me I must be mistaken, because that wedding *had* taken place."

"Okay, Joey Davis, this has now gone beyond the pale. Get up off the floor! We're going to fix your life! Get up!"

"I can't."

"Look," I say at last. "This is a big, big grief. I get it. It's huge! But do you really want to waste any more of your precious life thinking about this? You don't get extra points for wallowing, you know. It's not like you hit a certain hours-spent-wallowing goal, and then she magically comes back."

"Yeah, I know I'm pathetic," he says. He looks away. "And just so you know, I haven't told anybody but you that I paid for their wedding. Not even Zach, not even my dad, because then they'd know I'm the biggest loser ever in the world. Which I totally am."

"*She's* the biggest loser in the world, not you. I actually think I hate her, and I haven't hated anyone in years."

"Yeah, but what if she just got taken in by him and she's temporarily forgotten what we had, but then she'll remember and want to come back?"

"Joey, no, no, no, no. She's not coming back. Also, you don't *want* her back. Can't you see that this is not the way decent people behave? This woman—I want to go over to her house and, I don't know, let the air out of her tires and then have like ninety pizzas delivered to her door that she has to pay for, and ohhh, then after that, maybe—"

"We were going to have three kids, and we were going to live in Boston, and she said I was the only one who really *got* her. I was her soul mate."

"Okay, listen, sweet cakes, we are done with this woman," I say. "She is over. I've *had it* with her. I've only known about this for two minutes, and already she's given me a headache. Come on, get up. The first thing we're going to do is clean up this place, throw out all her stupid underwear and those horrible photos of her smiling, and then—well, *then*, we're going after that petrified bologna sandwich, which I am scared of, if you want to know the truth. After that, *you*, my friend, are going to go with me into the kitchen and we're going to load up the dishwasher with these hideous coffee cups and we're going to run the damn thing."

"I—"

"No. Don't say another word. Stand up. Feel your spine. You are officially moving on."

He gets to his feet, reluctantly. But he smiles a little bit.

"Here," I say. "Pick this up. Take these T-shirts and put them in the laundry hamper, unless they're hers, in which case, give them to me so I can rip them up with my bare hands."

He actually laughs, a dry, husky sound, and picks up the clothing strewn across the floor. I finish stuffing items into the bag, and say, "Also, that bra you made me put back. I'm sorry, but it has to go. It's a lethal weapon." He laughs again, but he goes and gets the green python bra from the drawer and drops it in the bag.

"Good move," I say. "High five. You're officially on the road to recovery."

I march him into the living room, where we do a sweep of the coffee table—or rather, I do; he mostly just sags against the wall. I put back the couch cushion and stack the books in a pile by the bookcase. The beer can tower falls over, and I wave my hand at it. "This has to go! Let's put these cans in a bag and you can take them to the recycling," I say. "Also, for future reference, having a beer can tower is a big turnoff. No woman in her right mind is going to want to date you with that thing in here."

"No one wants to date me anyway," he says.

"They will. Believe me. I'm afraid you're not done with women yet."

"How do *you* know?"

"Because I know about love," I say. "It comes again, like a bad penny. It's always showing up looking for any trouble it can cause."

"It's not *always* trouble."

"Just most of the time. Ninety percent, in fact, by my calculations. But before you can even think about love again, we've got to get your power back from *this* so-called love."

"I don't have any power. *She* was my power."

My grandmother wakes up inside my head. *Good God, Billie,* she says, clear as a bell. *How long are you going to let this go on? You know what you have to do.*

I know she's right.

"Listen," I say. "We are going to do a thing that will bring all your power back to you, where it belongs." My heart is beating kind of fast. I lick my lips nervously. I'm way over my head here. "First you need to close your eyes and picture yourself grounded. Take a deep breath. Feel the power flowing back into you. Go on. Picture it."

He closes his eyes. "I can't feel any power."

"You will. Take a deep breath. Now turn on the switch in your head that lets your power back in."

He takes a shaky breath, but then it falters. I can almost see Saucy in his head. Simpering. Waving some other python garment at him.

"Okay, as we said, this is a big, big grief. It's going to take some magic. Are you okay with magic?" I can't believe I've just said this. I stand in front of him and square my shoulders.

He blinks. "I guess."

"No, you can't just guess. This is real magic. You have to have some intention behind it."

His eyes widen slightly. "Okay . . . I'm in."

"Good! Okay, first we're going to need some salt."

"*Salt?*"

"Salt."

"Okay, whatever. Are we going to get some fries to put under the salt?"

"See? That's good. You made a joke. And no, there will not be fries."

He stares at me for a moment, realizes I'm serious, and then lopes into the kitchen and comes back with a blue container of Morton salt. Little girl in a yellow dress with the umbrella on the side. *When it rains, it pours.* Profound for a box of salt, I've always thought.

I explain that we're going to put it in all the corners of the rooms, where her spirit remains. We're going to ward her off, get her essence the hell out of here once and for all.

"This is what we do for tough cases," I tell him with confidence, as though this is standard procedure with every Snap Out of It client. The truth is, I haven't done this since Victor left. "Unwanted spirits don't like salt. I myself have had times when I had to keep salt in the corners of all the rooms in my house. Just for safety's sake. Hell, one year I wore salt around my neck in a little silk bag," I tell him.

I take his arm and walk him step by step to the corners of the living room, as though he's a much-loved invalid. At each corner, I solemnly have him shake out a bit of salt. I pretend to know the right amount, sometimes urging him to sprinkle a little more, sometimes shaking my head when it's time to stop. The salt mingles with the dust bunnies in the corners. We both stare at the dust/salt clumps as though we are at a funeral, viewing the sacred remains. Next we go into the bedroom and sprinkle some salt there, too. There is a hush in the apartment, our footsteps on the carpet the only sound. Outside, a truck starts up, but it is very far away. There is only this space, this grief.

My grandmother says to me, *Now . . . come on . . . do the rest.*

"And now," I say, "now we hold hands and say this little chant my grandmother taught me when she was getting rid of warts."

"Warts?" He laughs.

"See? It's funny! Yes. Grief, in this case, can be a kind of wart. Believe me, this works for anything you need to be rid of."

Well? Maybe it's true.

And who knows the exact words she used to say? I wish I'd listened, but she said them under her breath. They were for all occasions, now that I remember—she and her witchy friends had words for getting a stoplight to turn green, and some for water to boil faster, and those that made cockroaches leave the premises. She didn't think twice about calling on magic whenever she needed it. As I start in, words just line up in my head and I say them out loud as they tumble forward, calling on the forces of good to eliminate this unhappiness from his life. I can feel energy coursing through me.

"Now ten times so it really soaks in," I say. "Calling on the universe to help us."

His hands are moist in mine. I can feel his pulse, quickening a little now. We sway as we chant. My blood beats in my ears, and my eyes are closed. Joey says the words out loud, too, his voice getting stronger with each repetition. And that's maybe why I don't notice someone standing in the doorway of the bedroom. I hear a tiny sound, and my eyes fly open.

Then: "Helloooo!" says a voice—a hearty man's voice, shattering the spell.

Joey and I both jump and let go of each other's hands like we've been caught injecting heroin or something.

"Oh God, it's my dad," says Joey under his breath. Which is good, I think. At least we're not about to be murdered by a ghost we've summoned by accident with the spell. Not that I believe in that sort of thing, but you never know.

I bring myself to look at the man. He looks like Joey, actually—an older, non-broken-down version of him. For one thing, he has a headful of beautiful, clean gray hair and a tan, and he's wearing jeans and a navy-blue barn coat. And smiling in what I consider a hostile way, given that he's scared us half to death *and* he has a heartbroken son who should not be subjected to such a blindingly good-looking smile. Also, disgustingly enough, his eyes twinkle like he knows he's the poster child for middle-age to early-old-age handsomeness and is used to being recognized for that accomplishment. I make up my mind not to ever look in his direction again.

"Now what is *this*?" he says happily.

"Dad!" Joey yells, furious. "Christ, Dad! You didn't ring the bell!"

"I used my key," says his dad. He's looking from one of us to the other, with a slightly confused smile, like he's ready to be let in on the joke.

I refuse all eye contact on principle, but I can feel my face growing hot. Damn! Why didn't I get out of here sooner?

"So let me guess what's going on," he says in a chuckling baritone voice. A trained voice if you ask me. All deep and homey. "Don't tell me . . . don't tell me. A woman dressed like a rabbit is . . . ah . . . teaching you ballroom dancing, my boy?"

Ah, dad jokes. No wonder Joey hasn't told his father the truth. I get it now. He's the son of a buffoon.

Joey scowls. "No. She's—uh—she's . . ."

"No, son, come on. You know me; that was a joke. I'm teasing you. I actually heard what's going on," his dad says in his rich chocolate voice. "I've actually been standing here the whole time your eyes were closed. You're getting rid of Saucy, and I say it's about time. Whatever means necessary. Magic, whatever you gotta do—although I do draw the line at animal sacrifices." He laughs and gives me a meaningful stare, eyebrows arched. (Okay, so I looked.) "Fact is, lady in a bunny suit, we're desperate here. Anybody willing to come over and perform a whatever—an exorcism, I guess you'd call it—I say go for it. By the way, I'm Mason Davis, this sad sack's father."

I can't think of anything I'd like more than to disappear—me and my suddenly dry mouth—and perhaps it would be interesting to kick this *sad sack's* father in the shins on my way out, but the police are already onto me, so I do the next best thing, which is to stalk over and grab my rabbit head. I feel like we were on the verge of a breakthrough, so I'm extra mad. So mad I can't quite bring myself to put the rabbit head on, not in front of his dad. Instead, I impersonate someone who is quite late—quite late and quite annoyed.

But this silver-haired guy isn't having it. "By the way," he says, as relaxed as you please, "I appreciate your efforts here." He's standing next to Joey now, and he ruffles his hair, which is brave, considering it may have four months of oil on it. "I try to come over and force-feed this guy a little optimism every few days, tell him a few jokes, maybe talk him into a movie, don't I, buddy? But I never did think of the casting-a-spell routine. That's a good one." When he says, "casting a spell," he does air quotes.

I hate air quotes.

"Nice to meet you," I say coolly. "I was just leaving actually. And just so you know, it's counterproductive to call someone a sad sack."

Joey sends me a grateful look.

"I stand corrected. And what is *your* name?" the father asks.

"Dad, would you please . . . just not?"

"I just want her name. That's a reasonable question, not too intrusive, I think. She can handle that."

"I'm Billie," I say, mumbling. "From Snap Out of It Company LLC. Gotta go!"

"No, no, stay. I'm sorry I interrupted you. Won't you stay and tell me all about what you do? What the words mean?"

"*Dad*, she's not supposed to talk. She's the Heartbreak Bunny. She removes items, that's all."

Oh God. This now.

"Good-bye," I say. I lift the bag of Saucy's belongings. "Joey, take care of yourself." I pass Mason Davis, who looks at me with eyes that glitter with fascination, and I walk down the hallway—twenty steps more, then ten, five, and finally I'm at the door, my hand turning the knob.

"Wait," I can hear Mason Davis saying. "I just want to talk to you! Let me do the chant, too! The Snap—what, company?"

"Snap Out of It . . . I think she said," says his son. "There's a contract . . . over here . . ."

I walk outside, letting the door close hard behind me, and I am free now. Out blinking in the bright, cold January sunshine. I take a deep breath.

As soon as I'm in my car, I call Kat and leave her a voice mail.

"Kat! Call me. There's a level beyond Level Four, and it's no laughing matter. Holy moly! I *transcended* all bunny protocols. Listen! This guy—he is the saddest guy imaginable! When nothing was really work-ing, I took the bunny head off, and just . . . related to him. I made him load his dishwasher and got him to recycle his beer cans, and then—well, then I got inspired and I did a spell my *grandmother* taught me, for getting rid of warts! I swear my old Southern granny just started talking in my ear, and it was *wonderful!* Like I was on automatic pilot or something, channeling her, I just knew what would help him next. It was amazing and liberating, and I loved it! We threw salt in the corners of all his rooms, and then we did a little chant together, and you would have died laughing, but he was really responding to it, and we would have kept going for sure, but then his father came in! This is a new direction for the business, and I'm so excited! Call me!"

I'm heading home, going over everything in my head and feeling all exhilarated, when a jolt goes through me. I suddenly realize who Joey Davis's father is. He's *the* Mason Davis, the morning show news-caster on Channel 12. Calvin watches him every morning while he does the crossword puzzle and eats his oatmeal. Mason Davis reads the news with the air of a baritone whose world knows nothing but calm. He's known for his supposed-to-be-amusing-and-maybe-they-are little feature stories—the deer who jumped through the window of a North Haven family's house and stood blinking in the living room while they were getting ready for work. The seventy-five-year-old lady who deliv-ers newspapers every morning on her scooter. The kid who raised five thousand dollars for a homeless family by painting greeting cards and selling them door to door.

He makes life sound like it could easily be distilled into four-min-ute feel-good segments. Mason Davis is just the type who would try to turn his son's life into a human-interest story with a lesson and a moral and a slogan.

No wonder his kid couldn't tell him the truth about his breakup.

CHAPTER FOUR

I live in a three-story, halfway run-down wooden house in New Haven, Connecticut. (Halfway run-down actually, by modern standards, but fully dilapidated by Louise's standards, even though she grew up here—happily, I might add.) Something is always in need of repair, which is the way of old houses, I believe. The oak floor in the downstairs front living room has seen better days, and the front porch slopes ever so gently down to the three splintery wooden steps. It needs paint, inside and out, and some decent gutters. But it has such charm, this house. It has tall windows, and there's a mulberry tree next to the front walk and some sugar maples in the back—everything is bare now, of course, but the yard is filled with color and shade most of the year. The porch swing is still hanging, and there are a couple of wicker rocking chairs that we probably should have brought in for the winter, but we're not the kind of people who bring things in. We like everything to be ready to be lived in. What if an unexpected spring day arrived and the rocking chairs were hidden in the basement? We like to spare ourselves that kind of pain.

Kat calls me back just as I pull into the driveway, squeezing beside the plumber's truck—REGGIE MCMILLAN: WE REPAIR WHAT YOUR HUSBAND FIXED is painted in red letters across the side.

"Good lord, Billie!" she says, laughing. "I can't talk long, but I just got your message, and, honey, have you gone crazy? You want to clean people's houses? The Heartbreak Bunny was supposed to be fun. A lark. Per. Form. Ance art, sweetheart! Hop in, remove a few items, hop back out? Remember? There's nothing on the flyer about running the dishwasher."

"I know, I know. It sounds like madness. But it turns out the madness was in thinking it was just a performance. This is *real*, Kat. I now see that we could do some real good! Sort of a cross between listening and magic and fun, all in one. I was thinking I could even play music while I go through the house finding objects to throw out. Revenge songs! There could be different playlists, depending on their music tastes. And then the chanting—to chase the bad vibes out. Celebrate the dispelling of grief!"

"Billie, honey, maybe you don't realize, but I've been *screening* the people you see. If they seem like they're psychotic wrecks when they call, I say we're too booked up. You've only been seeing the people who are already pretty much okay and just need that *one* little fun push, a little metaphorical bunny dashing in to seal the deal, pronounce the relationship over."

"Some people need more. There are people beyond Level Four, Kat. They need us."

Kat says, "By the way, I just heard that somebody released a TikTok video of you doing your bunny thing, and now it's getting a bunch of likes and shares—"

"TikTok? Did you say TikTok?"

"Yeah. It just went up. Two women in the video, and you—"

"Oh, God," I say. "That must be Amanda. That was today. I had no idea she was going to post that. Tell me this. What does my ass look like in the video?"

"Good lord, Billie! Who knows? I love that that's what you're fixated on. I'm literally laughing out loud, and I love you so much. But, sweetie, don't you think we've got to be a little bit careful here? I mean, what if things aren't always going to be so cut-and-dried? What if dabbling in magic brings out some weirdness in people? You know?"

"I know, I know. But what if it can really help? Today when I was doing this, I felt like I was really doing some good."

"Listen," she says. "I know what Bob is going to say. He'll say, what's our liability? What if you do magic spells, and the guy doesn't get over his problems, and then he holds you responsible?"

"No offense, but your husband is a big stick-in-the-mud. He doesn't believe in manifesting and magic like we do."

"Yeah, but—"

"But nothing. We'll say to him: What if none of that happens? What if it goes great?"

∽

After I go inside and change out of my bunny costume, I find Calvin in the basement helpfully informing Reggie, the plumber, about the state of water pipes when he was a boy growing up in Philadelphia. Now *that* was the golden age of plumbing. Reggie is grunting and shining his flashlight into the deep recesses near the washing machine, a place that only spiders and Reggie know about.

"What's it looking like?" I say.

"Roots, you know. I'm snaking them."

Our troubles are always due to roots. This house should be named Roots and Clogs.

"Where you been?" says Calvin to me. "You took so long bunnying." He looks at me closely. "What's up? You look like you just won the lottery or something."

"I'm excited," I say. "New direction for the Heartbreak Bunny biz."

"Oh," he says. "Well, let's eat lunch and talk about it. Reggie, you joining us today?"

"Nah, I got to go do some real work," he says. "Gotta help out some people who went on vacation and forgot that their house had pipes that need heat."

Upstairs, Calvin gets out the chicken salad sandwiches he made—because it's my birthday, he says, he made them all fancy by cutting off the crusts like his mother used to do for formal teas—and I heat up the roasted red pepper soup I made yesterday and put the kettle on. And as soon as we sit down, he says, "So, spill."

"Welllll," I say, "it's *possible* that the Heartbreak Bunny business may have gone a little over the top today." I take a spoonful of soup and blow on it. It smells divine. It's lovely here, with the snow just starting to fall outside. I can see it piling up on the branches of the maple.

"Impossible. The Heartbreak Bunny business *started* over the top."

Then I tell him the whole story, and when I get to the part about pouring salt in the corners of Joey Davis's apartment and holding hands with him and chanting, Calvin starts roaring with laughter.

"Aaaand . . ." he says, "the Heartbreak Bunny turns back into Billie. I was wondering how long that would take."

"Yeah, well. It got *even more so*, I'm afraid."

"More so? Am I going to find out that you've rented him my bedroom?"

"No, but Calvin, then his *father* came in and saw what we were doing. You'd think he would have been horrified to find his son prancing around with a dancing bunny rabbit, but no! In fact, he wanted to get in on the action, which I would not allow. And then when I was driving home, I realized that he's Mason Davis! From Channel Twelve!"

"Mason Davis? No kidding. Well, I'll be damned."

"And he's just as smarmy in real life as he is on camera. Odious, horrible man. All that I'm-too-handsome-for-my-own-good vibe just rolling off him. He wanted to know my name, and he then he wanted to know about Snap Out of It—"

"Deplorable," says Calvin. "How dare he?"

"Right?" I say. "Wait. You're making fun of me, aren't you?"

He tries to hide a smile. "I have to say that I'm not of the opinion that Mason Davis is an odious, horrible man. He's rather chatty and funny on television."

"He's too fake. But anyway, when I saw him there, I stopped doing the spell because of the way he was staring at us, but then when I was driving away, it hit me: this is exactly what the Heartbreak Bunny should be doing! This was what the whole thing was always leading to, but I didn't see it. I was meant to do this. You know what I just realized? In previous years, this guy, Joey, would have been the sort of waif I would have brought home with me."

"Excuse me," says Calvin, "but everybody is the kind of waif you want to bring home with you."

"We could have really helped him, Calvin. We could have taught him to cook, and you might have recited him some poetry, and then maybe he would have used the hammock out back when summertime came, and I'd be cooking, and I'd look out and see him there strumming away on the ukulele and feeling all at home."

"You haven't taken anybody in for a long time," he says. "Not since Marisol."

"I know. I was thinking I need to cut down. And then I meet somebody like this."

"That *is* one of your deepest impulses," Calvin says huskily. "Doing that."

Our eyes meet. Well, yes. This is how I got Calvin, in fact.

Eight years ago, I had a little business (illegal, as it turned out) giving people rides—and Calvin was a client I was scheduled to pick up. So I parked at the curb outside an apartment building in my VW bug, and I watched as this elderly, dignified little man, wearing a tan overcoat and shiny black shoes, came out, then closed and locked the door with a click. He trotted slowly down the walk lugging a big maroon suitcase. I jumped out of the driver's seat and helped him with it, and then he very gingerly got in my back seat. He told me in a solemn voice that I was to drive him to hospice, where they were expecting him. And then he was silent, sitting back and staring out the window with his hands folded in his lap.

Hospice! I hadn't ever taken anybody to hospice before, so I kept glancing at him in the rearview mirror in case he wanted to talk. I put some big band music on the radio, thinking that if you were moving into a final place like that, you might need some traveling music to see you there. Once, our eyes met in the mirror and I smiled at him, and he smiled back, just a little bit.

Then, when we were almost at the turnoff for hospice, he leaned forward and cleared his throat. He wanted to know if, before we settled him in there, I'd mind driving him around so he could see some of his old haunts for the last time.

Well, we drove all over the state, up and down the coast and through the back roads to the rural eastern part of Connecticut, where he had lived as a teenager. We looked at the outsides of the houses where he'd lived, and some places he'd worked—a gas station, a mom-and-pop grocery store that he was pleased to see was still going, and an old clapboard farmhouse that had belonged to his grandparents.

"Now I want to have me some baseball memories," he said cheerfully. I put on some Frank Sinatra and Tony Bennett and headed to ball fields where he'd hit home runs once or twice, and to the former site of a drive-in theater, where he'd lost his virginity to a red-cheeked girl named Virginia.

"Virginity!" he crowed. "Remember what a big-deal problem that used to be? We didn't know whether to keep it or not. And if we gave it away, would we give it to the wrong person? And what if you took somebody else's virginity and then you were sorry? There was a whole two years when I didn't think about anything else but how to manage virginity."

My generation, I told him dryly, didn't have that precise problem. We saw virginity as something to be disposed of as quickly as possible.

I told him about making out with Victor for the first time and how I knew I had to marry anybody who could kiss that good, and Calvin told me that once Virginia had lost her virginity to him, he thought he owed her a diamond ring, a house with a yard, and some kids. But then they drifted apart, he said, and she took their kids—a boy and a girl—and went off and married some other guy, a salesman who moved them to California, and although Calvin wrote letters to his children, he never went to see them because he and Virginia were so angry with each other. Worst decision he'd ever made, he said.

He sucked in his breath. "And then three years later, they all died in a massive car accident on the freeway."

"Your kids? They . . . died?" I said, my throat tight as I said the word.

"Gone. Just like that."

I started saying all the things you say, how sorry I was, how unfair, how tragic, but he held up his hand.

"No, no," he said. "It's not the main thing. Not anymore. It's only one part of who I am."

After a moment, he cleared his throat. "You know this already, I can tell," he said. "You know how it is that you start over. A piece of music plays, or the light slants in just so. You see that you've lost little pieces of your heart, but then, without your permission, other little pieces start coming back."

We talked then about our marriages and our almost-marriages, and I told him about Desmond, my third husband, the one who let me believe in security for the first time. The one who was going to see me through old age. We were only fifty when we married, but I had it all planned out, how we would spend our old age shuffling around the house in our bedroom slippers and our ratty old bathrobes, and we'd fall asleep, mouths open, drooling, in our matching rocking chairs on the porch.

But then, three months ago, I said, he had to go and die on the operating table getting a little mole removed. We weren't even old enough to collect social security.

Calvin said he understood perfectly how that felt.

After that, we ate fried chicken sandwiches in the car, dripping mayonnaise all over the seats, and I explained my long-standing philosophy of romantic love to him.

"After Victor left, I decided not to have romance in my life anymore," I said. "It seemed like the only sensible thing to do. And now that Desmond is gone, too, I don't want any of that all-consuming falling-in-love nonsense. All that drama. It's over for me."

"Very smart," he said, smiling. "You know, though, I've heard that everybody who comes into our life maybe brings us something we need if we're just wise enough to accept it."

"Nope, nope, nope," I said, and I wiped a big glob of mayonnaise off the steering wheel. "Not unless the wisdom they've brought is that true love is way more trouble than it's worth, and is also exceedingly rare, if it even exists at all."

"Well, I have to agree with you on that point at least," he said. "It's definitely rare."

"Good," I said.

"Good," he said.

And we smiled at each other.

"Kindred spirits," I said. He didn't answer.

After we had that established, the sun was sinking in the sky, so I asked him shyly if he might want to come to my house for a cup of tea before we headed on over to hospice. We sat out on my front porch in the rocking chairs, and after a while, he said he'd had a realization. He didn't believe he was ready to go into hospice after all. The doctors had told him he had two months to live when they referred him to end-of-life care, but he didn't really believe that for one second. Because for a while now, he believed he just might have himself a remission, and he'd rather have it on the outside of hospice than on the inside.

I put him up in Louise's old room. He stayed the night—and then he stayed the next night, too, and the next and the next, and eight years later, he still has not left, and whatever was making medical folks call him "terminal" seems to have gone away. I don't get it, and neither does he, but aside from being a little forgetful sometimes, he seems to me to be a healthy specimen. And he is now my best male friend in the world, the one I run everything by, the one I couldn't really live without.

What I mean is that he listens to me without rolling his eyes, and he thinks I'm just fine the way I am, even though he knows all the bad parts of me. He doesn't look away or change the subject when I start my ranting, and he doesn't think I dress weird, or that my hair is too short (it might be), and he believes that my two ex-husbands were crazy to leave me, and that the husband of mine who died is still sending me messages from the afterlife. Two of Calvin's late wives do that, too, he says.

All these people whom we miss. Calvin knows what that's like. We don't even need to put it into words.

∽

Reggie comes dragging himself upstairs just then and decides he does want to have a chicken salad sandwich after all. He plops down in the wooden chair across from me and announces morosely that he didn't want to say this before, but his wife is cheating on him.

"Evidence, please," says Calvin.

"Well, she bought new perfume, and she never wears perfume. She knows I don't even care about perfume."

Calvin makes the buzzer sound they use in game shows to indicate the wrong answer. "Nope. I know Cynthia, and she's devoted to you."

"But what if she's not?"

"She is."

"All right. I didn't want to tell you this part, because it's private, but"—he lowers his voice to a whisper—"she also wants to get her boobs done."

"For you," I say.

"But I don't care about boobs."

Calvin sighs. "Then tell her that."

"I shouldn't have to tell her. What if I tell her and she says she's doing them for somebody else? Then what?"

"She won't say that," I tell him. "There is nobody else."

"There might be."

I suppose it's true that there might be—anything can happen with humans—but thinking of Cynthia, who is as unadventurous a human as you're ever going to find, I can't imagine her suddenly developing a whole new side to her personality and leaving Reggie.

Calvin scrapes his chair back, goes over to the refrigerator, and gets the bag of potato chips from the top. "If she says there's somebody else, then come back and tell us that she's cheating on you, and we'll help you figure out what to do. Right now, though: no, not enough evidence," he says.

I say, "I think you're feeling paranoid, because it's been winter too long, and you're always kind of squirrelly in the wintertime. You need to take Cynthia on a vacation to a warm place. Get away from the frozen pipes. You hate frozen pipes."

"That's just it. She *went* on a vacation to a warm place. With her sister. She *said*."

"Why didn't you go?"

He shrugs, and his cell phone rings just then, and he hauls it out of his pocket. It's some more frozen pipes calling, he says. "Can I have my chicken salad sandwich to go?" he asks, so I make it for him and put it in a brown paper bag.

"If you want, bring Cynthia and Micah over tomorrow night and we can play bingo or something," I tell him. "A nice, normal night from the 1950s. We specialize in those around here."

After he leaves, I start clearing the table and doing the dishes. Calvin sits there, drumming his fingers on the table.

"What is it?" I say. "Out with it."

"I was just thinking about when you were telling me about that kid today. Your face was lit up like I haven't seen in a long time. This is who you are. The goodness of you."

I sit back down at the table. "Well. Not really." I laugh a little. "You want to know how bad I was? I said to him that he's a glutton for punishment. I held up a bra she'd left behind and called it a lethal weapon. I even said I hated her. I actually used the word *hate*. Also, I said no woman was going to be interested in him if he didn't get rid of his wall of beer cans, which I made him remove. I marched around there like I was his mom or something. Made him do the dishes. And then, it was when I was desperate because I couldn't think of anything else to do that I made him do spells with me. I did the spell my granny used to do to get rid of warts, and I told him that it would work for a bad love affair, too."

He shakes his head. "That's you all over!"

I laugh. "Well, I have to admit, I loved it. I love that for the first time this guy looked like he was taking some action on his own behalf. He wasn't just going to lie there on the couch letting food rot on the table in front of him anymore. And I know, I know. He still might take her back if he gets half a chance. And that kind of kills me, to tell you the truth."

"So what if he takes her back? That's just what humans do," he says. "But *maybe* because a bunny persuaded him to put salt in the corners of his house, tomorrow when he cooks his scrambled eggs, he's going to realize he's out of salt, and he'll drive to the supermarket, and he'll say something nice to the checkout clerk, and she'll smile at him, and he'll smile back, and they'll fall in love, and by this time next year they'll be married with a mortgage and a kid on the way. And it'll be because of you."

"Poor guy. I wouldn't wish that on my worst enemy."

"Yeah, but you're forgetting that love also saves us. We *want* this guy to find somebody good who'll love him back."

"More often, though, love hurts us and you know it," I tell him. "I feel like I'm walking around the world seventy-five percent heartbroken, and you are, too. Look at my record—two divorces, tons of love affairs, and I finally find a nice man and then he dies. And who knows? Maybe if he'd lived, I would have discovered that he was really a bad guy, too."

Calvin's eyes are bugging out at me. "You have gone completely around the bend on this topic. Listen. I'm with you on how most romances don't work out, but Desmond was a good guy. And if he were here, I know he'd be saying you should find somebody new to love." He puts his hand up to his ear like he's listening. "What's that you say, Desmond? Sixty is too young to give up completely? Yeah, I'll try to tell her."

"Nope," I say. "Don't even start with that. I've had my share of passion, and it was great, but everything on my body is either sagging or wrinkling or drying up, and I'm not getting naked with anyone again, unless he has a medical degree or I'm unconscious."

"Well," he says. "I'd just like to tell you that the vibe from the senior center is that people are alive until they die. And they all want love. Nakedness and all."

"Nope. My new position is that no one over fifty should even consider such a thing."

His eyes are dancing. "Okay, so maybe this isn't the perfect time to tell you something, but I'm going to do it anyway. I've gotten myself sort of enamored with a lady by the name of Bernice Coggins. And we have a little . . . agreement." He smiles slyly.

I search his face. "What? Please," I say. "Are you kidding me? Oh my God, Calvin. I suppose you want me to just say how wonderful this is, but you and I both know these things are fairy tales. Especially at the senior center."

He shrugs. "Yup. It may be a senior center fairy tale, but I'm in it," he says. "What have I got to lose? Being in love is fun."

Sometimes I can't help worrying about him.

CHAPTER FIVE

That night, I drive Calvin to Louise's house for my birthday party, because I don't happen to think people in their tenth decade of life should be driving after dark. Especially if there's been a little light snow.

"Okay, so this afternoon, while you were at the senior center making out with your lady friend in the broom closet," I tell him, "I made a playlist of revenge songs and strong-woman songs and getting-over-love songs for different genres: country, rock, easy listening, torch songs."

"And what do you plan to do with those, may I ask?"

"The Heartbreak Bunny will play whatever songs are needed while she throws out all the objects of misery," I say. "Maybe we'll even sing along and dance, the client and I."

"That's great, but you forgot opera, and also, just so you know, we don't make out in the broom closet."

"I suppose you start smooching right there at the bridge table?"

He is studying me from the passenger seat. "I'll have you know that we old folks are perfectly capable of going out behind the building and grabbing some action, like the teenagers do."

"And your STD rates are every bit as high, I've heard," I say. "So be careful."

I press the button and Katy Perry's "Roar" comes roaring out of the speakers. I turn it up and bang on the steering wheel, singing along. Then I turn to him. "You see? This counteracts all the romance propaganda songs out there!" I have to shout to be heard over the music. He nods.

"And," I say, "maybe I'll come up with a list of movies for clients to watch, to counteract the effects of the romantic comedies! And some books, too. People need to know there's a whole other world out there to be experienced. We don't all have to have romance! There are other things in life."

"Nothing as fun, though," he says. "You have to admit."

"Fun until it crashes and burns," I say. "Also. How can you believe in the Heartbreak Bunny *and* also in romance?"

He shrugs. "I contain multitudes."

⌒இ

My darling only child lives in a house that is perched—*precariously* perched, I tell you—on the side of a hill that slopes down to the shoreline, and how is that for a perfect metaphor for parenthood? From the day your child is born, you do everything to protect her, and then she goes and lives in a house that seems every day to be considering leaping into Long Island Sound. Leo's parents bought the house for them. His family got rich generations ago when their immigrant great-grandfather came to this country with twenty dollars and a plan to invent something basic like the fingernail clipper—and they've been wealthy ever since.

I nose my car in between five other cars at the top of the vast circular driveway. For a moment, Calvin and I sit there silently looking out at the sky and the snow softly falling, and then he says, "Oh! I have a birthday surprise for you. *I* am going to share one of my very, very legally obtained medical marijuana cigarettes with you, in honor of the fact that you are turning such an advanced age. And we are going to sit in this car and smoke a few puffs before we go in. How is that?"

"Calvin, nobody calls it 'marijuana cigarettes' or says 'smoke a few puffs.' Nobody, not even old folks."

"Too bad. That's what my friends at the senior center call it," he says, and he lights up the joint. The fragrance immediately fills the car, taking me back to my days with Victor, who always kept a stash in his underwear drawer because, he said, the police would never think to look there if they staged a raid. After Louise was asleep, he'd close all the shades and get it out. He called it "our daily bowl."

I no sooner think of him than my phone dings—and yep, it's Victor. My grandmother taught me about this kind of thing—synchronicity. You think about someone, and then they show up, Granny said. Pays to be careful who you think about. I wish life had a rewind button, and I could *unthink* about Victor just now.

happy birthday it is your birthday right and you are entering a
new decade of possibility and i miss you

Would it kill this guy to use a capital letter? I shut down the phone and take the joint Calvin hands me.

"You get the first puff," he says. "On account of it being your birthday and all."

I take it in, pressing it into my lungs, and then his eyes bug out so much that I start laughing.

"How do you *do* that?" Calvin says. "Take in so much smoke!"

"I practiced a lot as a kid," I tell him. And then he does the same thing, and we both laugh—and then he says, "So who was that text from?"

"What text?"

"You know what text. The one that made you so mad you couldn't turn it off fast enough."

"Oh," I say. "That one. Well, it was from Victor, if you must know. He's been sending me a lot of texts lately. I'm ignoring him."

"After all these years? What does he want?"

"God only knows. His wife has died, and he's suddenly terribly concerned about keeping in touch." I take another hit, basically so I don't have to react to Calvin's direct gaze. "Also, just so you know, today I realized the other reason why I don't want to fall in love with anybody ever again."

"Because Victor broke your heart in two pieces and then stomped on it, threw it in the dumpster, and then set the whole thing on fire?"

I laugh. "No. Although he did do all those things. The other reason is separate from Victor, who I never want to think of again. It's that it occurred to me that as soon as you love somebody, you have to start worrying about them. Love equals worry when you get right down to it."

He's frowning, holding in some smoke. "Untrue!"

"No. Very true. Like, every single time I've loved somebody, I've then had to worry about whether he has high cholesterol, and is he careful enough when he changes lanes in traffic, and then pretty soon I'm monitoring his doctor appointments, and whether he called his kids for their birthdays, and did he file his taxes."

"Huh," he says. "No offense, but you may be a little weirder than most people."

"Admit it. You're already starting to worry about this Bernice woman from the senior center, aren't you?"

He takes another hit, and then stares at the joint for a long time while he holds in the smoke. Then he says, "You know what? I'm not worried about Bernice, as a matter of fact. I think that there's a worry muscle and a love muscle, and they are two different systems, see? And you can't really be appreciating anything if you're also worrying about it all the time. So I prefer to just love her instead of worry about her."

That's when I remember that he lost his entire family in a car accident. Maybe when you've been through something like that, you figure out the difference between the love muscle and the worry muscle.

I lean over and give him a kiss on the cheek.

༄

It's not until we get to the front door, and are perfecting our smiles and trying to look respectable and not at all stoned, that Calvin suddenly says to me, "So, are you going to tell Louise?"

"About me never intending to fall in love again? I think she knows."

"No, you rapscallion. About her father texting you."

"No. I'm not. Absolutely not. She doesn't have to get mixed up with his foolishness."

"Well," he says. "I was just wondering. Because maybe—"

Just then, Louise answers the door, all dressed up in a lavender flowy caftan and long silver earrings, smiling so big as she hugs us—and Calvin stops talking and hugs her. I'm relieved to see she's wearing the Genuine Louise Smile, not the Instagram-ready one. Then Leo, handsome, brooding, always with his work face on, comes up behind her with his camera equipment and dragging a stadium's worth of lights, and he says, "Hey, Calvin. Billie. Happy birthday." He kisses me on the cheek and shakes Calvin's hand, and then Louise says, "Leo, not those lights. They're not the warm tones I want for this shot."

"These lights are fine," he says. "What you *said* was you wanted to get the greeting, and these are the ones I have right now."

"But there'll be shadows with these lights. Can't you just go get the others? I don't see why these are the ones we have to settle for."

Calvin mouths the word "eek" at me, and we both almost start giggling, and then because he lives a charmed life and does not have to be photographed for any social media thing *ever*, he slips away, heading for the party, which by the sounds of things, is already in full swing in the living room. Which is where I want to be, too. I glance at Leo, whose jaw is clamped down.

"Look," he says. "I know what I'm doing, *Lulu*. I'll shoot from a different angle. It's the expressions they'll be looking at anyway."

"We might as well not even take any pictures if we're going to have the wrong lights," my daughter says sharply. "Can you just *please* do it my way for once?"

Leo hasn't moved his eyes from Louise's face, but he smiles at her and shakes his finger playfully in her direction. "Let me ask you this. Who's the guy who makes his living taking photographs?" he says. "And just so you know, Lady Perfection, this *isn't* a fashion shoot."

"Oh, for heaven's sakes. This is hardly a fashion shoot!" I say, laughing. "Anyway, what does it matter? I'm sixty! No lighting is going to solve me."

"You're perfect," says Leo, still not looking at me. "Believe me, you are not the problem." He smiles coldly as Louise rolls her eyes, and then he runs his hand through his hair. He is tall and skinny, with a fringe of nearly white hair on his high, pale forehead and icy blue eyes. When she first started dating him, I have to admit I was thrown by his careful, measured demeanor. He and I have never got on the way I'd hoped for with a son-in-law; I haven't won him over. He always seems slightly distrustful of my exaggerations, my willingness to just dive into things without any heed whatsoever. Maybe when they have a baby and he sees how children love my spontaneity, he'll come to appreciate me. If they ever get around to having a baby, that is.

"See? This is why you are my very favorite son-in-law," I say to him, because I am relentless in my quest to charm him. "Louise, what if we skip this greeting and the whole picture thing and just rely on our memories? Besides, I need a drink."

"Mom. Just give me one minute," she says, frowning. "Would you mind very much going back out and coming in again? Leo, I know what you're saying, but I'm right in this case. I need this post!"

"Oh, for heaven's sakes," I say. And I tramp back outside. A song starts running through my head. It's Willie Nelson's "Mammas, Don't Let Your Babies Grow Up to Be Cowboys," but the way I'm singing it, it's "Mammas, Don't Let Your Babies Grow Up to Be Bloggers."

If I were at home, we'd be celebrating Martini Thursday, and Marisol would probably be running downstairs to the basement right about now, tracking down the linen napkins, and I would be working on our next recipe from *The Joy of Cooking*—mushroom soufflé with sweetbreads, served with a molded fish salad, which involves pouring boiling water over canned salmon. (Doesn't that just sound delightfully awful?) Edwin, who always makes baked potatoes no matter what else we're cooking (he calls them our safety food), would have the potatoes already out, oiled and dressed in their aluminum foil jackets. Calvin would be inquiring about the age of the sour cream; he says it can't be used if it's more than three days old, while I say it is already sour—that's why they call it *sour cream*—and what's the difference? And there would be music: Frank Sinatra or Dean Martin, perhaps, all in honor of Calvin, who still thinks of the Beatles as young upstarts.

I take a deep breath. I want to be happy but there is just the tiniest little knot of tension in my stomach: it's the old familiar Louise worry. I get nervous when she snaps at Leo, especially when it seems all she worries about is having everything *look* perfect so she'll get lots of clicks. I close my eyes and cram all the angsty feelings in a bubble, like my granny taught me, and then, just as she would have advised, I wish them away, sending the bubble floating out over Long Island Sound.

The front door opens—and I see that Leo has set up a whole array of warm lights all beaming right at the doorway, and at last I get in the door, and Louise greets me officially, and my picture gets taken at least ten times, as I'm smiling and hugging them both, and then and only then does Leo snap off the lights, and Louise thanks him and takes my hand and we go to the living room. "I can't wait for you to see the surprise!" she says.

In the living room—a high-ceilinged, asymmetrical room that gives off the slightly offended feeling of a room that's only rarely used—the party is small, but even so has coalesced into two separate groups, as parties always seem to do. Calvin is over in the corner, with Edwin and Mirasol, and his eyes are on high beams, they're twinkling so much. This is Calvin, happily stoned.

"Look, Mama, who's here!" says Louise, and I see a knot of young women drinking wine and talking—and oh my goodness, suddenly I realize who they are: Louise's friends from high school, girls who spent nearly every afternoon hanging out in my kitchen back in the day and whom I haven't seen in years. They all disappeared to college and partners and lives lived elsewhere—and now here they are!

"*Billie!*" they squeal, almost in a chorus, and then we're all hugging and laughing. They lean toward me, kissing my cheek, holding their wineglasses aloft like scepters while we hug.

"I haven't seen you in ages!" says a smiling, dark-haired woman in leopard-print leggings and a long black sweater. Miranda Thomas! My sweet Miranda. Her mother died when she was fifteen, and for that whole year afterward, the only thing that made sense to her was baking bread in my kitchen. We kneaded and pushed dough around and baked and ate—all kinds of bread, slathered with butter and jam, every kind we could think of, with Elvis singing "Love Me Tender" on repeat in the background.

And here is Hildy Kaufman—wry, sarcastic Hildy, in a purple velvet jumpsuit caressing her round, compact, pregnant belly. Her blonde hair is cut into a bob and she wears long, dangly earrings and lots of eyeliner. "Just look what I've gotten myself into," she says. "Apparently I'm in the business of making humans now."

And Phoebe Adamson—Phoebe, still the jock, with her trademark swagger, still thin and intense, hardly changed at all, wearing jeans with holes in them and a pixie haircut. She was nicknamed Title Nine, because she was always trying to get on the boys' varsity baseball team. She was certainly good enough, but the rules said no.

Oh, these girls, these girls—they were such loud, opinionated additions to the household. Back then, I liked to think of myself as everybody's older, wiser friend, but now I understand that I was really just the mom who would come and pick them up from a date gone wrong, the one they could ask about sex and relationships and not be judged. We talked about everything: sex and love and flirting, and how you drive on the highway, and how you change a tire, and how it's true that boys also have feelings.

Now, looking at these girls after all this time, in their mid-thirties now and bursting with life—well, I feel like grabbing their hands and making them dance once again with me to "Billie Jean" or the Backstreet Boys.

"May I get you some wine?" asks a young woman in a black-and-white uniform. Her nametag says she is Michelle. *Hired help?* I think. *Louise thought she needed hired help for my birthday party?*

"Really, thank you, but I can get it," I say, and she shakes her head and whispers, "Louise would kill me; it's my job."

"We can't have Louise killing you, so a glass of red, please," I say, and she heads off to a mahogany bar set up in the corner next to the fireplace. Louise, flushed and elegant, is talking about the moon with Calvin, who can't seem to stop smiling. He's explaining his theory about the full moon and its meaning in literature. Or something. Werewolves get mentioned, in passing. Or maybe not, surely not. I accept my glass of wine, smiling. James Taylor is crooning about Sweet Baby James through the sound system. Through the window, I see the snowflakes floating down like diamonds with wings.

"You look gorgeous, like Lady Bountiful," I say to Hildy. "And . . . ah . . . is Mister Hildy just delighted?"

"Meh," she says, still smiling and pushing her blonde hair out of her eyes. "I wouldn't know, since he left me at the nine-week ultrasound. Around Thanksgiving."

"He left you *at* the *ultrasound*? What? Did he go to collect the car to pick you up and then never returned? Like those men you hear about who used to go out for pickles and never come back?"

"*Was* it pickles they were going out for?" She laughs and thrusts out one hip, flutters her hands. "I thought it was cigarettes. Anyway, it was more that he vomited into a trash can when the pictures of the fetus came on the screen, and then he told me that he couldn't be a father. He said he was in love with someone else. Something he may have forgotten to mention while he was getting me pregnant."

"Oh, my! Hildy! I'm so sorry. What is the *world* coming to?" I lean forward and say in a low voice, "It was the same with my first husband, except he unfortunately waited to meet the baby before he split. Pretended like he really might be a father. But then, nope."

"That was Louise's dad?" she asks.

"The very one."

"And he's stayed out of the picture all these years, hasn't he?" she says.

I hesitate. We both look over at Louise, who is bloomingly perfect. I have a slight twinge then, wondering if perhaps I'm wrong for not telling her about her father's texts. Some might argue that she even has a right to know her stepmother has passed away. Except that Juliette was never really in her life. Even the couple of times that Louise went to visit them in France, she said that Juliette hardly paid her any attention. And it's not like Victor ever made all that much effort either. I had to remind him about every single birthday, so he would send a card. Why get her stirred up?

"He hasn't really been in touch all that much," I say to Hildy.

She shakes her head. "Look at what he missed out on: this wonderful daughter he never bothered to get to know," she says. Louise is still talking to Calvin. Once she told me that Calvin is like the grandfather she never knew, even though he didn't come into her life until she was an adult. *We all need family*, I think. *Every single one of us.*

I turn back to Hildy. "Yeah. Well. What are you gonna do? These guys have to live with the loss, right?" I say.

Her eyes are sad. "Well. I'm coping. You did, too."

She is so not coping. I put my hand on her arm.

"No, really. I'll be *fine*," she says. "My mom is going to help me with the baby. She's even going to take childbirth classes with me. And according to her, we're going to recruit a whole *community* of fathers to take the place of that scumbag. Handsome ones, too."

Calvin, finished with explaining the moon, has materialized at my elbow. He says to Hildy, "You know, it's good you're telling Billie about this, because as you may not already realize, she happens to be the Heartbreak Bunny. And she's an expert on helping with this—this love-gone-wrong stuff."

Phoebe turns and says, "Wait! *You're* the Heartbreak Bunny? I keep seeing flyers about your business. Louise! Hey, Louise! Why didn't you tell us?"

Louise ducks her head. "Oh, I forgot. Also, to be fair, it seemed like it was a temporary thing."

"Sort of like temporary insanity?" I say happily, from my stonedness. Michelle hands me another glass of wine, and I take three big swigs.

"And now it's gone from temporary to *ongoing* insanity," says Kat, who suddenly shows up behind me, as if the mention of the Heartbreak Bunny summoned her out of thin air. She gives us all air kisses and exclaims how amazing it is that the girls have grown up. I'm sure she's thinking of her daughter, Kelly, who at times used to hang out with Louise and the others, too, at least until junior year, when Kelly took up with a more academic crowd. These days she lives in Southern California and runs a tech company.

"Hi," I say to Kat. "I didn't see you here before. Where were you?"

"Oh, I was in the powder room," she says. She fluffs up her streaked blonde hair and smiles at us. "I went in there because my phone kept buzzing. There are about five new messages for the bunny." She squeezes my arm. "Get this: one woman said she saw you pulled over by the side of the road with a cop yesterday, and when she told people at work about seeing a woman in a stuffed bunny costume getting a ticket, her secretary told her she knew all about your work. So she looked you up and wants to make an appointment."

"Oh, no, no, no," says Louise. "Could we just . . . not?"

"But why?" says Miranda, who then wants to know how the whole Heartbreak Bunny system works. I have unfortunately finished my glass of wine and should not have another, so there's nothing to do but try to explain about the hopping in and hopping out, removing sentimental items, yada yada, and how it's all to help people realize they don't have to stay steeped in unhappiness due to something silly like *romance*. Over thirty satisfied customers, I say.

"If you want the scientific, sociological explanation of why it works," says Calvin with a twinkle in his eye, "*I* think it's that there's something whimsical about a grown woman in a bunny costume and it lets people know that they don't have to stay so serious. It says: life has lots of surprises in store."

"But as you surely would admit, Calvin, it's a little bit ridiculous as an *occupation*," says Louise. "It was just for a lark, never a long-term thing, the way I understood it."

"Right, and that's because we invented it when we were *drunk*, if that tells you anything," says Kat. "But now, quite beyond all reason, it's taken on a life of its own. And can you imagine how much more it's going to explode when people realize you're also throwing in a little bit of witchcraft, free of charge?"

"Witchcraft?" says Louise, her eyes wide. "Oh, Mamacita, what are you *doing*?"

I can't seem to keep from laughing. "Oh, it's nothing serious, Lulu," I tell her. "Just a little salt thrown in the corners—that happened today for the first time, and—"

"And some chanted spell words," adds Calvin. "From your grandmother, I believe."

Kat nods. "Aaaaannd I believe there was also some *practical* business going on, too. Like, did you or did you not load the guy's dishwasher? And clean up his living room?" Her eyes are dancing.

"She took down a tower of beer cans, too, so I hear," says Calvin. "A shrine to his drunken unhappiness."

"Stop, stop," I say, laughing. "You're going to make Louise faint, and then how will dinner ever get served?"

"Wait, Mama. Why are you *doing* this?" Louise says. "This sounds like it's gone way beyond just dressing up like a bunny, which was already crazy enough—and now you're doing *magic spells*?"

"And cleaning houses!" says Kat.

Everybody looks at me.

"It was part of the healing process for him," I say. "The guy was living in a hellhole. I could see that he needed some hope. Some supernatural hope. I say we drink to supernatural hope!"

"To supernatural hope!" says Kat, and we all raise our glasses. Except for Louise.

"Already I was thinking you were going to get arrested for stealing," she says. "And now there's all this—this *magic* stuff you're adding to the situation?"

"I know," I say. "It just keeps getting bigger and bigger in my head. Everywhere I look, I get so many ideas of how to make this even better."

Miranda says, "Well, I think it sounds wonderful. And I think it could be really helpful to our Hildy here."

"I told you, I'm perfectly fine," says Hildy.

"Oh, sweetie, how could you be fine?" says Miranda. "This is us you're talking to. Don't try to shove the bad feelings down. It always comes back to bite you."

"Well, how could *you* be fine?" says Hildy. "You also don't seem to have any love in your life since Moe Waggoner. Wouldn't you consider your divorce a heartbreak?"

Miranda laughs. "I don't have a guy in my life because I'm concentrating on my career, and I'm just fine, thank you. My divorce was a blessing in disguise."

That's when Phoebe says cheerfully, "Not that anyone's asking, but *I'm* a bit of a heartbroken wreck." I look over at her, at the two blotches of color on her cheeks, her large brown eyes, the way she's pushed out her lip into a pout. This is just the way she used to be—always with her feelings slightly hurt, always needing to be the favorite. I remember that she has four older brothers, and her exhausted mother had no time for a daughter, especially one who was always mad about not having the freedom her brothers had.

I put my arm around her. "Why are you a wreck, you little poochums? Don't even tell me it's *also* some man. We are seriously going to have to reexamine the usefulness of that particular gender."

She looks off in the distance. "No, I've got the right guy. Now I'm trying for a baby, but so far no baby has signed up to get born to me." She makes a face. "I have to work very, very hard not to be jealous of all these people who just keep popping out kids like it's nothing." She gestures at Hildy.

"Wait a minute. What *is* this? I've hardly been popping them out," says Hildy. "This is only the first, and I haven't even successfully popped it out yet. The scariest part is still to come."

"You'll do great, like you always do, and you know it," says Phoebe. "You get everything you want. Watch. You're even going to get one of those substitute fathers to end up marrying you and raising this child."

"How long have you been trying, honey?" I say.

"Oh. Forever. Almost a year."

"See? That's nothing," says Hildy. "They don't even start thinking it's infertility until it's been over a year."

"I didn't *say* it was infertility, did I? It may not be infertility, but it still sucks. Every single month being disappointed. And anyway, it's soon going to be a year—and then what?"

"I know it's hard," I say.

"It's Louise who has the perfect guy *and* the perfect life," says Hildy. "And how many followers do you have now, Lulu? Last I looked it was like half a million people all hungry for the details of your exquisite life so they can try to copy you and your fabulous wardrobe. And here I am, wearing my sister's hand-me-down pregnancy jumpers to a party, like some kind of slob. I should be ashamed of myself."

Michelle shows up just then, clapping her hands and announcing dinner. We all move into the dining room, and I walk next to Louise, who puts her arm around me. She smells like roses, and her brown hair shines in the lamplight, and she leans down and says something in my ear about how she hopes I like the scallops dish—and how wonderful it is to have all the old crowd together again. Was I surprised? They were so excited that I was coming.

There's a little catch in her voice and her eyes are just a little too shiny. Something only a mother would see. I squeeze her hand.

⁓

The dinner is perfect, yet I am so achingly tired of "perfect." I'm tired of even hearing that word, tired of it even being a thing, but that's just what dinner is—and everybody keeps declaring it: perfect, perfect, perfect. I see the slight twitch of Louise's jaw and the intensity in her eyes as she watches us react to the beauty she's spread out: the beige linen tablecloth, the huge centerpiece of beige roses and white tulips (who except Louise can find *beige* roses, I ask you? In late January!) and the white bone-china place settings and the (yes, beigey gold) linen napkins pleated into little peaks, the crystal water goblets. Long tapered white candles everywhere! Every place setting with four forks and three spoons—and butter knives, sharp knives, table knives! It looks like a flatware boutique. And all of this is set off by the large floor-to-ceiling windows that look out over Long Island Sound, with the night so clear you can see the twinkling lights on Long Island. The moon is a glowing crescent, hanging outside the window like it was commissioned to show up.

"I wonder how much getting that moon to show up cost her," whispers Kat to me.

"Plenty, you can be sure," I say.

As the guest of honor, I score a seat at the head of the table, with Louise on one side and Hildy on the other. I look around for Leo, but Louise tells me that he's upstairs doing some work.

"No dinner for him then?" I ask, and she rolls her eyes.

"He's *fine*," she whispers. "He's just in a weird mood tonight."

"Could it be that he needs to eat? Even prisoners of war are fed and hydrated."

Her eyes darken. "Mom. He's been in the kitchen working for the last *thirty-seven* minutes photographing the *wineglasses*, which are just generic shots we can use for anything, nothing to do with tonight at all. When he should be out here photographing all of this. The party. But no. He thinks I should just have a 'goddamned birthday party' without it having to be a social media event. So let him eat later if he wants to be this way."

"Well," I say, and realizing I'm taking a huge chance here, I add, "he might have a point, you know."

"Uh-uh. Don't start with me," she says, but she's smiling. She pats my hand. "It's a *lifestyle*, remember. He signed on for it."

I look around at everybody seated so expectantly, smiling, waiting while Michelle serves bowls of butternut squash soup. There's a coolness and precision to Louise's dinner parties—admirable, really—that I have never been able to master.

Michelle and her two uniformed coworkers bring out the salads, layered with tomatoes and chard, crunchy with exotic lettuce. Then comes the main course—scallops and steak, asparagus with hollandaise sauce, and beets done up in goat cheese. And hot fluffy snowflake rolls with butter.

For a moment, looking at Louise's intense expression as she waits for our approval, I can barely swallow. I wish—I wish I could spirit her out of here and oh, I don't know, turn back time and take her for another road trip across the country or maybe just walk with her down to the beach where we'd look in the sand for sea glass or up in the sky for meteors like we did all those summers ago. I'd meant to show her that life could be fun and spontaneous, but was there *too* much spontaneity? Was everything too fast? Too wild? Is that why she has to have everything arranged so perfectly? Is that why we have to have *so many* damn forks?

What was it about our life that made you need to seek perfection, my baby? Where did I scare you?

I look at her worried face and think what a stressful life she's chosen, measuring her success by the numbers of clicks and comments. Always putting herself on display, always being judged and critiqued.

I wish—I wish that she'd realize that she only has to please herself and that her life could be so much fun.

Calvin clears his throat.

"I'd like to give a toast, and I can't wait for dessert because I'm already past my expiration date," he says, and everybody laughs. He holds up his glass and smiles, ready to ham it up big-time. "To Billie, who is always herself. It's your deepest calling to help other people find out where the fun lies. And if sometimes you have to summon a little bit of wart-removing witchcraft for a stranger's bad love affair, so be it!"

"Hear, hear!" says Marisol, and everyone raises their glasses.

After we're finished eating, the dishes are stacked and removed, and dessert is served by Michelle—it's the famous chocolate mousse, a celebrity in its own right, having garnered 325,689 likes this morning, according to Miranda, who has whipped out her phone to check. No doubt people all over America are right now envying my birthday cake. Some are perhaps even running out to buy the ingredients so they can approximate the wonderfulness of the cake made by @lulu&leo.

"I'm so mad that Leo isn't photographing this," mutters Louise under her breath, and I whisper that it's better this way.

"We can eat and not have to see ourselves online with icing on our faces," I tell her.

Because we all see that we have a sad hostess, we praise the mousse again and again, and finally stir ourselves from our food stupor. It's a weeknight, after all. Time to move along. We stand, down the last of our drinks, start murmuring about next time. Hugs are given. We move as one organism to the front hall, where polite good-byes and happy birthday wishes are murmured. Louise is wearing a tight smile. I get my coat.

Hildy comes over and whispers that the girlfriends are going to hang out for a while longer—and would I stay, too? Calvin says he'll go home with Edwin and Marisol, so I hang up my coat once again.

And then they're all gone, and the left-behind party—which Miranda declares is the "confidential steering committee" consisting of me, Louise, and Hildy, Miranda, and Phoebe—drifts toward the den, which is my very favorite room in this house. I love it for its overstated tackiness. It has laminated wood-paneled walls and contains not only a sagging blue corduroy couch with throw pillows in primary colors, but also beanbag chairs and TV tray tables. I can't imagine how this room has escaped the decorating frenzy of @lulu&leo, but somehow it has.

I look down and notice with surprise that my wineglass is full again. Hildy smiles knowingly and holds up the bottle. "I'm doing vicarious drinking, which I trust will not harm the baby," she says.

I take off my shoes to run my toes through the avocado-green and gold shag carpet, left over from the previous owners, circa 1968. It's a hideous, unconscionable carpet that you can just see is trying to lord it over more sedate rugs, bragging about how it doesn't show any dirt, and I am always astonished at how happy I am to see it again.

"This is exactly like the rugs I grew up with," I say. "Furry and fuzzy and hiding all the secrets. Would it be weird if I stretched out on it and rolled around?"

"Extremely," says Miranda. "But on the other hand, we need the sixty-year-olds to show us thirtysomethings that it's okay to be weird."

"If I fall asleep on it, just continue your lives all around me, and try not to kick me, okay? Wake me up when it's time for me to drive home."

"Are you kidding? I was hoping this was going to turn into a dance party," says Phoebe.

"Also, Mamacita," says Louise, "there is no way I'm letting you drive home. You need to spend the night. I had the bed in the guest room made up for you."

"Well," I say. "All right. Thank you. Is this because I've had three glasses of wine and am not suitable to drive, or is it because you're going to try to get all of my witchcraft secrets out of me?"

"Both," she says. "First, I'll sit here and do some deep breathing while you explain to me exactly how in the hell the Heartbreak Bunny got mixed up with doing a freaking magic spell on a guy today."

"Why is this such a big deal? All I did was say some words that my witchy old grandmother probably said one time, and I'm not even sure it's going to work. It just—it just helped at the moment. I could feel him gaining some of his energy back, and that got me to thinking that we all can use a little bit of otherworldly thinking from time to time."

"But your grandmother was crazy!" says Louise. "She thought she could take away people's warts!"

"She could," I tell her. "You didn't ever know her, my dear."

"Yeah, but Grandma said it was completely a myth. She said her mother loved to scare people she didn't like. Didn't she once send some frogs over to a friend's birthday party she wasn't invited to?"

"All family legend," I say. "Granny wasn't ever petty."

"But what words did *you* say?" says Miranda. "To the guy today."

"I don't have any idea. Even at the time, it was like I was chanting some words that came to me. Like I was maybe channeling them. You remember how slapdash I am, honey."

"Oh, God," says Louise. "See? It's not real. So stop encouraging her, you guys."

"It's fascinating," says Hildy. "You know it's fascinating, Louise."

"No, I don't know that. And I don't even think the Heartbreak Bunny idea is all that sound either," says Louise. "Like, how do you *know* people should stop loving the people they love? Maybe they should hang on, be persistent, keep trying."

"They shouldn't," I say.

"But who are you to decide?"

"Louise, child, I didn't decide. Somebody broke up with them and moved on. The thing is *over*. People who keep going back again and again—well, that's a form of mental illness. There's no point to beating a dead horse, as Granny used to put it. So, I help them get over it. That's all."

"And how do you know they don't simply go right back after you leave?"

"Oh my goodness, I have no idea if they go right back. The rest of their life is up to them. I only provide a way of looking at things differently. If they're ready, they'll see it. I believe that you can bring about change by opening the channels of energy, by picturing what you want and then allowing the magic to come."

"If it turns out you knew magic spells all along, why didn't you ever do one to get Victor to come back?" says Louise.

"Well," I say. "I thought of it, but it's not right to do any kind of manipulation to get people to do something they don't want to do. It's considered black magic. Not done. I would never do anything like that."

She's looking at me with suspicious eyes. Her arms are folded across her chest. "Okay. Tell me this: Did you even *try* to get him to stay with us? Not with magic, but with words? You didn't, did you?"

I feel my face turning warm. Maybe it's from the wine. But I'm also thinking of Victor's texts, all lined up in my phone. The last one, sent before dinner, said:

what years i threw away on dreams that lay stillborn on my pillow never blooming as i thought they would and now i am at the graveyard of all i thought would keep me

Can you believe this stuff? I haven't answered him; of course I haven't. But I'm wondering if I'm going to have to block his number. What would Louise think if she knew he was writing to me after all this time?

Miranda says, "Men! What *is* it with guys, anyway? Look at how many men can't seem to love. Look at how you've had to start an entire business based on heartbreak, all because men are always walking away! What is going on?"

"It's not only men," I say. "They're hurting, too, believe me. It's the system we've somehow set up that's faulty, the one that says romance is supposed to be dramatic and suspenseful, and that if you don't have a certain amount of agony, then it's not really love. What I want to know is why romantic love has to be this lifelong goal that everybody *has* to conquer, when it's so over the top and doomed to fail, and then, when it *doesn't* work out—and it hardly ever does—then everybody feels like a discarded piece of dryer lint. I say we stop all that. Pay attention to things that make us happy. Why tie your happiness to something that's so fleeting? Why not discover what makes *you* happy instead?"

Phoebe clears her throat. "Well, I, for one, don't have any problem with magic. And wouldn't it be amazing if Billie did a magic spell for me to get pregnant?"

Everybody looks at me. Miranda claps her hands.

"It *would* be amazing, but I don't know how to do a spell like that," I say after a moment.

"But you could figure it out! You've got some kind of power thing going on, so you can figure out how to make it stronger," says Hildy. "We could all do a circle thing and maybe with all our intentions mushed together, we could call in a baby."

Phoebe laughs. "Yes! Let's call in a baby."

Louise throws her head back and rolls her eyes. "I can't believe this is happening," she wails.

"That's because you're completely grounded here on earth," says Miranda. "Always have been. You're about perfection and organization, and how many followers you have. Which, by the way, how were the photos from tonight received?"

Louise picks up her phone and scrolls, and her eyes flash. "Oh, for God's sake, he didn't post anything!" she says. She stares at the screen, her brows forming an angry line. "If I'd known he wasn't going to post, at least I could have taken some pictures on my phone. And now I've got fifty-six messages from people wanting to know if I'm okay." She scrolls through the messages with her index fingertip, polished with a special purple gel she discovered at an Instagrammer event last week, something she's posted about with a series of exclamation points and sparkles. "Oh, lord. Here's @Lucy34 who wants to know if I went underground since she hasn't heard anything since ten a.m. Gah!" She types something quickly and then puts the phone down and rubs her temples.

"Do you mean to tell us that you can't even get one day off?" I say. "Is that true?"

"*No*, Mom. I can't take one day off. People are waiting to hear from us. And Leo knows we have to post a certain number of times, and he hasn't posted a thing since this morning." She sighs and puts down the phone.

We all sit in silence.

"Never mind," Louise says. She looks up at her friends with tired eyes. "What were you saying, Phoebe?"

"I was saying that all I want is some hope," Phoebe says. "So, could we do that, do you think? All of us get together and have a spell for me?"

"Okay, but with the disclaimer that I don't *really* know what I'm doing," I say.

"You mean, you don't know *yet*," says Phoebe with a smile. "But you will. The right words will come to you, just like they did today."

I look at her sweet, upturned face. "My grandmother was getting rid of things like warts, not calling in babies," I say. "But you're right. I can work on summoning the energy for bringing in a baby. When is the full moon? I think we should definitely work with the moon on this one."

Phoebe gets out her phone and scrolls. "A week from Tuesday," she says. "Could we meet then?"

Everybody checks their devices and says they can come.

My phone dings across the room, in my bag. A text message. Louise looks at me, but I shake my head. I think I probably know who it's from, and I don't want to invite Victor's lower-case energy into the room.

"Yeah, but what if the spell doesn't work?" says Louise. "Then what are you going to do?"

"But what if it does?" says Phoebe. "And what's the difference if it didn't? I'm no worse off." She smiles at me.

My phone dings one more time.

It occurs to me that it could be important. Calvin, Marisol, and Edwin left long ago, and it was snowing. My heart turns over in my chest as I go over and rummage through my purse.

There's a stirring of movement behind me. "Oh my goodness, I just remembered this is a Thursday night!" says Hildy. "I've got a doctor's appointment in the morning."

Kat has sent me a message.

"And I've got to be at work at nine," says Miranda.

Everybody gets up, yawning and stretching.

"Who is it, Mama?" says Louise.

I sink back down on the couch. "Listen to this," I say to them. "It's from Kat. She's forwarded a message from Mason Davis, the morning anchor on Channel Twelve. It says: 'Heartbreak Bunny, this is Mason, whom you met this morning. I want to feature the Heartbreak Bunny on the morning show for Valentine's Day. A new approach to the usual roses-and-hearts stories we do at this time of year. Why romance is dangerous. And also, my son and I had the first good talk we've had in years. Wanted you to know. So, thank you. Please call me.'"

"So here we go then," says Louise, throwing her hands up. "Oh my God, you guys. Why do I even bother trying to pretend I came from normalcy?"

Miranda goes over and gives her a hug. "Because, um? Maybe this isn't about you at all, Lulu my dear. This is your mama's brand of fame."

"But I don't want any fame," I say.

"Exactly," says Louise. "Hear that? She doesn't want any fame."

"Might be too late for that," says Hildy. She's holding her phone and scrolling. "OMG! You've gone viral, Billie. Want to see a TikTok video of you? 'Cause, famous or not, you look adorable. And you have eleven thousand clicks."

CHAPTER SIX

I wake up at Louise and Leo's house the next morning, in the guest room she calls the Santa Fe Room—and let me just say it: the air is not good. It's furious air, is what it is, seeping under the door and around the heating vents. I can hear the low undercurrent of angry voices coming from the next room, like dogs growling. Footsteps pound on the floor. A door slams.

I throw back the covers and swing my legs over the edge of the bed. My head hurts a little bit, and my mouth feels cottony. Oh, yes. Too much wine. Perhaps even waaay too much wine. Let's see: in this order, I need a drink of water, coffee, another drink of water, a shower, some ibuprofen, some protein, and to get home to drink more water. And I have to call Mason Davis, to tell him I'd love to be on his show.

So far, being sixty years old is turning out to be complicated.

I gaze around the guest room for a long time, taking it all in. Since the last time I stayed here—probably four months ago—it's been redecorated to look like a scene from the Sundance catalog; the walls are now a stubbled stucco, bleached pure white, and there's a distressed, rough-hewn dresser the color of tree trunks against the wall, and a muslin quilted bedspread in azure and teal and burnt umber hanging over a clothes rack. A picture on the wall depicts an old broken-down pickup truck parked in the desert.

I take a deep breath.

I hear Louise now saying, loudly, in the hallway: "What about our usual 'woke up this way'? You're not even going to photograph *that*, Leo?"

I hear him laugh. "Louise, Louise! The 'woke up this way' shot is the worst! It's exactly what I'm talking about. You *didn't* wake up this way. It's a fake, artificial shot that we spend a half hour on every day. Who needs this? Why are we doing it?"

Oh God.

"People like it," she says right outside my door. "It's our trademark, Leo, in case you don't realize. People say they look at it every morning before they start their day. You know how many likes we get just from this one post every day?"

I hear his bitter laugh again. "Why are we responsible for starting someone's day? How has that become our job? *My* job?" His voice trails away. I hear him going downstairs.

Then she yells, "Fine! Fine, then. You go do what you want. Who cares what you do? I'll do the photo with my phone. That's just perfect, Leo, just perfect."

There's a silence and then she knocks at my door. "You awake?"

Like anybody could sleep through that.

"Come in," I say with a certain amount of dread. I smooth out the covers to make room for her, and sure enough, she flounces in and lands on my bed with a thud. Her hair is a tumble of curls, already styled and glistening, and she's wearing a flowered kimono and purple socks. She sits on the edge of the bed and stretches her legs out in front of her and wiggles her toes. Then she turns and looks at me.

"Are you hungover?" she says. "You are, aren't you?"

"I, um, seem to be approximately ninety-two percent hungover. And you?"

"I was, but not anymore. I've been up for hours now. I'm already in a fight with Leo."

"So I heard."

"Then you probably heard that he's being impossible." She flings herself backward on the bed and then scootches around, so her head is on the pillow next to mine. "You saw how he was last night. He's going through a midlife crisis or something. I'm not going to put any energy into it. That's what you always say to do, isn't it? Just withdraw your energy?"

"That's one way."

She snuggles up closer to me, puts her head on my shoulder. I rub her temples, like I used to do when she was little, back when everything would be too much for her at our house. Then she says, "He's sick of doing Lulu and Leo."

"I see. And how long has this been coming on?"

"I don't know. A while, I guess. But it's getting worse. He says being an Instagram influencer is all fake and artificial anyway, and that we're not doing anything to help people, and he keeps talking about whether it's *honest*. He says we've made enough money, and we should think of something else to do."

I massage her temples. "And you don't want to quit?"

"*No*, I don't want to quit!" She props up on one elbow. "Why would I quit? I feel like I'm at the top of my game here. And just by the way, we *are* helping people. I can't tell you how many people are responding to the blog every single day, and then *he* goes and says that's all fake, too. He says we're just bragging about our lives. When that's not it at all. We give tons of money away. We support foundations that help women and kids and the environment." She flops back down onto her back. "What's not real about it, is what I want to know!"

Well, I think. I look over at the dresser again. It's a little precious, this room. A little tiny bit artificial, with its fake-adobe walls and southwestern blankets and the framed print of the old pickup truck in the desert. But I don't say that. Instead, I say, "Maybe you two just need a break. You've both been working so hard. How about going on vacation together?"

She sighs. "We can't take a break, Mom. That's the very thing you can't do with social media. We're in this and we have to stay in it."

"You can't just declare to your fans that you're in need of some quiet couple time? Wouldn't people respect that? They might even relate."

"You don't get it," she says. She sits up, moving away from me. "We have sponsors. We have people relying on us. We're a love story. Did you miss that? We're a commodity."

"A commodity!" I say. "Wow. That's harsh. I'd much rather be a human couple than a commodity. And you know how I feel about being in a human couple."

"I'm going to have to have this out with him. I can feel it coming." Then she flashes a smile in my direction and squares her shoulders. "But I'm strong and empowered and confident. That's my mantra. Strong, empowered, and confident."

"But, honey. A mantra for yourself is fine. But maybe there's a compromise." I can hear the ice crack—the ice that I'm currently treading on in this conversation.

Sure enough, she whirls on me. "Yeah. Right. I tell you I'm strong, empowered, and confident, and you immediately say I should compromise. Do you hear yourself?" She rubs her eyes. "Just forget I said anything. It's a conversation I have to have with him, and I'll do it, and things will get fixed like they always do, and *you* are not to spend one more second worrying, you with your Heartbreak Bunny eyes looking at me."

"I am not looking at you with any *Heartbreak Bunny* eyes."

"Yes, you are. I know you." Then she gets up and goes over to the antique mirror and fiddles with her hair, turning her head from side to side, tucking her curls behind her ear. "Hey, want to take a photo of me? For the 'woke up this way' post?"

"Me?"

"Sure. Here's my phone." She gets back in the bed, and I get out of it. "Ooh, this is going to be a good one. I woke up this way in Santa Fe!" She smooths her hair, but only a little—it's supposedly a wake-up picture, after all, and she fluffs the turquoise and orange pillows and then leans against them. "See if you can get the truck in the shot, too."

"Okay, okay, hold your horses."

I hold up the phone and look at her there, smiling and stretching. I take one with her arms in the air, clasped over her head, and one with her in a kittenish position, with her hands curled just so under her chin. She manages to make her face look both sleepy and sexy at the same time.

Ah, my little Louise.

"Okay!" she says when I show her the phone. "That's great." She throws back the covers and bursts out, suddenly energized. "Okay then. *I'm* going to go post this and write the stuff, and probably ignore Leo a little longer, and you—what about you? Want to take a bath? We got the whirlpool jets installed in this bathroom, so you are in for a bath treat extraordinaire. It'll wipe out those hangover cobwebs in your brain and body! And then you'll come downstairs, and we'll have breakfast. Dolly comes in around eleven to clean, so we have a lot of time. A nice, leisurely breakfast this morning! Sound good?"

"Sounds good," I say weakly.

"And no more worrying about Lulu and Leo," she says. She kisses me on the cheek. "Because this is all going to work out the way it's supposed to. Isn't that what you believe?"

"That is what I believe," I say.

"Perfect! Then whatever way it goes, that's the way it's meant to be. The Heartbreak Bunny said so."

∽

Five years ago, when Louise called me to say she'd fallen in love with a guy named Leo Cabot, she was practically giddy. I'd never heard her that way. He was "all that and a bag of chips," she said, laughing. She'd met him at work. She was working as a fashion correspondent at the Stamford newspaper, and he was a freelancer doing a series of photographs fifteen years after 9/11, photographing family members of the Connecticut people who had died in the Twin Towers. He was *quite* serious, she said—serious, competent, talented, brilliant. "He is all the best adjectives!" she said.

"Wow. When can we meet him and his adjectives?" I asked her, and there was a long pause. And then I knew. "Oh," I said. "I suppose you need us to clean up our act around here before such a paragon of brilliance comes around."

"It's not that," she said, and then she laughed. "But . . . well, yes."

So I painted the foyer and planted some annuals, spruced up the wicker furniture on the porch. We decided that the two of them would drive out for a Sunday afternoon visit. He'd never been to New Haven. She said she could perhaps take him to look at the Yale campus (always a crowd-pleaser) and then out for genuine New Haven pizza after he'd met us.

The day they arrived was a hot one, and he wore a suit the color of vanilla ice cream. I had made oatmeal lace cookies, the crunchy, buttery kind that everyone loves. I was ready for whatever. Even had a pitcher of lemonade. The kind with real lemons.

I was struck at first by how very tall he was—six-three, he said—and how very light his thin little fringe of hair was and how pale his skin. His eyes looked like they came from a chip right from the sky.

Also, he carried a spray of wildflowers, like a suitor in a nineteenth-century novel. All that was missing was a boater hat and some suspenders.

He sat perched on the edge of the couch, politely refusing cookies, nodding at questions we asked, clearing his throat often, blinking those ice-blue eyes over and over again, while Louise sat pressed up against him, smiling, her arm linked through his. It seemed like he didn't dare to look around, as if he'd be frightened by what he might see. When prodded, he told us about the 9/11 project, and Louise said he was going to win a prize for it, and we congratulated him. He kept flexing a little muscle in his jaw and gazing at Louise. She bubbled over with conversation—there'd been some sort of fashion scandal she was shocked to discover that none of us knew about. And oh yes, she might get hired full-time at the paper. And wasn't she so lucky to get to write about culture this way? That's what she said. Because fashion really was the newest outpost of culture! It was practically an art form now!

Leo's eyes begged to be removed from the premises.

After they left, I told Calvin that it was too bad we'd gone to all that trouble to look good when this relationship was obviously doomed. This guy was something of a stick. But Calvin, who is wiser than I am, predicted that we hadn't seen the last of this Leo character. And sure enough, five weeks later, Louise called me to say they were getting married.

"Married!" I was so surprised I had to sit down and think of what it is you're supposed to say to this news. "Why in the world are you doing that?"

She laughed. "Mother! That is not what nice people say to such an announcement."

"Well, it's just so sudden," I said. "May I ask if this is because you're expecting a little Leo or Louise?"

"No!" she said. "God, Mom! You've gone from bad to worse. Can't you just be happy that I've found the man I want to live with for the rest of my life? And anyway, even if I *were* pregnant, that wouldn't mean I needed to get married. It's not the 1950s, you know."

"Of course not," I said, recovering somewhat. "I *am* happy for you, Louise, but I guess I'm just surprised. He seems sort of . . . muted. I wouldn't have picked him to be your type."

There was a silence, and then she said, "Maybe you're not recognizing that he is a truly intense individual. Mom, he *smolders.*"

"I must have missed the smoldering," I said slowly. "I think the danger with this guy is that his power cord is going to malfunction, and you're going to have to send out for some spare parts."

"Well, you're not really seeing the real him," she said curtly. "Believe me, he's on fire."

I apologized, of course, and said we'd invite his parents and have a little engagement party for them. Jonathan and Renata Cabot accepted my invitation, and they arrived from New York City on the train on an oppressively hot, humid day a few weeks later. Leo had the same unblinking blue eyes as his mother and the same lean stick figure as his father.

I put out one of my most ambitious spreads—chilled gazpacho soup with dill and little pieces of avocado, cold Korean noodles with bok choy and asparagus, and farmstand heirloom tomatoes with fresh mozzarella and basil leaves. Calvin helped me make a pitcher of sangria. Marisol and Edwin and Max—Max was a tenant we had back then, and he had a sheepdog named Buddha—were in attendance. Marisol had set the table with the linen napkins and the silver and the candlesticks. Edwin had mowed the lawn and put pots of geraniums on the porch.

Thunderstorms threatened all afternoon. The air conditioner in the living room was on the fritz, and Calvin was trying to fix it by taking it apart, piece by piece, and letting all the little screws roll under the couch, narrating his progress as he went. "Now you *see*," he said to Leo's father, who stared at him from behind thick glasses that could only be described as *spectacles*, "a lot of people think *compressor* when they hear about an air conditioner gone bad, but what *I* find . . . what a *literature* professor can think of is different, you see . . . our minds work in *different* ways . . ."

I was in my element, sashaying around in my long skirt with little mirrors and sequins sewn into the fabric and my filmy red tunic. I passed around appetizers and asked everybody questions and kept up a conversational patter. I had just had my blonde hair cut in a pixie style—this was back when I still dyed it—and I was diligent about using mousse to make it stick up in spikes. I was on my game.

Leo's mother, dressed in a blue linen suit, with her almost white hair curled in little pin curls around her face, sat on the edge of the couch just as her son had a few weeks before, gazing at us with wide, concerned blue eyes, looking quietly terrified by nearly everything going on: the storm clouds gathering outside, the metal pieces of the air conditioner that Calvin tossed into an ever-growing pile, and the hard-breathing Buddha who was determined to steal everyone's crackers. The sky grew so dark that we soon had to turn on the lights. Thunder churned in the distance.

I was asking Mrs. Cabot about her trip when suddenly all our cell phones beeped at once—an unearthly cacophony courtesy of the emergency alert system. There were tornadoes in the area! Flash floods! Lightning kept flashing with the thunder right there on top of it, rattling the house.

Max shouted that we needed to close the windows because lightning could strike us through the screens—and Calvin yelled that the house would blow up from all the air pressure if we did close the windows. So Max was closing them, and Calvin was going along behind him opening them again.

And then—there was a huge bang, and the power went out.

"That's it," I said cheerfully. "Let's all reconvene in the basement for some light refreshments!"

I coaxed everybody to their feet. I held Renata Cabot's arm and gently led her to the basement door. She peered down the stairs. It was dark down there and smelled like spiders. (Calvin says spiders don't have a smell, but everyone knows they do.)

Leo held on to his mother's other hand until we got downstairs, but then he handed her over to his father and disappeared. Thunder roared like a freight train above. I ran upstairs to get the pitcher of sangria and some plastic cups—we were at a party, after all—and then hurried back down. I tried to put everybody at ease. Mrs. and Mr. Cabot had turned back into mannequins, and Calvin was recounting the five times he nearly died but didn't. I started handing out drinks. Leo and Louise had seemingly vanished.

"Just a little bit of excitement," I said as I gave Jonathan Cabot his plastic cup. "My parties always have an element of surprise with them, and I want you to know a tornado was *not* so easy to arrange!"

He looked alarmed, mumbled something into his drink, and pulled his wife closer.

I looked around, craning my neck to see into the dim recesses of the laundry section—and it was then that I spotted Louise and Leo. They were pressed against the wall between the washer and the dryer, partially illuminated by a weak gray light from one of the casement windows.

I craned my neck farther to see and then jumped back. They were making out—going at it full-tilt, movie-style, in fact. His eyes were closed and he was pressing her against the wall underneath him.

Well. I wanted to burst into applause. Really! What kind of man goes in for the full-body, devastating kiss in the middle of possible death and destruction? With his parents and his prospective mother-in-law standing just feet away?

Let me just say that I understood for the first time what it was Louise saw in him.

They were going to make it after all.

I don't have one jot of respect for romance, but passion is a language I understand.

∽

When I go downstairs nearly an hour later, after taking a long bath, Louise and Leo are in the kitchen, in separate corners like prizefighters, silent.

Whatever they've been doing for the last hour didn't improve their situation, from the look of it. Too bad they didn't think of making out, a language they clearly both understand.

Nevertheless, I have my orders not to worry. So, I stride forward. I will cook these disagreeable little babies some breakfast, slather them with love food, plump up their red blood cells, and then get the hell out of their way.

"Good morning!" I say. "I see all the known survivors are gathered here. How's everybody doing? I myself could use fourteen Advil and three cups of coffee and maybe a sledgehammer."

A kind of a sucking-in sound comes from Leo. If there is a sound that is the opposite of a laugh, that's what this is. Louise glances up and gives me a baleful look. She's still wearing her kimono and the purple socks, and Leo is in a green hoodie and sweats, leather bedroom slippers and aviator sunglasses. He's standing at the counter, frowning, scrolling through his phone. The two of them look like marionettes who some-how lost the person who was supposed to be holding the strings and they're now in danger of collapsing into a heap.

"Look at that snow—still coming down!" I say. "Are they saying it's going to stop soon?" I wish I could just teleport myself home so I wouldn't have to drive in this stuff, although with the tension in this room, I would gladly run home in my bare feet just to get away.

"In an hour or so," Leo says. He goes over to a contraption that resembles a moonshine still, and he presses some buttons and coffee streams into a mug that looks like it came from ancient Greece. He hands it to me, his mouth in a grim line. "Here. Coffee," he says. "Good morning. Rough night all around, I'd say."

This was way more conversation than I was expecting from him. "Thank you. Keep 'em coming, will you?" I say. "And maybe have a dozen or so for yourself." I take a sip and then set the cup down on the counter before it sprains my wrist. It weighs approximately ten pounds. "Shall I make everybody one of my famous omelets, get the blood circulating? Some nourishment? Get the pheromones waked up? By the way, that whirlpool bath is just amazing! That's new, right?"

Leo doesn't answer, but Louise sighs and puts down her phone. "It's new. Yes. And I guess an omelet would be good, if you feel like making it."

"Leo, you?"

He grunts something, which I take to mean that he would eat if food appeared in front of him, and I go over to the refrigerator—which is disguised as a regular teak cabinet right next to the other teak cabinets. You have to have an eagle eye to spot just which door opens the fridge. But because I've been here before, I do it on the first try and manage to locate the eggs and some swiss cheese and some spinach among the leftovers from the party last night.

Louise gets out a pan, sighing, and I find the butter in a special contraption on their counter, a system of bowls that keeps the butter both softened and cool at the same time. This is the benefit of being on Instagram night and day; people send you stuff you didn't know was even possible.

I must be extra nervous if I'm thinking so hard about the butter. I steal a look at Leo, who is staring grimly into his phone. "So, I just heard back from Jack, and he'll draw up the agreement," he says in a low voice. "He says it will be amicable, of course."

Louise doesn't even bother to look over at him. "Fine," she says. "Of course, I'm going to want to see what he considers amicable."

"I would expect nothing less," says Leo.

I feel my whole body tighten. I have never liked the word *amicable*. It's only used when things have broken down so badly that it's like a consolation. If you can't be nice, be amicable.

"Hey! What do you say? Could we have some nice, mellow, amicable jazz?" I say. "And where are those snowflake rolls from last night? I'll make us some toast. It is my personal opinion that every problem can be solved by either buttered toast or a trip to the ocean."

Good heavens. Who *is* this woman chirping away like this? Clearly she has taken over my personality this morning. Whoever she is, she doesn't seem to be able to overcome the thick mood of despair that has settled into every nook of this kitchen.

Louise hands me the snowflake rolls. And after a moment, Leo wanders out of the kitchen. I would like to know who Jack is, but I'm also afraid to know who Jack is. I turn on the peaceful jazz station on their Sonos system, which I just recently learned how to operate. The music curls out of the speaker, meets with and kisses the light coming in through the long windows, sunshine filtered through snow.

Louise picks up her phone. "I guess I should probably get a photo of the snowflake rolls. People love seeing melted butter on top of bread. It's like food porn. All that gluten and fat." She sounds like Eeyore talking to Winnie-the-Pooh.

"Sure." I put the rolls on the stoneware platter that she hands me, and she arranges them for their photo. Butter slides across the top in a glistening, photogenic puddle.

Louise just looks at them, no signs of life in her eyes.

She takes a shot of the rolls and then a photo of the orange egg yolks in the blue bowl and one of my hands buttering the rolls. The last one is an artistic shot, showing my beaded bracelets and the chunky ring that I bought at a jewelry fair last fall, and Louise says she'll post it this morning.

The January sun sparkles on the snow, on the sound below, and the light streams and streams into the kitchen, touching the marble countertops and bouncing off the white ceramic stein I'm drinking out of.

She and I eat at the kitchen island, sitting on the stools, looking out at the water. Leo never does come back down. Louise keeps staring off into space.

⁓

Later, after the snow stops, she walks me to my car. She has her phone with her, of course, and she listlessly snaps a few photos of us brushing off the car. My stomach is arguing with the eggs. Also, this may be the wine from last night talking, but my legs and arms feel heavy with dread. Whenever I look over at Louise, she quickly composes her face to hide whatever horrible emotion lies underneath. She keeps snapping pictures.

Suddenly, I can't take it anymore. "Um, could you sit in the car for a minute and talk?" I say tentatively.

She gets in without speaking and then sits there fiddling with her beaded bracelets.

I start up the ignition and turn the heat full blast. "Okay, what's going on? Did you and Leo have a big talk? And who is Jack? And why are we talking about things being amicable?"

She lets out a long sigh. "Okay, Mom, don't freak out, but we're splitting up."

"Splitting up? Just since this morning?" I rest my hands on the steering wheel. "You see, this is why people shouldn't have big talks when they're hungover, too mad, or it's the middle of winter, is what I think. You need some time together. Go on that vacation we were talking about, give yourselves some time off away from everything." I look up at the house, hulking over the driveway, all its pointy windows looking particularly ominous with the sun glinting off them. "Go do something fun!"

"Mom, you don't know what you're talking about. It's over." Her voice is monotone. "He's leaving. He's packing right now. He didn't want me to tell you yet."

"What? You have a night when he doesn't take any pictures, and then *boom!* Just like that, your whole love story comes crashing down? What kind of nonsense is this? Wait a second. You made this decision *after* you left my room this morning?"

"It's not *just like that.* It's been coming for a long time. But yes. I tried to talk to him this morning, to get him to agree to take pictures again, and he told me he's leaving." She answers me in a tired voice, like I'm not keeping up. She leans her head against the window.

"I knew I shouldn't have taken that long bath," I say.

"Yeah, that's right, it was your bath."

We both stare out at the water. When I look back at her, I see her eyes filling with tears. I lean over and put my hand on her shoulder. "Oh, baby. I'm sorry. This is very hard. I can't even imagine."

"What I have to figure out is how I'm going to run this whole business without him," she says, and swipes at her tears. "He takes all the pictures! How am I supposed to do that and make it look professional?"

"I don't know," I say. "I'll help you any way I can. You know that."

"There's nothing you can do. He's a professional photographer. That's what made our blog different from other people's. That, and the love story we claim to have." She closes her eyes. "*That* was certainly a bust."

"Well," I say. I look out through the windshield again at the rocks and the water. The wind has blown all the clouds somewhere else. The sky is as blue as a banner. "I think there's a good possibility that you two are going to patch this up. It's a spat, honey. If my life has taught me anything, it's that marriages are filled with spats."

"Thanks, but I don't think this is just a spat, as you call it. He wants to do something more *meaningful* than take stupid, meaningless pictures of me in evening gowns. That's what he actually said."

"Oh dear," I say.

"Yeah. He's a *photojournalist*. So, for the time being, he's going to New York to stay with friends, and we agreed that I'm going to continue @lulu&leo, keeping it just like it is. Pretend he's still there, taking the pictures."

"Well," I say again, "I guess it makes sense to hold it together until you decide for sure what's going to happen. Right now it may seem like the marriage is over, but—well, who knows what will happen? You have a marriage, you have a business . . . Both are susceptible to changes and arguments. And differences of opinion. But you can find your way back together if that's what you want."

"He says the marriage *was* the business. He thinks that's all there was."

"Really? He's going to try to make us believe that the only thing holding you together was the blog? Because I've seen you two, long before you were influencers. You have passion! He can't take his eyes off you, Louise."

"Stop. Please. This is ridiculous." She shifts her weight on the seat. "Don't be thinking you're going to have to prop me up. You're not. I've got people counting on me to post every day, and I'm going to be fine." She shrugs and wipes her eyes. "Really. Stop looking at me all worried like this."

"Well, if you need any help . . . If you want to come back home for a while . . ."

"Nope, nope, nope. I don't need a thing," she says. "And I definitely don't need the Heartbreak Bunny coming around and psychoanalyzing me or doing magic spells. I'm going to be okay. I have to figure out how to make this business work on my own. But I will. It's going to take me a minute, that's all." She wipes her eyes again.

"I raised you to be strong," I say without any conviction whatsoever. "And I know you are."

I sit there and feel all my feelings rolling around under the surface. All my Louise buttons—and there are many, expertly installed over the years in nearly every part of my body and mind—have now been pushed, and the alarm bells clang inside me.

The thing is: when all is said and done, I'm not shocked that they've made this decision, or even that my own child has a flawed love story— so the passion didn't see them through; what else is new?—but what kills me is that she hid it from me. What kind of mother could miss something this enormous? For God's sake, she lives only two towns over from me, and I talk to her nearly every single day. I see her life unfold on the internet, and I see the life that's *behind* that life. Or I thought I did. I feel like the breath has been knocked out of me.

My phone dings, and I ignore it until I've kissed her good-bye and she's gotten out of my car and is walking back to her house.

It's Victor again.

i need an app that tells me how to get back to myself please tell me how i can do that

Suddenly I want to throw not only my phone, but *all* phones everywhere, out of car windows, over cliffs, into landfills. The whole system of blogs and phone calls and text messages seems deeply, deeply horrible. What have we human beings done, tying ourselves to these hideous little computers that interrupt us and keep us plugged into communication with others we learned once to do without? I'd gladly do without this phone, just to keep from ever having to hear from this man again, but I manage not to throw it.

If I threw my phone out of the car window, then I wouldn't be available when Louise needs me.

◠◞

Naturally, I have to consult with my friends about this Louise and Leo breakup. Calvin reminds me that Louise and Leo were never what anyone would call a sure thing.

He looks at me over the top of his reading glasses and says in a very mild voice, "Do I have to remind you that you are the Heartbreak Bunny specifically because you know this kind of thing isn't sustainable? Also, their whole relationship seemed like it was based on pretending. On making their life look like it's easy and carefree, when it's anything but that."

"I know, I know."

"She'll figure it out," he says. "She's strong. And she has a lot of talent."

When I call Kat, she reminds me that our children have their own lives to lead, and that it's tempting to believe we can solve everything for them, but the truth is that we can't do much but look on and offer encouragement from the sidelines.

"Encouragement that they don't listen to," I say.

"Well, sure," she says. "But we didn't listen to our parents either."

They both say it's a good sign that Louise has such drive, and that she's moving forward. "She has a plan," says Calvin. "And she's implementing it."

Kat says, "It's Louise's life. If she wants to continue pretending that she's still blissfully happy, why would you want to interfere? Just live your own life and have faith that she'll figure this out."

This sounds suspiciously like advice I've given people a time or two, perhaps even to Kat herself when Kelly moved far away to be with a guy nobody thought was any good. In a long friendship, that's what you do—toss the wisdom back and forth, like a big beach ball.

◠◞

Two nights later, my phone rings in the middle of the night. After I've fumbled to find it on the bedside table in the dark, I don't hear anything but heavy breathing and sniffling on the other end.

"Hello?" I say. "Louise? Honey? Are you all right?"

"Oh, Mama," she says. "Mama, I miss him *so much.*"

"Of course you do. Of course, of course," I say, instantly jarred into wakefulness.

She is like my baby again, her voice young and uncertain coming through the darkness, listing everything that's wrong. That house: it's too big, too unfriendly, too *pointy.* Also, she's having so much trouble organizing the business without him. Taking selfies that look good is *hard.* Writing the copy, keeping up with the commenters. Unopened boxes of merchandise are piling up in the hallway. She wants to hire an assistant, but she doesn't have time to interview applicants. Also, no one would be as competent as Leo. And besides all that, the commenters need attention. They're feeling neglected, she says.

"I know it's just because it's four a.m., which is the hour of the black dogs, but I honestly didn't know I would be this lonely," she says softly.

"I know, baby, I know," I say. "Try to get some sleep. Maybe drink some hot milk, or take a bath, read for a while."

"You've been left. How did you get through it?"

I try to think of any elderly, maternal wisdom I might impart. How it is that those middle-of-the-night hours might be good, actually, how they somehow lead you to examine what's important in your life and to learn to trust yourself. How valuable, really, heartache can be when it brings you closer to a true version of what you want out of life. (Possibly this would be a version that doesn't require thousands of Instagram followers to praise you every time you put on a new outfit.)

However, even I know that none of this would be helpful.

"You just do," I say.

In the morning I get up and go over to help her. We do five days' worth of #wokeupthisway photos with her in different nightclothes, and I unpack the boxes—consisting of a levitating light bulb, a big stick that claims it can sanitize your clothing in twenty seconds, a jacket that has a Bluetooth connection so it can keep your arms at different temperatures, and some mysterious electronic thing that turns out to be a microscope you can attach to your phone.

That's the thing that pushes me over the edge and makes me go upstairs to find her.

She's writing copy for the blog and weeping.

I wave the phone microscope in the air. "How do you live this way? With all these useless, ridiculous things arriving daily in box after box! Is this what being an influencer is all about?"

She looks up with her tearstained face and nods.

"No wonder you're in tears. How are we to live in a world where people need levitating light bulbs?" I say. "I don't even want to *know* about this crap! Not to mention there's a jacket downstairs that can keep your right arm warmer than your left at the flick of a switch. Seriously, tell me. Who ever wanted that in a jacket?"

"With my luck it would set my right arm on fire," she says quietly.

"Exactly! And the levitating light bulb would hit you in the head."

She starts to laugh and cry at the same time, which causes her to start hiccuping, which then makes her laugh harder. And then cry harder.

I stare at her.

"Really," I say. "For the sake of all that is good and sacred in this world, you need to walk away from this job. Send all the stuff back to their inventors, and walk away quietly. This is not a normal life, Louise."

"And hopping around in a bunny suit *is* a normal life?" she says.

She may have me there.

CHAPTER SEVEN

The following Monday, at two in the afternoon, I find myself sitting in a booth at the Athens Diner, across from Mason Davis.

He has the appearance of somebody fresh from seeing both a hairdresser and a manicurist—and possibly just off the plane from a week's vacation in the tropics as well. *I* look like a person who possibly got dressed in the dark recesses of a boxcar and who can't find her comb. (If truth be told, I'm a little harried because before I left home, I had to find, trap, and then escort outside four basement spiders who were terrorizing Micah, Reggie's five-year-old son, who had come to work with Reggie because his school had closed for a teacher in-service day.)

I'm also a little worn out, perhaps, from constantly trying to take the place of Mr. Leo Cabot, photographer extraordinaire, in the world of @lulu&leo. Not only am I useless at taming the boxes of paraphernalia that are in the foyer, but I have realized I'm also hopeless at snapping a picture that communicates the amount of glamour and beauty that a simple Instagram post calls for. I simply cannot measure up. In between chasing away heartaches on my bunny calls and trying to take stunning photos of my daughter's life that don't reveal that she's a mad wreck, I'm ready to take to my bed, where I will do crossword puzzles and nothing else.

I can't even remember why going on television ever sounded remotely like a good idea. Driving over to meet him, I kept repeating a new mantra: *The Heartbreak Bunny is not going to go on television. The Heartbreak Bunny is not going to go on television.*

I know I was once excited about the prospect of going on Mason Davis's show, but now I know it would break Louise, having me go so public. I figure I'll simply meet him, be polite, have a cup of tea, ask about Joey, and say a firm "no thank you" to anything else.

Mason Davis and I pulled into the parking lot at the same time, and then threaded our way to the door, while myriad admirers of his, people who sniff out his presence like dogs who have just realized there was a rib eye steak flung somewhere nearby, threw themselves in front of him, smiling, waving, gushing about today's show. And once we made our way to the table, he signed at least five autographs.

Celebrity life. Spare me.

Still, I like that he is gracious and that he smiles at everyone, even chucks a little boy under the chin, and calls him *buddy.* The waitress comes to take our order. She is Penny, according to the name tag on her black jersey, and she is busy hyperventilating from breathing the same air as Mason Davis. When he tells her that he loves her earrings and asks for her recommendation on pie, I think she will faint. I like it that he smiles kindly at her.

I also like it that he orders the coconut cream pie she suggests and doesn't act all coy like he has to watch his weight.

But that's it for his good points. Otherwise, I am on my guard against his silver-gray hair and his crinkly eyes and that voice that sounds like he drinks gravy for breakfast.

We do the preliminaries. Small talk that surprisingly turns deep for a man with a fake tan—or what I think is a fake tan. He tells me that his wife died seven years ago, and that he has found being a widower to resemble falling into a yawning crevasse, and he admits that he can't ever imagine being romantic with anyone again. "Dating," he says sheepishly, "is not in my skill set."

I tell him dating is the *worst*, especially if you're older than sixteen, and then I go into my less than stellar marital history—the two divorces and the death—as if it's a badge of courage, which is how I see it on a good day. I figure I might as well just put all the crazy right out there, so I throw in the news that I have a grown daughter who's an Instagram influencer and therefore a perfectionist, and that I also have a bunch of housemates, and that I haven't had anything but seat-of-the-pants employment for my whole life, giving classes in my home and taking in boarders, driving people to appointments.

"I may have needed a Heartbreak Bunny a time or two myself," he says in a low, confiding voice. "Back in the day, I mean. Before I got married. I was always getting my heart stomped on."

"We all did. That's because we all listened to the same stupid love songs and watched the same stupid movies," I say. I'm sitting back in the booth, stacking up sugar packets, which is handy because it keeps me from having to look straight at all that handsomeness, which is like looking into the sun. "Sold a bill of goods, we were. We all got addicted to the idea of romance."

"And now you're here to put us all in romance rehab," he says. He smiles with twinkling eyes and leans forward. "And, if what they say is true—that in the future we're all going to be famous for fifteen minutes—then I'd say that the Heartbreak Bunny is already two minutes into full fame, wouldn't you? And now when our viewers see you, you're going to get even more attention."

"Actually," I say, "I'm not one of those people who thinks she needs to be famous. In fact, I want to keep the business small. And so I don't think I should go on your show."

"Oh!" he says. He looks shocked for a moment, but then his expression softens. Those crinkly eyes melt into a smile, and he smoothly glosses over any disappointment he may be feeling. "Well, then. May I say that I'm glad you came to meet me, so I can thank you for what you did for Joey."

"How *is* he?"

"He—he's doing great. Great*er*. Great for him, that is." He leans even closer, which forces me to look into his eyes. My pile of sugars falls over. "Sadly, I have to say that he finds adulthood rather challenging. Which makes it difficult for—"

Just at that moment, fortunately, Penny glides up and plunks down the plate of coconut cream pie and two forks, smiling at him. The pie wobbles on the plate, all spongy meringue and glistening cream with little pieces of white coconut sticking out here and there. For a moment, we can't do anything but admire it.

Then Mason nods and grabs a fork and takes a big bite. He sits back and closes his eyes and moans.

"Didn't I tell you, hon?" Penny says. "You want a piece, too, sweetheart?" Looking at me.

"Oh. No. No, thank you."

She shakes her head like she can't believe such ignorance on my part, and then a man at another table calls for coffee, and she hurries off.

"Oh my God, this is good," Mason Davis says. "Where was I? Oh yeah. I was thinking about how hard it is with adult kids. You think you've been through all the hard parts, gotten them through teething and acne and bullying, and then they turn into grown-ups who insist on locking us out of their heads. When they still clearly need our help!"

"You got that right," I tell him. "I suppose that's natural when you think about it. Evolutionarily, at least." What I don't say is that I suppose it's natural for *other people's kids*, not mine. Certainly not mine—until now, at least.

Mason Davis sits back in the booth and spreads his hands out on the table. We both look at his manicure. "Before you went to Joey's," he says, "everything I said or did made it worse. I'd try to get him to go outside, to exercise, to call his old friends. I got so worried that I even suggested he should move back in with me for a while. Which he took to mean I didn't trust him. And he was right. I figured I'd have to sleep on the floor next to his bed so I could watch him. You know?"

"Absolutely," I say.

"And then a week and a half ago I arrive at his house, and my heart is just as heavy as it can be, and I'm heading to his front door thinking that something radical has to happen to change the situation here—and then like magic, damned if there isn't a bunny rabbit standing in front of him, and he's smiling! Smiling!" He grins at me and lowers his voice. "After you left, when I discovered the python bra and the bologna sandwich were both gone, there was no way I *couldn't* hear how you managed to accomplish that."

I smile back at him. "Were you as afraid of that bologna sandwich as I was?"

He shudders. "Afraid? That thing was haunting my dreams. I was thinking I'd have to call the police on it."

"Sure. Well, you'll be glad to know that once it realized it had to go, it walked right over to the garbage can and jumped in."

"How did you get rid of the beer can tower? That probably didn't go willingly."

"No. I had to dismantle that myself. But then Joey helped when I said no woman would be interested in him as long as he had that thing."

"Ha! Only you could have gotten away with that. If I had said that to him, he would have taken away my house key and not spoken to me for a week."

"Yeah. It was the python bra that was the real stickler. I had trouble getting him to give that thing up."

We're silent for a moment, and then he says, "So how did you know what to do? Are you a witch?" He asks the question with a straight face, like that might be a respectful, legitimate question anybody might ask.

"Oh, well. That," I say. I narrow my eyes and think hard about what to say. How much to tell him.

And then something says to me: *What the actual hell? Tell him all of it! I'm likely never going to see him again.*

I tell him about my grandmother and how she once relocated some warts from a man she loved to a man who had cheated on her friend, and how she could also do other things, little chants and stuff, and that she carried around some herbs wrapped up in a handkerchief and wore something around her neck, too.

"My mother told me not to listen to my granny, but my mom would go off to work, and then my granny and I went around town, moving people's warts and turning stoplights green and keeping shopping carts from zooming into cars just by using our minds. We had nothing but fun running all around and doing what we wanted."

"So, you've just been honoring her legacy by changing stoplights and rearranging lives all this time?"

I laugh. "No! The thing was, I didn't really do any of that until the day with Joey. Even when my first husband told me he was leaving me for a witch, and I had every intention of bewitching him right back to me, I sort of forgot about it, and I never did anything with it."

"If I may ask, what was it about Joey that made you do magic on him?"

I think about it. "He just seemed so sad. Like he needed another layer of help." I take a sip of tea and then say, "Actually, if you want to know the truth, I was sitting there with him, and I heard my granny's voice in my ear, nudging me forward. She said, 'Good God, Billie. How long are you going to let this go on? You know what you have to do.'"

"She said that?"

"Yeah. Inside my head."

"So the Heartbreak Bunny business was never supposed to be about magic, then? That wasn't the way you planned it?"

"Nope." I tell him the story of how Kat and I came up with the idea—getting drunk, screaming with laughter, the whole bit.

"Do you know the current ratio of unhappy love affairs to happy ones?" I ask him, and he shrugs and says he does not.

"Well, neither do I, to be perfectly honest, but I'm sure that if the divorce rate is fifty percent, then the unhappy romance rate has got to be close to ninety percent. It's the most disappointing enterprise in the history of the world, I'd say, and yet we just go back into it, again and again, banging our heads against the wall. When we could be so happy without it!"

"Wow," he says, looking steadily at me, in that way I am so allergic to with men.

My phone dings just then, and I look down, grateful for modern technology that can interrupt conversations.

"Go ahead, take it," he says. "But you know what? The waitress was exactly right about this pie. Do you want a bite? It's like taking a bite of a cloud made of whipped cream and heaven."

"No. But thank you." It's a text from Calvin:

Reggie and Micah seem to be moving in today. Problems with his wife again. You don't mind?

I type back.

Course not.

He says: Just temporary. But his eyes are wet. Never seen Reggie like this.

Oh boy! Put him up in Max's old room. And Micah can go in the study across the hall. I can get the trundle bed down from the attic. YOU ARE NOT TO GET IT. I WILL GET IT.

Calvin sends a string of emojis—the smiley face, the scared face, the strong man arm, a heart, a balloon, and two beds. If I know him, this means he's already gone up the attic stairs and gotten the bed down. I look back up at Mason Davis. "Sorry. Apparently, our plumber needs to move in with us. With his little boy. Temporarily. Another so-called love story bites the dust, and now he needs a place to live."

"I hate to be pushy, but I would be remiss if I didn't insist that you taste this creamy pie. It's otherworldly."

"Well, then. A little bite. I love otherworldly pies." I poke my fork across the table and get a scoop. "Oh, yes. That is good. Now what were we talking about?"

"Well, I can't remember, but what I now want to know is why your plumber is moving in with you. I don't think I've ever had a plumber ask me if he could move in. Mostly he just wants me to move my car out of the garage so he can get to the pipes."

"Maybe your pipes aren't as bad as ours, which is why our plumber is always around patching up something. Half the time he eats lunch with Calvin and me, and this has been going on so long that now he just sort of fits in with everybody in the house. It won't even be a stretch, having him actually living there. He's bringing his little boy, Micah, who is unfortunately very afraid of spiders. I'll be involved in a Spider Relocation Project, which could turn into a part-time job, what with my old house being what it is."

"And . . . this Calvin? I believe I spoke to him once when I called your landline. Is he your uncle?"

"Oh, no. He's one of my housemates. The main one, really. I met him when I had a little ride service I ran—and I was supposed to drive him to hospice, only we spent the day together talking instead, and then, one thing led to another, and he decided he didn't want to die, and so he moved in with me. Anyway, he's been there eight years." I lean forward and say in a low voice, "He claims he's immortal."

Mason looks startled. "Immortal?"

I laugh. "Yeah, now *that's* the person you might want to have on your show. He says he was supposed to die five times and he didn't. So now he's pretty sure he's going to live forever." I shrug. "The side effect of all this is that it causes him to live the freest, happiest life you can imagine."

"Well, sure."

"I should add that *I* don't think he's immortal. I'm quite aware of every little thing that could take him out at any second. But so far he seems quite thrilled with everything and does exactly what he pleases. Which makes him sort of the resident philosopher at our house."

We both take another bite of pie and smile at each other.

He clears his throat. "Can I ask you a question? Does the Heartbreak Bunny believe in . . . love?"

"Love! Of course I believe in love!"

"Okay," he says softly, looking a little embarrassed. "I just wondered . . . I mean, I know you don't like romance . . ."

"Love! Sex! Passion! All of it!" I say, probably too loudly. I've had another bite of coconut cream pie, and I'm a little wound up. "It's wallowing I don't like. Nobody should dedicate their whole life to suffering over lost love after you've anointed somebody The One. But love! It's the full human experience—I believe in every kind of love!"

"Well," he says. "That makes me feel better. Because love—well, it's what makes the world go round. Or so I've heard."

I have another bite of pie and look at Mason. "Remember the eighties? This is a pie that would have been completely comfortable in the eighties. Decadent."

"Indeed, I do," says Mason. "A decade of plot twists. Back then, love was so prevalent that you could meet somebody in the morning and be living together by two p.m."

"My first marriage was a little like that, come to think of it. Lasted about a year and a half. We had a baby, and then he ran off to France with a poet so he could be free. Such a cliché he was."

He hums a few bars of "Born Free."

"I think that was the sixties," I say, "but the same idea." I take another bite of pie. "It turns out that love has been pretty much a problem since the beginning of time."

"I hope you at least got the house," says Mason.

I nod. "I did." I'm actually feeling as though this pie may have medicinal qualities. I say to him, "Do you think one can get drunk on coconut cream pie in a diner? I'm so glad my daughter isn't here to hear me. I'm always embarrassing her, it seems, being a bunny. She thinks that if I want to help heartbroken people, I should get a degree in social work and set up a counseling practice. Can you imagine me doing that?"

"Where's the fun in that?" he says.

"Exactly! If I could have my way, you know what I'd do? I'd go into heartbroken people's houses, and after we threw out all the stupid remnants of the romance, I'd take off the bunny head and get them to dance around the room with me. Then we'd make a list of all the other things they have in their lives to be happy about—and then, you know, maybe do a few magic spells for good measure, and I'd leave them believing in themselves and their ability to make a new start."

He is watching me closely. And then he says in a low voice, "Billie, I'm not trying to put any pressure on you, but why won't you consider coming on the show and talking about *that*? People need to hear it."

"Well, no. If you must know, it's my daughter. She's going through a rough patch, and I'm helping her, and so I have to cut back for a while on being the Heartbreak Bunny while I help her with her business."

"What's her business?"

"She's a blogger—you know, an *influencer*. A person who's perfect. And now her husband has left her, and she's—well, she's a wreck, is what she is."

"So the Heartbreak Bunny has a kid in heartbreak." He shakes his head.

"And when you're an *influencer*—well, it's devastating also for the brand," I tell him in a low voice. "You can't let people know."

"Of course," he says.

Penny comes over to see if we need anything else.

"Maybe more pie," says Mason, but I shake my head.

"I can't. Pretty soon the bunny suit will be the only outfit I fit into, and then I'll have to wear it out in public all the time. Which will be embarrassing, and then my daughter will *never* speak to me again."

"See?" Mason says. "If you're going to be wearing the suit, you might as well do all the calls you want. People need you out there. We need the Heartbreak Bunny to exist."

"Wait! You?" says Penny, looking at me. "*You're* the Heartbreak Bunny?"

I nod.

"Get out of town! It's you? No, really. I've heard of you. My neighbor Sylvia has a daughter who used you," she says. "And she was, like, over at my house last night, and that was all she could talk about. She showed me a TikTok video of you. You got something like forty-six thousand views, you know that?"

"Interesting," I say. "I haven't seen it."

She plops herself down next to me in the booth, and sort of shoves me over and digs her phone out of her pocket. "Wait. Let me show you the video. You'll die when you see it. You really helped Sylvia's daughter, you know—Marie's her name. Pretty girl, but big boned, you know what I mean? And maybe too sensitive for her own good. Anyway, never able to find a good guy. Dated a whole lotta duds on account of no self-esteem. She said you walked in, looked around, and immediately saw her ex-boyfriend's football jersey and said it had to go." She keeps scrolling through her phone and then she sighs. "Can't get it to come up. The reception in here is terrible."

I lean over and whisper to her, "Tell me the truth. Is my butt huge in the video?"

She looks at me and smiles. "What? No! Your butt is fine. And anyway, you're a celebrity," says Penny. "You can have any size butt you want." She's beaming at me. "Imagine that. I got two celebrities today at my station. Wait till I tell Marie."

"Penny!" A shout comes from a man in a white paper hat, poking his head through the order window. "Order *up*, Penny!"

"Be right there! We got us some celebrities in here!" she yells at him, but she doesn't get up. "Say, Mason Davis, you might want to get her on your show."

"I need a few more minutes to make my case."

"ORDER UP!"

"Well, I'll make it for you if you need any help," she tells Mason and stands up with another big sigh. "I, for one, want to know how she does it. She just identifies the objects, Marie said. Like that jersey. Marie loved that jersey, wore it to sleep in, and she did not want to give it up. Said it was the comfortablest shirt she ever had. But she knew she had to because it had bad vibes. And she's felt better ever since. Seeing a new guy now, I believe."

Mason Davis looks uncomfortable. "I hate to be the bearer of bad tidings, but apparently you had an order up some time ago, Penny, and now a guy in a dirty apron and a paper hat is taking some plates to a table and he's looking like he's going to murder somebody."

"Oh, him. That would be me he's planning to murder," Penny says. "Luckily, he's a blowhard. He needs a Heartbreak Bunny for his entire life." She saunters away, calling to him that she's coming, and he should hold his horses, and snapping her towel as she goes.

A few people turn and look at me, and a man sitting at the counter swivels around and gives me a thumbs-up. "You helped my nephew the other day!" he says. "You took away his ex-wife's wedding bouquet that she kept in their freezer!"

"See?" says Mason to me. "The bunny is important."

"I think I want to get out of here," I tell him. "This is feeling a little bit weird now."

Once we've paid the bill and extricated ourselves, Penny hurries after us to shout out the door, "Farewell! And don't forget to look up TikTok! Your butt is honestly fine in the video!"

"Thanks for that," I call back, laughing because people in the next town could probably hear her say that.

We get to my car first, and we stand there lingering a little. I pull my coat around my shoulders, kick at a little patch of snow on the asphalt.

"This was fun," he says.

"Yeah."

"Now I'm not going to try any more to persuade you—"

"Thank you."

"—but here's my card with my number on it. Could we maybe see each other again?" He looks suddenly flustered, which is probably a facial expression he developed to wow women who don't immediately fall at his feet, but which is totally, totally fake. "I mean, maybe for dinner somewhere, out of town, where people wouldn't hound you about your TikTok video."

"Mason," I say. I shift my bag to my other shoulder, putting a few more inches of distance between us. "I know that you're really a great guy and a nice man, but I have to be honest with you. I'm absolutely telling you the truth when I tell you I don't believe in romance. I think it's just a rotten system nature devised to get people to procreate and take care of the next generation—and Mother Nature figured if she made it seem suspenseful and fun, maybe people wouldn't notice they'd been hoodwinked into raising children. But I intend to enjoy my later years without even one smidgen of caring about all that anymore. I'm not going to go on dates. It leads to a bunch of wrongheaded endeavors."

"Wrongheaded endeavors?" he says. He's smiling.

"Yes. You know. Dating leads to dieting, hair coloring, shaving of legs—caring about what other people think. What *men* think."

He looks at me blankly. Then he recovers. "Well, it wouldn't have to be a date then. Listen," he says. "I interview a lot of people about things they're passionate about, and I'm a pretty good judge of when something is important. And your face—you get a certain look when you talk about your granny or the spells you did for Joey. This is a business that wants to take off, big-time. And you'd be doing a favor for people who have a rough time on Valentine's Day. And now I'll shut up."

"Well," I say. "Thank you."

"Are you thanking me for the compliment or thanking me for shutting up?"

"The second one," I say, and we both laugh.

He reaches over and shakes my hand. I make my own hand go limp in his grasp to illustrate how hopeless his cause might be. "Thank you for meeting with me," he says. "And if you change your mind—let me know. If you ever want to come hopping into the studio—or we could tape at your house—"

"Mason."

"—and you could explain how anti-love you are. How really wrongheaded the whole romance system is. It could be 'Tips for Surviving a Lonely Valentine's Day.' Or 'Reclaim Your Power by Throwing Out That Football Jersey.' We'll promo the hell out of it, and you know how many viewers will tune in?"

"Four?"

"Everybody. Because everybody has had a heartbreak."

❦

When I get home, I find Calvin at the kitchen table finishing up a crossword puzzle and listening to Tony Bennett on the radio. It's four o'clock, and the February sun slants through the dusty kitchen window, making a flat, white square of light on the red linoleum floor next to the radiator. A tabby cat is stretched out precisely in the spot where the light hits.

"Oh! Who's this?" I say. "Did we acquire a cat today?"

"We did. She's Reggie's cat. Her name is the Queen of Sheba."

She opens one eye at the mention of her name and then closes it again and stretches.

"Seems appropriate. And where is Reggie?"

"He's gone over to pick up more of his stuff and probably have another fight with Cynthia, and to get Micah from his after-school program. They'll be back here for dinner, he said."

"Wonder what we should cook." I start stacking up the newspapers. "So, Cynthia really was seeing another guy, huh?"

"Oh, who knows? She told Reggie she was going to visit her sister in Florida, but *he* thinks she really went to see this other man, because she came home with a tan and apparently no tan lines." He lifts his eyebrows suggestively. "And then I, an elderly personage, had to explain to him that there are such things as tanning salons, where you come out with a perfect allover tan. But he's not having it. Says it was another guy."

"And we both know he's probably right."

"We do *not* know any such thing, you love curmudgeon," he says cheerfully. "I think, in fact, that, tan lines aside, he and Cynthia are going to work things out. I think they've just got busy lives and they've forgotten they like each other. So how did your meeting go with Mason Davis?"

"Oh, fine," I say vaguely. "Did you know that the Athens Diner has the most amazing coconut cream pie in the world?"

He looks at me. "Great. So, how was Mason Davis?"

"Nicest man ever, but he has a fake tan, I think. Still, I didn't dislike him as much as I expected I would."

Calvin laughs. "Why did you expect you'd dislike him?"

"I don't know. I figured he'd fall into the category of being too rich and too jokey and—you know, all fake-nice."

Calvin shakes his head. "But, after meeting him, the only thing you're still holding against him is that you think his tan is fake?"

"Pretty much."

"Maybe it's makeup that he has to wear on his show. Did you think of that?"

"His teeth also may be too white. I didn't tell you that part."

"I see. How's his hair?"

"Silver. Might be too shiny. And I suspect he gets manicures."

"I see you've got all your defenses up and working."

"Well, but we had a good talk anyway. I explained to him that I don't want to be on his show, and he took it very well."

"Wait. Why don't you want to be on his show? I thought you were excited about that."

I sigh. "I don't know, Calvin. It's just that I'm busy doing all this stuff to help Louise, who can't seem to stop crying, and I feel like I shouldn't expand the Heartbreak Bunny stuff until she gets Leo to come back."

"I hope you're listening to yourself and hearing how truly ridiculous that is."

"I can't do it all. As it is, I'm trying to take pictures for her blog and keep her spirits up, and do occasional bunny calls. And if I went on his show, and then even *more* people wanted me to help them—well, it would just make it worse for Louise."

"I don't like to give you advice—but I feel forced to point out that Louise's life isn't your responsibility. You can't solve her problems with Leo *or* with her blog. That's not your job."

"I know it's not my job, but my kid is unhappy!"

"Your *kid* is thirty-five years old, Billie. She is a fully functioning adult."

"Supposedly." I look out the window at the bird feeder, which needs more seeds; I've been neglecting that. "Hey, you want to know something? All the way home from the diner, I just kept getting one idea after another for Heartbreak Bunny stuff I could do. It was like a voice in my head that I couldn't get to shut up."

"Yeah?" he says. "Like what?"

"Well, I'm probably not going to be able to do any of it. But I thought that besides playing revenge songs, I could get them to dance to those songs! Teach them a dance routine they could do anytime they need to move their bodies again! Help them remember the joy of feeling good about their bodies! And then, what if I gave them a list of movies to counteract the romantic comedies. Or—novels! We could do a book club with revenge novels! Wouldn't that be so much fun? And then I realized I could do repeat calls, follow-ups, reinforce the plan to never, ever go back. Support groups who get together and cheer on the newly heartbroken!"

"Again," says Calvin. "I hope you're listening to yourself. This is all brilliant stuff."

"I know. And maybe someday I'll get to do it. After Louise doesn't need me." I get up and put on my apron. "Anyway, we need to get dinner started. We've got a little boy to feed, and from what I've heard about little boys, I guess it's going to be mac and cheese and chicken nuggets."

"While he's here, can't we teach him to eat real people food?" says Calvin. "I can't be eating chicken nuggets. They make me too sad. And mac and cheese—oh please!"

"I'll do it the good way, the way you like it." When I make the mac and cheese, I always add in three different kinds of cheese—and then I make a roux and bake the whole concoction in the oven with buttered bread crumbs. We have to keep our cholesterol levels up, as Calvin claims. Instead of chicken nuggets, I tell him I'll broil some chicken thighs with butter and garlic and white wine, and I'll roast some green beans with sesame oil.

By the time Reggie and Micah return, the whole house is filled with the aroma of garlic and butter and bubbling cheese. It's almost dark outside, and I've turned on all the twinkly lights in the windows and put on music. After dinner, Calvin and I play Go Fish with Micah while his dad goes upstairs with his phone, probably to yell at Cynthia some more. And later, when I'm putting him to bed, he tells me in a serious voice that his daddy and mommy are mad at each other, and he wants to know if I know the good-night song his mom sings.

He's not sure of the name of it. He brought along a little bag of his books and his teddy bear and a deck of cards. But nothing about what song it is. "I kind of need that song," he says and sticks his thumb in his mouth, looking like he might cry.

I look down into his big saucer eyes, and he looks steadily back at me. I tell him I can sing the song I used to sing to Louise—"Over the Rainbow"—and he whispers that that would be okay. He shuts his eyes tight, holding back tears, and holds on to my hand while I sing.

How wonderful and terrifying it would be to have a grandchild. If Louise and Leo had a kid, this is what I would sing to the child when Louise and Leo were too busy, or when they were fighting. Because I can't picture them ever being together without fighting.

For a moment, I squeeze my eyes closed and think of how lovely it would have been to have a sweet little shmoopy to hold in my arms, to look down into a baby's bright eyes, to see that perfect little rosebud mouth and the fat cheeks. The gurgles, the cooing. Even the crying would have been all right with me. Back at that stage, as I remember, you can fix just about everything.

I think of it so hard that for a moment I almost can't catch my breath.

Around nine o'clock, with Reggie and Calvin in the living room watching a spy movie, and Edwin in his room and Marisol out on a date with 3M, as we refer to him—Marisol's Married Man—I go out on the back steps and look at the oak tree where I sometimes used to perch on a branch with Louise when she was little. We'd come out here to sing songs when she felt overwhelmed.

Louise is an adult, and I can't fix her life anymore, but I sit there for a long time in the cold, watching the branches brush lightly against the side of the house. The moon is nearly full, which reminds me that tomorrow night I'm supposed to do the spell for Phoebe to have a baby. I feel a little thrill thinking about that.

My nose is freezing, but I don't want to go inside until I figure this all out. Am I really going to do spells? Heal heartbreak? Or is my job to help Louise?

The oak tree rattles in a sudden gust of wind and says I don't have to turn myself into a blog photographer. It points out that I'm kind of great as a Heartbreak Bunny, but—no offense—rather an abject failure at being a Leo Cabot Imitator.

I'm lousy at it, in fact. That's from the forsythia bush.

And the big round moon, sailing along behind the branches of the tree, reminds me that one of my deepest beliefs is that people should only do what they love.

I go inside and find my bag, where I tucked Mason Davis's card. The Queen of Sheba is nesting in it, but she jumps out when I ask her politely to leave.

"I've been thinking it over," I say when he answers, "and I want to go on your show. Also"—I take a deep breath—"I'd like to talk to Joey. About maybe a return visit sometime. Make sure he's still moving forward."

I try to make my voice sound light and breezy, but it sounds to my own ears like a chorus of trumpets, all loud and definite.

CHAPTER EIGHT

The next evening, when it's time to do the spell, I pull up to Louise's house and sit there in the car, listening to the ticking of the engine. Concentrating. The full moon is spreading out its diamonds on the water. Little sparks blink in the black sky.

Good lord, how did I get myself into this?

Louise sent out a text message to all of us this afternoon:

Dress in clothing that you love. Remember that we are supposedly summoning the spirit of life, ladies! We gotta look good.

I know that tone: she is making fun of the whole thing.

I'm actually late. I couldn't seem to get myself to leave the house. I kept checking in on Micah, who sat on the living room rug, drawing whiskers on the front of his toy dump truck and making meowing noises while he ran it again and again in a circle around the coffee table. At one point I actually sat down on the couch and asked him if he wanted a hug. He said he was not a boy anymore, that he was now a big man who owns cat-trucks. Still, he got up immediately and came and sat on my lap and put his arms around my neck, breathing his little-boy peanut-butter breath on my neck. His skin was like warm peaches, and I told myself that holding on to a child before you go off to summon spirits to bring about a baby might be a very wise thing to do. None of the spell books I consulted mentioned this as a prerequisite: *Go and hug the sweetest-smelling child you can find before you summon the universal life-creating energies.* But maybe they should.

After hugging him for as long as an owner of cat-trucks could tolerate, I went into the kitchen and opened the refrigerator, trying to think of things that might symbolize fertility that I should bring along. Eggs, you know. Olives. A jar of capers, because they seem like little balls of salty, briny life force. I included anything that called to me.

Calvin tilted his head and gave me a look. "You want me to come with you?" he said. "I was thinking of heading out to see Bernice, but I could come with you if you want."

"Nah, thank you anyway, but I think this has been advertised as a female-energy night."

"Well," he said. He stood there with his arms at his sides, looking a little bit sunken in. "You'll be great. Just don't overthink it. And remember to have fun. If I was there, that's what I'd remind you to do: make it fun! Maybe throw confetti. That sort of thing."

"I don't think Louise would appreciate confetti being thrown all over her perfect yard."

"More's the pity," he said and shook his head.

◌

And now I sit looking up at the windows of Louise's house, unable to get out of the car. Waiting for a sign. Do I *really, really* believe in this? I don't know! Maybe all my grandmother was doing with her magic was saying affirmations. Maybe none of it was ever really, really real, even to her. She had bright, laughing eyes, my grandmother, filled with mischief. Maybe she just wanted to be mysterious, a little bit outlandish, in her staid, conservative community. She loved the idea of being a little bit kooky.

My mind is like a hive of bees. The opposite of calm. If I close my eyes tight, I wonder if I could summon her. I could ask her: *Was that real, Granny? Did you actually believe?*

Just then my phone dings.

Ah! Some help is coming in. Instead it's Victor again.

do you remember that little disk of dried-up syrup in front of our refrigerator gotta know if it's still there

How is it that *he* is the person who shows up when I'm attempting to summon my grandmother? You see? None of this makes a bit of rational sense.

I sigh and turn off the phone and look out at the near darkness.

☙

Hildy's car pulls in next to mine. She gets out, patting her little pregnant belly, wearing a black dress that features silver lightning bolts.

I get out, too. "Look at *you*, all pregnant and inspiring like this! Lightning bolts, yet!"

"Yeah, inspiring—that's not the word I would have used," she says. "Tell me this. How do people drive cars by the end of pregnancy? I've still got to make it to early July, but before this is over, I'm going to have to get arm and leg extensions so I can push the seat all the way back and still reach the steering wheel."

"How are you feeling?"

"I'm good," she says. "Only the usual indignities: acne, backache, sleepy all the time. I won't mention those things to our little Phoebe, in case it makes her change her mind."

"Oh, that wouldn't change her mind," I say. "There's nothing more determined than a woman who wants to get pregnant, don't you think so?"

"Especially in Phoebe's case. You got the spell all ready?"

"I've been practicing all afternoon," I say, which is only half true. I've been watching spell videos about how you summon spirits. But why tell her that I have no idea what I'm doing? "Also, I've brought along some eggs and olives and capers to help out."

"Oh, good. I brought some grapes and avocados. And round candles."

"Round things seem to be very important," I say.

"Anything to help." She looks at me. "You look like a bona fide spell-caster, I have to say!"

Yes. I have dressed the part by wearing a long purple satiny skirt and a black silk tunic with little gold stars along the front placket. It has voluminous filmy sleeves and lots of sequins. It looks serious and officially witchy, this tunic. Like something a high priestess would have worn. And then there's the cape, of course. Magical!

Inside, it seems that everybody else has also dressed for the occasion. We look like we're going to consort with wizards. Phoebe wears a hat with colored spangles and sequins, and Miranda is holding an actual magic wand.

For now they are all gathered around Louise, who is talking about Leo's departure in that flat, understated tone she uses lately. She's dressed in plain black leggings and an oversized shiny gold tunic, and although her hair is combed and she has on makeup, anyone can see that she's a wreck. Her eyes look sunken, and her mouth is tight. And when she talks about Leo leaving, her voice is nearly inaudible.

"Yeah, he left, just like that. Sick of our life—and now he's gone off to do something more *important*, something his parents would see as justifying that degree they paid for."

"Oh, Lulu. I'm so sorry. This is the end of one of the most beautiful love stories of the internet!" says Phoebe. "What are you going to do, honey?"

Louise sees me and shrugs. "My mom's helping me. We're trying to keep it going. But it's not the same, is it?"

I laugh. "No, it's definitely not the same. My photos resemble nothing Leo would ever even put up with. They're blurry and off-center half the time. And I don't know how to crop things right. But it's just temporary."

"Sweetie . . . so when are you going to tell the followers he's gone?" asks Miranda, turning back to Louise. "Shouldn't they be told soon?"

Louise doesn't answer, which is a shame because I, too, would really like to know. Whenever I bring the subject up, she just bursts into tears and says, "Not yet."

"I don't want my followers to freak out," she finally says. "It's going to disillusion people to find out our love story is over. I have to let them down gently."

We're silent as we all take that in.

"Wait! You're the one who's been left—and you're worried how your *followers* are going to take it?" says Phoebe. "Why don't you just tell them what happened? Lots of people will be able to relate. I'll bet you get even more followers."

"Aw, honey. Are you sure it's not that you're thinking he's coming back?" says Hildy.

I look at Louise, hoping for the answer to that one. But she doesn't seem inclined to comment. "Listen," she says, and claps her hands. "This isn't the night to talk about me. This is about Phoebe!"

Phoebe's eyes suddenly grow wide, and she hugs herself.

Hildy says, "Come over here, Phoebe, and rub my belly and maybe some of this pregnancy mojo will just transfer over to you. You know, osmosis. Isn't that what osmosis is?"

"Probably not," I say. "But everything we do tonight is going to help us call in a baby. We're going to follow inspiration."

"Calling in a baby!" says Phoebe wistfully. "You know, I almost wanted to bring my husband with me so he could add his voice to the whole proceeding."

"No!" the other three say at once. Hildy adds: "He gets his chance at the actual conception. Which is at least as important as this."

"In fact, maybe the only important part, if we're being honest," says Louise.

"I think we should go outside," I say. I want to get this going before we end up spending a lot more energy talking about Leo splitting up with Louise. I take her by the hand. "Come on, sweetie. Let's grab some candles and round objects and go out on the lawn."

We go outside, and holy moly—it's chilly. A breeze ripples off the sound, blowing against the shrubbery, which trembles in response. Louise goes back inside and gets some gray fleece throws—and we wrap ourselves up in them, which makes us look like Druids. I arrange everybody in a circle on the lawn and put the candles and all the round foods in the middle, like I saw on a YouTube video. Then I take off my shoes and explain that I need to connect with the energy of the earth.

Louise rolls her eyes. "Just don't connect with pneumonia," she says.

"Ssssh, from now on we are going to say only things we want to be true," I say. "We are going to call a soul to us, like a casting call."

"Do we need to be serious and solemn?" says Miranda in the darkness. Her face is only partly illuminated by the lights from the house.

I think about this. "No, absolutely not! We want this to be fun and amazing! We're doing a ceremony that will attract the right spirit. Don't we want to make the earth look like a fun place? I'll start." I hold hands with Phoebe and Miranda, and I raise our hands in the air. "Whoever is out there, listening. If you're trying to make up your mind whether or not you want to try living inside a human body, here's something to think about. This woman is going to be a wonderful mom and a true guide to life here! She'll take you to all the fun places, and she knows how to play softball and soccer, and also she knows a lot of knock-knock jokes."

Phoebe raises her arms and yells at the top of her very capable, athletic lungs. "You can have your own room! And your father happens to like amusement parks, so you'll have lots of chances to ride on fun rides!"

Miranda laughs and says, "She never gets tired! Or in a bad mood! She can do that dance that Michael Jackson used to do—what is it?"

"The moonwalk," Louise says.

"Yes! The moonwalk! You'll find it very amusing when you see it."

"Also, she is always up for doing adventurous things! And she makes the best cupcakes of anyone." This from Hildy. "Aaaand . . . if you need hand-me-down clothes, I intend to have a lot of them to give to you. You'll have the best wardrobe. You and my baby can be built-in best friends."

"I second that about the cupcakes," says Louise in a low voice, looking down at the ground.

There's a long silence, and then Phoebe clears her throat and says, "You might be a little nervous, wherever you are, with all that you hear about the state of the world. I don't know if the news gets to you entities, or whatever you call yourselves while you're waiting out there. Souls, maybe? But in case you've heard some hard stuff, I'd just like to say that it's not so bad here. Probably not like what you're hearing, if the TV news is any indication. Whoops—I shouldn't say anything negative, should I? Okay." She takes a deep breath. "Starting over. I just want you to know there's so much love and kindness all around us. So much love for *you*. And so many of us are trying our best. We're opening up to solving problems. If that's all that's keeping you from coming, rest assured that I'll watch out for you."

"Also, there are great beaches here," says Miranda.

"And we've got a lot of good movies! And lots of music. Right away, you'll get to hear some lullabies." This was Hildy. "I myself am learning some already, and I'll teach them to your mom."

"Oh. And if you're wondering why your father isn't here, it's because we decided tonight would just be for women. Life grows in women's bodies, and so we thought it would be a good idea for just us to call you at first," Phoebe says. "But he's into it, just so you know."

"And he is really very nice! And he wants you!" says Miranda.

Then we're quiet.

I look over at Louise. Her head is bent, and she is squeezing her eyes shut tight, and in her gray fleece cocoon, she looks like a collapsed sack of flour. I see her heart there, out in the open, but nevertheless trying to run back into the shadows. That sad, sweet, tender shattered heart. She wants a baby, too. I suddenly see that.

I walk around the circle and touch each one of them on the shoulder, like a benediction. "Now close your eyes and meditate for a moment on this little soul who's out there, who is hearing our words," I say. "Picture this little person who is not yet a person, but who has a place just the same. You can silently say all the things you want to tell it. Words of encouragement and promise. Be grateful for this chance to connect."

I'm talking, I'm saying these words, and then suddenly, it's like a gong goes off in my head. The sound is so loud that I look around the circle to see if anyone else heard it. But they are all swaying, with their eyes closed, except for Louise, who is looking out at the water.

It's like, with the possible exception of my suffering daughter, we're flowing all together.

I send her over some love, and I almost think I can see it swirling toward her.

Suddenly I feel something warm moving through me, some little scritching of certainty, like something softly knocking on the side of my brain, asking to be let in. It's tentative, this asking—ready to be turned away. And then it gets stronger. I swallow, look around me. The moon has come out from behind a cloud, and the women are bathed in the light. Little sparks gleam down from deep space. Maybe that's where the souls are hanging out, listening. Maybe one is thinking over our offer.

I don't know how this stuff works. Mostly, the way I see it, we're adjusting Phoebe's mindset to allow conception to take place. We're opening the channels of energy, just the way I do as the Heartbreak Bunny—it's the *allowing* we have to believe in. And yes, it is possible to move the universe.

But the truth is that no one knows what the universe is made of, how things get made, how happiness and love and new people just appear. All the cells arriving and doing their individual work, breathing, and dividing and fulfilling a purpose that's been handed down in the blueprint made millions of years ago. It makes my head feel like it's going to explode, thinking this way.

The moon shines so brightly it's almost like daylight now, silvering the blades of grass, the branches of the oak tree in front of me, the outline of the stone bench just ahead. If I listen, I can hear the waves tiptoeing up to the beach and breaking ever so gently, making soft, swishing noises. The little waves coming faster and faster now, and then sliding away, sucked back into the big, vast, safe ocean.

"It's done," I hear myself say.

"And now we wait," says Phoebe quietly.

"And now we wait," I say.

"Oh, for heaven's sake!" says Louise. "Can we go in now? It's freaking cold out here."

CHAPTER NINE

The first thing to know if you're going to be on the morning show on Channel 12 in New Haven is that the green room is not green; it's a shade that could only be called industrial peach, and it's furnished with a brown nubbly sofa facing a table covered with danishes and some strawberries that might be left over from last year's strawberry season, from the looks of them. There's a massive clock on the wall, ticking loudly, and a bank of television screens, all of which show what's being broadcast right now.

Bring a friend if you possibly can. The two of you can stare at a dark, pompadour-haired man with a big, white-toothed smile waving his hands to show a warm front coming across the map of Connecticut.

On this particular day, as Kat and I nervously await my turn to go on the air, the caption scrolling underneath the weather guy says: STILL TO COME: HEARTBROKEN ON VALENTINE'S DAY? WE MAY HAVE SOME GOOD NEWS FOR YOU.

"What's the good news about being heartbroken on Valentine's Day?" says Kat.

"I'm not sure. I think it's that I'm supposed to cure it?"

"Still," she says. "It's better news if you're not heartbroken at all." Then she says, "Oh God. I'm getting a stomachache. Why are we doing this, again?"

"Uh-uh. None of that kind of talk, or you have to go," I say. "We're here because we thought up a freaking awesome business venture, and the world needs to hear about it, and this is an amazing opportunity. And also, you're not even the one who's agreed to go on camera, so I don't think you get to be all that nervous. I should be the one freaking out, not you. And I am not freaking out."

"Did you tell Louise about this?"

"I did."

"And?"

"And she thinks I shouldn't do it. I think her big worry is that people will realize that she and I are related, and they'll think it's weird that a big-time Instagram perfectionist would have a mama who dares to go out in public in a bunny suit."

"She should embrace the weird."

"I'll tell her you think so."

She crosses and uncrosses her legs. She's wearing a lavender sweater and black pants and a gold chain. Her hair shines in the fluorescent ceiling lights, and I tell her she looks so good that she really ought to be the one on camera.

"Oh God, no," she says. "I can't even believe I'm here! I'm hyperventilating just being in the green room."

I shake my head. "You're not supposed to be making me more nervous, you know."

"So," she says after a moment. "Has the producer given you the script yet?"

"There is no script. Mason and I are just going to chat. We've talked about the whole thing several times."

"Oh," she says. "So it's *Mason* now, is it?"

"*Yes*, it's Mason. What am I supposed to call him?"

She smirks at me. I can see Fifth Grade Kat showing up in her face. I'll bet she got beat up a lot on the playground in elementary school.

Just then Mason Davis appears at the door. Grinning, and rubbing his hands together, looking delighted. Wearing a casual suit and a black turtleneck. "You must be Kat!" he says. "How wonderful to get to meet you in person!" He goes over and shakes her hand and then, much to my alarm, gives me a hug. A hug! I see Kat smirking. And she doesn't even know how good he smells. Like soap and some spicy, swoon-worthy aftershave.

"So," he says, "we're just going to chat about the bunny business and people's expectations of romance. All the things we've talked about before. Maybe a couple of little surprises, but nothing you can't handle." He turns to Kat. "You should have seen this woman in the diner last week. The waitress was practically ready to run away with her."

"Oh, I *know*," Kat mumbles. "She's amazing."

"So, Billie," he says, frowning and smiling at the same time, showing off his white, even teeth. "What I'm picturing is that you'll hop in wearing the bunny suit and come over to the chair next to me, and I'll introduce you, and then you can sit down and take off the head, and I'll ask you questions that allow you to explain what you do. How's that?"

"Perfect," I say.

"Just be careful, because there's a little step up to get to the interview area," Mason says. "We don't want you to trip."

"That would be unfortunate, to fall on my face on live television," I say.

He laughs. "Well, I'd shift to a commercial right away, and come and rescue you," he says. He turns to Kat. "So, Kat, are you quite sure you don't want to be on camera, too?"

She says, "No, no. Billie will explain it better than I ever could." She turns to me. "You might want to go get into your bunny suit and practice your hopping."

"Yeah, your segment is on in, um, eighteen minutes. Does that give you enough time?" says Mason.

"It's perfect," I say. I can feel my grandmother sitting right in the center of my head, smiling. I think she's making popcorn. At least that's how I picture her. It's showtime, and Granny always did like a good show.

༄

Fifteen minutes later, Mason Davis is standing at the entrance to the studio, smiling at me, as a young woman deposits me there, warning me to be quiet. As we walked down the hall, she'd said, "I can't wait to hear what it is you do. Apparently, Mason is *very* excited for this segment!"

And there he is, smiling hugely. For a moment, I can't breathe as I look around. The studio is a vast room, rather like a big-box store or a warehouse, with high ceilings and cables strewn about. Little sets are everywhere: there's the news desk, darkened now, and over there is a large blue screen. Cameras idly stand by, like behemoths waiting at a watering hole. In one brightly lit corner, two women—one of them the co-anchor Lily Malone, whom Calvin has a crush on—are in a pretend kitchen talking about a soufflé and how easy it is to make, while two cameras point at their bright, made-up faces.

Soufflés are not easy. I know this for a fact, but the women are laughing and smiling over one that apparently defied Murphy's Law of Soufflés and decided to stay puffed up. I am impressed. It probably is a plastic soufflé—that's the way this whole place strikes me. Fake, fake, fake.

Then the cameras start moving away from the soufflé situation, and everyone gets lively. Apparently, a commercial comes on, because Mason squeezes my arm and goes over and sits himself down in an armchair on a little platform. He's getting adjusted with microphones and earpieces. A technician dressed all in black comes over and helps me put the bunny head on and straightens it. "Can you see?" he says, peering into my eyes.

"Yes."

"Okay, then I'll tell you when to go on. You'll hop over to the platform, and then go up the steps. I'll be there to hold your arm if you need me. We don't want you falling."

Mason waves from his perch. He points to the armchair next to his, where presumably I will sit after I'm done hopping around. In between the two chairs is a table with a potted plant. I think of Calvin instructing me to put my hands up underneath my chin. A bald man runs over and starts tucking a microphone behind me. He says I should lean forward a little bit when I sit down, so the microphone won't fall into the chair.

I feel dizzy, like I'm already forgetting everything. Lean which way now—forward or back?

And suddenly someone starts counting and the lights come on. I stand in partial darkness while an illuminated, lively version of Mason Davis introduces himself once again and says something about how this next segment is about a very inventive new business—something that has become very near and dear to his heart, because it involves his *family's* well-being.

"Have you ever had your heart broken?" he says into the camera. "Maybe you're spending this Valentine's Day lamenting lost love. If you are, then you know that climbing out of the wreckage can be difficult indeed. That happened to my son a few months back—and I thought we just had to wait it out until he rejoined the human race with his usual verve."

He beams a crinkly, endearing dad smile into the camera. "And then one day I went to visit him, and to my surprise, I found a woman dressed up in a stuffed bunny costume at his house. What was she doing there? Well, she was taking away his heartbreak! I'll let her tell you herself how she does it!"

I am nudged gently out into the spotlight.

"Hop!" someone says in my ear.

And so I do. I hop myself over to where Mason sits, where all I can see are blazing white lights and his white teeth, beaming at me, like beacons. "Welcome!" he says. "Fantastic hopping!"

Then he turns to the camera. "So," he says, "usually we don't talk so much here about our personal lives. I've been an anchor on this station for over twenty years now, and I've never talked about my own family—but a few weeks ago I came across a phenomenon so interesting that I wanted to bring it to public attention. And that is—this furry woman standing beside me. Her name is Billie Slate, but she goes by the moniker Heartbreak Bunny. I'm sure you have just as many questions as I do. *I've* seen her in action, and I *still* have questions! So, Ms. Billie Slate, won't you sit down and tell us what the heck is a Heartbreak Bunny?"

"May I take my head off?" I say.

"Hahaha!" he says. His eyes are too bright, I think. Maybe it's just the lights. "A question that has never before been asked on this set! 'May I take my head off?'"

"Well?"

"Oh! Yes. Yes, of course. Take your head off! Live a little."

I gingerly take my bunny head and place it on the table between us, right next to the plant. The ears flop over, knocking into the plant. I have to steady everything. Then I smile at the camera and shake out my hair. I can see in the monitor that it's all smooshed, so I peer at my reflection and fluff it back into little peaks again. My heart beats so hard I worry it will be audible in the microphone.

"Cameras make great little mirrors," says Mason Davis, laughing. "But now that we've got your hair all spiffy, let's talk. From what I understand, you and your best friend were hanging out one night having a wonderful time visiting, and the next thing you knew you'd decided to create a new venture—the Snap Out of It Company, where *you* would dress up just like you are now and go out in the world calling yourself the Heartbreak Bunny. Tell us exactly what a Heartbreak Bunny is, and why the world needs it."

I find some words somewhere. "Well, a Heartbreak Bunny is . . . me! I come hopping into your house—after you invite me, of course—and I help you get over your heartache by removing any painful mementos you might be holding on to after a breakup."

"Like what kinds of things are you removing?"

"Ohhh. You know: the handwritten love notes, the photographs. Memorabilia. Basically, anything that keeps your ex's memory alive and holds you in agony."

"But why would anyone want to stay in agony?"

"Well, Mason, have you ever been dumped?"

"Dumped?" He looks embarrassed, glances down at his paper, then grins boyishly, charmingly. "Hmm. I don't see this subject in the notes. But okayyyy. Have *I* been dumped?" He holds out his hands. "Oh boy, have I been dumped!"

"Yes. We've all been there at one time or another. Happens all the time. And it hurts."

"Well," he says. "It's no fun."

"And what makes it worse is that our culture—I hate to say it—just hammers it into our consciousness that romantic love is the only thing worth living for. That if we're alone—if we've been left, if our romance didn't work out, then we've *failed*. From the time we're little kids listening to the radio, all we hear is love song after love song *after love song*. If we don't have passionate love, we're trained to think that our lives are empty, and that we have to remedy that immediately. So we tend to run from one bad relationship to another, hoping that things will change for us." I gesture so big that Mason has to lean back a little. "We're trained to think love is going to solve *all* our problems, and make us *complete* and *fulfilled*. Heaven help you if you're not *in love* all the time! But I'm here to tell you that it's a big lie. Romance makes us miserable just as often as it fulfills us."

"So . . ." He looks concerned. "Are you anti-love, then?"

"No, not at all. Love is great. I'm anti-*wallowing*. I'm anti–feeling like it's all your fault when it doesn't work out! I want people to see breakups as something everybody goes through and something you can put behind you."

"And . . . how would a person do that?"

"Stop living in the past, for one thing! Tell yourself a different story about who you are. Make up your mind you're not going to suffer. Throw out all the photographs, and then get rid of the love notes, dispose of the items of clothing that your person left behind! Move, if you have to! Stop listening to sad songs and watching sad movies. Look for ways to be happy that don't depend on the approval of another human you can't control. A breakup can actually be useful."

"Useful?"

"Yes! You can learn what makes *you* happy! Life is supposed to be *fun*. This is a secret that most people don't realize. You can change things. Pick work that makes you happy, surround yourself with people who get you, and forget about relationships that don't work out. Just *move on*. I go into people's houses and they're wearing clothes they haven't changed out of for a week, and they're so consumed with grief that they're just watching daytime television—"

He chuckles nervously. "Um, we like daytime television here."

I smile. "Fair enough. But you and I both know that watching daytime TV can be a cry for help if a person isn't doing anything else. And for some people, feeling bad becomes a way of life. They drive to their ex's house in the middle of the night just to *see*, you know, if they're home alone. *Don't do that, people.* And don't play sad songs over and over again, on repeat. Or watch *The Notebook* every night.

"The worst part is that people start losing their friends because they can't let go of the story that they are now lost and alone. They eat frozen pizzas without even bothering to heat them up. Here's a rule of thumb: if you've been broken up more than two weeks, and you find yourself thinking that heating up frozen pizza is too much trouble, you may need some help."

"And that's you? You come and talk them out of it?"

"Oh, no. No, no!" I laugh. "I don't talk anybody out of anything. That's what their friends and family are for. What I do is I hop around their house in my bunny suit, and I help them figure out which things are keeping them stuck in wallowing mode, and I take those items away. Just doing that can jump-start them into moving on."

"So what's the weirdest thing you've ever had to throw out?"

"A jar of dill pickles!" I say.

"No! Pickles? Seriously?"

"Oh, yeah. One of my clients felt awful every time he saw the jar of dill pickles in his fridge—because it reminded him of a picnic he'd been on with his boyfriend. That was a trigger, believe me. And it's not unusual at all to find the ex's underwear scattered about. One woman kept some jumper cables in the living room—her boyfriend had bought them for her before he left her."

"So what do you do?"

"I put everything in a bag that I bring along, and I get those suckers out of there."

"Okay. Well." He rattles the piece of paper he's holding. "As I was telling the audience, our family has had personal experience with your services. I've been given permission to tell the story of my son—"

"Wait," I say. "I don't discuss specific people's cases. I can't. It's confidential."

"But he *wants* to come onstage and tell people how you helped him. You changed his life, and he's happy to talk about it. Ladies and gentlemen, here is my son, Joey Davis!"

And then, before I can say anything else, a totally transformed Joey Davis comes out, ducking his head and smiling at the camera. He's wearing clean clothes, jeans and a white turtleneck, and his hair is cut close to his head on the sides and fluffy on the top. He holds out his hand to me, and then thinks better of it and leans down and hugs me. I realize there is another chair next to Mason's—how had I not seen this before?—and after hugging his dad, he sits down.

"Thank you!" he says to me. "I look a lot different from the last time you saw me, right?"

I laugh. "You do! You're completely different!"

He says, "Yep. After you left, I even threw out those sweatshirts and sweatpants I'd been wearing for days."

"Days?" I say.

"Well, months really."

"And you got your hair cut," I say approvingly. "You're a new man!"

"Joey, tell the audience what happened," Mason says.

He smiles at me. "Sooooo . . . my fiancée broke up with me in a really embarrassing way—almost five months ago. And I was . . . uh, stuck. Well, to say I was stuck is the understatement of the year. I'll just say it—I was freaking out. I called in sick a lot, and I sat in my living room and just stared into space. The only thing I did that whole time was make a beer can tower to see how high it would get without falling over. And I thought about her. And, uh, I looked at stuff. Of hers."

"What kinds of things?" says Mason.

"Oh . . . you know . . . ticket stubs and pictures and . . . slippers, some of her clothing. Haha. One thing—there was an item of underwear—okay, a bra with a python print—that when the Heartbreak Bunny saw it, she said it was actually dangerous." He lowers his eyes and chuckles a little bit. "It was green, and I thought it was awesome, but she—the bunny, that is—hopped in and said it had to go! And then—well, she did a spell."

"A magic spell?" says Mason. "Like . . . what did you do, Heartbreak Bunny?"

"Oh, dear," I say. I can feel myself getting flustered. "*Was* it really a spell? I just chanted a few words with Joey here, you know, calling on healing to come for him, and—I didn't really know what I was doing, but it felt right at the time."

Joey's smile is way too big. I didn't know he had that many teeth. "What? *Totally* it was a spell!" he says. "You even said at the beginning that you wouldn't talk, but then you took off the bunny head and said we had to do some magic."

"Well. Something extra seemed to be needed," I say weakly. "I wouldn't say it was magic."

"I'll say something extra was needed!" says Joey in a burst of enthusiasm that seems to resound through the studio. "I was a basket case. Like I'd gone all dark matter. Black hole stuff. And then you said we needed to clean the place up. I didn't know that keeping everything all messy like that was keeping me in a bad place."

"Well," I say. "Sometimes—"

"And oh yeah, I was pretty resistant." He chuckles. "I gave her kind of a hard time. We took salt and put it in the corners—and then we said some spell stuff that you said your grandmother used to say. What was it she used to cure?"

"Well, it was warts," I say. "She could get rid of warts. She said."

"Yeah. Warts. Warts are like heartbreak, that's what you said."

"Did I?"

"Yep! And I think you might be onto something. My whole life felt like warts. And now it doesn't anymore."

Mason clears his throat. "And then *I* came in while the Heartbreak Bunny and my son were saying some magic words, and after that, after she left—well, over four months of suffering started to disappear," says Mason. "Poof! I mean, I've heard of the placebo effect. I thought maybe that was what this was. You can make somebody believe something just by the power of suggestion—but it's weeks later, and my son here is better than I've seen him even *before* he started dating that woman. It's like—it's like he's been restored. I promise this is not a product endorsement, just a feature story about a fascinating woman in our midst. So tell us, Heartbreak Bunny, what's the takeaway here? What do heartbroken people need to know this Valentine's Day when they're watching their friends get roses and diamond rings? What do you want to say to them?"

I square my bunny suit–clad shoulders. My grandmother would say I should own this one, so I smile a nice wide smile. "Life is supposed to be fun! *Love* is supposed to be fun. If your relationship is over, or if you're hanging on to something that's no good for you, don't beat yourself up. Just know this: sometimes love isn't supposed to last. Sometimes it runs its course and—and then it fades away. It may sound crazy, but grief is just love that doesn't have a place to go. So love yourself! Love your life! Love your work and your friends and what it's like to be alive right now. And trust that you'll love again and open your heart up to new experiences."

"Grief is just love that doesn't have a place to go," intones Mason. He pauses and shakes his head. "And now, to a commercial break, and when we return, Lily Malone is going to tell us what winter heat does to our hair and skin and how we can combat the drying effects of the furnace. We'll be right back, so stick around." He does a little pistol gesture with his right hand and makes a clicking sound.

And . . . we're out. The dinosaurs recede in the darkness, Mason takes off his microphone, Joey jumps to his feet. Different lights come on. There is movement and bustling everywhere. A commercial plays.

Mason says, "That was *great*! Everything I'd hoped! People are going to love you, Billie!"

My face feels hot, and adrenaline may be the only thing running in my veins right now.

"That was so much fun!" I tell him. "And, Joey, you were wonderful! I hope you don't mind that you told thousands of people about your heartbreak. And I'm so glad—so glad that the spell helped you! Oh my goodness! I hardly know what to say!"

"He'll probably get some dates from this. Look at this handsome dude." Mason cuffs Joey on the back of the head. "I've got to get back for more segments coming up, but thank you, Billie. We'll be in touch."

The assistant comes over and hands me the bunny head with a shy smile.

"I thought you did really well," she says.

"Thank you. Thanks so much. I'm just a little bit flustered after that. I mean, I had no idea how fun that was going to be! None."

"I know," she says softly. "I think people are really going to respond. Somebody said the switchboard is already lighting up."

༄

"Speechless," says Louise a few minutes later, on my voice mail. "I am totally and utterly speechless." And then she proceeds to talk for five *non-speechless* minutes about how *stunned* she was, seeing me hopping on television—hopping and laughing! *And* telling people about my grandmother! "And for Mason Davis's *son* to come on *television* and talk about his fiancée's python-print bra! I had about four heart attacks during that segment, Mom, and I'm not sure I'm out of the woods yet. I may have to go downstairs and look at all the boxes that have arrived and hope there are some heart paddles in there so I can revive myself!" There's a pause, and then she says, "You, however, looked adorable. A raving lunatic, but adorable."

She calls back seconds later. "And thank you for not mentioning me. Because if you had, I would have to file dissolution papers to declare we're no longer related. If there even is such a thing."

CHAPTER TEN

Honest to God, the next few weeks proceed as if my perfectionist daughter's senior prom, Mardi Gras, and all three of my own bizarre wedding receptions are taking place simultaneously. It's like one of those old Buster Keaton movies, where he keeps moving forward while houses fall, trains whiz past, and automobiles collide all around him.

I hear from a radio station in Belgium. No, *two* radio stations in Belgium. One from Atlanta. And Pasadena. Also eight women's clubs, two suicide prevention newsletters, and a man in Oklahoma who wants permission to be the Heartbreak Burro. (I said yes; why not?) Also, network affiliates want quotes. Apparently, the clip of my interview with Mason went out all over the country. Four newspapers want to do feature stories, including *USA Today*. Oh, and about a bazillion people need help with breakups dating as far back as the Reagan administration. People who never reclaimed their happiness and now realize it's time. And what advice do I have for them?

A woman leaves a message saying she needs a spell so she can stop dreaming about her ex-wife. A guy stops me in Stop n' Shop and says he's being stalked by his ex-girlfriend, and he thinks if he removes her things from his house, maybe she'll go away. Because, he says, maybe the things themselves have magical vibe-producing properties, and did I think so? Was it the things themselves? Maybe I could go to *her* house and get *his* things out? He'd be glad to accompany me.

And then there is Mason Davis himself to be coped with.

He calls me every morning with the Heartbreak Bunny Consultation Report. Chuckling, he gives me the names and phone numbers of people who need a heartbreak visit. Apparently, folks are pouring out their stories to the switchboard operators at the station.

Still. And it's two weeks later. I haven't had time to trim my toenails or get my hair cut or have the oil changed in my car. I'm averaging three bunny house calls a day, and often now, my heartbreak customers have invited guests, who want to watch to see how the whole thing unfolds. At one house, yesterday, an entire dormitory floor cheered and helped drag objects out to the dumpster in the driveway.

And here, once again, is Mason Davis purring on the phone.

"Soooo," he says and there's something about the fourth *o* of that drawn-out syllable that signals we're moving into a new phase of things. Call me a weirdo, but I have a kind of sixth sense for when a man is attempting a relationship upgrade.

"I thought maybe I could actually stop by your house this afternoon after the show and drop off the list of people who want to hear from you," he says. "Instead of just reading you the names." He clears his throat. "I wouldn't stay or anything. Just hand over the list. It'd be nice to see you."

I immediately think of the *If You Give a Mouse a Cookie* story. You let Mason Davis talk you into going to the diner, and then he wants you to go on his TV show. You go on his TV show, and then he wants to call you every day. You let him call you every day, and then he wants to come to your house. You let him come to your house, and God knows what happens next. I suspect that he'd want to meet all the housemates; he'd certainly take over my position as Favorite Person to sweet little

Micah, and there'd come the day when he'd want to play the ukulele or attend Martini Thursday or . . . whatever.

I have him on speakerphone, because I'm busy making Micah a deviled egg for his lunch to take to kindergarten. That's what he wants each and every day: one deviled egg, cut in half, and with a little face on the yolk parts, with eyes made from sesame seeds and a sliver of carrot as the mouth. Also, I am to include two carrot sticks with a little container of vanilla yogurt to swish them in. And a rice cake.

Calvin the Romantic can hear everything. He's leapt up from the table, and now he's pulled out the stepladder. Oh, I see what he's up to. He's standing with his hands on his hips, contemplating climbing it to change the light bulb on the ceiling fixture, which keeps blinking. Calvin is not allowed on stepladders. I keep shaking my head at him, but he keeps pointedly ignoring me.

"Actually, I have a very busy day," I say to Mason Davis. "Two radio interviews, and then I'm helping Louise again with some more photos . . ." *Then there's that hair-washing. And possibly driving Calvin to the ER when he falls off this damned ladder.*

"Which is why I mentioned that I wouldn't stay," Mason says.

"Well," I say.

"What's your hesitation?"

"Mason, I've been really honest with you. I am not looking for a relationship."

"HELP!" says Calvin. He's standing on the bottom step of the ladder, grinning, and as far as I can see, there is absolutely nothing wrong with him. He is making the throat-cutting gesture at me.

"Hold on a second," I say to Mason, and put the phone on mute. "What are you yelling about? And you need to *please, please* get off that ladder. I'll change the bulb."

"Oh, I'm not going to change the bulb, believe me," he says. "I just brought this ladder over here so I could monitor your call and yell 'help' if you were being mean to Mason."

"I'm *not* being mean to Mason."

"Okay, so you're not being exactly *mean*, but there is no reason on earth to be telling him you don't want a relationship when all he wants is to bring you a list of names. It's rude, and it's beneath you."

"*Rude?*" I say. "What—I should pretend that I'm going along with this? He might as well know right now that I am *not interested in him.* Calvin, stop looking at me that way. You have no idea what it's like out there for women. You have to keep making it clear with these guys!" I click the phone off mute. "Hi. Sorry," I say. "Emergency here with my housemate on the ladder."

Mason clears his throat. "Um, sure, okay," he says, and his voice is a little shaky. "Just so you know, Billie, I'm not interested in a relationship either. I really only wanted to bring by the list of people interested in your business."

A silence ticks by.

"So the phone wasn't on mute?" I say finally.

"No. Not so much."

"Shit," I say.

"It's fine. I'll be over around one then?"

෴

I spend the morning on the telephone talking to disk jockeys. I'm happy to be talking to them. They are a universally cheerful brand of human being, although, frankly, they seem as though they are mainlining caffeine. They also have names that make it sound like they were born to either strippers or zookeepers. And they are prone to sudden, violent yelps when they need to interrupt to announce something about traffic or weather.

I'm settled in at my desk, my smile pasted on just right. Even though I'm not on camera, you can hear smiles. I know this.

The disk jockey, a man named Chaz Cat (clearly the spawn of a stripper *and* a zookeeper), is all sparkles and verve: "Sooooo! Good morning, Anoka, Minnesota! Drive time is eight oh five. We're seeing some increasing traffic on the highway right about now. Watch out for that snow melt that probably refroze. And this morning we're talking about luvvvv. Specifically, what lengths people will go to in order to get themselves over a bad love affair. We're talking here with an expert, a woman who goes by the name Heartbreak Bunny, who's recently taken the world by storm by—get this—hopping into people's homes and then *taking their stuff away from them*. Okay, I know. It sounds sketchy. But tell us, Heartbreak Bunny: What's the rationale behind even trying to help people get over a bad love affair? Won't they get over it eventually all on their own?"

Me: "Oh, who knows? Eventually. Probably. But I think the longer we keep ourselves in unhappiness and heartbreak, the more our neural pathways become adapted to a level of sadness that translates into feelings of lack of self-worth and—"

Chaz Cat: "Okaaay, well, one level of sadness here is that there's an accident on Thurston Avenue that's caused the stoplight to go out. So use caution there, folks. And now, I gotta ask: Are there Heartbreak Bunnies here in the Midwest?"

"I am the only one in captivity so far."

"Well, it's going to be thirty-seven degrees in Anoka this morning. Pretty much a heat wave compared to yesterday. And here's a song to celebrate the weather *and* the fact that love leaves us all a big mess: 'Heat Wave' by Martha and the Vandellas, asking the musical question: What's love supposed to be about, anyway? Or something like that. I forget the lyrics."

Then, because he didn't cut the phone connection, I hear: "What the hell are we doing interviewing somebody who isn't even available to our listeners?"

And *then* the line goes dead.

⌒⊙

"Good morning. I'm Raven Wildness, talking here on the morning commute with the Heartbreak Bunny. A woman who will come hopping into your house *in a bunny suit* and take out all the stuff that's keeping you in tears over lost love. So tell me, Heartbreak, um, Rabbit, why do you dress up in a rabbit costume? What do rabbits and heartbreak have to do with each other?"

"Bunny. Heartbreak Bunny. It's because I want people to lighten up about love. I want them to laugh and—"

"You want to be *zany* then, am I right? We all want zany!" He blows an air horn.

"Well, perhaps not zany in the sense of being a cartoon. But I—"

"That's all the time we have. Sunny skies today, temperatures in the twenties. Brr! Take along that overcoat! And remember that life can be heavy sometimes. The Heartbreak Bunny says you gotta dress up in a costume."

"No! I—"

⌒⊙

And, at 11:30 a.m., a call with Ivan the Terrible: "So, Heartbreak Rabbit, um, are you trying to be Rabbit from the Winnie-the-Pooh books?"

"What? No."

"Well, what made you think of being a rabbit then?"

"Drunkenness. I got too drunk one night."

"Happens to the best of us. We'll be back after a commercial, with weather and sports. The message is: Don't drink, boys and girls. Get stoned instead."

⌒⊙

Mason shows up right after lunch just as I'm coming downstairs. I open the front door, and there he is, grinning.

"So *this* is where the Heartbreak Bunny lives!" he says gleefully, doing his own brand of bunny hopping on the front steps and looking around like he's entered a museum space. "Quite a nice porch you have here! I love the gingerbread touches on the porch pillars. Are they called pillars when they're just pieces of wood connected to the roof? I've never known. Home repair—not really my talent." He turns and looks at me and smiles. His eyes have high beams.

"Not mine either, as you can see," I say. I hold out my hand for the piece of paper. "Do you have the list?"

He's still looking around and smiling. He walks over to the railing and examines the gingerbread curlicues up close. "It's so cool the way you painted the porch ceiling sky blue. I read somewhere that that's what the Victorians did."

"Is it," I say.

"Just what I'd expect in the Heartbreak Bunny's house," he says. "Quite, quite the appealing place. My, my. You've been here a long time?"

"Yes. A very long time. The list?"

"I know I have it here somewhere." He reaches into his coat pocket, fumbles around, comes up with nothing. Tries the other pocket. Pats both pockets, looks at me blankly.

"Come in, why don't you?" says Calvin. He's come up from behind me. "It's freezing out here."

"I'm just looking for the list," says Mason.

"Well, have some coffee to warm up," says Calvin, glaring at me. "It's that kind of day. Supposed to snow again late this afternoon, I think."

"The snow just won't stop this year," Mason says. He's still patting himself down, searching through pockets.

"It *is* only March first," I point out.

"Yeah, but I always have hope that March first is the beginning of the end of winter," says Mason. "Especially on a day like today, when I'm off. I was thinking it's the kind of day I'd like to drive out to Niantic and visit the Book Barn. Maybe get me some used books and then procure a lobster roll from somewhere." He looks at me questioningly. "If the snow holds off, that is."

I don't say anything. Calvin nudges me to step aside and let him in.

Having Mason here is like having an exotic animal standing in the kitchen—with that too-much-handsomeness and the smell of his aftershave and his sweatshirt that looks like it's been ironed. And all this delighted restlessness that he's giving off, as though he's actually *throwing* pheromones about the room.

Oh, I am on my guard.

He finally manages to locate the list tucked inside the kangaroo pocket of his sweatshirt, and he makes a big show of taking it out, unfolding it slowly, and perusing it. He puts his reading glasses on the end of his nose and stares at it.

"Very touching," he says. "You've hit a nerve, that's for sure. Here's a woman who was dating a guy for six months, and he left her when he discovered that she had a kid she hadn't mentioned."

"That seems like grounds for a breakup to me," I say, reaching into the cupboard to get a mug for him.

"Yeah, the kid was staying with his father during the week when this couple dated, so the mom never felt the need to mention him, until she thought the relationship was solid. And now she's bereft. She can't get over him."

"Ah, the humans," says Calvin. "They can always think of new ways to screw things up, can't they? Endlessly inventive."

Mason turns and smiles at Calvin, and his face lights up. They've talked on the phone before; they're fast friends, I can tell. "So, Calvin! Billie here told me you've lived here for, what? Nine years now?"

"Eight," Calvin says.

"Eight! Isn't that something! What a remarkable house to live in!" Mason walks around the kitchen, examining things. The mixer stand seems to fascinate him; it's a stainless steel model from the 1950s. The dishes hurriedly tossed in the porcelain sink elicit a smile, as does the decoupage peeling off the cabinet doors. And nobody, he exclaims, has a wall phone anymore—especially not a big yellow one with the circular dial you have to put your fingers in. "Only the Heartbreak Bunny!" he says. "Wow. So how many people live here now, in addition to the plumber?" He gives me a big smile.

I hurry and plunk down his cup of coffee on the table, hoping he'll stop exploring before he gets to our ancient, teal refrigerator, the top of which is currently piled high with potato chip bags, mixing bowls, and anything else we can't think of what to do with or don't have room for. The martini shaker sits on the counter, along with a half-finished bottle of vodka. Mason lifts his eyebrows at those, and Calvin dives in, bragging about Martini Thursdays. I hold my breath and exchange a glance with Calvin that means *DO NOT INVITE MASON DAVIS FOR MARTINI THURSDAYS. DO NOT.*

He drifts over to the table, lured there by coffee, still asking questions, in wide-eyed amazement. Is that a *ukulele* he saw in the entrance hall? He hadn't seen one in years! Who plays that? (We all do, to some degree.) And was that a bowling ball over by the couch? (Yes, Edwin is on a team.) And didn't he see a red scooter on the porch? (Yes. It's Micah's.) Ohhhh! He smacks his head at that. Of course! The plumber's son! And how's he doing with the spiders?

Does this guy remember *everything* anybody's ever said to him?

I want to rush him out. But Calvin—exasperating, lovable Calvin—answers all his questions in his affable, easygoing way, pouring more coffee, and even taking him on a tour of the rest of the house. I hear them clumping around in the living room, opening the draperies in the dining room, plunking notes on the piano in the entryway. Yes, there's a piano in the entryway. It was the only spot, and besides that, the entryway is so large that one tenant used to refer to it as the lobby.

They come trudging back into the kitchen, Mason exclaiming once again about how thrilled the station is with our interview. It's gotten more hits on the website than anything except murders. "Crime will always beat out feature stories," he explains. "But I think we've proven that heartbreak recovery has a good shot, too."

He smiles at me, and his eyes are so full and liquid that I worry I could fall into them and drown if I'm not careful.

But I *am* careful. I start furiously washing up the breakfast dishes. He and Calvin seem very well suited to each other, sitting at the table with their arms draped over the backs of the chairs, talking about Calvin's former department at Yale, and how Mason got into the news biz. And on they go, Mason talking about his wife who died, and Calvin talking about his ex-wife who died and then the other exes whom he thinks of fondly now that he doesn't have to deal with them anymore.

Oh, I *know* what Calvin is doing. I see through him. That little elf, always promoting love and togetherness and forgetting the past and moving on, and all the rest of it. He'll keep Mason here as long as possible, drawing him out, hoping I'll soften. I know his game.

"Well, I've got work to do!" I say when I've dried and put away the last dish.

They look at me indulgently, smiling, but it's as though I haven't spoken. Calvin starts talking about his new love. A delightful woman who is the belle of the ball at the senior center. Probably they wouldn't have looked twice at each other back when they were young, but now look! Perfectly matched. It's all due to Calvin's ten-year plan, a plan to reinvent himself and be happy again every decade. A gentleman of ninety can have a fine love life, he is saying.

"A ten-year plan!" says Mason Davis. "Extraordinary!"

"Thanks for the list, Mason. Calvin will show you out when you're ready to leave."

"Oh!" says Mason, startled. "Maybe I should—"

"Have another cup of coffee?" says Calvin, and Mason laughs, and I've almost, almost made it to the back stairs when I hear a ruckus at the front door. And then there's Louise standing in the doorway of the kitchen, holding a box of something, and looking as though she'd planned to come in and immediately burst into tears but is now going to have to be brave and social.

"Hullo," she says. She's wearing a fox-colored faux-suede car coat with a faux-fur collar, and her hair is all done up in a French twist with little tendrils expertly framing her cheekbones. She looks at Mason Davis, and I see by her face that she's registered who he is. She scowls appropriately. He's the one, in her mind, who has kept the Heartbreak Bunny situation alive. Little does she know that I used my own stubborn streak to keep it going.

"Hi, honey," I say. "What a nice surprise to see you! This is Mason Davis. And Mason, this is my daughter, Louise."

"Louise! So *this* is the beautiful Louise!" Mason says. He takes in the vision of her, and also notes, I'm sure, that she resembles a very well-dressed emotional wreck, wobbling in her knee-high black velvet boots just enough to make her look unsteady. She smiles at him, says some polite thing about how much she likes his show, and they chat briefly about an influencer who comes on Channel 12 regularly to talk about home-care hacks for people who hate to clean house.

"What's your blog about?" he says. "And my apologies for not knowing already."

"It's fine," she says dully. "It's, you know, fashion and lifestyle. It's a love story blog—goes by the cutesy name of @lulu&leo—even though Leo split a few weeks ago. Now it should be called Lulu Trying to Figure Her Way in Life and Doing a Bang-Up Job of Absolutely Nothing Especially Now That Her Mother Doesn't Have Time to Help Anymore. Which is too long to fit on a title."

"You're rocking the positive-thinking aspect, though," I say.

She makes a mad face at me.

"No, I just meant I liked your post yesterday."

She'd posted about her thoughts when the doorbell rings: she first thinks it must be a serial killer, or the police arriving to arrest her for unpaid parking tickets—and then she remembers it could be the notebook for the positive-thinking course she signed up for.

It was meant to be a joke, and it was accompanied by a selfie she'd taken of herself next to the front door with a frightened look on her face.

"Do you want some coffee?" I say.

"No. I'm on my way to meet with a nail polish client, and I just stopped in to drop off these spring bulbs," she says. She seems a little subdued, pale and beautiful in that Uma Thurman way that makes you want to take care of her. "Paperwhites. I thought we could both start them indoors."

"Paperwhites!" Calvin says. "My favorites! Say . . ." He leans back in his chair, tipping back on two legs, which I just hate when he does—and then he says, "So I never did hear how the pregnancy spell went the other night."

Mason Davis's eyebrows practically leave his face.

"Calvin," I say. "We don't have to bring all that up . . ."

He's looking at Louise. "It was for your friend, right? Phoebe, isn't it?" He turns to Mason, who looks so excited he might soon levitate. "Our Heartbreak Bunny here has discovered in herself a possible new calling for her occasional magic," he says. "Calling in babies who might want to join us here on the planet!"

"All right, that's enough, Calvin," I say. "We don't need to share that with everyone."

"Especially the media," says Louise.

Mason clears his throat and says that he's completely discreet; he's certainly not here as the *media*. But what is this about a pregnancy spell? His eyes meet mine.

"It was nothing," I say. "A little experimental spell, calling in a baby to a woman friend of Louise's who has been trying to conceive. We did some chanting and said a few magical words and passed around some round objects. It was a lark."

"We're quite sure it didn't work," says Louise. "Believe me, it was *not* my idea."

"We have a lot of magic denial in our midst," I say to Mason, and he laughs. Then I turn to Louise. "So, honey, I was just getting ready to go out on some bunny calls. Want to come upstairs and talk to me while I get ready?"

"No," she says. "I can't stay." She lowers her voice. "I really came over so that you and I could . . . you know, do the thing."

"The thing?"

"Never mind. It's fine."

"The thing?"

"*Mom.* Don't you remember?"

Calvin clears his throat and asks Mason if he'd like to see the garden shed. Like there's anything at all that would be interesting in the garden shed on March first. But Mason is game for anything, and he gets up from his chair and says he hasn't been in a garden shed in ages, so he'd love to.

Once the two of them have clunked out the back door, shrugging into their coats while chuckling about something I can't quite follow, I turn to Louise.

"I'm sorry, but I don't know what you're talking about," I say.

"The other day you said you thought it was time for us—for *me*—to rededicate the blog. Let go of the @lulu&leo moniker and admit that I'm doing this myself," she says in a low, trembly voice. She stacks up the napkins on the table, quite unable to help herself from straightening things. "Sooooo . . . I think the time has come, and I decided a good name going forward would be @LuluAlone. And I thought maybe I'd take you up on your offer to help me write a letter to the followers . . . explaining this new step. Why I'm not in love anymore."

I give her a look. "You're not?"

"No. I have to get over my marriage. Because it's gone. *He's* gone. So I was thinking even of making a TikTok video of me, sitting down and telling people how . . . strong and empowered I feel heading out on a new path. You know. Being brave and all that."

"Darling!" I say. "I'm so proud of you."

"Yeah, I'm ready," she says quietly. "I mean, I have to be. He came over last night, and we talked for ages, and although there's still so much love there, I can see that it's not going to ever work out. So." She takes a deep breath and closes her eyes for a moment, and then opens them and smiles at me. "So, I'm moving on."

"Let's go up to my room," I say. "We can do it right now. That is, if your nail polish client isn't going to be kept waiting?"

Her eyes flash. "I just made that up. The truth is, my whole business is going belly-up. That's why I've got to do something."

CHAPTER ELEVEN

To all my lovely subscribers and friends: this is a very hard post to write, but, my sweet little ducklings, it is time.

To all of you who have been loyal followers of @lulu&leo over the last few wonderful years, I have to tell you some news I never wanted to share. In fact, I have been hiding the news from you for several weeks now, hoping that maybe things would change. (Maybe if I closed my eyes and turned around three times, and said a magic chant, everything could go back to the way I'd prefer.)

But magical thinking isn't going to solve this.

And so now I need to tell you the truth: Leo and I have split up.

With 50 percent of marriages ending in divorce, perhaps it's no surprise. But I had always thought our love would wrap us up in its cloak of togetherness, and that we would someday be two centenarians, rocking on a porch somewhere and sharing Instagram photos of our hearing aids and granny glasses—as well as our great-grandchildren.

It's hard to say good-bye to a dream, but that is what we have to do.

Leo has left, gone off to practice REAL photojournalism, in a world that he feels needs his services and his talents more than @lulu&leo. I am grateful to him for making a clean break, for pursuing his dream, even if it's one I don't share.

My dream, my loves, is to remain with you in the soft world of beauty and comfort—sharing with you fashion pics, hairstyles, manicure tips, new coffee makers, and yes, even inventions that seem so outlandish and dazzling that it's hard to believe they exist. (Looking at *you*, levitating light bulb.) I want the wonder and the excitement and the enthusiasm for everything to continue just as it has: to share with you all the beautiful sunsets, sunrises, as well as bedspreads and hair ties and braided bread and washable markers and sound systems and eyelash curlers. I want us together to see the beauty and joy in everything, just as we have been.

I am now @LuluAlone. I am #alone but not #heartbroken. Like so many empowered women, I am striving forward. I've spent the last few weeks considering everything, and I'm working with a consultant, my mom, who's helping me figure out how to do this alone. The photographs may look different because the boundaries are shifting and that's part of the process and needs to be normalized. What I need from *you* is support for my new inflection points as I set my intention to operate out of personal strength and not abandonment. Empowerment and not passivity.

Please. We will stick together!

All my love,

@LuluAlone

⌒೨

Needless to say, I objected strenuously to the last two paragraphs, which I find incomprehensible. Jargon! But she is adamant about including information about her "inflection points."

As soon as she leaves, my phone dings.

It's Victor.

i don't mind that you don't write me back because i am a complete enough entity to simply hover there in your world where you don't have to acknowledge me even though we both know you hear me but someday i would like to know about louise I feel horrible about louise on those nights when i wake up in the deep and know that the life i chose was the life of emptiness

I shouldn't do this, I know I shouldn't do it, but I hit the button and type furiously:

WOULD IT KILL YOU TO USE SOME PUNCTUATION, YOU NARCISSISTIC, SELF-AGGRANDIZING, FAMILY-ABANDONING CREEP!

It was either that or I would have had to throw the phone through the window. And I need the phone.

CHAPTER TWELVE

"It's time," says Calvin the following week, in his I've-made-a-decision voice, "that you meet Bernice. I've invited her over for dinner tonight." He folds up the newspaper, having finished the crossword puzzle. And gives me one of his meaningful looks. I can feel it, even though I am doing the breakfast dishes and have my back to him.

My heart turns over. It apparently is not a fan of meeting Bernice. Call it intuition or dread or whatever you want, but my heart is pretty sure she will take Calvin away.

"But it's Martini Thursday," I say weakly. "Do we really want to expose her to Martini Thursday right off the bat?"

This is not nice of me. No reason Bernice can't come to Martini Thursday.

In my (admittedly weak) defense, I'm cleaning up the kitchen after a hectic morning, and I'm getting ready to go out on two bunny calls, so I have a million things on my mind. Just in the past four days, I've done nine bunny calls, and with four of those, I played revenge songs while we threw out bags of love notes, old sweaters that smelled like perfume or aftershave, and a couple of handwritten poems. I did my

love-as-a-wart-removing-spell three times. And two times I took off the
bunny head and we danced. I have never felt more like I'm doing what
I'm meant to do.

It's exhilarating.

It's just the rest of life that's crap.

For instance, this Calvin and Bernice thing.

Standing there at the kitchen sink, I feel the tears backing up
behind my eyelids. I bow my head and swipe at my eyes.

"Uh-oh," he says.

"Stop it. It's nothing."

"No. It is something."

"Never mind."

"You know you're going to feel better if you say it."

"I won't. I'll feel better if I ignore it, and it goes away."

"Except that when has it ever gone away?"

"All right." I take a deep breath. "I think it's that I'm sick of people
claiming they're falling in love when it's not even remotely real."

"Who are you talking about?"

"Well, *you*, for starters."

"Me!"

"Yes. No offense, but you declare out of the blue one day that you're
embarking on a romance, and then you throw yourself into it, even
though it can't possibly work. And you *know* it's not going to work! It's
all going to fall apart, because that's the way these things always go."

"With all due respect, Heartbreak Bunny, everything *doesn't* always
fall apart."

"Yeah? What doesn't fall apart, Calvin?" I whirl around from the
sink and look at him, waving the wooden spoon in the air. "Be realistic.
Right here in this one house, we've got Reggie and Cynthia separated
and probably about to get a divorce, and just look at little Micah, trying his best to make everything be all right with them again. And then
there's Edwin, who's been in love with seven or eight women since he

moved in, none of whom ever takes him seriously—and Marisol not giving up on 3M, her moony married man, who is *the* weakest individual, stringing her along! For years! And even Kat. Look at Kat's stupid marriage. Bob has no sense of humor, he doesn't get her at all, and yet she sacrifices and compromises and becomes whoever he wants her to be. Unrecognizable. Nobody has a great love. Everybody's selfish and looking out only for themselves. Look at poor Louise! I thought she and Leo were going to make it to the finish line, but now he's walked away and isn't coming back. And she's miserable."

"What's this finish line you're talking about? There's no *finish line*. And also *you* had a perfectly good relationship with Desmond. He didn't leave you."

"But, Calvin, don't you see? It wasn't love with Desmond. It was a late-in-life match, that's all. A compromise. There were no fireworks, no romance, no chases. No hearts beating extra fast. And even that fell apart!"

"Well, but only because he died. I don't think we can hold that against love, can we?"

"But that's what I'm saying. It *wasn't* love. Any more than what you feel for Bernice is love. And you know it. Admit it that deep down, you don't love her. You're just—just—grasping at what you think is one last chance . . ."

He draws himself up. For a moment I think I'm about to see him angry for the first time in eight years. I suck my breath in, preparing. But then he composes himself and gives me a long, mournful look.

"More than anything, Billie, I wish you knew what love can be. You're right that humans are imperfect. We're selfish. We're misguided. We make mistakes, but, honey, we're also capable of such deep connections with each other, and sometimes we recognize in another person something that's so moving and divine and otherworldly that we know we can't live without having that in our lives. And it can happen at any time in life. It's one of our best human powers, to love, and then pick ourselves up after a loss and love again and again."

Sometimes Calvin says things that absolutely kill me.

⁓

I go off to do two routine bunny calls. The first one is for a woman whose boyfriend left her after two months of steady dating. He told her he loved her. He said he had never met anyone like her, blah blah blah. And here she sits, the typical bunny customer, with the haunted eyes, the downturned mouth, the willingness to suffer long-term in the name of love. It strikes me that for some people, it must seem that the length of time they're willing to be sad translates roughly into how meaningful and important that relationship was. Maybe there should be an algorithm: one day of sadness for every month of the love affair. I don't know. People could work it out for themselves, see what it's worth.

But this woman—the whole thing only went on two months.

I say, "Sweetheart, two months isn't even long enough to break in a pair of shoes. So it's certainly not long enough to put your heart in mothballs. Snap out of this funk you're in. Right now. Give me that photograph of the two of you and unfriend him on Facebook and unfollow him on whatever other social media madness you've got going on. And square your shoulders. You're stronger than this, girl."

To my surprise, she does exactly what I say.

"You're already just fine," I say grouchily. "Calling me to come over means that you already knew you were over him."

With the second client, I feel myself losing it the moment I find out he's hiding his boyfriend's sweater underneath his pillow. "Out with that! Out!" I say. "Now open the drapes and call some friends! Remember what your life used to be! You've got to stop pining. Right this minute!"

The guy looks at me with round, surprised eyes. "No, you're right," he says in a wobbly voice. "Here—take the sweater out of here. And if I call you saying I need it back, don't give it to me."

∽

By the time I get home, Martini Thursday is well under way. I find Bernice and Calvin in the kitchen, and he has the music cranked up—Glenn Miller's big band sound is blaring—and Calvin is running around the kitchen with a dish towel over his shoulder, like a New York chef, twitchy with happiness. He introduces Bernice and me, and he must have done a good job preparing her because she doesn't even blink at the fact that I'm wearing a bunny costume. We shake hands and then we hug, and Calvin pours us both a glass of sherry, beaming.

In fact, Bernice has been well prepared for everything about Martini Thursday. She's all dressed up in the spirit of the evening, wearing an old-fashioned red wool suit with a little fur collar and black pumps. She does a little shimmy when "In the Mood" comes on and Calvin spins her around. She yells over the music that she'd always intended to run away with a man—any man—who knew how to play the trombone. Calvin laughs and points out that he plays the ukulele, which is even better because he can play and sing at the same time.

"Just try to get your trombone player to do *that!*" he says. He pulls her to him, and she puts her head on his shoulder and they two-step their way around the kitchen.

Marisol and I raise our eyebrows at each other.

Calvin is a purist when it comes to Martini Thursdays—according to him, we have to make the recipes in *The Joy of Cooking* in order, which means unfortunately that tonight's dinner is deep-fried stuffed carrots.

"More and more, I think this explains why women in the 1930s couldn't go to work. Who has time for anything else when you've got the responsibility of trying to stuff a carrot?" I say, and Bernice laughs. I like her laugh.

She has two bright pink spots on her cheeks. It's awfully warm in the kitchen. I offer to take her jacket, but she says no. So I go over and open the back door and then run upstairs and change into my flouncy skirt à la 1940 and my powder-blue cashmere sweater. When I come down, Edwin has set the table with the linen tablecloth and the silver, and Marisol has lit the candelabra. And everyone sips vodka martinis in the kitchen and talks about spring coming and how nice the carrots smell. Reggie and Micah come downstairs, and I end up eating dinner with Micah on my lap, which is his preferred seat lately. He takes a pass on the stuffed carrots and instead has some leftover macaroni and cheese. I love the way he rests his head against my shoulder, munching steadily on his pasta, with his eyes wide at the sight of all the adults dressed up in their finery and the candles burning in the big fancy holder.

I straighten my skirt and then look over at Calvin's face in the candlelight. He seems concerned about something, leaning forward and looking quizzical. And I see him reach over to touch Bernice's arm. She's gazing vacantly into space.

"Bernice?" says Calvin. "Honey?"

"Well," Bernice says in a very careful, soft voice. "This was certainly delicious, but now I feel like I really need to get back home. Maurice, will you drive me, please?"

Maurice?

Calvin gets up quickly—I see the alarm flickering in his eyes as he helps Bernice to her feet. But then, without any warning whatsoever, she crumples, as if she's a piece of paper folded into an accordion, and she slowly, slowly, *slowly* falls over—an eon of falling, and before I can even move or form words, she's landed headfirst into her now empty plate. It makes a thin little cracking sound as she hits.

We leap to our feet. Calvin's face is grim with worry, but he catches her before she slides any farther, and he and Edwin help her over to the sofa. I have already slid Micah off my lap and dialed 9-1-1 before I have even a moment to think.

$\sim$

The EMTs come tromping into the living room, all capable and respectful, and I see them taking in the scene of candles and dinner and the Glenn Miller music in the background, but mostly they're looking at the sweet, smiling elderly lady who is now lying on the couch in the front parlor with her collar loosened and her shoes off, looking perfectly normal and waving her hands in the air whenever we "make a fuss," as she calls it.

"This happens sometimes," she says. "It's nothing, I'm sure. I get overheated."

"Maybe you were just dehydrated," says Calvin.

The EMTs check her vitals, and their walkie-talkies crackle as though we're in a scene where things are about to go terribly wrong, but no—everything seems to be okay. Her blood pressure is normal, and her eyeballs seem okay, and they feel her pulse and look at her ankles. She knows the date and who the president is, and she remembers her name. They tell her to drink more water and avoid warm rooms. To get some rest.

She thanks them warmly, squeezing the hand of the one closest to her. And she ducks her head just a little and says in a confessional voice, "My doctor told me to schedule a *procedure*, and I didn't do it."

"A procedure?" he says and nods.

"For one of those things, those devices, that help your heart stay . . . straight. You know, with the beating."

"A pacemaker?"

"Yes. I think so. Yes, that."

He is packing up his stethoscope, and he turns and smiles at her. "Ma'am, you should definitely call your doctor and schedule that."

"I will, young man. And thank you. Sorry to trouble you when it was my own fault."

I see Calvin melt when she says this. He puts his arms around her so carefully, murmurs into her hair that it's not her fault, they're happy to get her fixed up, it's a privilege to be here with her, to be helping.

After they've left, we all try to shake the whole incident off. We help Bernice get to her feet and get her things. We hug her and she smiles and tries to make jokes about being a troublesome dinner guest—and then, despite my protests, Calvin drives her home.

Once they arrive, he phones to say he's going to stay the night at her place. No, he's not sure when he'll be back. He wants to keep an eye on her.

Just to make sure she's okay.

I look around me. The kitchen seems like the scene of a horrible accident, with unfinished food and spilled wine on the tablecloth and knocked-over chairs from everyone jumping up in such a rush. Marisol and I do the dishes wordlessly, but I notice she keeps stealing little glances at me. When we're drying the pots and pans, she clears her throat and says, "I wanted to let you know that Clark is going to come and spend the night here tonight."

It takes me a moment to remember that 3M has a name, and it's Clark.

I smile at her. "Wow, this is a big change!" I wish I could tell Calvin this news.

She clears her throat nervously, one more time. "I know you don't believe in love, and you think I'm a victim of a heartless man, but I want to say that he's left his wife, and I think we'll be moving in together soon. I wanted you to know," she says quietly.

I stare at her, unsure what to say. Marisol has lived here for three years, and 3M has never seemed real; I wasn't sure he really existed. After all, she rarely spent time with him, even at holidays. They didn't take off for secret trysts. She didn't seem to suffer the way you'd think. One day she confessed that they didn't even have sex because of his marital status. They *mooned* after each other. Those were her words. Calvin once said we should adjust his name to 4M, Marisol's Moony Married Man.

"Well," I say. "Wow. Again, wow."

She laughs. "I know. It's the only response possible, isn't it? All these years."

"Are you happy? This is a big change. Sex, love, cohabitation, the whole nine yards. The end goal. The whole ball game. I mean, you **won**. How does that feel?"

I don't know why I'm talking in sports metaphors, but she nods and adjusts her huge plastic glasses.

"I think I'm ready," she says. She licks her lips and swallows, looks up at the light fixture. "I saw a psychic, and she told me that I'm going to have three kids and a house in the country, and all the kids will play musical instruments. And I'll be married to him for fifty-plus years, which means that I'll be in my nineties, and maybe we'll be like Calvin and Bernice, only we will have had a whole lifetime together. I think it's going to be awesome, and please don't say it's not, because I *want* this, damn it! I have waited and now I want all of it: the house and the children and the mother-in-law problems and roses on our anniversary, and him across the pillow from me when I go to sleep at night . . ."

I go over and put my arms around her. "Shh, shh, Marisol. You are going to have it all."

And she bursts into tears.

⁓

I'm in my bed later when my phone dings.

i want to see you so can i see you can i see you

I don't answer such a stupid message.

you haunt me do you know that you are present in my room right now and i am remembering your smell your touch your halfway crooked smile the way you close your eyes the delicate curve of your ear like that shell we found on the beach that time

Well, that is just enough. He is out of his mind.

I grab the phone and type back to him, all in caps with plenty of punctuation:

WE NEVER FOUND A SHELL ON THE BEACH AND YOU ARE OBVIOUSLY IN A LOT OF PAIN IF YOU'RE SO MISGUIDED AS TO THINK YOU ARE WRITING TO YOUR DECEASED LOVER, WHEN YOU ARE REALLY WRITING TO BILLIE, THE WIFE YOU ABANDONED 35 YEARS AGO!!!! THIRTY-FIVE YEARS, VICTOR. ALSO, DO NOT WRITE TO ME ANYMORE! JUST STOP!!

Then, for emphasis:

I DON'T WANT TO HEAR FROM YOU AGAIN!

Once more:

EVER! EVER!

With that taken care of, once and for all, I talk to Mason on the phone. I actually call him up, which my mother would have said was a crime against nature, a woman calling a man on the telephone. I still hear her voice in my head whenever I do this. But I am not in love with Mason so it's okay, and also, I need to hear his rich, chocolaty voice, *and* I need to fill him in on Calvin and Bernice. He and Calvin are practically best buds now; I half expect that any day now they'll start wearing matching porkpie hats and hanging out at the golf range together on weekends. So it only seems right to report the series of tonight's upsetting events.

"And now he's gone?" he says when I finish describing everything. "Will he come back, do you think?"

"Of course he'll come back," I say. "He didn't take any of his things."

We have a moment of silence while we both realize that doesn't mean he's ever really coming *back*. He may have defected, for love. It would be just like Calvin to do something like that.

Mason says, "So, a new ten-year plan suggested itself to him, a woman from the senior center, and now that she fell over in her dinner plate, he needs to move along and take care of her."

"He's a little like Mary Poppins, I think, going where the wind blows him," I say. "But I'm already missing him."

"You know," says Mason. "I'm so glad you called because I was wondering if you might want to come on the show again. Picture it: the Heartbreak Bunny advises us how to make it through springtime. You know, when a young man's fancy turns to thoughts of love and all that."

"That sounds nice," I say.

"I would imagine springtime is a particularly dangerous time in your business," he says. "Second only to Valentine's Day."

"The station won't mind if I'm on again so soon?"

"Mind? No! They loved having you. Most-watched segment of the season. And we're still getting calls." His voice gets a little bit husky. "And you were my most favorite guest ever. I guess you know that."

"Well," I say. "Thank you for that."

My phone dings. I tell Mason I have to go. I don't have my reading glasses nearby, which means I can't read whatever message that just came in, and what if it's from Calvin? I tell him I have to hang up and go downstairs and get my glasses. Mostly, though, I want to get off the phone. I'm uncomfortable when Mason gets that throaty voice that sounds like he's about to declare love or something.

The message is from you-know-who.

> no we did find a shell on the beach on our honeymoon it was the color of the sunrise, and we could hear the ocean inside and you said our love would always last like the interconnected lines of the shell and do you remember the time we made love on the beach and could not stop

After that, I turn off the phone, but then I groan and turn it back on in case Calvin needs me.

Outside in the hallway, I can hear Marisol and 4M laughing together softly as they come upstairs.

I can feel it. She'll be leaving us soon to join him. If Calvin were here, I would say something like, *Another one bites the dust*, and he would say that Marisol deserves her shot at love—and who among us can predict what is going to happen? She might be fabulously happy.

And, if he were here, I would ask him how he thinks she will do without *us* and this house, where the *real* stuff of life lies? I think of her over the years, a whole collage of Marisol images: laughing and playing checkers with Calvin, finishing the crossword puzzle on Sundays, all the times she'd look at her phone and sigh because 4M sent a beautiful text with no mention ever of being together *now*.

And now he is going to be hers.

⁓

My phone dings all night, from the depths of the darkness.

Once or twice I glance at it just in case it's Calvin, but all I see is a blur of unpunctuated, uncapitalized words:

love

you

our daughter

sorrysorrysorry

Then:

forgive me can you ever forgive me remember how we laughed
and loved

CHAPTER THIRTEEN

For the next couple of weeks, I feel like a spinning top with all my Heartbreak Bunnying. The calls keep flooding in: between the people who contact Kat after seeing our brochures and our signs, and those who call the television station and are dutifully reported to me by Mason, I am rushing out to solve people's heartbreaks all over New Haven County. Call after call.

When I am not racing to someone's house, I'm talking on the radio. One evening I even drove twenty-five minutes to Ansonia to talk to a women's club. And the next evening I spoke at a library to a group of divorced young moms.

⌒

Meanwhile, in my own home, a deep silence reigns. Calvin is still with Bernice, and hasn't come back for even one item. I talk to him every day, and he is cheerful as ever. He says that Bernice had her pacemaker installed and she's doing so much better that they're now taking on little house projects.

"Be careful," I say.

He laughs. "Too late for that! I'm in love."

"I meant be careful and don't go on ladders," I say. When what I want to say is, *Come back! Come back, where I can make sure you're fine!*

And speaking of love, Reggie patched up things with Cynthia, and he and Micah moved back home. Marisol, radiant and beaming, has signed a lease on an apartment with 3M and packed up all her things and moved out. (He's back to being 3M since they are no longer mooning.) And even Edwin decided that he could handle sleeping over at his new girlfriend's house, even though she has two children and two dogs, and he is allergic to both of those species.

Spring, with all its dangers and pheromones zooming around, is in full bloom. All of my little charges are finding their way. Only Louise is still thrashing about in unhappiness.

She calls me one morning and says in a stuffed-up voice, "Ohhh, Mom."

"Hi, Lulu. What's the matter?" My heart twists into its familiar pretzel position hearing her sad voice. Kat once said that I'm scared of Louise, and I think she's partly right: I'm scared of her unhappiness.

She sighs. "I don't want to bother you. I know you're busy with all your bunny stuff. But it's just that . . ."

I wait, but she has stopped talking. I close my eyes, wishing for the millionth time that my daughter found life the tiniest bit easier.

I square my shoulders and say, "Tell me what's going on, baby."

"Ohhh, Mommmm! I'm losing followers right and left." She pauses to blow her nose. "Every day more of them leave, like we're on some kind of a sinking ship, and they have to run for their lives. And I know what you'll say—that it's because I'm not *energetically* in the game anymore. I know that. But, Mom . . . I miss Leo, and I miss his photos, and the whole blog seems to be just blah, and I don't know what to do. And I'm probably going to have to move out of here because he told his parents that we've split up, and he told me they're thinking about selling this house and kicking me out, and I'm just a wreck. A wreck!"

I go into the Mom Pep Talk. Here are the major points:

- It's going to be okay.
- You don't have to figure it all out right now.
- You are strong and talented.
- You just need a good night's sleep.
- Eat some protein.
- Maybe drink some water, too.
- Things always work out for the best.

"Well," she says, sniffling even more, "I was just sort of wondering if . . . you could come over, and if we can go through all my evening dresses and photograph me in them one last time, and then I can donate them. I think that if I downsize maybe at least it'll be easier if it turns out that I *do* have to move."

I don't want to remind her how inadequate my iPhone shots proved to be and how unhappy she was with nearly every picture I took, and rightly so.

"Please say you can come," she says.

"Well, sure. But didn't you hire a photographer?"

"I had to let her go, Mom. She was very judgy. And anyway, what we'll be doing today isn't really a big deal. It's just to document that I once owned these dresses. And get them packed up. I probably won't even post these photos. So can you come? Please?"

I realize then that it's not about the dresses. It's that she needs me. *Me.*

"Of course I can come," I say nervously. I look at the clock. "I don't have a bunny call until three, so I could come this morning. How would that be?"

"Thank you, thank you," she says. I realize that she's now started to cry.

⤢

I find her in her bedroom, knee-deep in a sea of dresses—on the bed, on the chaise longue, even on the floor. Yards and yards of colorful silk and tulle and netting and a million other fabrics I don't know the names of. She's standing in the middle of it all, wearing a nightgown and no makeup with her hair uncombed. I don't think I've seen Louise without makeup in years. I don't think she's even *been* without makeup for longer than ten seconds after awakening, not since she started this blog at least.

She looks beautiful, I think. Kind of vulnerable and young. And tired.

"You look like you could use some coffee," I say.

She sighs and picks up one dress after another, examining them for stains or tears. "What do you think of this color? Maybe this one could be somebody's prom dress, do you think?"

"Maybe it's me who needs some coffee," I tell her.

But she doesn't answer. She has that focused look she gets sometimes. I look around.

I can do this for a while, but ten dresses in, I am twitchy from trying to pay attention. Who really has so many dresses? Give them all away, I say.

"Let's go do something else," I say.

"I need to get this done. And anyway, what would we do?"

I push a pile of red dresses off to the side and plop down on the bed. "I don't know. Jump in the car and drive to Nashville, maybe, and stay in a hotel and eat some barbecue. Or, we could rent some bikes in New York City and ride down the West Side Highway and eat those German waffles they sell in the park by the Hudson River. Umm . . . go to Boston for the rest of the week. Come to think of it, I always meant to take you to Paul Revere's house."

"Why would you want to do *any* of those things?"

"Why? Because being in this house reminds me that you have pretty much sentenced yourself to prison. You need to have some fun. It feels like this house is where fun goes to die."

"Nice, Mom. I'm having a hard time, okay? I'm trying to get stuff done." She goes over to a pile of white lace dumped on the floor and picks it up. "Oh my God. Look at this! I brought down my wedding dress by accident. Ohhhh, and look how beautiful it was! *Is.*" Her jaw tightens and she holds it up in front of her, her eyes filling with tears. "Remember how scratchy it was, and how I said I hated it? And now I look at it, and I just . . . I don't know. It's beautiful, isn't it? But what should I do with it?"

Toss it, I think. But what I say is, "I don't know. What do you want to do with it?"

"I feel like you're supposed to save wedding dresses. You know, in case you have a daughter who wants to wear it sometime." She looks at me. "What did you do with *your* wedding dress? You sure didn't think of saving it for me to wear!"

"I wasn't much into the sentimental saving of dresses. I was more or less a hippie, remember? Also, divorce. Who wants to wear her mother's dress when she got divorced?"

She is burying her head in her lace dress.

"Oh hell, Louise, just keep it for now. Hang it back up in the closet, and don't think about it. I think I have to go make some coffee. Or did you already make some? Is there any downstairs?"

"I'm not drinking coffee lately. It upsets my stomach. And why didn't you have some at home? Doesn't Calvin make, like, the best coffee known to man, according to him?"

"Oh, I didn't tell you, did I? My household has completely changed. Calvin has pretty much gone to live with Bernice since she had that fainting spell I told you about. And *Marisol*—well, she and 4M have gotten an apartment together now. She left."

"What? I thought he was *3M*. And he left his wife?"

"He turned into 4M when we found out they weren't having sex. They were just mooning—oh, never mind. Yes, he left his wife. And *Edwin* is now spending most nights at his girlfriend's house, bravely confronting allergy attacks. And *Reggie*—well, now Reggie could make coffee, but he had an interesting interlude in the middle of the night last week, and so now he's gone."

She stares at me and shakes her head. "I do not know how you live your life."

"It's just a little complicated right now, is all. With people sorting themselves out. It's one of those transition times. It'll all be fine eventually."

"What happened to Reggie in the middle of the night? Or do I want to know?" She's abandoned her wedding dress and is now sadly picking up dresses and then dropping them again into different piles. There's obviously some sorting system here.

"*Well*," I say. "It *is* quite a story! You know how Reggie thinks that Cynthia is seeing someone else, which she is *not*, but he's got it in his head that she is and he can't be reasoned out of it? It's been nice having him living with us, especially because of Micah, who's five, and I just love him."

She nods, barely listening, so I get more animated, telling her how Reggie and Cynthia were fighting on the phone all the time—and how it was even worse when they stopped fighting—when there was no talking at all. Just moping.

"And then at eleven last Thursday night, I'm getting into my bubble bath, and really looking forward to just having a soak, when I hear Cynthia outside, *shrieking*, calling Reggie's name and then rattling the door and banging on the porch windows . . . and stomping. *Stomping!* Well, I haul myself out of the tub and put on my robe, and start down the hall, hoping she doesn't wake up Micah or the whole neighborhood, and just as I get to the head of the stairs, I see Reggie running to the front door, and he throws it open and says, 'Cynthia! What the hell is wrong with you?' And she just starts hitting him and he yells for her to stop, and then he steps outside and closes the door. For a while I can hear them on the porch, and then after a while, they get in his truck, and at one point I looked outside to see if one of them had killed the other one and was looking around to hide the body, and what do you know? They were *kissing*. Like going at it, right there in the truck. I could see them in the streetlight, just making out like they were on their second date, and—"

"I *get* it, Mom. You don't have to write a whole erotic novel here. They were missing each other. Skip to the end. What happened?"

It irritates me to be stopped in the middle of a story, but I make allowances, given that Louise is a wreck. "So, the next morning, Reggie and Micah were gone, and he'd left a note on the kitchen table saying he'd be back later for his stuff, depending on how things went."

Louise looks at me blankly. "So what's the takeaway from this, in your mind?"

"It's just further proof that love can be crazy bad for people. Makes ordinary, decent citizens stand outside caterwauling instead of getting a good night's sleep."

She shakes her head. "It's very sweet, actually."

"Is it?" I look at her. "I guess we've all been there once or twice—caterwauling in the darkness, or being caterwauled *to* . . . and that, my friend, is why the Heartbreak Bunny stays in business."

"Uh-huh. Speaking of which, what's going on with your TV guy? Are you the one doing the caterwauling, or are you being caterwauled to?"

"Neither, and I never will be!"

"Uh-huh," she says. "Then why, may I ask, does he keep calling you and coming around? Sniffing around like an old hound dog."

"It's just that he wants me to come on his show again."

"Of *course* he does! So he can put the moves on you."

"Nope. It's strictly ratings. He wants me to talk about how spring is hormonally a dangerous season for people."

She laughs. "The Heartbreak Bunny: saving lives, one hormone at a time!"

"Louise, I need coffee if I'm going to keep up with the dresses up here. I. Must. Have. Coffee." I do a zombie walk toward her, but she doesn't laugh.

"All right." She sighs as if I am such a pain. "Come *on* then. Let's get you some. We've got a lot of work to do."

We go downstairs to the kitchen. It's pristine, as usual, but today it has kind of an eerie quality to it. Spotless. As though she's not even cooking meals for herself. I look at her closely. She looks positively gaunt.

"What have you eaten lately?" I say.

She ducks her head. "Don't worry about me."

"I do worry! You've got to eat."

"Mom! I'm eating. Okay? Probably too much. It's just nerves." She sets up the complicated coffee-making device, the contraption that looks as though we're going to have moonshine instead of coffee, and gets a mug out of the cabinet. I go over to get the cream out of the fridge, but there isn't any. In fact, there's hardly any food in there at all: two blackened bananas, a jar of capers (did I leave these here after the calling-in-a-baby ceremony—and what ever happened with that, anyway?), and four red grapes that look like they're well on the way to becoming raisins.

"I certainly hope you've been eating out," I say. "This refrigerator is a cry for help."

"Please stop," she says. "Just stop."

"How do you plan to live if you don't eat?"

She closes her eyes. "I'm eating, okay? I don't have much of an appetite right now. And I haven't been to the store."

I close the refrigerator door. "Okay, new subject. So, do you hear from Leo?"

"Oh, yeah. I hear from him. He stopped by the other night, a few weeks ago now."

"So you said. And, was it . . . friendly?"

She hesitates just the tiniest bit, looks away. A mother could fit a whole lifetime into that little sliver of silence. "You could say that. He's just so pleased to be out of the marriage for the time being, so he can afford to act quite, um, *solicitous*. As long as I don't expect anything from him, he's quite accommodating. Even took a few pictures for me to post."

"Huh."

"Did you and Victor ever think of getting back together after he left?" She doesn't meet my eyes.

Oh, Louise. I swallow. I've never talked to her about this part of our breakup. But she's an adult now. So, I decide to tell her the truth. Before he went to France, he came back. Briefly. We tried to get back together, for the sake of the past. And for Louise. Seeing what might be left. But there was nothing.

"He was in love with someone else," I say, "and it was over."

She stares at me. "So, you just let him go? Just like that? You took *one* measly attempt to get back together, and then that was it?"

How had I not foreseen what a land mine this was going to turn into? "What was I going to do? I'd read somewhere that it's illegal to hold somebody hostage when they want to leave, and you're also not allowed to murder them. So, I signed the papers, and that was that."

"But what about me?" she says. "I was just a baby."

"That's right. You were a baby. So you didn't get a vote. I'm sorry about that."

"No. I mean, did you ever worry back then that maybe *I*, as a child, needed to see a marriage working? Like, I'm not saying this is absolutely true or anything, but what if I'm not going to be happy with a guy *ever* because I didn't come from a house that had two parents? Because I don't know how it's supposed to be between men and women."

"Oh, for heaven's sake. I hate to break the news to you, but nobody knows how it's supposed to be between men and women," I say. "Marriage is a flawed system, Louise. We all make it up as we go along. You know that."

She pours coffee into my mug. "Please don't start telling me again that this is why you're the Heartbreak Bunny."

"Well? You can see for yourself why I thought of this business. It's self-evident, I think."

She looks at me with eyes of deep, mother-blaming despair. "Come on. Let's get back to the clothes."

So, we tramp back upstairs, and she picks one dress after another off the bed.

"I rather like this one," she says, holding up a teal satin dress. "What do you think?"

"It's fine. It's lovely, in fact."

"Would you photograph me in it? I can post it on the blog today."

"All right." I sigh and get out my phone. There's a new message from Victor. Of course there is. Louise pulls her nightgown over her head and slips on the teal dress. With just a few swift tugs and smoothings, it looks like she's ready for a formal dance. She slips into the bathroom. "I'll just brighten up my cheeks a little bit," she calls back to me. "I'll try to look like an actual living human being."

I look down and read his message.

im in newyork on wednesday meeting with my agent i miss you
will you come

Really. Some punctuation would be ideal. Also, I thought I had made clear I was done receiving texts from him, with my all-caps message, which even a guy who doesn't believe in a simple comma or a capital letter should know means screaming.

"All right," says Louise, coming back into the room. She's added a little slash of lipstick to her mouth and pinkened up her cheeks. "I'll stand over here next to the curtains because they really set off the color of the dress, I think. Go ahead . . . whenever you're ready." She thrusts one satiny hip out and puts her hand on the other hip and smirks at the camera.

Damn it. He's in New York? What's to stop him from showing up here? I prefer to have an ocean between him and me.

"Mom?"

"Okay, honey."

"Snap the picture, will you?"

I click out of the message and start taking photos. She smiles for some and frowns for others and looks over her shoulder at me, and then looks angry and then looks delighted. I press the white button again and again.

"Great," she says. "Lemme see what these look like." And before I have time to think, she's swept over and grabbed the phone right out of my hands.

I stand there as she frowns, scrolls through the photos, biting her lip, evaluating.

"Well, they're clearly not Leo quality, but they'll do," she says, continuing to scroll.

"Thanks," I say. I hear the ding of another text message coming in, and I reach for the phone, but she pulls it away from my outstretched hands.

"Louise, do you mind?" I try once again to take it, but she spins away from me and holds it in both her hands, staring at it for a long, silent moment. And then she starts flipping back and back, reading everything. She looks up at me, her eyes wide with shock.

"Victor? You're talking to *Victor*? What's going on?"

"Give me the phone," I say.

She holds the phone away from me. "No, wait. He's texting you! Victor is in *New York*?" She holds the phone up high where I can't reach it and keeps on scrolling and reading. Then she stares at me. "And Juliette died? Look at all these messages he's sent you. Has he been texting you all these years?"

"No, of course not. Texting wasn't even invented until recently."

"Mom!"

"Louise, please. He's just going through some weird stuff now that he lost his wife. Come on. Give me the phone back. This is meaningless."

"I just can't believe how you keep secrets from me. He's saying he loves you. He wants you to forgive him! And you didn't even tell me that? We were just minutes ago down in the kitchen, and I was asking you about him—and you couldn't have mentioned this *then*?"

My mouth goes dry. Kat may be right, that I am afraid of Louise. "Do I seriously have to tell you every single thing that goes on? I didn't know that was part of our relationship contract. You certainly don't tell *me* everything."

"This is my *father*! I have a right to know! I mean, maybe the two of you *are* going to get back together. Would you think to mention that to me, at least? Look at these messages." She stares at me. "Wow. He abandoned us, and now he wants another chance."

"Stop. Stop it."

"Oh my God, Mom. You obviously have been seriously screwed up about love all these years, telling me that love isn't really real—and now Victor, the man who broke your heart, is wanting to come *back* and that's not something you think I should know? When were you going to tell me?"

And then she puts her hand over her mouth and the next thing I know, she throws up all over the teal dress. I have to jump out of the way.

I steer her toward the bathroom and turn on the cold water and wet one of the beautiful embroidered hand towels she keeps on the marble vanity. "Here, wipe your mouth with this," I say, even though it's clear that these towels aren't supposed to be used for such purposes. They're probably meant only to be photographed.

But she takes it and does what I say. "Stop looking at me like that! I'm not sick!" she says to me. "I throw up all the time! It's stress, Mom. Stress! Can't you see that I'm stressed out to the max?"

She rinses her mouth and brushes her teeth, and I stand there staring at her in the mirror, at the dark circles, at the gaunt look of her face. It's all becoming clear. I feel like I'm in that dream where I've just stepped off a staircase and now I'm falling through space. You know the one.

I say to her, "What do you mean, you're throwing up all the time? Are you throwing up, say, every *day*? Every morning, perhaps?"

"Don't!" she says.

"*You* don't," I tell her. "You're in some serious denial. How long ago was Leo here?"

"It's not that."

I just look at her.

"This is *stress*, Mom. My husband left me! I have a business to run! I can't make the mortgage payment! You try living my life!"

"Here. Just sit down over here. Take a sip of water. We're going to figure it all out. I'll help you. First, though, I think, we need to go to the drugstore. And I need to cancel my bunny calls for this afternoon."

She rolls her eyes.

CHAPTER FOURTEEN

The pregnancy test that we buy at Walgreens is positive. Two little pink lines bloom as bright as you please right there on the stick.

The pregnancy test that we buy at CVS later that day is also positive but more hesitantly so, less bright in the lines, and so we need a third one, a different brand, so back to Walgreens we go, and the new one is positive plain and simple—it literally spells out the word *PREGNANT*, which you would think would be the definitive answer, but no, it only means we have to go out and procure pregnancy tests numbers four and five, purchased from a specialty pharmacy in North Haven, just in case. These also make it look pretty damn convincing that, hormonally speaking, there is an embryo somewhere in the vicinity of Louise.

We sit in her bathroom contemplating the limits of medical science.

"We could go out of state, see if any pregnancy tests in New York or Massachusetts might give a different result," I say, and she throws a balled-up tissue at me and also asks me to kindly shut up.

After a little while, she says, "I suppose you think this was the spell you did."

"Actually, I was thinking it was probably because you had sex with Leo when he came over a few weeks ago, being—how did you put it?—*solicitous*. Just an amateur guess, however."

"Well, *yeah*. That's what *I* would say caused it. Since magic isn't real, and that spell you did wasn't even directed at me, so even if magic was a thing, which it is not, this would not be the successful result."

"Speaking of which, have you heard from Phoebe?"

She stretches out on the bathroom floor. "She sent out a text day before yesterday that she got her period. So, no baby. I thought you were on the text chain."

"Oh God."

"What?"

"Nothing."

She sits up again and fixes her eyes on mine. "Wait a second. You think you did the spell wrong, don't you? You think you caused this to happen."

"I . . . don't know what to think."

"I know you. And I just want to tell you for the millionth time that this kind of thing is not real. Pregnancy doesn't come from chanting something, even in the full moon, even if you want to believe in something so badly. You can't make it so."

"Okay. No, I'm sure you're right."

Her voice gets even louder. "Otherwise, what would be the point of adoption? No one would adopt, would they, because all they would need to get their own baby would be somebody saying some damn fool chant. Think about it."

She's right. But what she's *not* right about are the unknown factors swirling out there; the chances that this particular egg and this particular sperm coming together at *this* particular time may have been guided by something other than propulsion theory and hormones and whatever else . . . I decide not to tell her what I believe about intention and the mystical properties of chances. And how situations can be nudged into being by chance, or a spell.

"Anyway, this—what you're thinking—is not the way the world works," she says firmly.

"Have it your way."

"I will."

"So . . . what are *you* thinking?"

"About what?"

"What do you mean, about what? What do you think I'm talking about?"

"I'm not thinking about that right now."

"Because you're in shock?"

"Hell, *yes*, I'm in shock! Is it nighttime yet?"

"It's six thirty. I really, really think you should have some food."

"I don't want any."

"Eating is pretty important."

"Mom. I've had no appetite for a week. I throw up all the time, and I'm trying to keep this business going, and trying to keep Leo's parents from kicking me out of here, and then he comes over for some stuff, and he looked so damned good, and we both started getting sentimental, and then we ended up sleeping together—and now look at me. Knocked up!"

"So, an obvious question that comes to mind. And forgive me for this, but why didn't you guys use a condom?"

She bugs her eyes out at me. "We're not condom people. I've been on the pill for years. And then I went off of it, and I got a diaphragm, and I didn't like the goo . . . oh, never mind. Why am I even telling you this?"

"Well," I say. "Be that as it may, now at least we know why you've been feeling bad."

She puts her head down. "Mama, what am I going to *do*?"

"Come here, honey." I do points one and two of the Mom Pep Talk. "It's going to be all right. You don't have to figure it all out right now."

"No, it's not going to be all right. How can you even say that?" She sits there with her knees up and her forehead resting on them. I move over and wrap my arms around her.

"I don't think I can be a single mom," she says.

"Sssh, you don't have to make a decision yet."

"But I don't think I can end it either," she says two minutes later. "And yet, when I think of nine months of being pregnant, I don't think I can do that either. And Leo wants to go off and have a big-deal journalism career. I don't think he even wants children at all. So, there's that."

"But you said before that you were going to try in two years."

"I know. I figured I could talk him into it by then."

After a moment, she puts her head on my shoulder, and I rub her temples, and she starts weeping. I can feel her shoulders trembling. Her breaths get long and slow as she falls asleep, poor thing.

But you know what I am thinking while I let her sleep against me? I remember that when I was doing that spell—and not really knowing what the heck I was doing—there was a moment, just a flash of a moment at the end, when I was saying the words and chanting away and thinking about the moon and Phoebe . . . and well, my attention was snagged by Louise. I stopped thinking about Phoebe, and I turned and looked at my daughter, and . . . here is my question for the universe: Did that redirect the magic over to her? What if? What if somehow, I *am* responsible for this?

Because it must be said: I *have* wanted a grandchild.

I know that I do.

But *this* would not be the best way to go about it. This would be deplorable. So unethical.

Which is why I didn't do it.

I didn't.

The universe works in mysterious ways, ladies and gentlemen. That is all I would like to say on that subject. Thank you for coming to my TED Talk.

CHAPTER FIFTEEN

As soon as I can get out from under my sleeping daughter and sneak away, I send a text to Kat:

> I can't talk on the phone, but I need to tell you what's going on. Life as we know it has gone straight to hell.

She writes back immediately:

> Are you being held hostage? Did a bunny client kidnap you? Should I call the cops?

> Hahaha. NO. That would be much easier! Complications with Louise. She found out that Victor has been texting me and is furious I didn't tell her. AND the pregnancy spell worked. Only it's Louise who got pregnant and not Phoebe.

> How did you manage to do THAT?

I did say I didn't know what I was doing when I did that spell.

Billie, forgive me, but I am laughing so hard right now. Call me when you can. And in the meantime, don't do any spells on anyone else, OK?

~♪~

Louise doesn't even argue with me when I suggest that she come stay at my house for a while.

We both know that her house is far too bleak and inhospitable. You can't solve the problem of ruined love juxtaposed with possible new life while you're looking out of those cold, jagged windows that stare blankly at the sea.

We pack her bags in silence. I was afraid she'd insist we haul the millions of dresses to my house to keep photographing them. As well as every appliance and hair care product and all the drawers of makeup. But nope. She just packs some sweatpants and sweatshirts, some leggings, a tunic or two. Pajamas, a kimono, the towel that has magical properties, which she uses to dry her hair. No lights, no equipment come along. She runs back inside to get her laptop and phone. She doesn't mention that she'll be posting anything, which is both reassuring and alarming. I thought she had to post multiple times per day or life as we know it would grind to a halt. But she shrugs and says she'll write *GOING AWAY ON VACATION* on the Instagram feed. And she says she will recycle material from years ago if she feels inspired. I didn't know that was something that could be done.

Driving along the dark roads, my headlights sweeping across the lanes, I tell her I'm glad she's coming back home. We can declare it a No Decision Zone, and just watch movies and eat popcorn and *not* post on social media while we wait for inspiration to tell her what to do.

In my heart of hearts, though, I'm relatively certain that she'll call Leo, in his newfound hotness, and she'll tell him the wonderful, complicated news—and there will be a few weeks of tears, arguments, amazement, adjustments of plans, rethinking the meaning of life, followed by laughter, perhaps some mild celebrating, and then my darling daughter will return to her home with the love-meister Leo, and we will all await the birth of a child.

In years to come, we will raise a toast to the miracle of conception. *Look at this exquisite child!* we will say. *The one who almost didn't come to be.*

I wonder if the story, as it evolves, will include my nefarious part in things. Perhaps that will be a secret I will whisper to this child at some future point. *I wanted you so much that I did a magic spell under the full moon with your mother and her friends—and you answered.*

⌒◎

My house has a neglected look about it now that everyone is gone. And it's Thursday, which means there should be martinis, *The Joy of Cooking*, Calvin. Somehow, that makes everything seem extra sad.

I walk through the rooms, turning on all the lights and then, for good measure, I put on Frank Sinatra in honor of Calvin. I need to hear some crooning to coax the life back into this kitchen. I get out pots and pans just to show I'm serious.

"Do you want to sleep in your old room?" I say to Louise. She is standing in the kitchen, looking weary, her hands by her side, her bags of stuff at her feet. I know she's contemplating how much straightening up my house will require in order to be livable.

"Doesn't Calvin have my old room?" she says.

"He did. But he's now living at Bernice's, remember?"

"Oh, right."

She goes upstairs and comes back down and reports that he's still got lots of stuff in there. And it smells like him. Old man smell, she says. She wrinkles up her nose.

"I think, if you don't mind, I want to sleep in your bed with you," she says. "Slumber party style. Like we used to do."

I know what this means. She's decided she needs to keep an eye on me. After all, I might just head out and get remarried to her father without getting her consent.

She doesn't want anything to eat, but I'm her mother and she needs to eat, so I make her favorite: thick, fluffy blueberry pancakes piled high with whipped cream. It may not be recommended by the American Obstetrical Best Dietary Practices Association, but hey, it's food she'll eat. That's what I explain to their board members convening a meeting about it in my head.

While she picks at her pancakes, removing all the blueberries, I say the thing that's been thrumming in my head ever since the very first positive pregnancy test, which now seems like eons ago instead of just hours. I say, "So. Should you perhaps call Leo?"

She gives me a ferocious look.

"I am *never* calling Leo," she says. And then she pushes her plate away and fixes me with her fiercest stare. "Even if I decide to keep the baby, I'm not telling him. And I am not at all sure I'm going to keep the baby. I would be a terrible mother, and I don't even have a place to live or a job, so it's impossible. So there." Then her face crumples up and she says, "But it's so sad because I'm probably never going to get another chance to have a baby, so I have to think about that, too."

"Well," I say. "It certainly bears thinking about it all very carefully."

She looks up at me. "And *you*! Don't think I've forgotten that we were in the middle of a *huge* conversation about Victor. In fact, do you know what makes me the saddest right now?"

"No, darling. What in the world could possibly be making you the saddest right now?"

"That it doesn't ever occur to him to contact *me*! Did you ever think of that? My own father!" She bangs her hands on the table, which unfortunately makes the plates and silverware jump in the air. "*You're* making it clear to him that you don't want anything to do with him—but maybe I do! I'm his daughter, his flesh and blood. And apparently he's planning to go on ignoring me for my whole life, treating me like I'm some speck of inconvenience in his otherwise perfect little life, except that—boo-hoo—now his wife died, and his ex-wife doesn't want to talk to him anymore. But does he think he could call his *daughter*? Doesn't he think maybe *I* should get an apology for him being gone for over three and a half decades, aka my whole life?"

"Last time I checked, I noticed that he's not a particularly insightful guy," I say at last.

"And you! I feel like I don't even *know* you," she says. "You're living this secretive life, talking to Victor and flirting with a TV guy, and meanwhile you're telling everyone that you know how to do magic spells, and oh, also, everybody everywhere should stop believing in love. And I'm out somewhere in the middle of the ocean, having to figure everything out for myself. My husband is gone, I'm losing more followers every single day, and now it turns out I'm *pregnant*, and my best friend who wants to be pregnant *isn't*, and my in-laws are going to make me move out of my house—"

"Louise. Stop it. You're turning everything into a catastrophe, when you don't know that any of this is true. Maybe when Leo's parents hear they're getting a grandchild, they'll be more than happy for you to stay."

She makes her eyes go round with fury. "Have you not been paying attention to anything I've said? I told you that I haven't made up my mind what I'm going to do. There may not *be* a grandchild for them! So why should I tell them anything? Also, if that's their only reason for letting me stay, then that's not good enough for me! They don't love *me*, Mom. Don't you get it?"

"Louise, Louise." I rub my eyes. We've only been at this for a few hours, and I'm already completely wrung out. "Sweetie, I know you're feeling emotional, but we can get through this. You're not alone in the middle of the ocean. You're at the house where you grew up, and I'm on your side, honey. Take your time. We'll figure this out. Don't go all warrior queen on me. Just take some deep breaths. Have a glass of milk."

"I don't *want* a glass of milk!"

"What do you want?"

She screeches then. "I DON'T KNOW WHAT I WANT! I WANT EVERYTHING TO BE NORMAL!"

Thank goodness, my phone rings just then, and it's a friendly person: Calvin. A lifeline!

I take the phone out onto the front porch, just like a guilty teenager who doesn't want to be overheard.

It's a fine evening—an almost-spring night, with just a little chill in the air. I pace back and forth on the porch while I listen to him talk. He rattles off random, amusing facts about living with Bernice: she keeps a neat little house, and she believes that all upholstered furniture should be covered in plastic, and who's to say she's not correct? I am, I say, and he laughs and tells me that her neighbors are the kind of people who stop by with pots of soup just because they love her. And she drives an old Cadillac that is as big as the Colosseum and needs two full lanes in which to make a turn. She is, he says, both difficult and delightful, and it was an excellent stroke of luck on his part to fall in love with her.

"There I was, fortunate enough to be standing near Bernice when the thunderbolt of love came and struck me right in the heart."

"Yeah, yeah," I say. I close my eyes, rub my temple. I get it. The plain fact is that he doesn't know when he's coming home. "But you *are* returning, aren't you? You have stuff here."

"Ah," he says. And then he doesn't answer, and I know what that means: he's on his next ten-year plan, and he doesn't care about his stuff. "What's going on with *you?*" he says. "Aside from the fact that you're going on television to tell us that spring is a dangerous time, and we all need to guard against falling in love. That's what Mason told me, at least."

"When did you talk to Mason?"

He chuckles. "I talk to Mason all the time."

"I'm not even going to comment on that. And anyway, I have bigger news, now that we've gotten the preliminaries out of the way."

"Bigger news than that your scoundrel ex-husband is stalking you?"

"This is way bigger than Victor. You might want to sit down for this one. Louise is pregnant."

There's a silence. Then he says, "Wait. *Our* Louise?"

"Yes. And, just to add to the interestingness of the situation, Phoebe isn't."

He howls with laughter. "Oh my dear, oh my dear," he says when he regains the power of speech. "Are you being blamed? Misdirection of spell? Is that a thing?"

"Maybe. It's only been a few hours since she took, like, five pregnancy tests—all positive—so we've tiptoed past denial, and dipped our toe in the fact that magic isn't real, and I've been scolded for my possible assumption that I might be responsible. But now, at this very minute, she's angry and sad and confused and all the things."

"I shouldn't have laughed."

"No, but I'm glad you did. Also, I brought her home with me. She's staying here for the time being. Also—" I take a deep breath. "She saw the texts Victor has been sending me, which have only intensified in the last few weeks. And so now she's angry at me about that, too. Nobody has ever done right by Louise, to hear her tell it."

"Well, well, well. Too bad the statute of limitations for blaming your parents expired when she turned thirty. And what does Leo think about the baby?"

"See? That's just like you and me, jumping to the conclusion that a pregnant woman would mention to her husband that they're expecting a baby. But as it turns out, she says she's not even going to tell Leo. And she doesn't know what she's going to do. All she's done so far is cry and claim she can't eat anything and life is terrible."

"Oh myyyy. I leave your house, and everything falls completely apart."

"Yes. So, therefore, I think I need you to come back. Bernice can live here with us, if you want. But you need to come back. Maybe even tonight. Like, in the next five minutes."

He laughs.

"And, speaking of other big changes, Marisol's guy has left his wife and found an apartment for them, after all these years, so she's moved out."

"What? So, you've got Reggie, Micah, and Edwin and Louise? That's an interesting configuration."

"Nope. I thought I told you. Reggie and Cynthia patched everything up, rather dramatically, actually, in his truck in our front yard. Spectacular optics. And then he came in and got Micah and all their things, and now our entire plumbing system could break down, and I don't think we'll get him back."

"Good God," says Calvin. "So, it's just you, Louise, and Edwin then?"

"Well, Edwin has decided to brave his allergies and move in with that girlfriend of his, the one with the kids and the dogs. He left."

"Holy smokes. So, it's just you and Louise? Together in the house?"

"Yes, and it's a house that cannot measure up to the high standards of a former Instagram influencer."

I can hear the laughter in his voice. "What has the world come to?"

"Now you're beginning to understand why I need you back here immediately. Tell Bernice you've made a dreadful mistake, it was lots of fun, but now the two of you have to come back. Bring the Cadillac and her medical records, and move right in. Your old room awaits you."

My phone buzzes just then. It's Louise, from upstairs.

201

"I gotta go," I say. "My cranky new roommate is calling me. Talk to you tomorrow."

"Can I reorganize your medicine cabinet?" says Louise when I click over. "I just looked for an antacid, and it took me twenty minutes to go through all the cosmetics."

"Oh, do you have heartburn?"

"Never mind me. The point is that nothing can be found in that medicine cabinet. And I want to fix it."

"Must you?"

"I can't believe how much *stuff* you have in here. And everything is expired! There are vitamins in here that are over two years old. Can't I just . . . regroup things?"

Ah, yes. Louise is home.

CHAPTER SIXTEEN

Two days later, having spent forty-eight hours being organized by Louise—she's moved all the bowls in the kitchen to a cabinet that she thinks is a "better fit" and she's threatening to steam off the sunflower wallpaper in the entryway—I am in the perfect mood for my interview on Channel 12. Feisty, fed up, overtired. Anna, the assistant producer, plunks me down in the green room, and Mason comes in and hovers in a way that makes me too aware of his twinkling eyes and his irritatingly perfect jawline. Also, I really do think the tan is fake, now that I've seen it close-up several times.

"So," he says, chuckling, "you ready to go out there and caution everybody about the horrendous side effects of falling in love?"

The promo copy for my segment runs across the bottom of the TV screen. It says, SPRING FLING? NOT SO FAST!

He says we'll just lightly touch on the fact that people associate springtime with love, and that maybe people shouldn't blame themselves if love doesn't come to them during this particular season. Could we reassure them that love will come eventually?

"No," I say. "No! People are not to be encouraged about love just now. I've had five clients in the past few days who were holding on to the most mundane of left-behind objects." I number them on my fingers: "A Rubik's Cube, a Tom Brady bobblehead, the ribbon from someone else's bridal bouquet, a half-empty can of shaving cream, and a condom wrapper. And three of them wanted to call the departing ex and insist that these pieces of detritus be *picked up*. Obviously, they're just craving another post-breakup discussion and possible chance for a reuniting. *Nobody's* returning to pick up a condom wrapper!"

Mason looks a little surprised at my vehemence. Maybe I shouldn't have had the third cup of coffee before coming to the station.

Instead I say, "Also. When a relationship ends, it seems that one of the high points should be that you no longer have to look at their Tom Brady bobblehead, wouldn't you say?"

He nods. His Adam's apple moves beneath his tan turtleneck. "Let's go get settled in," he says. "Shall we?"

He touches my shoulder while we walk out to the set. I sit down in the armchair to the right of him, wearing my bunny suit without the head—it sits on my lap in case anyone might need proof that I'm the real thing—with the potted plant between us. The bright lights shine in my face, and just beyond, I can see Anna holding her clipboard—and the cameras, roaming across the floor, in dinosaur mode.

"This is going to be good," says Mason. "I'm glad you're here."

Someone counts backward from five, and the red light comes on, and Mason looks into the camera, his face transformed.

"We have a special treat today. I'm thrilled to welcome Billie the Heartbreak Bunny back to our studio," says Mason. His smile seems wider than before as he explains to viewers what it is that I do. Then he turns to me: "And happy spring to you, Billie! It's the season of love all around us. And I have to ask: Why *can't* we just go off and fall in love? Do you really want to play the part of a killjoy? Why can't we have fun?"

I shake my head at him. "This is the most dangerous time of year, what with all those hormones running amok. And just so you know, I'm the *opposite* of a killjoy. Thinking you've got to fall in love in order to be okay is what's killing people's joy! The pangs of falling in love are *not* joyful. Romance is only going to make you tense and unhappy."

"But what if you're happy in love?" he says. "Don't some people *like* love and romance?"

"Look, if your love life is going along great, have a blast. Just turn the channel and don't listen to *me*—"

"Excuse me," he says, flirting with the camera. "She doesn't mean to literally change the channel. Please!"

"Stay on the channel then," I say, grouchy. "But don't take my advice. In fact, revel in your good fortune at finding love. Because for most of us, falling in love makes a mess of our lives. Passion takes up all your time. You feel nauseated and disoriented. You can't sleep. You're always bugging your friends with questions like: 'Will this last? Does my lover really, really love me? Will she still love me even if I get a haircut? What if this is too good to be true?' This is *no way to live*, people!"

"But what if we're programmed for love? And maybe we're programmed for it because it's fun. It makes life fun!"

I turn on him. "Seriously, you know how long it's fun? It's fun for maybe thirty minutes a day. That's the length of time people bask in the feelings of love. Otherwise for most people it's agony."

"Agony? Whoa!" He sits back in his chair, with a big grin, and pretends to be shocked by this.

"Yes. Agony! It's stressful. If it's not going well, you're living in fear, or guilt, or regret. But even if it *is* going well—even if you can see a dazzling future with this person, and you've never felt so beautiful or handsome or charming or witty in your whole life, chances are you're starting to second-guess everything, deep down. You wonder if it's all going to explode in your face. You're watching for things to go wrong—and believe me, things *will* start to appear wrong if you look hard enough."

"Well, how can we protect ourselves? What about playing hard to get? A time-honored tradition, the hard-to-get game."

I laugh. "Oh my God. You have *got* to be kidding! I want to tell you right here and now that the hard-to-get game is *the* worst game ever invented by human beings! To win, you have to withhold yourself from the other person until they realize how badly they want you and that they're willing to humiliate themselves to be with you. And who wants a humiliated partner? Stand up and be strong. Love is not about games!"

He looks startled. "So, what do you say to people who say you're anti-love?"

It's like something has caught fire in my chest, and I can't stop it from taking over. "Anti-*love*? I'm *not* anti-love! I adore love! We all need love in our lives! I am *anti–romantic heartache and suffering*. I say we should all go out in the world and enjoy our lives! There are lots of ways to have fun without having it all come down to romance. Love everything and everyone but stop with all the agonizing and the wringing of hands! Forget about trying to look gorgeous and appealing every minute of the day!"

I become aware that Anna is waving her arms from the darkness in front of me. Our time has run over.

Mason Davis says, "Well, that—"

But I don't seem to be able to stop. I look right into the camera, which you're not supposed to do; you're supposed to look at the person you're talking to, but I have more to say. "Listen, earthlings! Stop worrying about attracting people! For heaven's sake, do the things that you love doing. Read books! Take up clog dancing! Serve meals at the soup kitchen! Train for the space program! Volunteer at a homeless shelter or talk to dogs you see in the park. Dance! Or don't do any of those things—just lie on the floor and contemplate the ceiling fan if you want. Whatever! Do the things you like to do, concentrate on pleasing and loving yourself—and you'll be amazed at how much your life will improve. Romance isn't the way to happiness! There are so many other ways! Stop with worrying about attraction and romance! Just stop it!"

"And that's the advice of—" says Mason.

I keep going, staring into the camera and moving closer to it. "*No more pining for love or maneuvering yourself into love's path! Live your life and put your passion into things that make you feel good and stop worrying about all this drama! Just snap out of it, will you?*"

"And there you have it," says Mason, laughing a little bit. "We'll be right back after this commercial. Ahead, we've got some inspirational instructions on how to do your spring cleaning painlessly. Thank you, Heartbreak Bunny."

The lights go off, and the dinosaurs veer away.

"Wow," says Mason. He looks a little bit flushed. "We sort of went off script there." People come over and start wordlessly removing my microphone. I stand up and grab my bunny head, stepping around all the wires and stuff. No one looks very happy, especially Anna, whose mouth is in a straight, hard line as she tells Mason there won't be time for one of the scheduled segments because we went too long.

Mason says, "Well, that is unfortunate. But you've got to admit, this was a good segment."

She gives him a withering look. "We do have to stick to the schedule," she says. "If you had let us know . . ."

"We'll talk about it later," he says.

"Yes, we will." And she walks away, holding her clipboard in front of her like it holds the secrets to life. I glare at her as she leaves. I do not think she should be talking to Mason that way.

He leans closer to me and says in a low voice, "Don't worry about this. Your segment was wonderful. But are you okay?"

"I shouldn't have been on the show," I say. "I wasn't in the right mood for this today. I'm sorry."

"No, no, no. No worries at all," he says. He steers me through the wires and out the studio door, and down the hall, far from other people. "Has anything upset you?"

We've reached the green room, where my bag and coat are on the table. He closes the door behind us. I get busy picking up my things and can't bring myself to look at him. "I'm just grouchy today," I say. "All this love nonsense everywhere I look! And now I've gone all out of control on your show. Too talkative, too complain-y."

"Well," he says, chuckling, "if it's any consolation, I think people will relate to how frustrated you are. It looked entirely spontaneous and natural, which is what we're going for. Not some scripted interview. But, just checking in here: Were you irritated by the questions I was asking? Did I hurt your feelings somehow?" His brow is furrowed; he looks extremely concerned.

"No, no. It's not you. It's—life. How it goes off the rails. Bang zoom!" I make my arm into a rocket and shoot it toward outer space, and then when I'm bringing it down, my elbow bangs against the table. For a moment my eyes water and I see stars, which only makes Mason *more* concerned.

His eyes go all sympathetic. "Tell me," he says. "What's going on?"

Oh God. I sigh. I so did not want to get into this.

"Well," I say and give him a leave-me-alone-because-you-don't-know-what-you're-dealing-with smile. "If you must know, just about everything in my life has gone sideways. The main thing is I got my daughter accidentally pregnant—"

"Wait. You . . . what?"

"Yeah. The spell. I did that pregnancy spell for her friend Phoebe, and somehow the embryo or entity or whatever it is went and landed in the wrong uterus. I keep explaining to everyone that I'm not cut out for witchcraft, that all I'm good for is just a little bit of channeling energy— but Louise is freaking out, probably rightly so, and now she's moved into my house so she can punish me more thoroughly by making me think about it every waking moment, and even some of the non-waking ones, too, since she's insisting on sleeping in my bed with me! *And* then my ex-husband is hounding me with text after text, and none of them have any punctuation, and she's mad about that, too—although not the lack of punctuation so much as just the fact that I haven't laid my full life out for her to review and approve. And now I've—"

There's a quick, hard knock at the door, and then it bursts open like the police have kicked it in. Anna stands there, looking from one of us to the other. She has her official sanctioning face on, although I wouldn't think she has any real power over Mason. Still, I notice he is holding on to a chair, and I think he looks a little pale.

"Aaaaand now I've got to go," I say quickly, even though that wasn't what I was about to say at all.

"Mason, you're wanted in the office," Anna says.

"I'll be there in a few minutes," he says.

"I think they want you now," she tells him and turns on her heel.

"She seems like the hall monitor I remember from elementary school," I say in a low voice. "You'd better go before the principal comes down here."

He isn't thrown in the slightest. He laughs. "You have the most colorful, interesting life of anybody I know," he says.

"Well, let's hope it gets a little less interesting soon," I tell him. "And as for colorful, I could also do with emotions that are more in the beige family right now."

"You've never had a beige emotion in your life," he says. "Why start now?"

❦

So what do I do when I'm rattled and overcaffeinated and also out of my mind? I go to the place that always heals my soul: the grocery store. I wander the aisles and stand forever admiring the rows of vegetables, perky and glowing under the pink lights. Today the red peppers look like animated characters, they're so bright.

I can't resist. I put three of them in my cart. I'll stuff them with spicy sausage and rice . . . except then I remember that Louise won't eat anything that has any flavor to it whatsoever, and I get mad all over again.

Honestly, if I had my life to live over, I think I might have skipped the part where I first went on television. I'd go back to being the quiet, competent Heartbreak Bunny, seeing one client at a time and focusing on removing offending objects.

I'm moving on to the lettuces and greens when my phone blows up with messages.

Oh my God. Sixty-four people have called the station and want an appointment with the bunny. A television station in New York wants to have me on next week. The General Federation of Women's Clubs would like to fly me to Chicago to be the keynote speaker in the fall, talking about love and feminism.

The last message is from Mason.

Just talked to Joey. Disaster. Saucy is back in town. And he's talking to her.

I pace through four aisles of the store before I can answer.
Then I write:

I don't think he's going to take her back, Mason. He's not a masochist. By the way, what happened at the station? Are you in trouble? Did the principal say you have to stay after school?

Three dots appear and disappear. Then appear again. Then disappear. I am all the way in the checkout line when he finally writes:

I think he's vulnerable. Possible latent masochistic tendencies where this woman is concerned. Also: station boss says to put the pause on bunny appearances. No biggie. Still highest ratings when you come on, so this is ridiculous.

I am about to write that I don't want to go on the show anymore anyway, and I don't blame them for losing their minds over the way I acted today, and also that Joey is not going to take Saucy back because: (1) she is the most selfish human ever, and (2) he sees that, and (3) why would *anyone* take someone back who married someone else *at the very wedding HE had paid for*? And (4) then gone on the honeymoon with that dude!

But all this is too much to type with just my thumbs.

So instead, I write:

Do you want to come over for dinner?

He immediately says yes.

I am feeling guilty, so I decide I'll roast him a chicken. Forget the spicy-sausage-stuffed peppers. Tonight calls for a healing lemon and rosemary chicken. With mashed potatoes and brussels sprouts sautéed in olive oil. I get out of the checkout line and put back the sausages and the peppers, and I go get a chicken and little red potatoes instead. No food says *I'm sorry I was something of a diva today* like a roasted chicken. After I feed him some nourishing food, I'll take him for a walk, and I'll listen to him talk about Saucy and Joey, and I'll reassure him.

And that will be who we are to each other: people who bond over their misguided-but-finding-their-way kids.

It will be a calm, mellow evening. I'll remind myself that there are ways to be friends that don't involve complications. Also, I won't hold his turtleneck and his jawline and his crinkling eyes against him, which I think is very generous and intelligent of me.

CHAPTER SEVENTEEN

By the time I get home, it's already five o'clock, and I find three cars in the driveway—surprise, surprise!—and Phoebe and Louise are sitting on the porch swing, their heads together, swaying back and forth. Bonnie Raitt is singing about heartbreak through the outdoor speakers.

It looks as if Phoebe may be crying, and Louise's arm is around her.

I park my VW on the street and give myself a stern look in the rearview mirror before I slide out and lug my bags of groceries up the walkway. I'm not going to lie: my heart is filled with impatience and dread. Louise looks up at me.

"Hi, Mom," she says quietly, like she's welcoming me to viewing hours at a mortuary. "Everybody's here. We're all processing what happened."

"Processing," I say weakly. "Hi, Phoebe. How are you, honey?"

"I'm okay, I *think*," she says. And then she bursts into tears, and Louise wraps her arms around her again, and looks up at me, her eyes filled with worry. She waves me away before I can try to hug Phoebe, too. I am not the one people want hugs from just now.

I take the bags to the kitchen, where Hildy is leaning on the counter while Miranda pours some red wine into the goblets we use on Martini Thursday.

"Hi," I say. "Are you the indoor processing team?"

Miranda smiles. "We're giving them a moment, is all. Lots of complicated feelings out there. Too big for indoors. Would you like a glass of wine?"

"Sure," I say. I turn the oven on to preheat and then sit down on the floor so I can rummage through the lower cabinet for the roasting pan. Louise hasn't gotten to this cabinet yet: the pans are still haphazardly stacked and, as usual, are threatening to fall on me. I lean farther in to wrestle the bread pans to the very back of the shelf, which creates a big racket.

"How are *you* doing with all this?" says Miranda when I resurface. "As the spell-caster."

I can feel that my face is flushed. "Well, no offense, but I think I did mention that I had no expertise with pregnancy spells."

Hildy laughs. "Certainly you had no expertise with *directing* pregnancy spells."

"How do you think it happened this way?" says Miranda. When she sees my face, she smiles and says, "No, no. I'm not criticizing you. I really want to know. Did you have any idea?"

I rub my head, where a little headache of irritation is beginning to bloom. "Of course I didn't," I tell her. "I'm completely at a loss at how this happened."

"It's like the plot of an episode of *Bewitched* or something," says Hildy. "It would be hilarious if we didn't know the people involved."

"Except it's real life, and Phoebe wants a baby, and Louise doesn't," says Miranda, and Hildy says, "So what we're here to do—and it's no small task—is get them both to the point where they can be okay with this."

"Well, I may be alone in this, but I think Louise really does want a baby," Miranda says. "I think deep down she's going to be a little bit happy about this, once the shock wears off. She's always talked about having a kid."

"I hope so," I say.

"Just maybe not while she's breaking up with Leo," says Hildy. "Timing is everything. Breaking up and having a baby sucks. And I'm sure I haven't made this look like a piece of cake."

"Nor did I," I say. "Being a single mother isn't for sissies." I unwrap the chicken and put it in the pan and get busy rubbing it with butter and lemon. "You guys staying for dinner?"

"Sure. I guess so," says Hildy. "If you don't mind, that is."

"It's fine. Can you peel some potatoes? The peeler is in the second drawer on the left."

"I remember where the peeler lives," she says.

Miranda takes a big sip of wine. "Gotta say, you two are making me feel just brilliant for not getting myself entangled," she says.

"You are brilliant," says Hildy. "Brilliantly *lonely* as hell, but brilliant." She starts washing the potatoes.

"Here, shouldn't you be sitting down? I'll do the potatoes." Miranda pulls out a chair, and Hildy sinks into it.

"Anyway," she says, "what if tonight we do a different spell?"

"*Another* pregnancy spell?" I say. "I don't think so."

"No. Another *kind* of spell," says Hildy. "An acceptance spell. An all-is-perfect, appreciation spell. Something like that. I don't know. What the hell could make this better? You're the one with the spell book. You tell me!"

"I don't have a spell book. I tried to explain all that. I just mumble some words."

"Well, where do the words come from?"

"They just pop into my head."

Miranda hands me a glass of wine and looks at Hildy. "Do they really say no wine for the *entire* pregnancy?"

"The entire pregnancy. Yes, they do," says Hildy.

Phoebe and Louise come in, and Phoebe comes over and gives me a tentative hug. Her eyes look wide and wet, her lashes matted together.

"I'm sorry I'm such a lousy witch," I say. I pull her to me and rock her back and forth. "I really hoped you'd get a baby from this," I say into her ear. "Maybe we shouldn't have played around with something that was so serious, you know? Too much riding on it, perhaps?"

"I know," she says.

"But you know it could still happen. I mean, all those little vibes out floating around in the universe . . ." says Miranda. I hadn't been aware she was listening. I look up to see them all looking at me. Miranda is dabbing at her eyes.

I slide the chicken into the oven. I'm thinking that now we're going to have a lovely kumbaya moment, and everybody will wipe away their tears and we will have a group hug, put aside the drama, and when Mason gets here, it will be all unicorns and roses—but no. Phoebe pulls away and says to Miranda, "Shut up, will you? It's not going to happen without a fight."

"And what do you see as a fight, if I may ask?" Miranda says.

"Interventions. Shots. Medical appointments. Doctors. Disappointment."

"Just because one spell didn't take doesn't mean—"

"Don't you see? *Nothing* has taken! You don't get it, do you? I'm in for the whole heartbreak here."

"Oh, honey, I'm so sorry, but you need to hold out hope," says Miranda, and she goes over and hugs Phoebe, which seems to be a little bit like hugging a porcupine, judging from their two expressions.

The doorbell rings just then, and I can see Mason on the front porch, walking past the windows, talking on his cell phone, gesturing. I hear him saying the words "don't be a damn fool." It looks intense out there. It's intense in *here*. Really, someone should check the astrological charts to see what the hell might be going on.

"Wait," says Louise, narrowing her eyes at me. "Mason's here? Mason Davis? What is *he* doing here?"

"I invited him for dinner," I say. "He's got something going on with his son. Needed to talk." I head through the dining room toward the front door.

"But I invited everybody over!" she says. "I thought we'd hang out."

"It's all good. We can all be here," I say, although she knows—she's got to know—that's the way I would feel. I've always maintained that good things happen with an assortment of people at the dinner table, and that these things can't be planned in advance. "We can all be here together," I call back over my shoulder. "I'm roasting a big chicken and mashing up some potatoes. There's plenty to go around."

Mason smiles but waves me away. He's still pacing and talking on the phone, so I go back to the kitchen.

"But we're processing!" she says. "And, Mom, he'll find out everything that's gone on. All our business!"

"He already knows," I say. "I don't think he'll put it on the news, if that's what you're worried about."

She looks at the rest of the women with a *do you see what I have to deal with?* expression.

"I think it'll be fine," says Phoebe. "And I'm the one who's mostly a wreck, so if I say it's okay, then it is fine."

Louise says, "Listen, I'm a wreck, too, you know. I would like to point out that I'm throwing up four times a day, and also that I hate everything! Everything in life! Smells drive me crazy, and my boobs hurt, and I'm halfway in tears all the time. And I'm losing my entire career because I haven't posted anything in nearly a week, and my followers are leaving me like rats running from the *Titanic*, if that's a thing, and none of you seem to think anything of just cooking chickens around me and talking to me about how wonderful the miracle of life is. And I don't know what to do, and I can't even think straight anymore. I've lost my whole mind."

"Oh, poor Lulu," says Hildy. "Of course you're going through the wringer, too! Oh, my poor, poor, sweet baby!" And she goes over and wraps Louise in her arms, or tries to, but her belly gets in the way, and Louise draws back and says, "Oh my God! Look at you! Is this going to be *me* in a few months?"

"I think if you keep doing nothing, yes. This will be you," says Hildy. "And trust me, you will come to love it. All its little bumps and thumps and gurgling sounds. Even the fact that it wakes you up to pee three times a night. And you want to know why?"

"Because you're programmed to feel this way by mysterious biological processes over which you have no conscious control?"

"No. It's because you know that you get to trade it in on a real live human being soon."

"Oh God, oh God," Louise says, and she puts her head in her hands.

"So, what *are* your plans, if I may be so bold?" asks Phoebe.

We all look at Louise.

She looks up at us. "Well, *duh*, I'm having a baby," she says in her cranky voice. "Can't you tell? Otherwise, I'd have already ended it."

And this is how my lovely daughter announces her intentions to the world. It feels like the rubber band that's been constricting my heart has started to loosen. Which surprises me, this feeling. There might be some extra air in the room.

"And it's going to be a shit show, because I don't know what I'm doing. And I'm setting myself up for some kind of lonely life with a kid who'll grow up to wonder why her father isn't around, just like I did, but what else can I do? I'm completely over my head! I'm a train wreck of a human being!"

"But you're keeping it, and that's wonderful!" says Hildy. "And you're not going to be lonely. Not for one second. This is going to be so great! You and me being moms together."

So, it's true. It's real. I'm going to be a grandmother, I think. *My grouchy, heartbroken daughter is going to have this baby. And it's going to be difficult and wonderful and all the complicated things.*

I can feel my eyes filling with tears. Louise, standing near me, touches my arm, and starts to cry. Phoebe bursts into tears too, and then Hildy dissolves, and pretty much after that, we're all goners.

"Mama, please tell me you think I can do this," Louise says, and Miranda, standing across the room, lets out a loud wail. I throw my arms open wide, and they all kind of fall into me and into each other, and we're all in an orgy of crying, which is the very best thing in the world.

I look up to see Mason standing in the doorway.

Really, that guy has some serious stealth moves.

༄

"Just a fair warning: you seem to have entered a crying zone," I tell him, still holding on to everybody. "We could try to stop, but we probably can't. So, if you can't take the sight of women crying, you might want to go back outside until we can regroup."

"Which might be years," says Louise. "I, myself, am planning to cry for at least the next nine months and then for possibly the next eighteen years after that."

"If I could just join in on the crying fest, I'd be happy for the rest of my life," Mason says. "There's so little appreciation for a good cry these days."

"Around here, there's plenty of appreciation," says Hildy, dabbing at her eyes. "At least there was when I was in high school. I came over here and cried every damn day."

"It hasn't changed all that much," says Louise.

"Wait a second. It's not that bad. There's laughing, too," I say. "Come in and have a glass of wine."

"Otherwise known as crying juice," says Phoebe. And then she holds out her hand and says, "Hi, I'm Phoebe. Chances are you might know me as the one who was supposed to get pregnant from the spell, but Louise did instead."

Mason looks at me, baffled and amused.

"It's okay. They know you know already," I tell him. "It's well established that I have a big mouth. But trust me, we've processed this, and we're not going to feel the need to keep talking about it all night. Right, my lovelies?"

"But the real question is: Can you ever finish processing something like that?" says Miranda. She goes over to Mason and hands him a bowl of peanuts she's gotten from the counter. "I'm Miranda, and I'm possibly the only person here who is not contemplating some form of family addition. I have my work, thank you very much."

"So, Louise, congratulations," says Mason, his eyes glowing. "Although one wonders if saying congratulations is appropriate in every case. I suppose if it's being announced, it's a good thing. Am I right in assuming that?"

I look at Louise, who shrugs. "I don't know what you're supposed to say," she growls.

"You did just say you're keeping the baby," I say. "So, people are going to offer congratulations."

"Well, I'm Hildy, and I'm very pregnant, as you can see," says Hildy, as she rubs her belly, which seems to have acquired a dusting of crumbs. I see that she's gotten a package of crackers out of the cabinet and is munching on them.

"Congratulations to you then," says Mason. "Now let me see if I have this right . . . There's Phoebe . . . who you did the spell for."

"Well . . ."

"She did. She did a spell," says Phoebe. "She's probably going to try to disavow it now, but she did chant some words under the full moon, and ask the universe to send me an embryo, and it did not do that. It sent it to Louise instead."

"Interesting," says Mason. "Okay, so . . . then there's Hildy, is it? Hildy who is definitely pregnant . . . and was there a spell for that one, too?"

"Absolutely not. I got pregnant without magic. Then I got blind-sided by my husband leaving me."

"Notice how this conversation has gotten awfully deep, awfully fast," says Louise. "In another hour, you'll know everything about all of us if my mom has any say in it. She lacks a sense of privacy."

Miranda smiles. "Right, and now that you know all this about us, you have to tell us something devastatingly personal about yourself. I personally would like it if you started with your son. I saw him on your show a few weeks ago. How's he doing?"

"Well, funny you should mention him. His ex-fiancée is back, saying she's sorry."

"WHAT?" We all say it at once. I say it even though I already knew it.

"The woman who left him and married somebody else?" says Louise.

"It was her boss, right?" says Miranda. "We all watched the segment."

"Well," says Mason stiffly. "I don't believe she *married* someone else. I think she just left him for her boss."

I take a moment to compose my face. Mason doesn't know the story of the wedding? Of the deposit? The honeymoon trip Joey paid for and then didn't attend? Joey never told him *that* part when they sat down together and supposedly discussed everything?

"Well, at any rate, he's very cute," says Hildy. "Does he happen to want children, by any chance? How would he feel about being a step-father? He'd only have three months to wait."

Miranda hits her on the arm, and Mason laughs. "I don't know what he's doing, frankly. All he told me on the phone is that they're talking again. For now."

"For *now*? What does that mean?" Phoebe says.

"That's what my husband said when he moved in with the woman next door to us," Hildy says. "He was just doing that *for now*. Just going to see how things played out."

"And how did they play out?" says Mason.

"He's still there. I've moved in with my mom. Just so I don't have to watch him going into *her* house every afternoon when he gets home from work. Or watch him washing his car or whistling when he's coming home from the liquor store with a case of beer for the weekend." She lowers her voice. "And the worst was when I could see the time at night when they turned the bedroom light off."

Her eyes fill up, and I pass her the box of tissues.

"So is Joey . . . susceptible, do you think, to Saucy?" I say, and everybody nearly falls over hearing that her name is Saucy. As they should. Miranda clutches her heart.

"Please, you pregnant people here, do *not* name your babies anything moronic, okay?" she says.

I ask Mason to scoot over so I can open the oven and baste the chicken. "Would you mind reaching up to that pot hanging up there?" I ask him. "Fill it about three-quarters of the way with water, please. Are the potatoes all peeled and ready to go?"

"I like it better when they have peels on them," says Miranda.

Louise says that looking at the peels is making her ill. Hildy spirits her away to the living room with a box of crackers that she says help combat nausea, and on the way, she's talking about raspberry tea and special pregnancy yoga classes they can take, and how she knows a nurse practitioner who also does acupuncture, as well as a place to get lovely maternity leggings and stretchy tops.

Phoebe looks after them sadly. It pierces me, how much she wanted this to be her. Miranda goes over and gives her a big hug, and when I look over at Mason, he's watching them with eyes so soft and luminous that for a moment I think I'm going to have to comfort *him*.

 ∽

As planned, I take him for a walk after dinner. I, for one, am saturated with drama. I feel like a damp dishrag that's been wrung out. It's a lovely spring night; early April, which can go either way here, has decided to behave itself. People are out on the street, sitting on their steps, or tossing baseballs and Frisbees in their front yards. A few daffodils are about to burst into bloom. If you squint, you can see that the trees have pink fuzz on them.

As we pass Archie Moore's restaurant and bar, Mason says we should go in and have a drink. "The antidote to the rough parenthoods we're experiencing might just be a noisy bar."

"Is that what this is—rough parenthood?" I say, laughing.

"Well, what would you call it?" he says. "Let's see. My son is currently flirting with going back to a self-absorbed narcissist, and your daughter—"

"Is right now sobbing in my kitchen because she got pregnant from a spell I did, only she doesn't believe in spells, and she isn't completely sure she wants motherhood, and also she's decided *not* to tell her husband about her pregnancy, even though she's keeping the baby."

"And, for a witch, you seem to be having an awfully tough run of things. Misplaced pregnancy, and now Joey seems to have lapsed. He, I believe, was your big success."

I sigh. "I know. I should turn in my Witch Registration Card. Oh, right. I don't have one."

He laughs.

"But also, I don't think he's going to go back to her. Why would he?"

"Because he's still in love with her? Because he's an idiot who thinks it could still work out?"

I want to say, *But she's married to someone else! And she took all his wedding and honeymoon money WITH the new guy!*

But I don't. I don't because Mason has stopped walking and is giving me a funny look. Like, one of *those* looks. And his face is getting closer and closer to mine. He looks into my eyes and hesitates for only a moment and then places his hands on my hair, my wiry, sticking-out hair, and he leans down and kisses me. Just like that. Kisses me. At first it's a little kiss right on my bottom lip, and then, maybe because I don't pull away, his mouth moves over mine, and things turn pretty miraculous rather fast. I haven't had any kissing this intense in a very long time, and I really have forgotten how it loosens you up. Like, it unlocks your knee joints or something. Makes you want to lean completely against the person doing the kissing, crash into things—walls, or beds.

By the time I pull away, I am without words. I stare at him.

"I'm sorry," he says. His eyes are searching mine. "Oh, for God's sake, what the hell was I thinking? I'm sorry, I'm sorry, I'm sorry."

"Well," I say. "It was quite a kiss, actually. Unexpected, which is the best kind. But I don't think you should do it again."

"Of course not," he says.

"On the other hand, we are grown-ups, and we've got two spectacularly screwed-up children, and we've had some alcohol, so I think it's completely understandable and even fine for us to have another kiss if we really want to."

He cocks his head, looks at me questioningly, as though this might be a trick.

"I don't have a rule about things like that," I say. "What I have a rule against is romance. This, however, falls into the category of a kiss that is not inviting romance."

"No one's going to get their heart broken over that kiss," says Mason. "Is that what you mean?"

"Yes. Even though I suspect that you yourself believe in romance and happily ever after and all that stuff."

"No!" he says. "I don't. I swear I don't."

"Well, then, in that case," I say, "let's stop making out on the sidewalk and go into Archie Moore's like grown-ups and have something to drink, even though it may be inadvisable, and maybe by the time we go back to my house, the young folks will be over their crying fest and their processing, and we can do indoor kissing."

"Okay," he says. "Although this is confusing. You must admit this is confusing."

"I admit nothing of the kind. You have to keep up."

We sit at the bar and have a couple of grown-up cocktails with olives in them, and some apple crisp because it's irresistible, and then, after we're tired of having to shout to hear each other over the basketball game that's playing on both television sets as well as all the loud talking from the people around us, we walk back to my house.

All the lights are still on, but no one seems to be around. And in fact, there's a long note from Louise on the counter saying that she's gone back to her house for the night or a week or whatever. She says she's going back to "face her life."

I get it. She needs to be in her own home now that she's decided to have the baby, to walk through the rooms and see herself there as a pregnant woman and maybe even a mother. To pace around and figure out what place Leo has in her life, and where she'll put the crib, if indeed she stays, and what she'll say on her blog, and what kind of diapers she believes in, and whether she'll breastfeed, and if there's a special kind of pacifier and baby carrier she'll be needing.

I read the note, and then I take Mason by the hand, and with all the stern practicality the occasion calls for, I take him upstairs.

I unbutton his shirt as we go. And when I finish with his, I start unbuttoning mine, and by the time we get to the top of the stairs, I slip out of my skirt and leave it there in the hallway, and I take him into my bedroom. There is no artifice or coquetry here. This turns out to be the right way to do it when you're sixty and a bit imperfect and there's no romance. You don't need to see or be admired; you just fall together under your grandmother's hundred-year-old quilt, and you try not to make too much of the wonderment and gratitude in his eyes, but just stay in the moment. The touches are sure and deliberate, and you smile at each other a lot and you both take your time, and after you make love (which doesn't hurt because you have some old goop in the drawer that you rummage around until you find), you put on your flimsy kimono and give him one of Calvin's bathrobes, and you take him to the kitchen, where you whip up some blueberry scones and a glass of brandy just like you're in a Nancy Meyers movie, and the two of you eat them standing at the counter with just the stove light on, while you tell him your theory about how everything is ephemeral, and how it's perfectly okay with you that nothing really works out in the end, because you've learned that you can seize the moment and have a perfectly wonderful time and then never do it again.

And then you say he has to go home.

He grins and asks if he could be permitted to go back upstairs and put on his pants and shirt, or if he has to wear this ratty old bathrobe to drive home.

You pretend to consider this, and then let him go up, but tell him that he has only five minutes.

Because you need him gone. You need more than anything to be alone, to reclaim all the parts of yourself. To cast out the memory of his smell, of his stubbled cheek next to yours, his deep sigh, his warm hands that thawed out every place they landed on your body.

CHAPTER EIGHTEEN

Kat sits in my kitchen three days later, complaining about her husband. He's controlling, he has no sense of humor, and he gives her bulletins from C-SPAN all day long. He also eats toasted cheese sandwiches with a knife and fork, and he wears black dress shoes with khaki shorts—sins that I don't think are technically grounds for divorce, but Kat thinks they should be.

She's just winding down from her list of complaints when my phone rings. It's Mason, and I look at it and click it off.

Of course she sees. "So, what's going on with you and him?" she asks. Then, even before I can answer, she looks at me closely and suddenly she's figured out that I slept with him. She laughs and gives me a high five because she always thinks people getting to have sex is pretty wonderful. It is not love. She knows this. It's just sex. Something a person might need, medically speaking. Like food or air.

Then we get down to business, and she tells me about the new requests for me to speak. The world has gone insane, so there are lots of calls. So many that I've ordered three more bunny suits so I won't look bedraggled.

Next week I've been asked to give a talk in Brooklyn—*Brooklyn!*—as well as at two women's clubs in Fairfield County and fifteen house calls; then next month, two television stations, and a keynote speech to a group of women in California.

"You seem to have hit on something people want to hear about. I've gotta tell you, I'm a little envious."

"No, you're not."

"I am. The excitement of it." She pushes a strand of her blonde hair out of her eyes and rests her chin on her hands. "Being wanted. The fact that your days aren't consumed with figuring out whether to serve a man steak or chicken, and would steak be bad for his cholesterol."

"Well, you *know*, now that I have extra bunny suits, you could get in on a little bit of this bunny action."

"Bob would kill me."

"No, he wouldn't. And you wouldn't have to do it for very long. Just until I come back. It'll be fun. And it'll help the business. Come on, live a little."

"Wellllll," she says. And I know I have her.

We go upstairs and she tries on the bunny suit. She looks adorable in it, and she turns in front of the mirror, back and forth, admiring herself. "It has . . . it has a certain . . . panache, doesn't it?" she says. "You really think I could do it?"

I remind her that she's the woman who can do anything—I've known her to stare down scary teachers and mean moms at the playground, back when our girls were little. "You are the bravest person I know."

"I'm not brave anymore."

She's right; she's not. Kat could be Exhibit A of how marriage can drain a person of their true essence.

I put my hands on her shoulders and look her right in the eyes. "Well, girl, then you need to get brave again. Maybe this is a good start."

She looks at herself in the mirror. "You're right. Maybe I don't even have to tell Bob."

"Whatever you think, but just maybe you could consider being honest. He can deal with the real, undiluted Kat, who doesn't care much for C-SPAN and rather likes adventure. That's the woman he fell in love with, after all."

She considers this, but I can tell it's already settled. She'll take the bunny calls each week on Mondays and Fridays, and then when I go on tour, she'll do all of them.

I haven't seen her so excited in a very long time. In fact, she calls me three times that night, just to review the whole protocol: how you take the items away, what you say if they're extra sad, and what to say if they're not.

"You got this," I say. "Say whatever comes to your head."

∽

A week later, I go to Brooklyn, where it's storming and windy, yet the streets are filled with people all hurrying about carrying to-go cups and take-out containers of dinner, presumably. The air smells like car exhaust and rain.

Inside Hallowell Hall, where I'm scheduled to talk, the mood is more laid-back after-work anticipation. Downstairs, some people are playing bocce, while in another section, a woman is setting up folding chairs. Everyone is sloshing a beer, it seems, and the air feels buzzed, like something great might be about to happen. After I check in with the bartender, I go into the restroom to adjust the bunny costume and to spray stuff on my hair to make it stick up in little fun peaks. I stare at myself in the mirror and repeat: *There is no reason to be nervous, there is no reason to be nervous.* A woman in there tells me that she's just been left by her fifth boyfriend in a row—and all four of the others are now happily married and living in lofts somewhere.

"It's devastating trying to find love in this city," she says.

When at last I get on the little makeshift stage, after being introduced by a young man who has a shy smile and a long dark beard, I look out at the audience and take a deep and shaky breath.

"Ohhhh, poor Brooklyn!" I say. There are about a hundred people sitting on folding chairs. "Are you so heartbroken, darlings? I look around me, and I think what in the world could bring people out on a rainy night like this if you all aren't out of your mind with suffering? Who in here is currently suffering? Don't be afraid. We're all in this together. We won't judge you."

People raise their hands. I squint into the audience. There's a light shining in my eyes, and I ask if it could be turned off so that maybe we could sit and chat. Informally. A man runs over and makes that happen, and I settle down in an overstuffed armchair that smells like it probably has soaked up at least a six-pack's worth of spilled beer.

The guy who introduced me says, "Maybe you could tell us why you're wearing a bunny suit . . . and just what a Heartbreak Bunny does."

"Oh, yes, that," I say. "I know, this looks ridiculous, doesn't it?"

"It looks comfortable AF," someone calls out.

"Thank you. It is. Okay. You probably can't relate to this, but one night my best friend Kat and I got wildly drunk"—they laugh—"and at around three o'clock in the morning we came to some amazing realizations. One of them was that between us, we'd been married five times and had an untold number of relationships, and we'd spent over three-quarters of our precious lives trying to mold ourselves into being the right kind of women for men who didn't even appreciate us. We were always trying to look good and make everybody feel great about themselves, to give out performance trophies if the guy so much as came home from work on time—and we realized that even though we were old enough to know better—damn it, we were *still* caught up in the myth that love was going to save us. We were *still* listening to love songs on the radio and watching movies where people who hate each other turn around and start loving each other so much they have to run through an airport to prove it. And everywhere we looked, we saw people simply knocked over by what love had done to them! Decimated! Unable to move on! Punishing themselves, staying stuck, really invested in suffering. Like that was going to make things all right again. We were so drunk that we decided right there and then that *we* were the people to fix this! Two fifty-nine-year-old women who'd been through the wringer, love-wise."

There's a smattering of laughter.

"Yeah. We were pretty cocky. We figured we'd shine some light on things, and that I—it had to be me because Kat is shy—that *I* would dress up in this crazy costume, and I would hop into people's houses and remove everything that was holding them back. Love notes, photographs, dead flowers, bedroom slippers, stiletto shoes, a garlic press—you name it. I'd remove it. And people would then be able to see themselves as free!"

"Hey, I think falling love is fun!" someone yells.

"Greetings, visitor to this planet!" I say. "Many of the humans here on earth find the rituals of love quite fun. But I think you'll find, as you spend more time here with the earth animals, that it's fun the way jumping out of an airplane is fun. You don't know if you're going to make it out alive, but for the moment your adrenaline is pumping and your lungs are taking in air and your brain is wheezing—and if that's your idea of a good time, then have at it. But studies show that hit of falling in love lasts approximately thirty-six days—okay, I have no idea if that's true—but after that, you'd better have something else going on or else you're in for trouble."

"What happens after the thirty-six days?" someone calls out.

"Disaster," I say calmly. "That's when you find out if there was something there besides the mad adrenaline rush. Which, by the way, is chemically the same thing that happens to your brain when you eat chocolate. So, I say, why not just eat some chocolate?"

I can feel myself getting so gloriously wound up.

A woman asks if she can talk about her situation, and I say, "Yes! Yes! By all means!"

It's the usual: a guy moved in with her, they loved each other, he started growing cold and distant—"reptilian," she said, which draws a laugh from the audience—and then one day he simply packed his stuff and told her that he couldn't do it anymore. No reason given. And she's still thinking about him. Wanting to call him back for one more talk. For *closure*, she says. The audience groans.

"I just can't move on. I call up all my friends and we talk about how horrible he was. I cry on their shoulders all the time, and I'm—"

"Okay," I say. "First of all, do not ever use the word *closure* again for the rest of your life. There is no such thing. No more crying on your friends' shoulders. Here's what you do: tell them you broke up with him because you were only helping him get over his sexual hang-ups, and he showed no signs of ever getting any better at sex, and so you broke it off."

The audience dies.

"And then be your own Heartbreak Bunny. Be ruthless. Throw out every single thing that he gave you or anything that reminds you of him. Burn his letters. Delete his emails. Purge him from any social media accounts you have. Then—and this is important—you have to use all that anger to make change. Put yourself on a strict diet of healthy foods. Eat greens and nuts. Start exercising for an hour every day. Read a book a week. Start learning a foreign language or start writing a book with you as the heroine. You may have to boil the sheets on your bed, I don't know. Or paint the walls. If you have to, you have to. Do this for three months like it's your job or your religion. And then see how you feel."

"What if he wants to come back to her?" asks someone else.

"No, no, no! Never!" I say. "He doesn't deserve her anymore."

"But what if he's changed?" she says. I feel my heart soften.

"Sweetheart, lambie, he hasn't changed. He has not changed one iota. So, if after the ninety days, you're still tempted, *then* you may have to draw on magic to rid yourself of him. Stay on your healthy regimen, of course, but now you must also call upon the universe to help you. Write affirmations. Go outside during the full moon and chant that you are driving him from your heart. Do conscious breathing. Read about positive magic. Summon your power. Tell yourself the story of yourself as a goddess ridding the land of wickedness and weakness."

"Does it ever happen that the person can come back and be very, very sorry—and you can begin again?" someone calls.

I say, "Oh, you poor misguided babies of Brooklyn. All right. I will tell you something. This is very rare—one in forty-three million—and so it will probably never happen, but *if* after some years of healing, after you've reclaimed all that energy, you can *maybe* be ready to let love come into your life the quiet, refined way. And then, *if* he's the one who shows up offering long-lasting good feelings, a friendship that's like a partnership, *and*—this is critical, so listen up—*if* he's no longer keeping you off-balance and making your heart skip beats and your knees wobble, and if he has done at least ninety thousand hours of true penance for what he did to you, then *maybe*. But keep your guard up. Don't go for the falling-out-of-the-airplane feelings anymore. And don't neglect the penance part of this. He must do penance."

And then I look at the back of the room, where there's a slight stir. A man lounging against the wall raises his hand halfway.

"What kind of penance would he have to do?" he says.

The air starts to feel like it's fried—little sizzles form around all the light bulbs, and it appears that a good deal of oxygen has left the room. I squint so I can see to the back of the room—and then I feel like I've been knocked over.

Oh my God. The man is Victor.

Victor Steidley stands there, in all his glory, wearing a leather jacket and jeans. He's bearded and his hair is thinner, and his head is cocked to the side, and he's smiling his wide, expansive, we're-in-this-together smile. And lounging. He looks like he should have a piece of straw in his mouth and a cowboy hat. I used to love men who could lounge.

"Well? What would he have to do? What's enough?" he says in the same nonchalant tone. His eyes, however, are boring into mine, even from that distance.

The floor has dropped out of the room, although no one else seems to notice. I'm too smart to let anything like the blood leaving my face keep me from my mission—I'm the fucking Heartbreak Bunny, after all—and so I say very quietly, in a steely voice, "Actually, there's nothing he can really do. What I meant to say before is that once you've gone through the three-month fueled-by-anger cleansing time, that's the best revenge. Because by then you're over him."

"Oh, really," he says.

"Absolutely," I say. "You're done with him and everything he represents."

And that's it.

When my talk is over, I'm surprised that people stand up and clap. I hear whistles and the stamping of feet. A standing ovation. I stand there, flushed and pleased, until it dies down.

CHAPTER NINETEEN

I'm sorry. I think I may have neglected to tell you some things about Victor.

Maybe I should have mentioned that he is charming. He prides himself on that. He is actually *beyond* charming. He is also drop-dead funny. And, okay, a bit arrogant. He's accustomed to the deck being stacked his way. He's handsome enough to get by on his looks. He knows how to get what he wants.

That is Victor.

He used to call me William to be funny. I hated it at first, and then I loved it. We had tons of fun—and a reckless, zigzagging, big-love kind of life. We had our own language. For nearly two years we slept on a mattress on a wooden frame that would fall apart when we made love, and we'd go sprawling across the floor, laughing. Every night. He liked sex a lot, and so did I. The trouble was, he liked it with lots of people, and he didn't really see how that might be a problem for me. He believed in something he called CSR—Casual Sex Rights. Everybody should be allowed flings, shouldn't they? They didn't mean anything, he told me. I, myself, did not partake. I was busy loving my role as a new wife and mother. Who had time for extracurricular sex? Who would want me anyway, in my state of maternal wedded bliss, all milk and soap and sweetness? I had no sex appeal to the outside world whatsoever.

But he did. He was a mechanic, fixing cars in a garage downtown—and women would come to the shop just to hang out with him. I'd take him dinner—me in my long skirt and peasant blouse and with my hair in a braid—and find some woman with cleavage and sunglasses talking to him about rods and pistons. He would be leaning against her car, looking like a cross between Elvis and Bruce Springsteen, and then he'd see me and say, "Hey, baby," like I was just another woman who admired him. No one should be permitted to be that good-looking. He never introduced me as his wife. It didn't matter to him like it mattered to me. I was put in the ridiculous, shameful position of having to flash my wedding ring at whatever girl was there, eyeing him. To make sure she saw who I was.

Later, after the baby came, I couldn't stop by the garage so often. I was busy playing the part of Earth Mother and being happy. By then, we were living in the row house, with my mother on the top floor and his mother on the bottom floor, and he had an old antique car in the backyard that he worked on restoring. I could look out the window and see him there, and that made me feel good. But then, seemingly out of the blue, he decided to take a poetry course at the community college, and that's where he met the one who couldn't be accommodated in a casual sex situation, I guess.

Juliette.

What else?

Oh, yes. This.

He called himself a wolf and said he couldn't be satisfied. Nobody and nothing could contain him, he said.

And this: after we broke up, after he'd moved away to France and some time went by, he missed me. For years he said he missed me. He'd write me poems and send them in huge brown envelopes. He asked to get back together one time—no, two times. Once was when his mother died, and he came back from France and broke down after the funeral and told me he was unhappy with Juliette, and he wanted to come home to me. But he said it all wrong, and I knew it was only a symptom of grief, and it wasn't to be taken seriously. A foregone conclusion that he could simply swan back in and take his place in the house, in the family. He was arrogant, as I might have mentioned.

I reminded him that he was a wolf who was never going to be satisfied. He would always want another woman in addition to me.

Okay, he said. There would be no more Juliette. He promised.

No, I said.

No other relationships with other women ever, he said. That made me laugh.

I said no again. The place he had occupied in my heart had been locked up, closed down for the rest of my life, I told him. I laughed when I said it. I told him he would never unlock that part of me again, which he took as a challenge because of course he would.

He sent French chocolates, poems with no punctuation or capital letters, and some empty promises. I didn't answer any of his missives. I threw everything in the garbage.

I could see through him. He didn't want me. I was just the one who got away.

My bitterness made my teeth feel like I had chewed on metal. I wanted only to get away from him.

That is how it happened that I denied my daughter a chance to grow up with both her parents in the house.

So sue me.

And now he's here, walking toward me. I see his blue eyes—those eyes still filled with laughter and arrogance. Before he gets to me, he's blocked by all the Brooklynites swarming me. They have questions: they want to know why a bunny suit; they want to tell me their unhappy love stories; they want to talk about their roommate's cousin's girlfriend's crush, the stepfather who had left their mother in tears. All of it. I am happy to listen.

When the crowd thins out, I go to the restroom to change into my Brooklyn outfit: black jeans and boots and a black scoop-neck shirt with strategically placed lightning bolts here and there. I stare at myself in the mirror. Hating myself for doing this, I put on lipstick.

He will be there; he will be there when I come out of the restroom. I know this.

And sure enough, as soon as I come out, still fiddling with my bag, I look up and there he is. He's leaning again, waiting for me, looking handsome and thoughtful. Now, in the light of the hallway outside the restroom, I can see that his beard is gray and his eyes are crinkled, but they still look smarter and more sincere than anybody else's eyes. *He's so interested in you; you're the whole world,* his eyes say, and his salt-and-pepper hair is ruffled and casual, and he's wearing a black leather jacket and tight jeans, and . . . he's grinning.

"William," he says softly. He comes toward me. "Look at you. My gawd, woman. If you aren't a sight for sore eyes."

Just then, though, a group of people swoop over. The women are laughing and teasing the men. One of the men clasps my hands and tells me I may have saved his life. He's going home and throwing out everything his ex-girlfriend left behind, and then he's going on a ninety-day plan. Victor can't resist telling them that *he* is the Heartbreak Bunny's heartbreak. "If it weren't for me," he says, "none of you would be hearing her speak." The woman standing closest to him socks him in the arm, and he pretends to be mortally wounded. "I'm here to get penance," he says. "Tell this bunny that I deserve penance." It's forever until they move away.

Once they're gone, Victor looks at me and smiles.

"How is it that you found me here?" is all I can manage.

"Signs," he says.

At first I think he means signs, as in signs from the universe, but then he points to a poster that's still hanging on the wall. BILLIE SLATE, it says, IS THE HEARTBREAK BUNNY.

Of course.

He laughs, knowing what I was thinking. "Well, certainly there were those *other* kinds of signs, too," he says and makes jazz hands when he says it. "Woo-woo signs."

He gathers me in a hug. The formal, quick hug that semi-amicable exes are allowed to give but then he lingers a little bit more, because he's Victor. "I was in Brooklyn for the past week," he says, "and I saw these signs hanging everywhere, and so I looked you up, and sure enough, my own William has turned into a magical Heartbreak Bunny, and so obviously I had to know what the hell that is."

"Billie," I say.

"Billie, William." He smiles and shrugs. "You win. Whichever way you want it. Let's go have a drink and we can debate the finer points of your name, and also you can tell me how it is that I find you here in Brooklyn, New York, wearing a stuffed-animal costume and being the rock star of heartbreak. This, I don't mind telling you, was not on my bingo card."

"All right," I say. I figure, why the hell not? It's just a drink. And maybe I can get him to stop texting me all the time.

"We don't even have to talk about hard things," he says and takes my hand in his as we walk. "I just want to sit in a dark bar and look at you while we contemplate our lives."

I withdraw my hand, and we go to a place around the corner. On the way he tells me that he's back in the States for a while; he doesn't know for how long. This is the best thing about his life, he says. He can go anywhere and do anything. It's just that now that Juliette is gone, he's at loose ends. He's trying to write poetry, but he's blocked. He's visited by the ghosts of the past.

He finds us a booth in the back, and he orders a bottle of wine—he remembers that I like pinot noir and makes a big deal of explaining that to the waitress, who is a cute young woman with red curly hair—and we get appetizers, too. An olive plate, some cheese. He calls the cheese *fromage* with the *R* rolled just so. He orders six oysters. We loved oysters. He tells the waitress that we used to be married and that on paydays, we'd go to a dive bar near the Quinnipiac River in New Haven and get oysters fresh from that day's catch. She is charmed by him and pats his arm as she sets down the wineglasses.

We touch lightly on memories after that: The time we drove to the White Mountains in New Hampshire in T-shirts and jeans, and a blizzard came up, and we tried to turn around, but our car got stuck in the snow and we had to be rescued. The time we thought we could have sex in an airplane bathroom, and it turned out you really can't. The time we were so poor that we cooked—*I* cooked—a full Thanksgiving dinner on a hot plate and toaster oven in our tiny kitchen and we sat on the floor and served it to the neighbors on mismatched plates we'd bought at the Goodwill store.

"And then there was that day when a woman came to the door and said she'd had a date with you the night before, and maybe you still had her earrings," I say, because I want to remind him of the bad stuff just in case he's heading down the road to possible reconciliation.

He laughs dryly and ducks his head. "I know, I know," he says. "You can't forgive me. I get that. I was horrible."

"I've done better than forgive you. I've grown indifferent to you. So why are you here?"

"Why am I here? Why *am* I here?" he says, looking into the dimness of the restaurant. Then he turns back to me. "I'm here because you're breaking my heart."

"Ha! This is a new one." I fold my arms.

"No. I mean tonight. What you're doing now. This Heartbreak Bunny gig or whatever it is. Going out and lecturing people about not trusting love anymore. I stood there listening to you and I heard people laughing and responding—you were great and convincing, and they loved you—but it made me realize it was all because of me."

"Of course you would assume this is about *you*."

"What I did to you." His eyes go soft. "William, my love. You used to be this sunny, happy person who believed in happily ever after, who believed in love and cooking and babies and sex, and you were taking care of everything, and I broke your heart."

"Oh, for God's sake!" I say. "Don't give yourself so much credit. Nobody gets to sixty without their heart taking a beating. And also, I'm fine."

"You trusted me, and I blew that trust out of the water. And I just want to say that I'm so, so sorry."

"Shut up, Victor. You did blow my trust, it's true. But I rebuilt. And the last thing I want—"

"I know you," he says and leans forward, his eyes locked on to mine. "I *know* you. Also, just for the record, everything you're preaching up there is bullshit. You don't believe a word of it. And if you *do* believe it, then it's because you've killed off some of your essence. And *that* is what I did to you."

"I don't know for sure," I say after a moment, "but it's possible that you are the true definition of a narcissist, somebody thinking that the whole damn world and everybody in it revolves around him. That what I've become and how I've lived my life and raised our daughter is all in reaction to *you*, a guy who took up about two years of my entire sixty years of existence. Which now seems about twenty minutes, if you want to know the truth."

He looks away. "Point taken," he says.

I look at my watch. "I need to get to Grand Central. I want to get home before midnight."

"You could stay in the city. I have a hotel room. Two beds. No hanky *and* no panky. I promise."

I laugh. "Not bloody likely."

He signals for the check and sighs. "Then I'll walk you to the subway. Because I need your advice about Louise."

"What do you possibly need my advice for? You've pretty much neglected her for her whole life. Why start asking for advice now?"

"I know. I've been abominable. And don't worry; she's giving me a rough enough time about that."

I squint my eyes at him. "Did you say she's *giving* you a rough time, as in the present tense? Meaning now?"

"Yeah, now. Her latest salvo was an hour ago. But I think I'm slowly winning her over."

"Excuse me, you're . . . what, now?"

"Winning her over. At least she's talking to me. And she seems willing to forgive me in some small measure, although I have a lot of work to do—"

"No, no. Wait. Back up," I say, putting my hand up. "You and Louise are talking? How did this happen? When? How?"

For a moment, my head seems filled with bees. I want to explain to him that Louise is *mine*. He is not to use all his overabundance of Bad Guy Charm on her. This isn't how the plot of our lives was ever supposed to go.

He's quite oblivious to this. "Yeah, we're texting, talking. Mostly texting. She yells at me when I call her, I try to apologize. She hangs up on me. But she always calls back." He smiles. "I think she likes the game of it."

I sit back in the booth. I feel like I've been punched in the stomach.

"Oh, I thought you knew," he says. "She got my number after she saw the text messages I'd left on your phone. And one day she called me up. She was livid at first, understandably. How could I have left her when she was a baby? Why didn't I care about her? All that."

"Yes, I'm familiar with those questions."

"I apologized, of course, which meant nothing. Just words. I expected that. But I kept talking to her, and gradually she went from being white-hot furious to simply being angry. I told her I understood how she felt. And also I told her how proud I was of her blog and her career, and I think that broke down some of her defenses. She didn't know I had been reading her stuff. Looking at the pictures. She's really remarkable, and I told her that I'd missed out on everything, and that I was so very, very sorry." He drinks the last bit of his wine and puts the glass down. Looks at me, spreading his hands out. Like an innocent man who's been wrongly accused but is finding his way back into grace.

"Jesus, Victor."

"That made her cry," he says. "Which I've learned is a good thing with your gender. One night we got so emotional that we were *both* blubbering on the phone. It was sort of epic." He makes his face go solemn. "I just wish I'd been different, Billie. I thought the best thing for Louise was for me to stay completely away, once we'd gotten divorced. That's what Juliette said: don't make her life confusing by showing up. Now I see I did everything wrong, and I have to live with that. But maybe I can make it right, a little bit at a time."

"I don't know how much more of this I can take," I tell him. "This is such bullshit."

"I know. I don't blame you. Why am I doing this?"

"Yes. Let's skip right to that. Why *are* you doing this?"

"Because, because . . . I want to make up for what I've done wrong. Is that so wrong? Maybe in my old age I think that I can be there for the people who should have been able to count on me long ago. I want to help. I want to know you again, and I want to know my daughter. And her baby."

"You know about the baby." It's a flat statement.

"I do. Hey, we're going to be grandparents, you and I! How wild is that, huh?"

"This is unbelievable. The way you're going about this."

"Wait. I hope you're not *jealous* that she's opening up to me! You're still her main support, I know that. I'm not trying to take anything away from you. You did an amazing job raising her. I didn't mean—I hope you know—to be a problem. I'm just going through one of those times in my life when I'm reexamining everything. What *would* be penance for me? Is there anything I can do? To make *some* things up to you, at least?" He has this look I remember. He tilts his head so charmingly, and he makes his eyes look all twinkly and sincere, and he turns his mouth down just slightly. It is a look that has always worked for him. I am not falling for it.

"You don't get to do any penance."

"What? I don't get penance?"

"Absolutely not. Go home, Victor." I get out of the booth. "I've got to get to Grand Central. I have a life to get back to."

And that's it. I get up and put on my coat. I grab my purse. And I leave. I walk to Grand Central. My phone dings when I'm hurrying to catch the 10:28 train.

i think i want the baby to call me pepe and you can be mere and we will take him to the sea and to the park and we will swing him up high in the swings so high he might go over the top into the clouds

CHAPTER TWENTY

Mason texts me when I'm on the train, right after I've settled in, wrapped myself up in my scarf, and stretched out across the empty seat next to me.

> I'm with Joey and Saucy. Please someone kill me now. He really thinks she's changed. She has not. Does the Heartbreak Bunny do interventions for bystanders?

I sit up and lean my head against the cold, hard window of the train, which vibrates so much that it makes my skull hurt a little bit. I realize I didn't think of Mason even once while I was with Victor. I remember this about Victor. It's as if his personality is so gigantic that it overtakes all your brain cells, blots out anything you were thinking about previously. He expands to fit whatever cranial space you have. It's awful.

And tonight—tonight was like thirty-five years of Victor distilled and jam-packed into just a few hours. I feel as though half the oxygen in the New York metropolitan area has been depleted.

But here is Mason. It's a comfort to hear from lovely, rational Mason—even Mason expressing his unhappy, fatherly concern. I smile as I text back:

Must be Ex Return Week. I was speaking to sad hipsters in Brooklyn, and who should I see but my ex in the audience! Ack! Went for drinks with him. He also claims he's changed and can make up for 35 years of absence. Worse, I think, is that he's been in touch w/ Louise.

For a long time after that, three dots appear, then disappear, then appear again. Mason is such a wuss. Why can't he just say what he wants to say? I smile and put away my phone.

As I'm getting off the train in New Haven at half past midnight, I hear my text chime, and there he is.

I think the world of love is more screwed up than I ever imagined. We need a better system.

I write back:

LOL. That's what I've been talking about! Now at last someone is listening to me!

I was always listening.

I walk through the tunnel to the parking garage, and I take the elevator with a couple who nuzzle each other the whole time. When the door opens, I make my way to my perky VW bug. It always looks like it's waiting so patiently, like a contented little animal. A hedgehog, perhaps.

I get in, close the door, and sigh. It will feel so good to be back at home. It's been a long day. I turn the key in the ignition and hear . . . nothing. Just clicks.

"Come on, car," I say, and try again.

Nothing.

I put my head down on the steering wheel so I can summon up some energy to decide what to do. My phone chimes.

Mason.

Not to freak you out, but I want to see you. Is that too much?

My car is actually dead at the train station. Too much what?

I'll come and pick you up. Meet me out front in ten.

Thank you. Too much what?

Nothing. See you in ten.

∽

He jumps out of the car as soon as he sees me on the sidewalk. There are a few cabdrivers hanging out, chatting and smoking cigarettes, and Mason, wearing a tan trench coat, hurries over, across the rain-slick pavement and takes me in his arms right there under the overhang. I feel like we're in a scene from an old black-and-white movie. The cabbies all stop talking when he kisses me.

"What the hell!" I say, but I'm laughing.

"Sorry. This is a result of my evening with my poor, deluded son, combined with the story of your ex showing up, and—I don't know— the rain," he says. "Let's get in the car. I'll take you home."

"Well," I say, as I slam the door and fasten my seat belt, "I do love me some spontaneity—and the cabbies may have learned a good lesson about old folks having some juice to them."

"So, it was all for a good cause," says Mason.

On the way, I tell him about the Brooklynites and the questions they asked, and how I hit upon the idea that everybody could learn to protect their own heart, even without a Heartbreak Bunny. How they need to put themselves on a self-improvement regime, fueled by anger. And he tells me about Joey and Saucy holding hands and talking about the future.

"And they so do not belong together in any future whatsoever!" he says.

"It's a mysterious power, that's for sure."

"What is?"

"Idiocy about love. It has a strong, successful history with the humans."

"I guess so." He sighs. "It makes me so sad. Just unbearably, unutterably sad that he would even *think* he could be with this woman who walked out on him. I—I don't get it. I can't stop thinking about it. Why would he ever trust her again? How would he go to work every day knowing she might be cheating on him?"

"Mason," I say. "I think the time has come to admit that we may have given life to some seriously deranged people."

He takes my hand. "We have no influence on them, do we? Nothing we say means a damn."

"Nope, and now, heaven help us, Louise is talking to her father! Who is *not* to be trusted, not to be listened to, and yet I can just see what's happening: he's going to try to charm her to make up for all the years he was away."

"So, he's charming then?"

"He is. The personification of charm. He walks through the world and people fall at his feet from all the charm he sheds as he goes. Look at me. Do I have any on me? I think it sticks to a person's hair."

"You look relatively unscathed."

When he pulls up to my house, we sit in the car for a moment. I should get out, but the whole place is dark, and it hits me hard that I live completely alone now—everybody has found another place to be. I shiver a little bit. And I realize I'm starving and not one bit tired.

"Are you hungry?" I say.

He looks at me. "Famished. I couldn't even eat with those two maniacs."

"This may be crazy, but do you know what I feel like doing? I didn't have much dinner, and now I feel like getting out *The Joy of Cooking* and making the next recipe. Do you want to?"

He cuts off the ignition and smiles at me. "I do want to. Although as an adult, I feel I should point out that it's nearly one a.m."

"But tomorrow's Saturday. We could sleep in. Maybe?"

"I can sleep in," he says softly.

We're silent for a moment, and then I say, nonchalantly, "And you *could* sleep here, if you'd like."

"All right," he says, "but don't start getting ideas about romance or anything. I know how you girls are."

"We have to stay on our toes. Fight romance wherever it rears its dangerous little head."

We go inside, and I turn on all the lights as we make our way through the house. I tell him that Victor never wanted lots of lights on, and his mother was adamant that we turn them off each and every time we left a room. As a result, I find I *need* lights.

Also, I say, "We need each and every light right now and music because we have to get rid of the dark chill that everybody else's problems has settled on us."

I can feel my energy flowing back into me with every passing minute. I go upstairs and put on my leggings and a knit tunic top and my green flowered kimono, and then I come downstairs and get out *The Joy of Cooking*. I read him all the possibilities, and, based on what we have in the house, we decide on Welsh rarebit over grilled tomatoes. I turn on the smooth jazz Pandora station, and the music curls out of the speakers, surrounding us.

Smiling, Mason pours us each a glass of wine, and I set to dicing the cheese. He melts the butter in the skillet, and I get the Worcestershire sauce and the ground mustard and start buttering the toast to put under the broiler. I'm so aware of the force field of *niceness* around him—the shy, earnest way he tackles all the cooking jobs, the little half smile that plays around his features. I keep stealing glances over in his direction. He's really quite, quite handsome—but not in the trying-too-hard way Victor specializes in. He's just kind of comfortably normal. I realize that's his TV persona, too: the friendly dad in the morning, telling you some fun stuff before you go on with your day.

He sees me staring at him, so I pretend I was thinking of something else. I say, "I think I want dessert, too. How about a cinnamon tea cake?"

We make a pact that we won't talk about the difficult people in our lives, but then of course, we do. We have to. He tells me that Saucy was dazzling Joey all over the place, that every move she made, every smile, every toss of her head had him completely mesmerized.

"It seems like it's going backward," I say, "but he won't stay there, Mason, I promise. This is just him basking in the idea that he might have won her back from the bad boss. But it won't last."

"I wish I could be sure of that," he says. "So how was your bunny talk? Before the Victor part, of course. You don't have to talk about him if you don't want to."

"It was great," I say. "So much fun, actually, with all those lovely young people in the audience wanting to hear what I had to say. Sharing their own experiences. But then . . . well, Mr. Charming decided to make his presence known. And naturally, being Victor, he had to make it all about him."

"He sounds like a real peach," Mason says. "You had no idea he was coming?"

"No. He likes to make things as startling as possible. I remember that about him. Life always has to be more dramatic than anyone ever wants it to be." I stir the cinnamon into the flour and baking powder. "And then he told me that he thinks I don't believe a word of what I'm saying, that he remembers me as someone who *celebrated* love."

"As I recall, your official policy is that you do celebrate love but not wallowing, is that correct?" says Mason with a smile.

I smile back at him. "Oh, but for Victor, this means that he's responsible, don't you see? He *ruined* me, *broke* me. And he just feels *sooo* bad about that."

"Infuriating."

"I know. It makes me so mad to hear him say that, but—"

"But what?" he says softly.

"I don't know for sure. But it's certainly true that I wouldn't have become the Heartbreak Bunny if he'd stayed with me."

"Oh my goodness, this is going in a bad direction," says Mason.

"But I don't think he broke me."

"Of course not. You're not broken."

"Maybe if he hadn't been unfaithful and I hadn't been so young and proud, maybe we even could have worked it out. But when I look at him now, all I can think is that he's a man who's always used his charm to get anything he wants. How does he get away with it?"

"I don't know, but may I say that I now suddenly hate the word *charm*?" He comes over and puts his arms around me, nuzzles his nose in my hair.

I pull away. "I have to say just one more thing, and then I'll stop. I'm worried about what his effect will be on Louise. All that charm."

"But won't she see for herself—?"

"Will she? Who knows?" I say. "It would be great if they could have a normal relationship, and if he could give her some support just now, with the baby and all. But I don't trust him. He might break *her* heart, too. He gets what he wants out of people, and then he gets bored and moves on."

"Here's the thing," Mason says. "Not that I have any wisdom whatsoever about families, because I don't—but what I know for sure is that we can't control what happens. She's going to see her father, and what she gets from him is going to be something you probably can't predict. So you have to let go."

"Let go, yes," I say. "That's exactly right."

"And now," he says, "let's agree that we are not going to let these people win the night here. We are locking them out of our heads." He makes the sign of a lock and key, and then tosses the key over his shoulder. We smile at each other, and then he leans down and kisses me on the cheek and then on my eyebrows and down to my nose, and then his mouth settles on mine, and I feel myself melting. He doesn't look like a man who can kiss better than 90 percent of the people on the planet—all that polite grooming, you know—but he's wild with kisses.

Let's just say that things escalate to the point that the Welsh rarebit and the cinnamon tea cakes get left on the counter, uneaten, and we stumble our way up the stairs, tearing our clothes off as we go.

Later, I realize I can dimly hear the music still playing downstairs, and I can see the glow of the lights still blazing. But I am too drowsy with happiness to go downstairs and set things right.

I fall asleep with my head on his shoulder.

⌒

The next morning we're eating leftover Welsh rarebit and drinking coffee in bed when Louise calls.

"Well, it's happened," she says. "You're not going to believe this. Leo's parents just left, and they want me out of the house. ASAP. No mercy here! Since *Prince Leo* isn't living here anymore, they've decided to sell the house."

My brain has not yet emerged from its warm and languid cocoon, and it struggles to think of something to say in response. But of course, she isn't in much of a mood to listen to anything anyway. She wants to vent. And vent she does. I fluff the pillows while I listen.

"They called me last night and said they wanted to take me out to breakfast. At first I said no, thank you just the same, but I have stuff to do, and then his dad gets on the phone and says in his most ominous dad voice that they know about me and Leo splitting up. And that they need to talk to me, and they said they would rather do it in a restaurant where things could be civil and nice."

There's a pause. I say, "What are they talking about, civil and nice? Couldn't they be nice at the house?"

"Right?" she says. "And then, of course, we get to the diner, and they raked me over the coals anyway. Basically they said they need the house back now. And then his *mother* said that *although* they liked and respected me, blah blah blah, they could see from the beginning that because I'm a *child of divorce*, that maybe I didn't know how to take marriage seriously. And clearly, she said, I hadn't."

"Oh, honey."

"Yeah, I know," she says. "It's terrible."

I speak up. "Well, I for one think you're better off out of there. I think it would be a horrendous place to have to live alone," I say, in the nicest possible way. Very constructively.

"Mom!" she screeches so loudly that I have to hold the phone away from my ear; Mason looks a little alarmed. "Believe me, I always knew I was going to have to leave the house! But to turn on me *right now*? To treat me like *I'm* the enemy when their son has left *me*? Plus, I have enough to cope with. Everything—literally *everything* is changing! My blog is three-quarters about this house and the photographs we take. So, I obviously can't continue *that*. And now I've got this baby coming, *and* I have to move, *and* I'm losing sponsors and followers. My whole life is in the spin cycle of the washing machine."

"Honey, honey, calm down. Did you tell them you're pregnant?"

"Are you nuts? Of *course* I didn't tell them that. They have no right to know what I'm doing." I hear her blowing her nose. "So, the way I figure it, I need to move back in with you. I've been sitting here in the parking lot of the diner, and I've decided to do a complete reordering of my life. This is what I've been thinking, just so you know: I'm probably going to lose the blog, so I'll just find a job doing something else. With my contacts, I could probably get a high-end retail job, don't you think so? And in the meantime, if I'm with you, I won't have expenses. So, I'll get a storage unit and a moving van to get all my stuff out of there, and if you'd tell Calvin I need my old room back, that would be great. He could get the rest of his stuff maybe? And we could share the cooking and all if you want."

My brain has gone numb, somewhere around the uttering of the phrase "move back in with you." I love my daughter—and I love having people around, but she is in no state to make sound decisions. I give Mason a panicky look. "Good lord," I say. "Take a deep breath. Slow down."

She laughs, a short bark of a laugh. "Try to keep up. I'm refiguring everything. People are leaving snotty comments on my blog because I'm not posting as often because I'm throwing up all the damn time. So clearly I'm not going to have sponsors before long, so I might as well just walk away while I can save some face. Maybe I can be a substitute teacher or work in a store or something until the baby comes, and then I can take it to work with me in a sweet little basket. But for now, you and I can get your place all organized and straightened up, and I'll eventually stop throwing up, and I'll sleep a lot while I'm building a human, and you can do your bunny thing, if you want to, and we'll agree on certain terms. Like you won't nag me to tell Leo about the pregnancy, and I won't fuss over all the stuff you should be throwing away. We'll have an ironclad *no men* policy. Just us and *Gilmore Girls* and lots of healthy food like kale and kefir, okay? And maybe we'll do the prenatal exercise routines together—they're good for everybody."

"Let me get this straight. Are you literally setting the terms for *you* coming to live in *my* house?"

She giggles. "See, this is the mama that I love! Come on. Admit it. It's going to be fun."

"I have some tours coming up . . . bunny things to do," I say.

"Fine, fine! This is perfect. I'll look after the house while you're gone. I'll be over later with the first installment of clothing. Although I guess I should hire somebody to help me. Being preggers and all. I wouldn't want to upset the little babester by lifting too much." She laughs.

I'm silent. Louise is going to be a handful. She wants to do even more reorganizing of my house? I look over at the man currently in my bed. What's this about a no-men policy? And . . . kale? Kefir—seriously?

She says, "Well? This is okay, isn't it? Say right now if it's not okay, and I can move on to Plan D or E or whatever the hell I'm at right now."

"No, no," I say. "It's okay. I'll help you."

Louise comes first. That's been my plan since her father walked out.

I can't remember if I realized back then that I was signing on to a lifetime of this.

CHAPTER
TWENTY-ONE

Mason and I look at each other when I hang up.

"So," he says carefully. "Sounds like further evidence that both of us kind of have our hands full with our spawn just now."

"She's moving back in with me. Today," I say weakly. "That was the high-octane Louise on display."

"I could hear her through the phone," he says, shaking his head. "She's got some energy to her, that one." He reaches over and puts his hand near mine and then withdraws it. "We can . . . you know . . . get together at my house . . . that is, if you want to continue . . ."

"Sure. Yeah, okay. We can continue our whatever-this-is."

"I was going to call it our non-romance," he says. He chuckles. "That's why, just now, I was going to put my hand over yours, but I realized that's something a romantic man would do, and I am *not* a romantic man. Not one bit. Which is why I'm all in for a non-romance, yes sirree."

I lean over and kiss his nose.

"Let's think of it as cooking sessions with benefits," I say.

"Well, we've only cooked twice."

"And we've only had benefits twice, so there you go," I say. "And one followed the other both times."

We lie there gloomily, propped against the pillows, and then he clears his throat and gazes at me. "Listen, whatever you need is fine with me," he says. "If we have to take a break, I get it. I'll wait until the coast is clear. Sounds like Louise is going to need a lot of mothering."

"I think that's true," I say. "Along with moving hysteria, I suspect we're dealing with pregnancy hormones, and then there'll be divorce hormones, and the needing-to-find-a-livelihood hormones. And of course there's all the let's-fix-Mom's-haphazard-life hormones."

"And I hate to say it, but then there's also her father showing up," he says.

"Yeah. That, too. I notice she didn't mention that she contacted him."

He leans over and kisses me on the forehead and climbs out of bed, gathers up the dishes. He smiles at me. "I just hope you won't let her fix you too much. I rather like you the way you are."

"Thanks." I clamber out of bed, too, and take our coffee cups and put them on the tray with the dishes and head downstairs. "And now I think I need to call Triple-A and have my car towed to a car hospital," I call back over my shoulder.

"Well, what about this?" he calls down to me. "I have jumper cables in my car, so why don't we just head to the train station and I can try to get the car started. Then, if you want, we can grab a last lunch out before all hell breaks loose, and maybe take a walk on the beach. Have the first lobster roll of the season. What do you say?"

Well, I say yes. Who wouldn't say yes? Why not have one more afternoon of sun shining on my face, and lobster, and this man who makes me laugh?

But I'm also the queen of mixed feelings, and I know there's something else at play in my thoughts just now. We've had a wonderful night of sex and a morning spent eating in bed. I know what a mess this can lead to, believe me: romantic feelings followed by heartbreak as someone (probably me) will have to say that things have gone as far as they can go.

So maybe, I think, this is a sign from the universe that we should call a halt right now. Why let things go any further, when it's all going to lead to a breakup anyway? We can part with no hard feelings. We both have to turn back to our kids who need us.

Time to call a halt.

One more day—and then it's over.

So, I say yes. He takes me in his arms and kisses me sweet and strong. I hold back just a little from kissing him back, a signal to him and to myself that all this is about to come to an end.

⌒⊙

Indeed, after getting my car running again and having a wonderful time eating lobster rolls at the beach, we say good-bye. We don't make a plan to get together. We don't act all sentimental. We don't linger over lunch, making moony eyes at each other. I don't blow him a kiss as I'm driving away.

I go home, sweep the kitchen, and wash the dishes, put away all evidence of my night of sex. Then, with nothing else to do, I make oatmeal lace cookies, and wait. I square my shoulders, ready for Louise.

Her stuff arrives an hour later, in a box truck driven by one handsome guy while another handsome guy rides shotgun. The truck has barely parked at the curb when they leap out like circus performers, wearing jeans and vests, their hair flopping in their eyes, and they go around to the back of the truck and lift the roll-up door, and start pulling out cartons. Cartons and cartons and cartons, which they place on the lawn.

I stand at the living room window watching in something close to shock. There is so much stuff! Louise's Tesla glides up and parks right behind the truck, and she gets out, gesturing and pointing, holding a to-go cup of coffee. She turns to point to the house, and then she sees me and wrinkles her nose and shrugs.

I understand that shrug. The shrug speaks volumes. It says, *I know there are way too many boxes here, but I can't do anything about that, and anyway, I don't want to put all my stuff in storage while I figure out my life and where I'm going to live.*

That Louise can pack a lot into a look, let me tell you.

After I compose my face into something that looks hospitable and warm, I go to the front door, and say, welcome home, darling, and she says thank you, and where shall all this stuff go—upstairs?

I say the attic would be nice, or the spare room on the third floor. And then I watch as the circus men, now stripped of their vests and wearing muscly T-shirts, carry in the cartons, tromping up the stairs obediently, dropping things into the spare room with various grunts and groans. Louise and I direct them as best we can. I offer them iced tea and cookies.

"I suppose we'll have to rent some storage units if you think they're serious about selling the house," I say cheerfully, after the men leave, and she bursts into tears.

"Are you living in a dream world?" she says. "Mom, this is my life now! We both need to get used to it. They *are* selling the house. They've listed it."

"Well, then, storage units are definitely the way to go," I say. "That's all I'm saying. Clearly this house doesn't have room for all of this stuff. Not that it's anything we need to worry about just now."

"*Thank* you," she says in a slightly hysterical voice. And she settles herself into the couch, exactly as she has been doing her entire life, and the cushions seem to close around her like a fortress, exactly as they have been doing her entire life, and she closes her eyes. This girl can sleep absolutely anywhere, and God knows she will need that talent in the months and years to come. It makes me tired just to think of it. I go into the kitchen and fiddle with pots and pans and then cut up all the vegetables in the refrigerator and make vegetable soup, thick with cream. Outside, it grows dark, and I remember the time when it felt like every day we were protecting ourselves against the darkness by filling the house with people. Maybe my whole life has been about warding off the night.

Louise comes into the kitchen, trailing the blue fleece throw from the couch like she used to do when she was little.

She plops down in one of the kitchen chairs. "I can't seem to get enough sleep. I'm so, so, so tired."

"Don't worry. This is all normal early pregnancy stuff. I'll take care of you." I like the way the words feel in my mouth.

"Also, just so you know, this isn't all my stuff. There's more to come."

"Oh?" I say. "Well, I guess then we'll go back and get the rest sometime. Is there any hurry, do you think?"

"Oh, God, I don't know. I was thinking Leo should deal with it since he hasn't really been doing this part, but his mom told me he's in South Africa."

"South Africa! I thought he was in Texas."

"Not according to his mom. I guess he gets around."

We sit down for dinner, the two of us at the big table. I think she's too vulnerable for me to ask her about her communications with Victor, so I don't. She doesn't want the soup I made—she says the smell of it makes her ill. So, I put it away, and she has saltines and yogurt, and afterward, at her request, we crawl into my bed and watch *Gilmore Girls*.

We're two episodes in—Lorelai and Rory are walking side by side and smiling when Louise slides off the bed and down onto the floor and says, "I can't do this!"

"Can't watch this?"

"No. I can't be a mother." She puts her head in her hands and starts to cry. "And I *really* can't be a *single* mother! I have no idea how to get a kid to go to sleep, or how to talk to the room mothers at the school, or how to breastfeed. I don't even know how to put a baby in a car seat!"

"There's plenty of time for figuring out room mothers and car seats. Right now, you just need to get plenty of sleep."

"*Everything's* a catastrophe," she says. "Don't you see? You got divorced and now I'm getting divorced, and it's because we don't know how to do life right. Leo's mom is right. I thought I wanted to watch *Gilmore Girls* so I could see how other mothers and daughters are, but it's just making me feel worse. What if I have a daughter, and I screw her up?"

"It's just a show," I say. "It's fiction. And, besides, we do have that life. We love each other, and we're on each other's side."

"I've been mad at you."

"I know. Because of the spell."

"It's just because I'm scared." She starts sobbing for real then— huge, rending sobs—so I scoot down on the floor and hold her.

"Listen, like everything in life, you'll figure it out as you go along. Nobody ever knows what they're doing before it happens."

"Everybody says it's not easy."

"No. But it's wonderful."

"Even without the father around? You can't tell me that part is wonderful."

"Speaking of fathers," I say, smoothing her hair. "Listen, I don't know if you're aware of this, but I had a drink with Victor in New York."

Her face flushes. "So . . . you know that I've been talking to him," she says. Her chin goes up the way it did the time she was in eleventh grade and I came home to find her showering with her boyfriend. Chin-in-the-air is her main defensive posture.

"Yep," I say now, striving to keep my voice even.

"I wasn't keeping it from you," she says. Chin goes even higher.

"No, no. Of course not. No need at all for you to have mentioned it!" I laugh. "In fact, I'm *glad* the two of you are in touch. It sounds like he's trying to reconnect. I'm glad. It's nice for you to get to know your father."

"Listen, Mom. I called him at first because I just wanted to tell him how mad I've been with him. Like, for my whole life. I thought he should know. And then . . . well, we talked."

"And let me guess. You found you weren't so mad anymore?"

"What I wanted to know from him," she says, and turns and looks at me, "is what kind of man could just walk away from his wife and baby, and never look back."

"And did you get your answer?"

"I did. I thought he was going to make it sound like it was your fault or Juliette's fault, but no. He completely blames himself for all of it." She sighs. "He owns it. He didn't even ask for me to forgive him because he says it's all unforgivable. I respect that, in a weird way."

I watch her face carefully. I wait to see what's going to come up next.

"Meanwhile, he's been reading my blog and following me on Instagram. All these years."

"Has he?" I say. "Huh!"

"Yeah. He knows . . . all this stuff about me. He's been keeping track of me from afar. He said he stayed a lurker because he didn't know how I'd feel if he just popped up as my dad. But he really seems to *get* what I'm trying to do. He says he loves my writing."

"Oh, Louise, be careful!" I say, quite involuntarily. I'm sorry. I can't help myself. I know for a fact that he only a few weeks ago became aware of her blog and her Instagram life. I know because I'm the one who told him; he had no idea. And now he's passing himself off as Fan Number One. I just can't stand it. A lurker, indeed. Maybe he does like her writing—she's good. But to act as though he's pined for contact for years . . .

Her eyes darken. "What? I knew you wouldn't be supportive of this. I knew it."

"It's not that I'm not supportive, darling, whatever that means in this case. It's just that I know this guy. And yes, he cares for you insofar as he can care about anyone. But don't be expecting anything from him. I guess that's what I want to say. He's . . . mercurial. He's utterly the most charming man in the history of the world, but then he just . . ."

"Leaves? Because he left you? Is that what you mean?"

We look at each other, and she has a challenging look in her eyes, like *I'm* being the impossible one.

"To hear his version of things has been very interesting," she says in a hard voice.

I sigh. "I'm sure he has a *fascinating* interpretation of the events that led him to leave," I say. "Luckily, it's thirty-five years ago, and doesn't affect any of us anymore."

"But it does affect us! It affects me!" she says. "This is the way it seems to me: you guys got married, you had me, and then he got sidetracked, made a big mistake by getting infatuated with this French woman, and then, when he regretted it, you wouldn't give him a chance to make things right again, so he went off . . ."

"Things are never that cut-and-dried," I say. "It's always complicated because the human heart is a twisty little rascal. But the upshot is that *my* husband, whom I loved, went to live in France with another woman. What was I supposed to do? Chase after him? Beg him to stay?"

"But what if you'd been a person who believed in love?" she cries. "Did you think of that? You might have waited him out, let him go through his little whatever it was, and then he would have come back, and we would have been a family."

"Louise, that's crazy."

"I'm just saying. It's like a chain of events from that moment on. You raise me by yourself with a houseful of *maniacs*, he stays in France and doesn't ever get to know me but meanwhile he's *pining* for you, but you won't let him make amends, and *I* grow up feeling scared and inadequate and trying to make things perfect and organized, and then I go and marry a guy who's distant and disconnected. And now *that* all falls apart, as could have been predicted! He never loved me. I never loved him. I don't know what love freaking is! Because I didn't ever get to *see* it in action! My mother-in-law is right about me not having the faintest idea of how to stay married."

I take a deep breath. "Listen to me, Louise. I did the best I could. I'm not perfect, but I loved you with all my heart, and all I ever wanted to do was make sure you were surrounded by people who loved you and that you had experiences and . . . liveliness . . . and . . ."

"Oh, it was lively all right! It was fucking chaotic here! All the time! There wasn't a moment's peace, unless I could pull you away and get you to come upstairs and watch television with me in your bed. To just pay attention to *me*."

I feel myself getting furious. "Louise, honey. I'm out. You need to find somebody to talk to about all this. Somebody who is not me."

At this she practically turns into a human volcano. She actually leaps to her feet and screams. "I AM SEEING A THERAPIST, MOM! How do you think I figured all *this* out? This stuff I've been telling you? Trust me! I see the patterns, I *see* what's gone wrong! I'M WORKING ON IT, okay?"

My voice is shaking when I stand up and say, "I am not going to sit here and be screamed at for life choices I made over a quarter century ago. I got divorced because I didn't think it would be good for you to grow up seeing a marriage where the husband does what he pleases, and the wife just puts up with it. That did not seem like a great way to raise a child, seeing her mother be disrespected. I'm sorry it wasn't a perfect life. Good night."

"Studies show," she says, "that children are *always* better off if their parents stay together and try to make things work out. Unless there's abuse, of course."

"I am done with this conversation."

And even though she's in *my* room, I go off and brush my teeth, and then I go downstairs and clean the soup pot and turn off the lights. My heart is pounding. Maniacs? *Maniacs?*

My phone dings, and it's Mason.

May I call you?

I hesitate. I have told Mason good-bye forever. Just today I did that. Only he doesn't know it; I may have forgotten to let him in on that fact. My hand is actually shaking as I type:

Okay. But, fair warning, I am not as you left me . . .

He calls, and I take the phone out on the front porch, and I tell him that things have gone bananas and that I probably shouldn't see him anymore. Louise has lost her mind, I say, and not only has she brought in fifty crates of stuff, which are stacked all over the upstairs of my house, but she's raging about why we're not the Gilmore Girls and why I had to leave my marriage.

"I think the decision to have a daughter might not have been my wisest one ever," I say.

"Yeah, well, sons are not exactly pieces of cake."

"What's yours doing?"

"Oh, he's going on and on about Saucy, and how do you know if someone is really, really sorry—and I say, but how would you ever trust her again, you lunkhead, and then he says that it was all the other guy's fault. He stole her."

"I specifically explained to him that people can't get stolen."

"I know. He mentioned that. He thinks the spell might have worn off. He's not sure about any of it anymore. He says he doesn't know what to think."

"I'll have to make a return trip."

"Quick before he changes his mind and marries her." We're silent for a moment. Then he says, "Could we go on a trip somewhere? What if we took a weekend away? Or a week. In the Berkshires maybe. Or—well, where would *you* like to go?"

I stare out into the darkness of the backyard. "I don't know. Well, I do know. We shouldn't. I'm not in any kind of frame of mind for anything like that. I'm sorry."

He's silent.

I say, "I mean, there's nothing like hearing the news that your child thinks their entire upbringing was wrong. And so wrong that it's caused their own relationships to fail—and probably to continue failing until the end of time and we all die."

He laughs. "Right? Well, if it means anything, I just want you to know that you're the wisest, kindest, funniest person I know."

"Yeah, but you don't really know me all that well," I say. "I'm weird."

"You need a hug. So I'm going to come over and run up to your porch and give you one," he says. "Also, I have cheesecake."

He arrives ten minutes later, and bounds out of the car, smiling and carrying a pink box high in the air. I make room for him on the swing.

When he sits down next to me, I take in his smell—not cologne, not anything artificial—just the natural, already familiar scent of him, his neck, the soap he probably used this morning. I should tell him that I can't see him anymore. But I keep not saying those words. Instead, for reasons that I can't quite understand, I just sit there.

"Forks?" he says. "Or should we just eat it with our hands?"

"Well, I would pick hands, but then like I said, I'm weird," I say.

"Hands it is!" he says. "I even have paper napkins so we can clean up afterward."

"Not me. I'm going to lick my fingers," I say. "I'm a lover of life that way."

His eyes study mine. He's laughing. "You are incredibly weird," he says, "but I'm in."

After we finish off the cheesecake (there was really only a half left), we walk down to Archie Moore's and play darts and drink beers in the back room. I beat a guy in his twenties, who shakes his head and tells the bartender that I should be in a league or something.

After the crowd thins out, we sit in the back at one of the wooden tables. It's late, and for a long time, we sit and talk. We have a contest to see how long we can go without mentioning our children. He tells me how he got into broadcasting. I tell him about all my odd little jobs.

He reaches across the table and takes my hand.

"Mason," I say. "I have to tell you something. I really, really can't do this right now. I'll be glad to talk to Joey one more time if he needs me to, but as for you and me, I just have to say that I don't have it in me. We have to stop. I'm sorry."

"Wow, if I didn't know that you and I were absolutely *not* having a romance, I'd have to say this strongly resembles a breakup speech," he says, withdrawing his hand. He smiles. "But how could we be breaking up when there isn't anything romantic going on between us?"

"I don't know how it happened," I say miserably. "But we have to stop whatever this is."

CHAPTER TWENTY-TWO

Over the next few weeks, the world becomes bunny-obsessed.

Even more bunny-obsessed. Which is good, because it keeps me from thinking so much about Mason Davis, and it keeps me from minding that Louise has taken over my house with her boxes and her organizational projects. She and I have been polite and careful with each other since the night she told me I raised her wrong. The next morning she apologized, blamed it on the fact that she's scared for her own future as a mom. She said she shouldn't have taken it out on me.

I start doing at least five house calls a day. I remove four boyfriend sweaters, a ceramic turtle, a spatula, a pair of red high heels, a set of wedding rings, and a test tube that contains belly button lint. I also removed a jar filled with years of used contact lenses, all curled up like clear little shells.

And then on an otherwise pleasant May afternoon, I come home from a call to find Victor sitting at the kitchen table.

I maybe should have expected this, but I didn't.

As soon as I come in the front door, I can hear him laughing from the kitchen. And then I get to the kitchen door, and there he is in person, laughing and clasping his hands together in front of his chest, sitting in the same spot where he told me thirty-five years ago that he was in love with someone else. Louise sits across from him. Only she is the grown-up, pregnant Louise, not the fat, gurgling baby smearing a muffin into her hair, and they are both laughing, as though the world is such a funny place to have landed in.

I suddenly feel self-conscious, wearing my bunny suit.

"Well, well, well. The bunny is home!" says Victor in his cool dude drawl. I haven't heard that in a long time; he didn't bother to put it on display the night we met in Brooklyn. He looks over at Louise. "I'm sorry, but it makes me so sad to see her in this getup."

"Ditto," she says. She looks over at me, smiling her huge Instagram smile, daring me to be surprised. "It's sooo heart-crushing."

I stop in my tracks.

"Hi," I say, struggling to make my voice stay even. "What a surprise to see you here."

I realize, seeing them there together, that they are a matching set. She has his eyes, his smile, and something that I can't define in the way she moves. And there's this, becoming abundantly clear by the second: She has opened her heart to him. The Louise who scowls, who scorns everything, who longs for perfection, has been replaced by a giddy person.

"I was just in the neighborhood," says Victor, "and . . ."

"No, you were *not* just in the neighborhood!" says Louise, laughing. "I had to beg you to come!"

She begged him? I put the bunny bag down on the floor. I can't think of what to do with my hands all of a sudden.

"Sit down and take a load off," says Victor, as though we are at his house instead of mine. He pulls out a chair. "There's coffee if you want. Louise and I were just talking about maybe going to her house and picking up another load of her stuff, and I thought we could pick up some lunch and bring it back. I was sort of thinking . . . Wooster Square? I've been wanting some New Haven pizza ever since I accidentally moved to France. They don't have white clam pizza like that on the French coast, did you know that?" His eyes are twinkling. He tilts back in his chair and grins at the two of us. "So good to be here where they know how to make a true pizza."

Louise says something about pregnancy cravings not including white clam *anything*, and he says she may need to adjust her craving meter. "Your mother certainly craved white clam pizza when she was pregnant with you! There was a stretch there when we had to have it three times a week. You may actually be *made* of it, come to think of it."

It's true, I tell her.

"Well . . . *yes*," says Louise. She gets up and puts her cup in the sink. "Dad here was just telling me about when you two met," she says.

Dad?

She has never called him Dad. After her last trip to France to see him, she called him Mr. Steidley for three whole months before she went back to calling him Victor.

"He says you were adorable. Wasn't that the word you used? Oh, and that you were a Pollyanna. I had to ask what that meant."

"How is it that this generation doesn't know Pollyanna?" Victor says to me. "I have half a mind to sit her down and make her watch the movie. So she can see what optimism looks like."

"Apparently I'm not optimistic *enough*," says Louise sarcastically. "I can't imagine why that would be."

"Doesn't matter why," says Victor. "We're going to work on it. No point in looking back, I say. Look to the future." He pretends to roll up the sleeves of his gray flannel shirt. "Operation Optimism is under way. Because if you're going to bring a baby into this topsy-turvy world, I say you need a hefty dose of optimism to see you through."

"Well," I say. "I wish you all the luck with that. I've got to go upstairs and make a call."

"To Mason?" says Louise, and it is then that I realize that in the short time she's been with her father, she's probably told him everything.

"Actually, it's not to Mason," I say. "An agent is interested in talking to me about a possible book."

"Really? A book about the Heartbreak Bunny?" says Louise.

"I think so."

"Huh. But don't you need a social media platform for that?" she says.

"Optimism, Louise," says Victor gently. "If an agent wants to talk to her, I think she might see the possibilities herself."

"No, no, of course," says Louise. "And actually, if you wrote Instagram posts or a blog about what you've learned about heartbreak through your clients, I could see where that would be good."

"Thank you," I say.

"You could maybe photograph some of the objects you collect . . ."

"Maybe."

"Or write about what you say to the people. How you jar them out of their agony."

At the mention of the word *agony*, Victor's eyes meet mine. That had been our shorthand after he told me about Juliette but before he left. He used to say it every day: "I'm in agony." It became a joke: this pillow is agony, warm on both sides; this baby is agony, won't go to sleep; this sink full of dishes—agony. This life—agony.

One day when he said, "I'm in agony," I threw a coffee cup across the room at him. One minute I was holding it, and then it was gone, flying toward his head. I had no memory of releasing it. I only remember screaming at him: "You and your fucking agony need to leave!"

And now, sitting here in the kitchen with the two of them I want to hate him, but I can't quite muster the feeling. I kind of like the way he's smiling at Louise, and how comfortable and fatherly he seems here.

270

And yes, I know, he is a master at this sort of thing—he can make you feel like you're the only person in the world, right up until the moment he disappears.

◌৯

They get ready to leave soon after, to go collect the rest of her stuff. Would I like to come?

"No," I say. "I'll fix us some dinner for later. Victor, are you staying for dinner?" I feel light-headed even saying that.

He bestows me the humblest of looks. "Well, sure, of course, if it's really all right. If you didn't have other plans . . ." He looks from me to Louise, and she nods enthusiastically.

She's beaming. How has he accomplished this so quickly?

"Mom, what I really want is to show him the house before that battle-ax mother-in-law of mine comes and changes the locks on me!" she says, slipping on her shoes. "Let him see what got ripped out from under me, through no fault of my own!" She says this in a cheerful, manufactured voice, the voice of a sarcastic, lively, and brilliantly comedic woman, making her way in life through obstacle after obstacle.

Well, fine.

He shrugs, jams his hands in his pockets, and rocks on his heels. His eyes are glinting. "I don't know if the goal here is to try to get the house back, or if we're saying good-bye to it, but I'm in for whatever."

"If you can think of a way to get the house back," she says, laughing, "I'd be all in for that! But mainly I just want to show it to you. Because it's a showplace. It's a little peek at my former life—former, meaning about four minutes ago."

She goes upstairs to get her stuff together, and he looks over at me.

"She's wonderful," he says, and his eyes have turned tender. He can change his eyes like that. "William, I've got to hand it to you. You've raised a delightful human, no help from me. And now I'll be your partner in helping her over this next hurdle."

He reaches over to touch my arm, but I move over to the sink, farther away from him, as though I need to pick up *that* mug at *that* very instant.

He gets busy looking at the wobbly leg on the kitchen table, gently shaking it a little. "I maybe could screw this back in for you," he says, straightening back up. "Maybe when I'm out, I'll get some wood putty unless you have some." He sees my face. "I mean, if you want."

"Sure," I say. "I've been putting paper napkins under it ever since Calvin left. It'd be good to have it fixed."

He looks around the kitchen, and I see his eye fall on a sheet pan sitting out on the counter. I'd baked cookies on it the other day. It's blackened and warped, used a million times for a million batches of cookies. He chuckles. "Now *this* is the way I like to see pans looking! Authentic. This whole place—it's so you. It feels very familiar and very awkward and very . . . humbling to be here."

"Great," I say. I won't look at him.

"Also, I just want to say that I'm not here to do any harm. Maybe I can fix this wobbly table and take her to collect some things at her old house and then get out of your way."

"Maybe she needs you," I hear myself say wearily. "She looks happy to be with you."

"I don't want to make you unhappy. Believe me. By the way, she told me you're seeing somebody, and that makes me feel a little bit odd about the whole speech I gave you on heartbreak the other night in Brooklyn. I should apologize for that."

"And now *what* exactly are you apologizing for?"

He shrugs.

"No, I would really like to know. Where is this apology coming from in you?"

"Oh, William, c'mon. You know what I'm apologizing for. I was an arrogant SOB, acting like I had been totally responsible for you having a terrible life and no love—and then it turns out that you're actually in love with somebody. Typical me stuff. Can't see beyond my own nose."

"Well," I say. "Apology accepted, but it's not quite as simple as I'm *in love* with someone. Because I'm not."

He tilts his head. "No?"

"Listen, we are not talking about this. If you want to help Louise, go right ahead. I'd love that. She's having a bit of a rough go at the moment, and anything you can do to help her is welcome. But so help me God, if you promise more to her than you can give, if you end up losing interest and disappearing again, if you break her heart, I swear I will hunt you down."

"Whoa," he says, and laughs. "I like seeing this passionate response from you. Now *this* is the Billie I remember and love."

"She's my baby," I practically growl. "I protect her."

"Well, she's my baby, too," he says. He stands up a little straighter. "And I may not have been here for her for way too many years, but all I can say is I'm here for her now. And, whether you know it or not, Billie, I'm here for you, too." He makes his eyes go all soft, as though he's onstage, playing to the back row. I practically expect him to drop to one knee and put his hand over his heart. "Whatever you may think of me, I never stopped loving you."

"Oh, for God's sake, Victor. Shut up. If this is what you think of as 'loving me,' please, by all means, do me a favor and don't love me anymore," I say. "Do what you want as far as helping Louise. She could use a father in her life just now. But I do *not* want you to think for one minute that you can waltz back in here and take up with me again."

He stands there, grinning at me. His eyes sparkle.

"I don't believe anyone spoke of taking up with you again, but I am so hoping that there will be talk of warts again," he says. "I'd be willing to get a new wart just to know you used your powers on me."

⌒

How to explain what happens over the course of the next few weeks?

I don't know precisely how it happens, but quite against my will, we turn into something resembling a family.

Maybe it's because nature abhors a vacuum, and we've definitely had a vacuum here since Calvin, Edwin, *and* Marisol have all left. Or maybe Louise and Victor are engineering some master plan. But whatever it is, suddenly I discover that I'm having family dinners again every single night—with the two of them. Victor remembers my osso buco, and so I grouchily make it again. He mentions my homemade strawberry ice cream and goes down into the basement to retrieve the ice cream maker. So I grudgingly make that, too. He used to make popcorn after supper, and he takes that up again. Good fiber for a pregnant woman, he says. I roll my eyes.

We stream TV shows. We play triple solitaire at the kitchen table, at Louise's request.

I try not to look directly at him, but one evening my eyes meet his, and he mouths the words, "I'm so happy."

He goes back to his hotel room each night—a little later every time—but I have a sinking feeling that soon one or the other of them will decide it's just more logical for him to stay upstairs in one of the empty rooms. After all, he's taking on chores around the house. He's putting together a jigsaw puzzle with Louise, and they work on it until quite late. They decide to do posts for her Instagram with the hashtag #fatherdaughterreunion.

He is paying attention to her, and I hate to say it, but she is flourishing.

Believe me, no one thinks this is a good idea.

"You're out of your mind to let this happen," says Kat.

"Do I have to move back there and guard your house against intruding exes?" says Calvin.

"No worries! No worries!" I tell them, laughing as I say it.

༄

But, in fact, two weeks after his arrival, Kat tells me that it seems I've disappeared inside a fantasy world and that she can barely track me anymore. I have to agree. The world has become somewhat muddled.

"But I know who he really is," I say to her. "I'm not falling for any of his tricks."

She just looks at me and shakes her head. "Thank God you have the bunny business to keep you remembering who you are and what you believe in," she says. "We've got some big items coming up—conferences and such. Those will bring you back down to earth."

Two weeks later, I wake up in the middle of the night, having had a bad dream. I lie there tossing and turning, and then I get up and go downstairs to make some warm milk. My head is filled with images of continents crashing and babies crying and a sudden, swift darkness befalling all of us.

And then Victor materializes. Of course he does, because this isn't really my house to roam about in anymore.

He's here.

"What are you doing still here?" I say.

"I was up talking to Louise, but she went to bed, and now I've just been sitting in the dark thinking how basically unequipped I was to be of any use as a human being," he says. "Back then."

"Well, yeah, you got that right."

"I would look at you being the mom and think that somehow you knew what you were doing. You knew how to fix things, how to make everything better. And I just didn't know how."

"Oh, that. I went to a special university," I say. "The University of How to Live a Life. I majored in Motherhood, with a minor in Fixing Things. You didn't know, but I got an A-plus in Fixing Dinner While a Child Screams After a Husband Has Walked Out."

"Sounds like a rough education," he says dryly. "I have a joint we can smoke if you want. Do you still do that stuff?"

"Not much anymore."

"Me neither, but tonight seems like a good time." He pulls out his wallet, and sure enough, there's a joint pressed into the section reserved for dollar bills. "Never thought this stuff would be legal, did you?"

"Nope."

He takes it out and admires it. Then he pulls out a pack of matches and strikes one and lights the end of it while he sucks in the smoke. "The day you told me you were pregnant, I had a panic attack. Did I ever tell you that? I was at the garage when you called to say the test was positive. You were so happy, just chattering away, and listening to you, I thought I was having a heart attack. Brandon had to take over the car I was working on, and hours later, after I could breathe again, I went and got stoned in the parking lot." He passes the joint to me.

"And then you came home late that night and acted like you were glad about the baby. Danced me around the kitchen. You kept laughing."

"I was high. And then, I went and wrote a poem about it, how it was new life, but it felt like the end of my life. And how lost I was."

"Shit, Victor. I don't remember that part." I take a big hit. "I would have—I don't know what I would have done."

"Yeah." He looks away. "So, listen . . . about that night. In Brooklyn. As usual, I was out of line. Not reading the room. I shouldn't have said the part about how I broke you . . ."

"Right, because I'm not broken."

"Even though—no offense, but you're dead wrong. About love." He laughs and ducks as I glare at him. "But now that I've seen more of you, I recognize that you're really still that same girl. You always had it together, except that now you've decided love is a hoax. Love is the realest thing there is, and if it weren't for romance, the whole planet would have to stop spinning." He takes another deep hit off the joint and holds it in. "But the truth is—and you might as well admit this— we went into parenthood long before we were ready . . ."

"I was ready."

"You—you have always struck me as someone who jumps right into things without ever worrying about what bad things could happen. Totally fearless and giving and impulsive." He takes another hit and presses the smoke into his lungs for a long time. Then he says, "Perhaps it's, um, indiscreet to mention, but could we talk for a minute about how hot we were for each other? Oh my God. I felt like whenever I touched you, it was like your clothing just disintegrated somehow."

He is correct. I had such a crush on him, and apparently my clothes felt the same way. Before him, I'd always had the upper hand with guys I went out with; I was the sought-after one. But Victor swept me away. Mostly it was his confidence, his saunter. I was the worst kind of dazzled, almost obsessed with him.

It was the epitome of a brain-rotting romance.

We dated for a very short time, and then at a friend's wedding he got carried away and asked me to marry him right there. He jumped onto the stage, grabbed the microphone from the DJ, and said he had an important announcement to make, and then he got down on one knee and asked me right there. It was seconds after the couple's first dance as Mr. and Mrs., so it was pretty much unpardonable, but so Victor. After I said yes he leapt off the stage, basking in the applause, and he twirled me out onto the dance floor. People clapped.

We had a thrown-together ceremony with both our moms in attendance and as many friends as we could jam into the American Legion Hall in Branford, where his father had been a member. We wrote our own vows, and we decorated with Tibetan flags (very much a cultural misappropriation, but we didn't know about that then). We drank spiked apple cider punch from a big punch bowl, and people brought food. A potluck wedding. I made my dress out of crepe de chine and sewed butterflies onto the hemline. I borrowed a veil from a friend whose marriage had ended in divorce. Later, the internet told me that was a bad idea. Never repurpose something from a broken marriage.

Louise came along ten months later. Victor remarked that it was like we lived in the 1950s or something, had never even heard of birth control. The reality was that the drugstore was closed.

But anyway.

He is looking at me. "Let's do each other a big favor and not talk about all that past stuff tonight, what do you say?"

"I've never been more happy with a decision," I say.

"Okay, let's just talk human to human, not like exes," he says. "It's the middle of the night. We can say whatever we want. Tell me about all the guys you married. I know of at least fourteen."

I laugh. I think I'm stoned. "Two besides you."

"And were these men not the paragons of husbandhood you were searching for?"

"If you want to know the truth, the first one was kind of great for a while. He looked nice in his swimming trunks, and he was nice to Louise in a fatherly kind of way. I thought that might be nice for both of us. But in the end, I realized you can't pick a marriage partner because you think he'll fit in nicely in your idea of family life. Turns out guys like to be wanted for themselves. Go figure."

He makes the sound of a buzzer, a buzzer that says you've lost the game. "Nope! Disqualified. Overuse of the word *nice*. That's a dead giveaway. Swimming trunks or not, you weren't into him."

I start laughing again. "Wait a minute. I think I was . . ."

"Nope. I know you. Not into him. Now how about Husband Number Three?"

"Well. Him. He came along about ten years ago. He was going to be the comfortable husband, the golden years guy, the travel husband—"

He's leaning back in the kitchen chair, and now he brings it down hard. "Good God, woman, you're not anywhere near your golden years!"

"I am, too. I am sixty years old, and I am definitely in the silver years, if not the gold."

"I think you're still in your ruby years. We'll take that up at a later time. What kind of disaster was he, then?"

"The kind that dies on the operating table."

He looks at me. "I hate that kind. Very unreliable of him! Like Juliette. People who can't stick the landing."

"Mean. No doubt they didn't want to die."

"Probably. I don't care. So, I'm getting the feeling that I was maybe the worst of the bunch."

"Oh, the worst by *far*."

"My record stands. I'd hate it if I came in second. I mean, leaving a woman and a baby has to count for something in this world."

"Especially when you leave for a French poet. Extra points for that."

"But cheating! That's what put me over the top. The other guys didn't cheat, did they?"

"Probably not. I didn't really care by then. I was done with all expectations of love."

"Well, and I already had an advantage, being the one who wouldn't clean up the spilled syrup in front of the refrigerator, which I notice is gone. Did you give in finally and do it after I left?"

"Louise did it. Louise, if you haven't noticed, is someone who disdains clutter and mess. Opposite of us. I would suspect she's not really ours due to a mix-up in the hospital, except that she looks exactly like you. So, I think I have to conclude that her disdain for clutter and chaos is a direct, conscious repudiation of my personality. Our personalities."

"As one does. Repudiation of the parents is required." He looks at me. "This is too many big words for this time of night." Then he says, "She adores you."

"We're close." I shrug. "She takes a lot of stuff out on me, of course. Mother-daughter stuff." Then I can't help myself. "In her telling of our story, I drove you away. I didn't fight for the marriage."

"I know. You were supposed to fly to Paris and break down my door."

"Apparently. Or at least register my dismay in a dramatic fashion."

"Hmm. I would have liked that. I might have come back. I was bored almost right from the beginning."

"You're always bored. It's your trademark."

He's looking at me in such a funny way.

We're both stoned. And you know what else? The first strains of light have appeared at the kitchen window. I need to go to sleep.

"So, you're doing magic now, I take it?" he says.

"Absolutely. I magic all over the place. Be very afraid."

"You know, Juliette was . . ." he begins.

I hold up my hand. "Don't. Do. Not. That woman was not a witch."

And he laughs so hard. It actually does my heart good, that kind of hysteria that can set in at 5:24 a.m. when you've stayed up all night and you're old and wrinkly and someone is standing there who remembers you from the past when you might have been firmer and glowier, but now you're just a tougher, stringier version of that past self, laughing with him as the gray light comes into the kitchen the same way it did on that morning so many years ago when he said he was leaving.

And now he is apparently not.

CHAPTER TWENTY-THREE

The month of June seems to fly by, and on the night of the solstice, I have a date with Mason. He and I are not calling it a date, but I'm smart enough to know that it is one. This is why it's okay: the first part of the date is simply us going to see Joey to try to talk some sense into him, maybe renew the magic spell. Mason says I should picture the three of us all chanting and dancing around his living room—but then—"*Then,*" he says, "we are going out to a non-romantic dinner, just the two of us. I need to sit at a table across from you and hear about what's going on in your life. I miss hearing about all your characters."

It's okay because it's just us catching up. We are transitioning our relationship to being good friends who know each other's stories.

"Okay," I say. "I'm in. Joey will be my first booster shot of a bunny call. And it's very auspicious that it's on the night of the solstice."

"It may open up a whole new avenue for you," says Mason. "Solstice magic."

He gets to my house at seven, and Louise yells to him to come in before I can stop her. I would have liked to slip out the front door and meet him in the street because Victor is there. He and Louise are trying to make homemade pizza—and much to my dismay, they drop the dough in the sink as they fling it in the air, and then crack up while Victor tries to shred the mozzarella. Things have gone off the rails. Also, Louise turned on the gas too long before the pilot lit, so the whole place smells like it's about to go up in flames, and I'm rushing around, looking for my scarf and my purse and my phone, and shouting instructions to them to open the windows, for heaven's sake, and to stop throwing dough around the kitchen.

"Five-second rule!" Louise yells, and I give her a fierce look. Who *is* this woman—who a month ago would have died before she would have eaten even a morsel that had touched an unsterilized countertop, let alone the floor?

And then Mason's standing there, with a quizzical expression on his face. I feel flustered suddenly, seeing him there.

Victor is fanning the oven with a magazine, and Louise is trying to unstick the window, which she cannot do, so Mason comes over and does that for her, which makes a horrendous sound like the whole window is going to crash onto the floor.

"Welcome to the crazy kitchen," says Victor, and I see Mason's feelings telegraphed across his forehead: *Billie's ex-husband. This is his kitchen. His daughter, his ex-wife, his window, his gas disaster.*

Mason is a lovely, non-jealous human, though, so that look quickly vanishes and is replaced by a disarming smile. "I hope I didn't break your window," he says and dusts off his hands. Sadly, there is a lot of dust in the window sash. There just is.

"Never mind, it's fine," I say. "Thank you for opening it. Now these two can live. And you and I can get out of here. Save ourselves."

Victor strides over to Mason, in a manly, friendly way, no doubt activating codes that only men know. Women can only guess how the antler comparisons are coming along or who's ahead. "Hi, I'm Victor Steidley, the world-famous worst ex and also Louise's dad," he says and holds out his hand.

"Mason Davis," comes the reply. They shake hands and do their masculine shuffle, sizing each other up.

This is so weird.

"Ah, yes. I've heard so much about you," says Victor, which I hope is not true. Although I have suspected—no, *I know*—that Louise has told him everything about my life that she can think of.

"We should go," I say.

"And I've heard so much about you, too," says Mason—to which Victor laughs, and says, "Uh-oh. That's never good. Exes usually don't come off too well, especially guys like me who stayed gone for over thirty-five years. I tell you what, though. I'll agree not to believe what she's said about you, if you agree not to believe what she's said about me." He does an imitation of a hearty laugh, which is very unnecessary. And he does a hip check on me, which is *absolutely* unnecessary. Maybe even a violation of some code.

"Oh, don't be ridiculous, Victor," I say. "Shall we go, Mason?"

"Wait," says Louise. "Dad and I were just talking about the decoupage on the cabinets. And these sheet pans of yours! They look like they're from World War I."

I shrug. "So? I like them that way."

"No, no," she says. "They're all burned and bent up. Tomorrow I'm going to my storage unit and getting my sparkling-clean sheet pans and bringing them here," she says, and kisses me on the cheek. "And as for this decoupage, look how tattered it's become. And stained. I think there's tomato sauce on this piece over here, and look—here's a little rip. Dad and I were thinking we'd steam this off and then repaint for you. How would that be?"

"No. Leave the cabinets alone, please," I say. I shift my purse to my other shoulder. I want to get out of here.

"Aw, but, Mom, I already bought some stuff to steam them," she says. "Come on, *please*! It will make the place look so much fresher."

I see something in her eyes. Her need to do a project, to be with her dad, to make this place her own. And I don't know what comes over me, but I acquiesce. Maybe someday I'll decoupage them again. They *are* tattered looking.

And it will do her good.

"It's out of the utmost love and respect," says Louise, and I haven't seen her smile so wide since she was ten years old and alphabetized the spice rack. "So . . . this is really okay with you, right?"

⌒⍥

We get in the car and Mason starts the engine and glides away from the curb. When we're a few blocks away from the house, he asks me how I'm doing *really*. He mentions how interesting it is to see the two of them together. Victor and Louise. His tone is measured, careful.

"They look alike," he says. "It's startling how much."

"I know," I say. "I don't want to talk about him, though, if you don't mind."

"Of course." We ride in silence for a minute, during which I'm trying to figure out if I have a magic spell for Joey. And then Mason says, "He looks so comfortable there, for lack of a better word."

"Oh, that he is."

"Spending a lot of time there, is he?"

"Mason."

"I know, I know. I'll stop."

"It's only that I don't know what's too much and what isn't. Look, this is for Louise. She needs him just now, for reasons I can only begin to try to understand—"

"No, of course she does. You don't have to explain to *me*. It's good that he showed up in her life when she's at such a . . . crossroads."

"Well, that's what I'm telling myself. And he does seem to be doing her some good."

"Well, that's wonderful, isn't it? Surprising."

"I guess," I say. "Who knows what tomorrow will bring, though."

"Sounds like it's bringing brand-new shiny sheet pans and cabinets that don't have pictures on them anymore," he says.

I look down at my hands. "Maybe it's a good thing. I don't know. I resist change, but sometimes it's all for the best."

He is silent, looking through the windshield.

"You know," he says after a while, "I'm your friend here. You don't ever have to pretend with me."

"Thank you," I say, and my throat is suddenly clogged with something trying to get out. What I'm thinking is that this is all too serious, and we need to have some fun. This is exactly what's wrong with love, and even though I'm not in love, here we are, being all serious anyway.

∾

"What I want to say is," says Joey, and he lets the sentence just trail off. I picture it wafting off into space, searching for the end. He's not quite in as awful a shape as he was the first day I met him, but he's not quite put together either. I study him while Mason hugs him and claps him on the back. Joey hugs back.

The apartment looks much cleaner. No beer tower. The coffee table doesn't have any old food on it. There's a thriving daisy plant by the window.

"I'm so glad to see you again," I say. "I wonder if I should have worn the Heartbreak Bunny suit for this, now that I think of it."

"Haha," he says. It's not a laugh; he literally says the syllables. His hands are jammed in the pockets of his jeans, and he looks nervous. He licks his lips. "Nah, good to see you—just a regular human person."

"Just a regular human person," I say.

"Maybe you'd like something to drink?" he says. "Carrot juice? Or how about a glass of wine, perhaps?" He looks tense. "I said carrot juice as a joke. You know. Because you're a bunny?"

Mason laughs. "I'll get the wine," he says, rubbing his hands together. "You and Billie get down to brass tacks. She and I have dinner plans. What are we hoping for here, son?"

Joey looks at me as Mason goes into the kitchenette. "I just—I just—well, I'm sort of back talking to Saucy again. And stuff is coming up."

"Sure," I say. "Like what, for instance?"

"She's sorry. She's unhappy with *the guy*. You know, her boss. He's turned out to be one of those people who, when he gets something he wants, he no longer wants it anymore. So, they're having a rough time, and she's turning to *me* to tell her what to do."

"Aaaand . . . what do you feel like when she calls you and asks you to do that?"

"I guess I feel . . . protective of her. I don't think she meant to leave me."

"Wait. You think she *got married* without meaning to?"

He looks down and says very quietly, "Ummm, my dad doesn't know that part. And I only meant she didn't mean to hurt me. She still needs me."

"What part don't I know?" says Mason pleasantly, coming back into the living room. He hands me a glass of red wine and gives one to Joey as well. Then he sits down on the couch, next to me, facing Joey in the armchair. "Well?"

Joey shrugs. "It's embarrassing, this part."

"I think I can hear something embarrassing and still go on loving you."

A whole bunch of expressions have a fight on Joey's face. Finally, he says, "Saucy got married."

286

"Uh-huh. I see." Mason's face changes only slightly. His smile stays steady. "So, she married the guy she left you for?"

"Yeah."

"Well, that's not so embarrassing. Why is that a thing? She was free to do that, wasn't she? I mean, *you* didn't marry her."

We're silent. I sip my wine and keep looking at Joey. I've lost all sensation in my fingertips, just watching the expressions scudding across his face, like dark clouds in the sky.

He clears his throat. "She, um, married him in the wedding ceremony we were supposed to have, Dad. The same one I paid for. Doves and everything."

"*What?*"

"Yeah."

Mason looks at me. "And you knew about this?"

I nod.

"Well," says Mason. He looks almost perturbed, but then he just shakes his head and smiles at me. I feel a little whoosh of relief that I don't have to explain how things I learn on the bunny calls are confidential. I don't betray confidences.

"And," says Joey.

"And? There's an *and?*" Mason says.

Joey nods. "Well, then they went on the honeymoon trip I'd paid for."

Mason leans forward with his hands between his knees. I can hear him breathing. "So let me get this straight. You paid for a wedding *and* a honeymoon, neither of which you were invited along on."

"Yeah, basically."

"Did you get billed for their drinks and dinners as well? Did you have to pay for the tips they left for the waiters?"

"Dad. It was all-inclusive."

"I was only kidding about the drinks and dinners part." He looks down at his shoe, pretending to be scraping something off the toe.

When he looks up, he says, "Come here, you big lug, and let me give you a hug. I'm beginning to understand what's going on with you. That's what all this has been about—you feeling ashamed because you got taken in by a woman who used you and humiliated you."

"Well, yeah." Joey doesn't move; he just stares at the floor, so Mason goes over to him and envelops him in a hug. I feel a lump rising in my throat, watching them.

When they pull away, Mason says, "And so now she wants *you* to rescue her from her own bad decisions. Believe me, you're not the first guy to get taken in by some confused young woman. Just don't let her take advantage of you again."

"She says she still loves me," he says. "She says she made a big mistake. Everybody makes mistakes. And now she wants to fix it."

Mason and I look at each other.

I reach over and take Joey's hands. "I see a woman who got herself in a bad situation and now is flailing about trying to get out of it and make *herself* feel better. She's scared. Did you ever hear how a person who's drowning thrashes around so much that they scratch and push under the person trying to save them? They can't help it; it's a reflex, to grasp on to something and save themselves. And Saucy can't help it either. But she can't solve the problem inside herself by using you. It won't work."

Joey looks down at his hands. "I know that," he says. "I just—it feels good to have her feeling sorry. I guess that's pretty terrible, isn't it?"

Mason laughs. "It's not terrible. It's human. It's the way we feel when we've been wronged. But it's not the same thing as loving someone. You don't love her anymore, and that's good."

I look at Joey. "Are you ready to let this go?" I say. "Because if you're not, there's no point in us working on it."

"Let's get her out of here," he says quietly.

"You have to be sure. If you need to hear a couple hundred more sorries from her, then maybe this isn't the time yet."

"Ironically, there's actually someone else in my life now," he says slowly. "Somebody who's a bit more normal, I think. It's funny. I met her soon after we did the spell. At work. She seems interested in me. She asked me out."

"The Law of Relinquishment!" I say. "It's one of the best laws. Once you give up, you find what you were looking for."

He smiles. "Yeah. I think there's potential for something good to happen, but I can't put Saucy out of my mind. And I ended up turning down Alicia because I went to see Saucy that night instead." He leans back in the chair and runs his hands through his hair. "What an idiot I am!"

"Okay then, so you're really ready?"

"I'm ready. Yes."

Mason rubs his hands together. "At last. I get to see the magic firsthand."

I close my eyes and feel the familiar surge of energy coursing through me. It must have been what my grandmother experienced when she trotted around town, casting her spells wherever she wanted to. It's a delicious feeling.

"Let's all hold hands," I say. "And close your eyes, both of you."

The words come, as before, spinning through the air, catching me by surprise, arriving, each one following the other as I reach for them. I am grateful for them, and grateful that these two men are solemn.

We hold hands, we say the words, and maybe it's ridiculous, but when I close my eyes and concentrate, I can feel the ribbon that connects Saucy to Joey start to fray, and then break and drift quietly away, off into the ether somewhere.

∞

I'm exhausted afterward.

Mason is chattering away in the car, smiling so big, thanking me again and again for agreeing to come. His hand, with its nicely trimmed nails, keeps leaving the steering wheel and coming over to touch my arm. He says it's all going to be fine. He says, "I was a little bit surprised to hear that he'd been taken for a ride *financially* like that. I had no idea the extent to which—well. That's just a lesson we have to learn sometimes." He shakes his head, a fond shake of the head, as though he'd found out his son ate all the cookies in the cookie jar. There's a way in which he's just a happy man, deep down and through and through. He doesn't get thrown. He forgives.

"But I think—I mean, I *know*—that he's now over it. I could see the difference in him after tonight. I hope."

"Well, good," I say. Mason is trying too hard.

We stop at a red light. Yale students walk in clusters, backpacks hanging off their shoulders like they just came from class. The streets are busy; there's no place to park.

He says, "Louise certainly looks like she's coming along nicely. Settling in, is she?"

"She's fine, I guess," I say.

Then I feel bad when he looks over at me quickly, sensing that my mood has shifted. He skillfully executes a left turn. We pass a row of stores, all lit up. At the stoplight, I watch a man and woman walking together, obviously having a fight.

"Where shall we go for dinner?" he says. "You have any hankerings for anything in particular?"

"No," I say.

"Is everything all right? Have I upset you?"

"No, no. You're fine. I just—I think I need to be at home. I'm feeling . . . I don't know what I'm feeling. I think I might need some alone time."

I can feel him making fourteen mental adjustments. But he says, smooth as chocolate, "Of course. You've been doing so much bunny work. And then with Louise. And your ex. And now I ask you to work on Joey."

"No, it's not Joey," I say, although it might be. "I just—I'm sorry, but I have to go home. Take a hot bath. Watch a baking show on Netflix in my bed and go to sleep."

"Okay," he says. "I get it. I really do."

We drive a few more blocks. I lean my head against the window.

But then it hits me that at home, Louise and Victor will be dismantling my kitchen. Scraping. And oh, they will be laughing. *Crazy, weird Mom! Dresses up like a bunny, keeps a house that is so disorganized, collects people like other people collect antiques—and now we can step in and intervene. Bring some sanity to the place.*

"Mason," I say.

He looks over.

"You know what would make me happy?"

"What?"

"If we went to the grocery store and got the ingredients to make crab cakes. With rémoulade sauce. And then we went to your house and cooked and turned up the music and had fun!"

I watch his face. Lights from the traffic sweep across his features. His mouth is grim.

"Well, sure. We *could* go there."

"But . . . ?"

"Well, it's a funny thing, that house."

"Is it?"

"Not all that funny, actually. When Tish died . . ." And then he stops talking. We go two more blocks. He's working his mouth around.

"Never mind," I say. "I don't want to force you."

"It's just that—I didn't change anything. I pretty much only go there to eat and get dressed in the morning. It's not really a *home* home."

"That's okay."

"It's one of those McMansions, as they call them. And now really lifeless. You'll hate it. It's the opposite . . . the opposite of what you . . . have. What you love."

291

"Okay."

"A wasteland. A shrine."

"Do you want it to be that way? A shrine?"

"No," he says. "No! I just don't spend any time there, so every day it stays a shrine." He barks out a laugh. "She would hate that. She told me if I hadn't found somebody new in two years, she was going to come back and haunt me."

"What if we just go in there and say hi to Tish and then do some cooking? Maybe she'd be so impressed that you have someone with you that she'd help out." Then I feel myself back up. "I didn't mean that like it sounded. I'm not a *somebody* in the sense that she probably meant, but it's something."

He hesitates so long that I think I'm going to have to go home to Victor and Louise after all. But then he clears his throat and says, "I just consulted with Tish in that place where she lives in my head, and she says it's a great idea."

I stare at him. "Did she now?"

"You're not the only one, you know, who dallies a little bit in the unseen world." His voice sounds a little bit ragged all of a sudden. "That's why, that first day, when I saw what you were doing with Joey—that spell, those chants—I wanted to know more. I wondered if you knew how to say good-bye to . . . well . . ."

"We'll see, won't we?"

∾

We pretty much have to buy every single ingredient at the grocery store because he says all he has at his house is instant coffee, some fake dairy substitute, a few overripe bananas, and some beer. Going through the aisles, he's like somebody who's never been in a grocery store before—exclaiming over all the choices! The colors! The different foods!

"She and I used to do this every week," he says softly. "Over seven years ago now. We bought groceries, and then we came home and cooked things."

"Amazing, isn't it?" I say. "It's like magic. So what have you been doing for food since then?"

"Takeout. And bagged dinners you can find in the frozen food department. We had those so often that Joey would just call them 'froze bag.' We lived on froze bag."

I laugh. I am very matter-of-factly pushing the cart. I know exactly where we're going and what we need. We get canned crabmeat and panko bread crumbs. I check with him, and it's true: he doesn't have Dijon mustard or mayonnaise or hot sauce or Worcestershire sauce. Or eggs.

We leave with three bags of groceries—in addition to our ingredients, he also gets a carton of milk and a loaf of whole-wheat bread and some butter. Some apples and oranges. A box of oatmeal. Maybe he'll make some toast and oatmeal sometime, he says to me proudly as we get in the car. Who knows what's possible?

"The sky's the limit," I say.

᎙

He lives in a modern, four-bedroom colonial with a center staircase, in a subdivision filled with lots of similar models, all tucked away on quiet cul-de-sacs. It's a land of houses with decks in the back and darkened windows in the front. All the life takes place at the back of these houses, in the dens and kitchens and backyards that don't show from the road.

His house is gray with a wall of rhododendrons just past their blooming season, and a circular driveway. The sensor lights come on as we pull up, and when he presses a button the garage door slides open, barely making a rumble.

Inside, the air feels cold and damp, a little unwelcoming actually. The kitchen is huge, with speckled faux-marble countertops and a center island with its own sink and a pair of barstools. A sideboard holds a soup tureen and some candles, never burned. Everything is tidy and sterile.

"As I said, I don't cook," he says when he sees me noticing. "And also, I have housecleaners who come in once a week to keep the place from being coated in dust." He smiles weakly. "I feel like I should apologize. I imagine that to you this feels a little soul-sucking."

"Not at all," I say. "We can warm this place right up. Cooking, music, conversation." On the wall hang a few wrought-iron decorations—one says KISS THE COOK. And there's a calendar from last March tacked above a small desk.

We turn on all the lights, and I ask if we can play some music while we cook. The stereo is in the living room, a vast and neglected space stretching between a brick gas fireplace and two overstuffed sea-blue couches and a home entertainment center. It's all sweetly old-fashioned, the maple end tables and coffee table, the needlepoint pictures hanging on the walls. A family portrait over the fireplace, of the three of them—Tish in the center, with dark curls and a slight smile on her face.

"I'd like to hear 'Season of the Witch,'" I say. "On repeat, if you can. And then let's go back in the kitchen and talk to Tish."

Is this crazy? I don't know.

I sort of sway and sing along to Donovan crooning about the witch. And we set to work. I narrate what we're doing as I hand him the egg and a red mixing bowl I discovered in the cabinet. He looks so baffled and yet dutiful, beating the egg with a whisk.

"Did she love to cook?" I want to know.

"Oh, yes. Yes, she did. But she was the type who shooed everyone out of the kitchen and furrowed her brow and went about it like it was her day job and she couldn't let the boss see her slacking off." He smiles, and the look of pain that crosses his features isn't lost on me.

When I excuse myself to go to the bathroom, I look at the pictures of her hanging in the hallway—first holding a baby and then swinging a toddler at the park, and then dressed up in winter clothes for a ski trip. At the end of the hall are photos of Joey as a little kid, then as a handsome teenager, and photos of Mason and Tish standing next to him at his middle school graduation.

When I come back to the kitchen, Mason is holding a snapshot of her with a scarf wrapped around her head—and she's smiling, but there's something haunting her eyes, something that isn't there in the others.

"Ovarian cancer," he says. "Six months."

"I'm so sorry," I say.

He begins talking, in a monotone. Joey was sixteen at the time, and after Tish died, he stayed mostly in his room. Sometimes Mason could lure him out to do a puzzle or to go to a movie. Joey liked *Minecraft*, and Mason tried to learn what the hell it was all about, he says. But sitting in front of a screen moving around little pieces of light and sound—well, it got to him. It made his neck hurt. At the suggestion of Joey's therapist, they adopted a dog, a mutt named Janice, and took her to the park to throw sticks for her. But she was a listless dog who never seemed to want to be in the same room with them, much less chase any sticks they threw.

"She could see we weren't the real deal," he says. "Can you imagine having too much grief for even a dog to deal with? So, after a while, she sort of moved next door to the neighbor's house, and when the neighbors asked if they could keep her, it was kind of a relief."

Mason said whole weeks went by—months even—when he couldn't remember smiling a genuine smile. At his job, in front of the camera, he plastered on a smile that looked like rigor mortis.

"I know those kinds of days," I tell him. I put mayonnaise in a different bowl and stir in the Dijon mustard. I give Mason the can of crabmeat to open.

"Then one day," he says, "about a year after she died, Joey comes into the kitchen, and he's written a song for his mom. He called it 'An Unfinished Mom.' And it was about how we all live under a ticking clock, and we are all unfinished songs . . . and we have no choice but to honor love by sewing up each other's wounds." He stops talking. "So. That night, we just sat on the floor and cried. I never hated anything in my life more than letting that boy see me melting down like that. But the therapist said it was a very good step, because supposedly after that we knew we were both in it together and could depend on each other." He laughs. "Apparently crying is supposed to be wonderful for us."

"So they say," I tell him.

"But now . . ." he says, "now I look at him, and he's so devastated by love, picking a woman who can't love him . . . and I don't know. It's my fault, isn't it, because I didn't know how to help him when his mom died. I couldn't talk about his mom to give him an example of what love is. I didn't help him become a man. I still don't know how to help him, and then . . . and then you showed up that day . . . and I thought—well, maybe this bunny witch with her spells can figure it all out. But you can't fix it either, can you? Because it's me. It's all my fault."

"Sssh. Nothing is your fault," I whisper. "Maybe not having bread and fruit and oatmeal in the house was your fault, but you took care of that. No guilt, you hear me? Wasted emotion!"

To my surprise, he smiles. It's a weak smile, but still. And then his eyes well up. I know he wishes he could stop himself. He turns away and leans against the counter with his hands over his eyes.

I go over and take his arm. Then I lead him past the family portraits on the wall, past an overflowing laundry basket, past a stack of towels all folded and ready to be put away by the housecleaners. I know where the master bedroom is in these massive houses, in the back overlooking the deck. His is a suite, and it's got a huge king-size bed with a pink flowered cover and pillow shams, and I'm touched to see that the bed isn't made, and the shades are still up from this morning. I catch a glimpse of perfume bottles on the oak dresser and some earrings in a dish on the bedside table. I know if I opened the closet, I would see her clothes, her shoes. Even after all these years, it's possible that her scent would rise up and envelop us.

I slowly undress him. He closes his eyes while I help him step out of his slacks and unbutton his shirt. And then I guide him over to the bed and gently get him to lie down, and I take off my clothes, too, and lie down next to him, facing him in the darkness. There is only the thin silvery beam from the outside lights. I look deep into his eyes, and I keep my arms around him tight, like I could hold him together somehow, keep him from flying apart.

I stay the night, watching him as he sleeps like I'm standing guard or something. We never did make the crab cakes, so at 3:00 a.m., which is the time he has to get up in order to get to the station for the early show, I get up with him, and while he showers, I put all the ingredients away in that cold, empty kitchen, and I make us some toast and coffee before he goes to work.

And then I call an Uber to take me home. I quietly let myself into my own house and crawl into my own bed.

As I'm pulling up my grandmother's quilt, it hits me what a huge mistake I have just made. I did the thing that was more intimate than making love. It was more intimate than anything, that holding. That being there.

Maybe I shouldn't have looked into his eyes. But I can't think about that now. I'll fix it all later.

CHAPTER
TWENTY-FOUR

"Leo is flying back from South Africa tomorrow," says Louise at breakfast later that morning. She picks the raisins out of a bowl of oatmeal that I made for her before I sat down with my coffee and the crossword puzzle. The television set is on—Mason's show—and I have to say, it's weird to have Mason Davis stepping right into the kitchen, talking brightly about five inventive ways to make a Welcome to Summer cake, after I have just been with him at his house. I can't look at him. It feels like he's talking just to me, a continuation of this morning's conversation. I wouldn't be surprised if he started talking about crab cakes. If he said my name.

"How many inventive ways can there be to make a *cake*?" says Louise.

"Five, apparently," I tell her.

I can feel her eyes on me. "That must have been weird for you last night."

This startles me. She surely isn't referring to the fact that I came home after three in the morning, which, just by the way, is none of her business. Or anyone's business. But if she doesn't mean that, then what in the world *could* she possibly be talking about? "Why should anything have been weird?" I say carefully.

"Oh, you know. Your two men. Just having both of them together in the same room made me so god-awful anxious, so I can't even imagine what it must have felt like to you—and it was funny really, watching them being all manly and flirty and possessive. It was quite a display of masculinity, I thought. I was sure somebody was going to suggest an arm-wrestling contest." She laughs; I don't.

Change of subject. "Why is Leo flying back home?" I say.

"Because . . . ta dum . . . I told him I was pregnant." She looks slyly triumphant. "I called him last night. After we took off the decoupage, which you didn't even notice. Dad and I rehearsed what I would say, and then I called him, and I just said it. 'Leo, I am going to have a baby, and we need to discuss the terms of the thing.'"

"'The terms of the thing'? What does that even mean?"

"Dad thought that was a good way to put it," she says. "That way, he said, it could be either just the financial obligations, or it could be the terms of whether we get back together or not."

"Get back together? That's even a possibility?"

"Well, Dad says I should keep in mind that nobody ever *really* knows what's going to happen. I mean, look how surprising it turned out to be that *he* came back! That's what he said. We can decide all that later."

I put down my pen. My head hurts a little bit. "Huh. Well," I say, "it's good you told Leo about the baby, whether it ends up that you get back together or not. How did he react to the news?"

"Well, obviously he sounded shocked. I mean, we *all* were shocked. Then he wanted to know if I was sure, and if I'd been to the doctor. And I said that of course I was sure. You can't mistake something like this. And then he said he's coming to see me." She smiles. "Dad says that guys have all kinds of reactions to the news that a baby's coming, and that Leo had every right to know about it so he can see if it changes anything for him. Also, the blog stuff. That changes things."

"The blog stuff?" I say.

"Oh! I didn't tell you. Well, in the last couple of days, I've decided to end it. The other night Dad and I were talking, and he made the most interesting point."

"Do tell," I say. I feel slightly light-headed.

"Well, he just said that I've made so much money from the blog already, and now that interest in it seems to be subsiding, he thought that maybe I could stop striving so hard to re-create what I had. If @ LuluAlone isn't hitting it as big as I want, he said, why not just let the whole thing go? Why keep beating my head against the wall?"

"Really," I say.

"This was funny. You know, we did a few of those father-daughter reuniting posts, and he was hilarious about it! He'd pose with me and we'd act out little scenes for fun, and then one day when we were finished taking pictures, he said to me, 'Is there any purpose on God's green earth for what we just spent three hours of our precious lives doing? What's the *point* of all this?' Isn't that so funny?"

"Very amusing," I say.

"Oh, stop!" she says, laughing. "You know it's hilarious. I had to explain to him how people love to see other people dressed up and looking like they're having fun, and he bugged his eyes out at me and he said, 'So the hell what? Who cares what people think about us and our fun?'"

"Did he now?" I say. "I believe I may have said something to that effect about five hundred million times."

She laughs again.

"Maybe I should have said it in a deep voice. Was that what was missing?"

"Oh, Mama. I don't know. I'm down to so few followers now, and I've been a wreck about the whole thing, and then when he said, 'Why not quit?' it just hit me. I might as well quit."

"Oh, Louise. You can think of a million ways to make me go crazy, can't you?"

She gets up and comes around the table and massages my neck. "Mom, I know. You've been saying all these things. But it's good what he's doing. He's making reparations. He's doing the right things. He's showing me that he can stand by me right now when I need him the most. And look at it this way: maybe I need this adult relationship with him more than I needed him around when I was seven, did you ever think of that? He's helping me see things from a different perspective." She leans down and kisses me on the cheek. "I want you to be happy that he's here, and that he's on my side. And, Mamacita, he's on your side, too. He says the nicest things about you. You know what he said? He told me he really likes this life you're making. He told me you're a really strong woman. The strongest, he said."

Oh, give me a break.

She brushes a piece of my hair away from my face. "Please. You don't have anything to worry about. I don't ever want to hurt your feelings or anything, but it's kind of an exceptionally lovely time, the best ever, living in the house with both my parents again. Who would have thought? I feel so much calmer . . ."

I hear a noise upstairs, and I look at her. "Is he—? Is this something else that's happening that I didn't know about?"

She giggles. "Oh, yes! It is! I said he could stay here for a while. Why should he spend the money on a hotel when he stays late here every night, and he's helping me so much? He's staying in your mom's old room. It's just temporary. You know that."

"It might have been nice if you checked with me first." I stand up. I have to get to Kat's house for a business meeting. Also, I need to get out of here before the top of my head flies off.

"Oh, Mama, you love having people here," she says. "And he's so easygoing. Please let this be okay for now."

Victor shows up just then at the door of the kitchen, wearing sweatpants and a T-shirt. He is charmingly in disarray, his hair all tousled from sleep, his face creased. "Good morning, ladies." He pretends to stagger over to the counter. "I'm in desperate need of a java substance, preferably the kind that has massive amounts of caffeine." Then he points at Mason on the TV screen. "Ah, it's our favorite TV man! Gotta tell you, Billie, I've been watching his show from my hotel room the past few mornings, and he really knows his way around a conversation. That guy can talk to anybody about anything." He pours himself a cup of coffee and then gives me a thumbs-up. "You two are good together, you know that? He's very nice."

"Thanks," I say. "I'll leave you two to it. I've got a meeting to get to."

"Sure," says Victor. "I think Louise and I are going in for an ultrasound today, did I get that right?"

"Yes! We get to see the baby today!" says Louise. "We'll bring you a photo, Mama."

"And don't forget to tell her about our plan," says Victor, his eyes twinkling at me.

I look from one of them to the other.

"Oh, yes!" Louise says. "We've invited Leo over for a family dinner next week. Dad here is going to talk to him about fatherhood."

Victor laughs, seeing my face. "Yeah, that's right. Because who on earth is better qualified than a man who's been acting like a father for, what? Almost two months now? I'm clearly the expert on how to do it right."

"So you've got to be here!" says Louise to me. "It's going to be quite an experience."

"Absolutely," I say faintly. "I wouldn't miss it."

When I'm getting ready to leave the house a few minutes later, they're talking about how he's going to get to drive her Tesla. He was always a car fiend, and now he's in love with her car. Also, she reminds him, they're going to stop at the hardware store and get shelf paper for my kitchen cabinets. Shelf paper!

"I'll bet you've never had shelf paper in your life," says Louise. And I have to admit that I haven't.

"It's going to be life changing," she says. "It brings beauty and personality to your kitchen cabinets. It will make you smile whenever you open the door to get out a bowl or a plate. You'll see."

"Does it bring about world peace?" I say.

"Possibly," she says. "But in this case, what I can promise is that it brings family togetherness. We'll work on it together."

∽

Kat's house is like a little piece of Florida that broke off and drifted up the coast to Connecticut and attached itself to an otherwise typical colonial in New Haven. Where other people up here grow rhododendrons and hydrangeas, she has tropical plants—plumeria, palm trees, hibiscus, and bougainvillea vines—in pots everywhere on her patio, which she calls the "lanai." Tiki torches sit on her deck.

Inside, the walls are covered with palm tree wallpaper. And here I find her, sitting at a new white wicker dining room table with a map of Florida underneath the glass top. She's got a deep tan, and she's wearing a coral T-shirt with a foil pelican and the words FLORIDA IS CALLING—I MUST GO on it.

"So, judging by the sheer number of Florida promotional items you've added, I'm assuming that Bob hasn't agreed to move down there yet, huh?" I say.

"Nope."

"Soon there won't be any need to keep lobbying. This place is already total Florida. I wouldn't be surprised if some sheriffs don't show up at the door demanding this part of the state be returned immediately."

"Yeah, well, they can arrest me and take me back with them," she says.

She gets up and fixes us a couple of Cokes (very Florida, she says, drinking Cokes in the morning) and then we get down to business. Which is booming. She has Snap Out of It papers spread all around her. So many requests, so many choices to make! I've agreed to do the keynote speech for a women's conference in LA next month, and while I'm there, I've been asked to do two morning news shows. And three women's clubs in the San Fernando Valley want me to come and speak, as well as a Meetup group in Encino that talks about relationships. As long as I'm in the LA area, a literary agent wants me to come to her Malibu Canyon home to talk about doing a book on the bunny philosophy. Or perhaps about the items people hold on to. Or maybe about romance and feminism. Damned if I know, but I'm willing to go.

Kat sits back in her chair and rubs her eyes. "Are you up for all this? I mean, it's *a lot*. And the list just keeps growing and growing."

I say yes to everything. All of it. "Bring it on! The more bunny stuff, the better. I'm ready to get out of here."

She looks at me closely. "Yeah, so, what's up with you? No offense, but you do seem a little . . . unhinged."

"I'm perfectly hinged."

"Don't forget I know you. What's going on?"

"Well," I say. I look down at my hands. "It's nothing, really."

She gives me one of her looks. "I beg to disagree. It's something and you know it."

"IsleptwithMasonagain," I whisper.

"Excuse me? Did you say you slept with Mason again?"

"AndVictorislivingatmyhouse."

Her eyes grow wide.

"Victor. Your ex."

"Yes."

"Is living at your house."

"That is correct."

"Please tell me you're not sleeping with *him*, too."

"No. I'm not."

"But I'm guessing he wants to."

"He will want to."

"Oh God, Billie. So, it's basically raining men? If this isn't the Law of Relinquishment at its finest, I don't know what is. You give up men; you even get famous for your stance on how terrible men and women are together—and now you've got men everywhere." She claps her hands. "This is monstrously fun! So, just to recap: the Heartbreak Bunnies are basically two old women—one of whom is dangling two men and one of whom is married?"

"It's not really raining men," I say. "I'm breaking it off with Mason before it gets any more serious. He seems to have gotten it in his head that amazing things are just around the corner for us."

"He didn't read the fine print and realize that you don't believe in love?"

"He knew, but I think he might have forgotten."

"Huh! And was that because *you* forgot?" she says teasingly.

"I don't know. It was all going fine. We've had some nice evenings together, and one thing led to another, as it does, and so we slept together—just two times, but it was very clear that it was *not* romantic. We both knew it. And then . . . well, I even hate to tell you this next part."

"Oh, but I insist," she says.

So I tell her about the crab cakes night, how his house seems like a shrine to his late wife, and that if I were acting as the Heartbreak Bunny over there, I'd have to rent a truck to haul off all the items that he's clearly hanging on to.

By the time I get to the part about him breaking down, and how it only made sense as a human being to take him upstairs and hold him—well, she is staring at me.

"You know, it may be time to revisit the idea that you don't believe in love. I know you. You're in love with him."

"No! I can't be in love with him, Kat. I mean, I just won't. It would be a disaster. For all my usual reasons—but in addition, *he's* still hung up on his dead wife—and, now, quite against my better judgment, Victor is . . . kind of a factor, too."

"Oh my God, Billie!" she says. "Do you hear yourself?"

"Well, he's settling into the house like he's been there all his life, and I'm in this state of . . . I don't even know how I feel about him being there. Sometimes I want to scream at him for the way he hurt me back then, but mostly he's just so different now, and he's pitching in and making me laugh and helping Louise. And he's . . . well, he's charming. Easygoing. Funny."

"No, Billie. No!"

"No, hear me out. Louise loves having him around. She's changed since he arrived. She's even given up the blog and she's embracing her impending motherhood. I don't know what to tell you. It's good. They've become Elvis and Lisa Marie. Nat King Cole and Natalie."

"Wait. She's given up the blog? The most holy, all-encompassing thing in her life? She gave that up?"

"She has."

"After all that convincing you tried and failed to do?"

"Yep. For months, I do everything I can to persuade her, only to get myself yelled at. Months! And then, enter stage left Mr. Victor Steidley, with his twinkling eyes and his fatherliness that seems to have bloomed in him from out of nowhere—and he tells her, 'This Instagram stuff is all rubbish. This is fake. Why do you want to waste your life taking pictures of evening gowns and appliances for people who don't have anything else to do but envy you? This is no life!'"

"This Victor is a wise man," she says dryly. "Maybe we should take him on staff." Then she looks at me, and her face grows serious. "But,

Billie, this isn't real, right? He won't stick around; it's not in him. We both know that. People don't change overnight. And then what?"

"I don't know, really," I say. "I don't know how to feel about any of it."

She puts her glass of Coke down on the table—a little loudly if you ask me. "Oh, for God's sake, Billie. Come back to your senses. I've never seen you like this. You *always* know your feelings. Why is this tripping you up?"

I think about it. Why *am* I so confused? "Because—because, here's the thing: besides the fact that he's helping Louise so much, there's also the way he makes me feel. I mean, he's the only person I have in my life who knew me when I was that young." I can feel my voice getting choked up. "He remembers a me that doesn't really exist anymore. He tells me that he can see through this bunny, no-romance stuff. He says he remembers when I believed in love and was optimistic. I don't know why that touches me, but it does. Maybe he's right that I'm harder and more cynical now. You know?"

"Hold on," she says. "You're not hard and cynical. You do this work because you're helping people move on. You're telling them you believe they can move on because *you* moved on. It's your belief in that that's at the center of who you are. And that's the opposite of cynical."

"Is it? Because obviously I've been sleeping with one man and hanging out with another. That doesn't seem quite in line with the bunny philosophy as we outlined it on our night of drunkenness."

"Billie. The bunny was never against sex. Or fun. She was against wallowing."

"Okay. Yes. That's right. And I've already decided to stop sleeping with Mason. I can't do this to him."

"You've done nothing wrong. You can maybe enjoy both of these men for what they can give you at the moment. How about that? Victor reminds you of your lost youth, and Mason is the one who knows you and respects you for who you are now. So, just go with that—and keep in mind that you do not need to tell yourself a whole story about love and romance. Right? Isn't that what the bunny believes?"

"Thank you. I might have to come back and get reminders of that every now and then."

"You got it."

When I'm ready to leave, she walks me to the door and takes me by the shoulders. Looking into my eyes, she says, "No ruminating. No second-guessing. Have fun. Live. Life is a freaking gift, remember?"

I've put my key in the ignition when she runs out to my car and says, "However, I would just like to say that if you end up telling me that you're going back to Victor Steidley, I'm dissolving the Snap Out of It business and also never speaking to you again. I can't have wasted thirty years of my life talking about the villain of your life, only to then hear that you've decided he's a superhero."

"Fair enough," I say.

"Because he's *not*."

CHAPTER
TWENTY-FIVE

A week later, Mason calls and asks if I'd like to come and make crab cakes at his house for dinner.

"Listen," I say.

"This time we'll really *make* the crab cakes," he tells me. He clears his throat in such a way that I know how much this call is costing him. "I won't fall apart on you, which by the way, I'm sorry for."

"No, no. It was fine," I say. "But unfortunately, I can't come tonight. Leo is coming for dinner. And we're going to talk to him as a family."

There's a beat of silence, and then he says, "You and Victor and Louise? That family?"

"It's important that I be there."

"No, no. Of course it is." His voice sounds far away.

"I know it seems weird. It's something that Louise should probably be handling on her own, but she's not. She wants Victor and me to help her talk to him, to help figure out what the future should hold with regard to this *child* they're having. It's crazy."

"I understand," he says. He clears his throat again, and after a few awkward seconds, he says something to end the call, the male equivalent of *I've got a pot boiling over on the stove.*

"Okay," I say. "Well, I'll let you go."

"Good-bye, Billie," he says.

As soon as I press the off button, it's like a cold wind goes blowing through me. I almost have to go sit down.

⟋◦⟍

I hate to say it, but we are kind of wonderful that night. Victor and me.

Without even planning to, I realize we're presenting such an interesting story: the doting parents, now seemingly reunited (even though we're not), reaching across time to encourage a faltering marriage that, according to our optimistic outlook, could so easily be glued back together. If you saw us, you'd think we were some kind of spiritual warriors of love, having survived the worst of the worst, and come back from it.

Look at us, and you will see that people can make it work. Love conquers all. Life goes on. Babies heal everything. Don't make the mistake this guy made, of leaving when the going was just getting good, and then waiting decades to find his way home.

Victor greets Leo so warmly that I'm again reminded why I loved him, what attracted me to him in the first place. There's something magnetic about him. He's expansive and self-deprecating and charming.

Leo is the same Leo—cool, careful—he's even wearing the same vanilla-ice-cream suit that's his outfit of choice for all functions involving parents, apparently. He is disarmed by Victor, I can tell. When I go to hug him, I notice that he's a little less stiff, even with me. He hugs me more tightly than he ever has, and he even looks me in the eye when the hug is finished.

He is polite and deferential with Victor at first, but then he allows himself to be embraced and to have his back patted, to have a beer thrust into his hands. He laughs out loud when Victor congratulates him and says, "You might think this is about the baby, but the *real* congratulations, my boy, comes from you getting the hell out of the photographing-the-evening-gown business!"

"Dad!" says Louise, laughing. "Stop it. We made a damn good living doing that!"

"Yeah. More's the pity. What has *happened* to the world that that's a thing that makes people into millionaires now? Whatever happened to being robber barons—I ask you."

She shakes her head at him, and she and Leo exchange a fond look. She looks young and eager and beautiful tonight, in a flowy flowered dress that shows off her pregnancy. Ever since she got back from fetching Leo at the airport, she keeps tucking her hand into his and smiling up at him like they have a delicious secret. Together, they pore over the ultrasound photo—which makes the baby look like a simple, shrimp-shaped blob, of course—but which makes them both smile. She tells him about what it was like hearing the heartbeat—it sounded so fast, she says. Like a little sped-up metronome, with a swishing noise. And Leo looks at her in amazement, like she invented life or something.

Really—there is so much love floating around that the air is almost blooming. Every sip of wine I take makes me feel swoony.

The men do the grilling, as is the American way. I coat the chicken pieces with my homemade barbecue sauce, and then take the platters outside, where Victor gives me an air smooch and then carefully places the pieces on the wire rack over the charcoal pit, everything just so, as if he's doing an art installation. While the chicken sizzles and spits away, the two men drink beers and play horseshoes. Louise and I go back inside and make potato salad and corn on the cob. We watch them through the kitchen window as they get to know each other. This requires us to duck away from the window frequently, as one or the other looks up and realizes they're being spied upon. Every time this happens, Louise giggles.

"So, he's taking the news well?" I say.

"Yeah."

"I guess he was ready for a baby after all?"

"Perhaps."

"A change of heart?"

There's a long silence. On the stereo, Aretha Franklin starts singing about respect.

I laugh. "You know, Lou, the reason I'm talking this way? Making everything sound like a question? Well, it's because I'm trying to get *you* to tell me what we're seeing here. Is Leo happy about the baby, or isn't he?"

"He seems to be," she says. "I haven't had that much of a chance to really talk to him."

"He seems different somehow," I say. "But didn't you tell me once that he didn't want children?"

"Oh," she says. "He said he didn't want children *yet*. But maybe yet is over."

"A good question, and one we should ask ourselves more often: When is *yet* over?"

"Maybe yet ends when there is an actual fetus and not a theoretical one," she says.

"But what do *you*—" I start to say, only to be interrupted by Victor coming inside triumphantly bearing the platter of chicken overhead like a man coming home from the hunt. Leo trails him, carrying their beers and smiling.

No one is taking any pictures. Maybe that's why.

The evening officially begins. The magic starts crackling around the edges of things, filling in the silences around the table. Victor is expanding his personality to fill all the empty spaces. Usually this is my role; I am the one who soaks up people's experiences and draws them out, and I'm generally the one talking too much, pontificating, leading the laughter. I'm the one pouring more drinks, anticipating what's needed, entering a kind of flow. I live for this, in fact.

But Victor! He is Hugh Grant, Johnny Carson, and George Clooney all at once. I can just sit back and watch him—his graceful, brown hands gesturing in midair, his sparkling eyes, his generous spirit, telling stories, and yet letting everybody else shine, too. Funny, I'd forgotten this side of him.

The cabinets, I think, actually look better without all that peeling decoupage that Victor and Louise removed. Louise has repainted them a nice, muted almond color. A kitchen color, like you'd see in a decorating book. In fact, the entire place looks clean and straightened. And it's not so bad. Ridiculous, though, that all the spatulas point in the same direction. So Louise. I smile at her fondly.

I get up and go to the bathroom and stand there for a long time, staring at myself in the mirror. Am I drunk? Possibly I am drunk. Or maybe this is just what relief feels like. An unfamiliar feeling. I wish Calvin still lived here. I would like to tell him about this relief.

"Wouldn't it be something," Louise is saying when I come back, "if things happen in the way that they're meant to? That all of this is a story we had a hand in creating—and we're all supposed to be together right now, despite all the forces that could have kept this from happening?"

I look over at her. She's looking at Victor, who smiles back at her with shining eyes.

After dinner, we make a fire outside in the firepit, and we get down to real talk.

Leo asks how the bunny business is going, and I tell him that I'm going to California soon. I'll be on television in LA and Oakland and speaking at a couple of women's groups in the San Fernando Valley. There's a keynote speech also, that I keep forgetting about. I'm thinking of making a week of it, maybe doing some sightseeing.

Victor leans forward, his face lit up by the fire.

"And don't forget, Mom, that you're meeting with an agent," says Louise.

"Oh, yes, that too." I put my hands up to my temples. "It's all moving kind of fast . . . I haven't even mapped it all out yet. I'm kind of disorganized. As usual."

"You know *what*," Louise says. "I could go along and help you. I could be your organizer and your travel guide and the person who brings you tea. And—wow! What if we all go? Dad could come, too. It would be piles of fun. How would that be?"

Leo blanches. "Um, I'm due back in South Africa," he says. "For a story."

"Well, no, I didn't mean you, silly!" she says. "I meant me and my parents." She looks from one of us to the other. "What do you say, guys? The First and Probably Last Family Trip of the Steidleys!"

Victor looks at me so hard it feels like he's boring a little hole through my temple. When I look across the fire at him, he grins and shrugs. It's one of those shrugs that says *why not*.

"Remember the trip we took to California right after we got together?" he says to me. "When we drove up the coast? I've actually been thinking I want to do that again. It was an incredible time."

Yes. It *had* been an incredible time.

But now?

Victor and me and Louise?

It's true that I could use a handler.

Louise spreads her arms wide and stands up and turns in a circle. "Look at me, Leo! Two parents! Who would have thought I'd ever have my two parents together? It's the dream come true of every divorced kid everywhere!"

I would like to say something, but I can't think of what. Like, how she's not a kid? And that we're not . . . together . . . unless she's talking about *together at this moment by the fire*. And the main question I have for all of us and for the conniving universe that pulls the strings here: Is *this* the narrative everything's been leading to? Am I tumbling toward something inevitable? Because there is no freaking way we're going to be reconstituted as a family unit. There just isn't. Do I need to stand up and squash this fantasy right this minute?

"Please," she says, and looks at me as though she's read my mind. "I know, I know. We're not a typical, intact family unit. But would it kill you to just let me have this one little trip—and then we can all go back to our corners and live the rest of our lives in peace?"

"Or not," says Victor. "Who knows what could happen?"

Louise's phone dings. She stops and looks down at it.

"Oh my God, oh my God! Hildy's in labor!" she says. She looks up at all of us, her face illuminated by the fire, her eyes bright. "I am so sorry, but I gotta go!" And then in a singsong voice: "Hildy's having a ba-by! Hildy's having a ba-by!" She looks at me while she slips on her sandals. "I don't know when I'll be back. Babies don't often come immediately, or so I've heard. But I'll call you all and let you know what's going on. Gotta run! Bye!"

"Wait, what?" says Leo. "Just like that? You're leaving?"

"I promised!" she says. "She said she'd call us all just as soon as she got to the hospital, and we're all going to meet her there so we can celebrate when little Cyril comes into the world. Ohhh, this is so exciting! So epic! The first baby coming!"

"*All* of you?" I say. "The hospital is not going to like that one bit."

"By all of us, I meant Phoebe and me. I think Miranda is showing up tomorrow."

"Wait. One more thing. Did you say Cereal?" says Leo.

"Cyril!" she says over her shoulder as she runs into the house. "Cyril, Cyril, Cyril!"

No one moves. The back door slams. I can see her through the window, rushing around, grabbing things out of the cabinets.

"Well," I say. "This is exciting."

Leo stares into the fire. Then he laughs. "I just hope she doesn't let those women name *our* baby," he says. Then he clears his throat and looks at Victor and me. "So, I guess we're doing this thing," he says in a gruff voice. "Having a baby, I mean. Not going to California. Not me, at least. It sounds like the three of you might be going . . ."

"Possibly," Victor says. "And congratulations, son, on being a dad. I feel like making a little speech."

Oh please, I think. *Don't ruin everything with a tone-deaf speech.*

But I shouldn't have second-guessed him. He's quite eloquent, as it turns out.

"Since I wasn't here when you and my daughter first got together, I didn't have an opportunity to pontificate, but now I do. So here goes, bear with me." He stops, looks momentously around at the two of us, and then says, "I think, watching you and Louise together, that you've really got something you can build on. Marriage is harder than it looks—I don't have to tell you that, goodness knows—but now you have this little one coming who may be arriving just in time to pull you back together. Or . . . if you're not lucky, pull you apart forever." He stops talking, looks up at the sky for a moment. Then he continues, in a husky voice: "My advice, for whatever it's worth, from an old marriage loser: Make your marriage your own thing. Don't let society define it for you. Figure it out as you go along." There's a beat of silence and he looks at me. "I sure wish somebody had told me that, way back when. You stick it out, you make it your own thing."

∽

That night, after Leo leaves, I go upstairs to my room and call up Calvin. Ostensibly, it's to see how Bernice is, and also to offer to bring him the trunk that he left behind. It's filled with his summer clothing. He might need that, I tell him.

But mainly it's just because I miss the sound of his voice.

He says that Bernice is fine. She's adjusting well to the pacemaker. Then he hesitates. "She's feeling good for the most part, but I think her daughter is one of those daughters who worries too much. She's trying to make Bernice think scary things about the future. And what's the point of that, I say. So . . . it's a little bit of a strain sometimes."

"What does her daughter want her to think about?"

"She wants Bernice to move to Ohio, to be closer to family. It's a very human impulse, I know. But Bernice is fine here, and I'm looking after her." He laughs. "I don't know why, but having a ninety-year-old boyfriend looking after her mother doesn't seem to make Bernice's daughter feel any better."

"Huh!" I say.

"And how are you?" he asks. "Tell me all about the bunny business."

So I tell him about the trip to California and about all the calls I've been making and still need to make. The conferences where I'm speaking. The agent who might want me to write a book. "It's all great," I say. "But, regular life seems to be a little out of whack here, if you want to know the truth. Victor seems to have moved in with me, Louise has quit being an Instagram influencer, Leo is now semi-excited about being a father, *and* I'm going cross-country with Louise and Victor pretending like we're a pleasant little normal family—"

He roars with laughter. "Victor is living at your house? Victor? Please don't tell me he's living in my old room."

"He's not. Louise is living in your old room."

"How did this happen?"

So I explain the whole improbable chain of events, starting with the speech in Brooklyn and ending with tonight's around-the-fire discussion with Leo. And everything makes him laugh even harder. Really, he's the happiest person in the world.

"And, while I'm telling the truth, I should also say that I slept with Mason Davis. Twice. Almost three times. Which I think has given him the wrong idea. And Victor has turned out to be a whole different human from the guy who left me. He's wooing Louise and also being very helpful around the house, and I think he imagines us all as a family again, which is, of course, impossible. So, obviously I need some of your wisdom. Tell me something wise. Please. Anything you've got."

"Um. Trust love. How's that?" His voice gets husky.

"Too general," I say. "What else you got?"

"How about this? Get over yourself and stop trying to figure everything out all the damn time," he says. "Just live. How about that? See where things land."

"So you think it's fine that I go to California with Victor and Louise, and I let myself be involved with Mason?"

"How do *you* feel? That's the important question."

"I feel I shouldn't do either thing. I think it's a mistake to let men in my life again."

"You know what? You need to just live your life, realizing how lucky you are that you have so much love around you. Goddamn it, trust yourself, Billie! Make mistakes if you have to. Make all the goddamned mistakes you need to make. Everything is fixable. Loving is never a mistake. Just take a leap of faith, why don't you?"

"No one is like you, Calvin, when it comes to love. Other people have some sense of self-protection, but you don't have any, that I can tell."

"Just tell me one thing, Billie. Do you love Mason?"

I hesitate a long time—too long by Calvin's standards. Finally I say, "I don't really know. He's got a lot of problems."

"Name one."

"He . . . misses his dead wife too much. And he tries too hard to be perfect. And . . . I think he gets manicures. And he has a fake tan."

Calvin laughs. Of course he laughs.

"I see that you're still exactly the same as you were when I left your house. You've still got this cockamamie idea that love is like some giant predator that's going to swallow you whole. But it's not, sweetheart.

Sharing your life with someone is a *good* thing. Give in to it. Let your heart have what it wants."

"I don't know what it wants! It wants to be unattached! It wants to be free!"

"Billie, that is the dumbest thing you've ever said. Go sit in a dark room and talk to your heart. You're not paying attention to it *at all*."

"I don't think my heart is speaking to me anymore."

He lets out a noisy sigh. "Who could blame it, the way you malign it?"

CHAPTER
TWENTY-SIX

The next few days are busy, busy, busy. I make the airline reservations for Victor, Louise, and me to fly to Los Angeles, and I do ten Heartbreak Bunny calls and four radio station interviews. (I'm the queen of the Drive at Five.) I firm up the details of the conference and my meetings. I rent a car.

Aaaaaanddd . . . I think about Mason, but I don't call him. This is bad, but I don't even return his calls. He leaves messages saying he'd like to see me, and only once did I text him back. And then it was only to say:

Would love to see u 2. So busy!

Sometimes I practice what I would say if I did call him up, and here are the leading contenders:

I am so sorry that I'm not the person you need.

*I wish your lovely late wife could still be alive, and that you never had
to go through the last seven years without her.*

I can't . . . I just can't.

You can see why it would be a mistake to say those things after what
we've been through. After the night when I held him.

Then one day he texts:

Something has come up, and I need to talk to you. Meet at the
diner tomorrow at 2?

So I say yes.

Of course I'm late.

I'm late, and he's already at the table when I arrive. I must say, he
looks awful. His face is drawn and his hair isn't exactly in its usual television style. Even his eyes seem opaque and ominous. I sit down warily
on the other side of the booth and say hi. I'm starting in on a rambling
list of apologies and excuses, but he holds up his hand to stop me.

"There's been a little problem," he says, without preamble.

"Don't tell me they've discontinued the coconut cream pie!"

He smiles painfully. "No. It's a Heartbreak Bunny problem, I'm
afraid. The station got a complaint about you."

"Uh-oh. What have I done?"

"You didn't do anything wrong. A man contacted the station saying
that you went to his ex-girlfriend's house and took some things that
belonged to him. He's accused you of stealing and says his ex would
never have let those things go if you hadn't insisted. He's threatening all
kinds of bad PR for the station for promoting Snap Out of It, which he
says is nothing more than a theft ring. He's told the station manager he's
going to post on Twitter and Instagram and every social media platform
he can find stating that you're unstable and not to be trusted, and that
the station is responsible because we've had you on for what he's calling
free advertising."

"Well, that's just crazy. He should have gotten in touch with me. I could have helped give him his stuff back."

"Yeah, I said that when they called me in to talk about it. Apparently he's not interested in that, though. He wants to cause trouble for you. And also . . ." He looks down at the table. I've never seen him look so miserable.

"Also?"

"My involvement with you has been called into question. It didn't escape the management's notice that I have . . . feelings for you. That last day you were on the show—remember when the producer came into the green room?"

"Yes, but we weren't *doing* anything."

"True. None of this is your fault. It's mine. I've been chastised for having my own son on the show, and for bringing you on twice. What I saw as adding a little personal touch to a feature story turns out to be grounds for—"

"For what?"

"For a performance evaluation and review so far. The possibility of a suspension is still on the table." He sighs and takes a sip of his coffee.

I look at him. "Oh, Mason! I'm so sorry about this. Are you . . . okay?"

"Yeah. Well, no. It's odd to think of my colleagues judging my intentions. I guess it was obvious that I felt . . . you know . . . connected to you. Which is not why I had you on the show, but it looks like a conflict. So for that, I'm a little embarrassed, I guess." He smiles. "But this will blow over. I'll be fine."

I immediately start tearing up my napkin into little strips and stacking them—an exacting task, which means I don't have to look up so often.

Penny brings over the coconut cream pie; we have to stop and admire it and hear about her niece who is finally over her heartbreak.

When she leaves, I turn back to Mason. He still looks slightly gray with worry.

"So, tell me the rest," I say. "I feel like there's more here than me just not going on the show anymore. Do you need me to do anything?"

He looks directly into my eyes, and my mouth goes dry. He's got the look on his face of someone who's about to say the worst possible news. "I'm just going to try to be an adult about this," he says. "I've done a lot of thinking since the other night, and I . . . want us to stop seeing each other."

"You want to stop seeing me?" I say, shocked. "Is this because of the station?"

"No. Not really. Well, maybe somewhat. But it's mostly because I'm finally hearing you loud and clear about love. You aren't ever going to love me, and I'm tired of pretending I don't care. That's the truth of it."

"Oh," I say. That feeling crawling around in my solar plexus feels a lot like disappointment, and for a moment I have trouble thinking of the next thing a person is supposed to say in these circumstances. I don't think you're supposed to argue about it. So I say, kind of faintly, "I understand," and he nods, and then I say, "Nobody should be depending on *me*. You're correct to take care of yourself here."

He laughs; he actually laughs. "I'm *correct* to be breaking up with you? Is that what you said?"

I nod.

"Well, you're right," he says. "You're back with your ex-husband, and I can't sit by and watch that. My heart has seen too much action already."

"But just so you know, I'm really not back with him."

"No? Is it possible that you're the only one who doesn't realize you're back with him? I mean, he *is* living with you now, I believe. And so is Louise. You're a family. Family dinners, family conversations. It's all there."

"It's not!"

He takes out his wallet and puts a ten-dollar bill on the table. "Well, whatever is going on, it's too much for me. I'm sorry. I have to do this."

"But I'll miss you," I say. "And since we were never having a romance, I would think we can still be friends."

"I'll miss you, too," he tells me. He reaches over and touches my hand. "You know what? Even though we *can't* still be friends, I want to tell you one thing that makes me the happiest. This may sound crazy to you, but I *do* believe in love. After Tish, I thought that part of me was completely dead, and you made me see differently." He smiles sadly. "Not that you meant to. Bless your heart, you wanted to get me onboard with your cockamamie idea that there's no good ending to a love story, but every single thing you did made me believe just the opposite. Isn't that funny when you think about it?"

"Is it funny?"

"Yes, it's funny. It's funny because we're breaking up, and what I'm coming away with is the happy knowledge that I know how to love again."

He looks out the window for a while, so long that I think he's got nothing more to say, but then he clears his throat and says, "And maybe we both get to have it our own way, you know? You're going back to Victor—and that will enable you to prove that love and romance *are* the wrong things. That they only cause pain." He looks away, shakes his head. "While for me, I'm realizing that I don't want to live without love in my life. I even want food in my kitchen again." He smiles. "Thank you for showing me that food wakes up a kitchen. I have real sustenance in the refrigerator now, thanks to you."

We both get up. My legs feel almost wobbly. And I'm suddenly angry.

"You're welcome," I say, "but I'm not going back to Victor."

"But you are." He smiles again. "And I get it. Hell, if Tish showed up right now and said everything could be put back—"

"That's different. She died. She didn't walk out on you."

"Exactly," he says. "Victor walked out on you, and yet somehow—well, it's not so different from the Joey situation, is it? Saucy comes back, and he's over his head again."

"This is why I hate romance!" I say suddenly, too loudly. "This is exactly what I've been trying to avoid! All this pressure! All this guilt! You see? I *was* right about romance all along."

"Maybe for you, but that's not the way I see the world. I want love, and I want romance, and I want a companion in life and somebody to wake up next to each morning and eat dinner with at night. And I want all the trimmings, too—sharing popcorn at the movies, and buying a dog, and even the arguments about whether to go on vacation in July or wait until September when the crowds have gone. I want every minute of that."

"I just don't want drama," I tell him, but I can feel myself in danger of crying.

He puts his arm around me as we walk to my car. "Nope. Billie, you're not right about that either. You love drama. You're the most colorful, dynamic, dramatic person I know. It's your superpower."

The last thing he says as I'm getting in the car is, "I know he's going to make you change—I already see it a little—but don't let him make you give up being the bunny, okay?"

"I do what I want," I say.

"Take care of yourself. I'll miss you." He pats the side of my car door and smiles before he walks away.

I would just like to say, ladies and gentlemen, that this is exactly the kind of scene I hate most in the whole world. I sit there in my car because for a moment I don't trust myself to drive away. I close my eyes and let all of the feelings churn around, showing up to take their turn pummeling me. First comes rage, and then disappointment and sadness move in. Guilt shows up to say hi.

But then the worst of all comes last: that old familiar feeling deep in the pit of my stomach, the sensation of being hollowed out. The shutting down is happening, just like it did all those other times.

◦ᤁ

Victor and I fly out of Hartford, from Bradley International Airport. Louise didn't come along. She called last night and said that she just couldn't stand to leave Hildy's house. Cyril was having trouble nursing, and Louise and Hildy were reading up on it and meeting with a lactation specialist, and—well, Louise wanted to stay behind. Needed to, was the way she put it.

I thought maybe that would mean that Victor wouldn't come either, but he said he was looking forward to the drive up the coast—and also, didn't I still need somebody to keep me organized? And also, he had an airline ticket. He didn't want to forfeit his ticket to California.

"It'll be fine," he said. "We can absolutely do without Louise."

But can we? I thought. Maybe we need her. Weren't we doing this trip to show we were just an ordinary, happy, reconstituted family?

Now sitting on the plane, I suddenly dread everything about this trip. I just want to hunker down in the seat, put on my headphones, and watch a movie. I want to be alone with the drone of the engine.

Victor, however, wants to talk, to stretch out, to open his book and then close it again. He yawns, cracks his knuckles, wonders about the weather in San Francisco. He orders a beer from the flight attendant. He can't help himself; he flirts with her, asks about the opal ring she's wearing. I can tell by the lilt in her voice that she finds him so charming. I roll my eyes; I can't help it.

He is basking. He told me that all those years in France, Juliette never appreciated his jokes like I do. He was lonely for the way I loved him and didn't even realize it.

I roll my eyes at that, too.

That bit I said at the beginning, about how when Victor told me he was in love with someone else, how I shut down? I said I clamped down on my feelings and got over it. I think I said that within a week I'd changed out some of the furniture and painted the kitchen, and that was it. I was done.

Well, I no longer think that's true.

Being with him is making me remember everything so differently.

It comes back to me now, sometimes, how much I mourned him. I stayed in bed. I brought Louise in with me. She nursed hungrily through the night, then broke away to sleep and I smelled her sweet baby head, holding on to her so she wouldn't fall on the floor. I wept buckets of tears into her hair.

The ache went on for so long. Maybe it never went away. Maybe I just pushed it down.

Also, I clung to our mothers.

Victor's mother, whose name was Lou, had a heart condition. She lived on the first floor because she couldn't do stairs. She seemed elderly even though she was only fifty-five, and most days she sat in a blue pleather recliner and watched daytime television and smoked cigarettes. Oh, and she made pancakes. The aroma would come up through the vents, and Louise and I would go down and eat with her.

She's the one who said I shouldn't have to go to work after Victor left; she said if I left Louise in the care of others, she'd struggle with abandonment issues her whole life. Lou had studied Freud when she was young, before she married. She believed Louise was probably already ruined. She suggested I stay home and make things and sell them—crocheted pot holders and watercolors. The sort of things you could never make a living from.

And then there was my mother, who was younger and still worldly and went out with men. She had never been very maternal. My dad died young, and my mom worked long hours through my whole childhood and left me with my grandmother. Even when my mother lived on the third floor of my house, it was as though she landed there by accident. She kept claiming she would be there only temporarily. She wanted to remarry, but that hadn't happened. She said men weren't worth much and that I was stupid for letting Victor get to me. There were a million just like him, she said. She talked fast, animatedly, with kind of a wildness in her eyes. And then she met a sea captain at a square dance in New Haven, and moved with him to the Virgin Islands—and I rarely heard from her anymore. She died when she was in her fifties, and I felt like I never really knew her.

I look over at Victor, who's fallen asleep now, studying the way his eyelashes sweep against his cheeks. The crinkles around his eyes only make him look more attractive, distinguished somehow.

For the longest time after he left, whenever I'd see a wedding taking place, I'd feel so sorry for the bride. It would almost be a physical sensation in the pit of my stomach. I'd see the white lace, a veil, flowers, and I'd think I was going to throw up.

I still feel that way.

CHAPTER
TWENTY-SEVEN

"So, who am I on this lecture circuit?" says Victor. He turns off the radio.

"Pardon me?"

We're driving to Santa Monica from the San Fernando Valley. Traffic is terrifying in California; and even though Victor is going nearly eighty, we're being tailgated by a yellow pickup truck, and three cars have just narrowly missed our bumper as they shot past us.

I've spoken at three women's groups in the last two days, and tonight is the big one. The keynote speech at the Women's Creativity in Independence Conference. Victor's been content to sit the events out, swim laps in the hotel pool or draft the beginnings of a new poetry series he says he's working on: Poems for Louise. He's also silently accepted the fact that I've insisted on us having separate hotel rooms. But tonight he's insisted on coming with me to the lecture—it's a larger event with more people, and he says he wants to be my escort. He thinks it looks more appealing for a woman giving a talk to have an attentive, proud man at her elbow. He's even wearing a suit. I'm not sure I want him there. It seems to me that he's been feeling neglected, and also that he wants to be the center of attention. I can sense the crackle between us that means he's escalating things.

And now here he is, trying to pick a fight.

"You know. Who *am* I?" he says. "Are you acknowledging that I'm your ex-husband? Or is it too messy to explain why a *Heartbreak Bunny* would be reuniting and traveling with the guy who should be persona non grata?"

"I hadn't really thought about it, to tell you the truth," I say. I rummage through my bag for my sunglasses.

"Kind of undercuts the whole premise, I'd say. Me being here. Unless . . . unless you want to tell a *different* story." He gives me a side-long look. "You know, it could be a story about reconnecting. About how love coming around for the second time means more. People have a romance, and then something happens and they learn to live without it . . . and then it comes back around again, and they learn that love is real."

"I think, in the interest of keeping things somewhat normal, I'm going to just stick with the speech I already have written. No need to go into the whole backstory of me and you."

"Huh," he says. "Well, okay. I just wondered if I needed to be ready, you know. It seems a little more authentic to mention that your life has changed since you came up with this Snap Out of It business. Maybe I could come up onstage and we could embrace and talk about how love can grow again. You know. If you want. I don't want to tell you how to run your business, but it seems that we could be messengers of hope."

I adjust my sunglasses and look out the passenger window. After we've gone about twenty miles without speaking, I say, "Do you feel you're in mourning for Juliette?"

"No," he says too quickly. "I get over things. Also, I have you. Maybe I was in mourning for you, and now that's the part of me that's healing. Did you ever think of that?"

"First of all, it's scary as hell that you say you're over Juliette, who you were married to for thirty-five years, and also, just for the record . . . you don't *have* me."

"Well," he says. And he taps his hands on the steering wheel and, even though I wait, he doesn't say anything more.

⟶

"So, I got this crazy idea one night," I say to the audience. I'm at a podium on the stage in a massive ballroom with gold-flecked wallpaper. About two hundred women of all ages sit at linen-covered tables, clutching notebooks and looking up at me. After this talk, they're going to break into small groups. I'm the keynote speaker for a weekend that is supposed to be about "empowerment and growth and nurturing the full-on, banging creative spirit."

I slip right into my regular spiel about Kat and me and our friendship through the five divorces and one widowhood, as well as the two children we brought up as single moms. And how we stuck together and comforted each other through all of it.

Then I hesitate, looking out at the audience and seeing Victor standing in the back, smiling at me.

"I was young and optimistic when I got married for the first time," I say. "I turned everything into a story that showed we were fun and impetuous and right for each other." I get a laugh when I tell them about the dried-up syrup on the floor and how that became a story about how unconventional and hilarious we were.

I let a beat of silence go by.

"And then he left," I say. "Fell in love with someone else, like they do sometimes. Smashed everything all up."

The audience groans.

"And when that happens, when our person leaves us . . . we put our hearts under glass and make a little beautiful altar to the gods of ill-fated romance. A little altar of heartbreak, made up of things that remind us of what we had."

The women make noises of assent. Victor is smiling. I think he enjoys hearing about the heartbreak part.

I switch gears then, start telling them about all the things I've collected in my forays into people's houses. "People save everything. It's not only what you'd think—love letters and photographs and ticket stubs," I say. There was also a toothbrush that had a trace of lipstick on it, a champagne cork. I tell them about the woman who took the dress she wore the night she first made love with her ex and cut it up after he left her. She made a fabric collage that she hung in her room, glorifying it even though it made her miserable every single day.

They make little murmuring sounds.

And then I tell them about the words I sometimes chant with clients, the music I play, the revenge dances we sometimes must do. I say that no one needs to hold on to suffering. We are fierce and creative, and we can find love and passion in other places besides romance. We can decide to say no thank you when the love we're offered isn't what we need.

"Hold off," I say. "And when someone has left you, turn to yourself. Be still and wait. I've seen that we can recover stronger and become more powerful when we throw away all the stuff that's keeping us stuck—the wedding dress, his hair trimmings, the valentine she sent in better days. Don't glorify that stuff with stories you tell about its importance. That's all a big lie that keeps you stuck. It's not worth giving over your fun, magical life to memories. Move on!"

I get more and more heated, as I feel the audience respond. Victor snorts from the back of the room. I can hear him over the crowd.

"So go live your banging creative life and instead of wasting energy on making a shrine to lost love, turn that energy into art and writing and music and dance and fantastic haircuts and tapestries and knitted scarves and cures for cancer and walkathons for causes you care about. Put that energy into the environment, into causes that move you, into holding each other up! Don't let yourself ever again give yourself over to a love that doesn't fit you. Don't," I say, "break your own heart."

Victor has disappeared from the back of the room.

I get a standing ovation. And afterward, people surround me and want to tell me their stories and ask me questions.

A woman takes me aside and says she's the agent that I'm supposed to meet with in Malibu. She decided to come and see me talk instead. This could *absolutely* be a book, she says. "People are hungry for these stories, and want to know about the objects," she says. She gives me her card. "Let's talk more when you're back east. You can come to New York, and we'll get a proposal together."

"Yes," I say. "Yes!" I can feel my cheeks grow hot and my mind clear. When it's all over, I don't see Victor anywhere.

I go to the bar with my newfound friends, and I stay until closing time, drinking wine and talking and laughing. Three women say they want to be Heartbreak Bunnies, too, and where did I get the costume? And maybe, they say, we should license this!

"We could be a league of bunnies curing heartbreak," one says.

"Just do it!" I say.

We practice Heartbreak Bunnying for the bartender, stopping to collapse in laughter just like Kat and I did the night we came up with the idea for Snap Out of It.

When I get back to my room, a message comes in from Louise, a picture with her and Hildy and the new baby—a sweet, blue-eyed cherub wrapped up like a burrito, staring off into space with that newborn vacant gaze. Hildy and Louise look bedraggled and whipped by life, grinning crookedly into the camera.

When I send her a smiley emoji, she immediately calls me even though it's the middle of the night there. She's up with the baby strapped to her front, walking him back and forth so Hildy can get some sleep.

"Mama," she whispers. "Oh my goodness, Mama! I have a new life. My job is getting the baby out of the bassinet and handing him to Hildy to nurse. I do it, like, thirty times a day. It's the most time-consuming thing I've ever done, even more than blogging. He's always hungry!"

"Is he just amazing?"

"It's . . . incredible. He smiles, and I think it's for real even though people say it's gas. Also, I think he knows me. He settles down in my arms, and then my baby kicks him from the inside, and that makes us both smile. And, Mama, I have to tell you something."

"What?"

"I'm going to live here."

"And is Leo going to join you?"

There's a long silence. "I don't think so."

"He doesn't want to be together after all?"

"No, he does. But I don't want to. He's so cold, Mama. And hard to get along with. When we had that night, all of us together, I realized I don't love him. I looked across the fire at him, and it just hit me. I mean, part of me was happy you and Dad were trying so hard to pretend you think marriage is a good thing—I'm grateful to you, I really am. But I don't want that life with him anymore. I'm not scared of being a single mom, and Hildy and I have decided that we're going to do this together. We're going to live here in this house she's rented because it's big enough, and Miranda might come and live here, too. And we're all going to share the work and help each other—and the babies will be friends, and, oh, it's going to be so much fun. And maybe I can blog about that! You know?" She's talking so fast I can barely keep up.

"Lulu," I say.

"Wait. Could I just tell you something else?"

"Yes."

"Dad's wonderful, but he's kind of a spoiled baby, isn't he? Am I allowed to say that? He called me tonight after your talk, and he was telling me that you insist on being the Heartbreak Bunny even when he's offering you a chance at all this happiness. Happiness everywhere! You'd think it was rainbows and unicorns he's offering. He says that after all this time he's put in, that you won't even stay in the same room with him on the trip. That you treat him like he's just your chauffeur or something."

I'm silent. I hear the baby making little mewling noises close to the phone.

"So I've gotta go," she says. "But just so you know, I might understand what you've been saying about him. You were right."

"Excuse me," I say. "But could you repeat that? Because I don't think there is any sound in the whole world as lovely as hearing your child telling you that you're right."

"Well, don't get too accustomed to it," she says. "You also said I should consider going back to Leo, and you were wrong about that."

☙

"You know, I figured it out," Victor says after we've checked out of the hotel, and we're back in the car.

This is supposed to be the day that we head out on the Rediscover California Tour, as Victor calls it. Heading north to see San Francisco and the redwoods as we had done so long ago.

"Have you, now?" I say. "That's good because I'm too tired and happy to figure anything out. I met the most amazing women last night and stayed up too late in the bar teaching them all how to be Heartbreak Bunnies, and then—*then*, Louise called, and we talked for a while. So I may need to sleep in the car."

He hasn't started up the engine. He's sitting there looking at me. I put on my sunglasses. The sky is so bright. "It's just so disappointing to see you this way," he says. "I lay awake all night thinking about this and trying to figure it out. I decided that maybe you're doing this for the money. Even though you and I have this daughter and this connection, you want to turn your back on all that and capitalize on the worst thing that ever happened to us. Because, let's face it, trouble is lucrative. People are willing to pay to hear you talk about it."

"It's not about *a thing* that happened to *us*, Victor," I say. "It was my life. Mine."

He acts like he doesn't hear. "And you—you *talk* a good game about creativity! What about real creativity, the spark that could go into creating the family life all three of us—four of us, even five of us—might need? What about that?" He jams the car into gear and pulls out of the parking lot. "We can make a life that's different from anything we ever imagined for ourselves! Freedom and respect for each person's individuality. A real marriage! Louise and Leo could do whatever they want—journalism or blogging about parenthood, whatever it turns into—and you could give talks about empowerment. I could write poetry. We could move into a bigger house and all live together. Raise the baby! Help with their lives! That's what I've been picturing. A family! And I thought you and I were on the same page. But no. You're like those people you say you're trying to save—stuck in the very worst thing that ever happened. You've made a business that's a shrine to unhappiness. And isn't *that* a shock to realize?" He bangs on the steering wheel.

"You would be surprised," I say in a small, even voice, "how little any of this is about you."

"It's everything about me," he says, and his lip curls. "You wouldn't ever have done this if I'd stayed."

"Louise and Leo aren't going to stay together," I say.

"You don't know that. You're encouraging her not to be with him," he says.

Then we ride in silence.

❧

It starts to rain after a while, big drops spattering against the windshield. There's an accident up ahead, and traffic is stopped—eight lanes of traffic all stuck in one long, unmoving parking lot of a freeway. I lean my head against the passenger door and do deep breathing.

"Looks like we're not going to make it to the hotel before I have to do that call-in show," I say. "Which is a problem, because I need to be someplace where I can hear well."

He purses his lips. "Well, I can't single-handedly move the cars, can I? What time is the call-in show?"

"In an hour."

"We're not going to be in Oakland by then. Can't you cancel it?"

"I don't want to cancel it. This is my job." The air in the car is so thick it's hard to breathe. "Maybe," I say, "we could get off at the next exit, once we're moving again. We could find a parking lot somewhere, and make sure there's a good signal and I could do it from the car."

My phone dings, and I root for it in my purse.

It's Calvin.

Bernice's daughter is insisting that Bernice come & live with her in Ohio.

I let out a big sigh. Victor glances over. "What? Is it Louise?"

"It's Calvin."

I type:

Oh, Calvin! I'm so sad to hear this. Are you going with her?

The three gray dots are on for a very long time. Then he says:

No. Not invited. This is when families circle the wagons. Bernice
is not well.

Your ten-year plan.

I know. It didn't make it ten months.

Come back to our house! Please! It will always be your home,
you know. Since you're immortal, I'm even planning to leave it
to you in my will.

Ha ha.

"What's going on?" says Victor.

"Nothing."

He's silent for a long time, tapping on the steering wheel. The traffic
starts moving; we achieve a velocity of twenty miles per hour. When he
speaks again, he says, "I feel like I have to say something. I shouldn't
have left you. And I shouldn't have stayed gone. It was a dick move,
and I did it for stupid reasons, and I've regretted it ever since. I know
you've had a full life in the years I've been gone. And I even know I'm
being awful again, just like I was before."

I don't say anything.

"But hey, at least now I'm acknowledging it before it gets out of
hand. That's worth something, right?" He walks his fingers over, sending
them marching along my thigh.

I move over just a bit. "Could we get off at the next exit? I'll do the
call-in from the car."

"There's a rest area in fifteen miles. Listen to me. I'm trying to make a speech here. I'm telling you that I'm sorry and that . . . well, I love you."

"Victor, please. I don't think we'll make it that far before the call is supposed to start. Maybe just get off at this exit, okay? We can find a parking lot somewhere . . ."

"No," he says. "I'm going to aim for the rest area, and if we don't make it, we can just pull over on the side of the highway if we need to. It'll be romantic, sitting on the side of the highway with the rain coming down, and you talking about healing from heartbreak. I'll cheer you on."

I stare at him. "Could you please just get off at the exit? Please!"

He sets his jaw. I sit in silence as we go by two, three exits. Ten minutes later my phone rings, and it's the producer for the show. She has a bright voice, and she says, "Nicky Mintz will be with you in a few minutes. Just want to make sure your mic is working. Say something so I can check the levels."

"I'm in the car traveling," I tell her. "But I'll do my best. I have you on speakerphone."

"Hmmm," she says. "Well, it seems to work. Let's hope for the best."

Victor smiles and gives me a thumbs-up.

Nicky Mintz is a fun host. She's got lots to say about relationships and people's high expectations, and she tells the audience how excited she is to be talking to me, a person willing to put on a costume to go out and root out heartbreak. "Because the Heartbreak Bunny, from the Snap Out of It Company, knows one thing for sure: you can keep yourself stuck for a long, long time—or you can take that one wild life of yours, with all its disappointments and its heartaches, and live it to the fullest every single day."

Victor winces a bit. "How are you supposed to do that?" he whispers. "Love is the answer. Say that."

I shush him.

"And the Heartbreak Bunny is taking your questions," says Nicky Mintz. "Call her and ask her anything! She'll tell you exactly how to do it!"

These are callers I feel I've talked to before. The first two calls involve someone ghosting someone else and a man who discovered his wife is having an affair—and when he confronted her, she moved in with the other guy, and now he can't move on.

I am sympathetic and encouraging. I say we all can survive these times. We can be our own Heartbreak Bunny. Throw out mementos. Eat vegetables, keep a journal, do things for fun, create a ninety-day plan.

Then a woman calls whose voice is so quiet that I can barely hear her. Nicky Mintz keeps asking her to speak up.

"I'm the bad guy here," the woman says finally, drawing in a deep breath. There's a lot of static on the line.

"Ma'am, could you turn your radio down?" says Nicky Mintz.

"Okay. Yeah, sorry." She's away for a moment. "Okay, I was saying that I'm the bad guy. I am. I just broke up with a guy who loves me." She goes silent.

"Yes?" says Nicky Mintz.

"He says he loves me. He thinks he does. But . . . I'm sorry, I just can't trust what he's saying to me. He . . . well, he tries too hard. He always understands what I'm going through, and when I don't want to see him, he says that's fine, and he goes away. And whenever we're together, he tells me how much he loves me and all the reasons why we're great together." She clears her throat. "But what I think is that he's just *trying* to love me."

"Wait. You don't love him?" I say.

"No. I *could* love him," she says after a moment. "But—I don't think I want to."

"Too scary?"

She laughs again. "Way too scary! My first husband walked out on me with no warning, and my father walked out on my mother, and my sister walked out on her husband. You know how people say they're happy and everything looks perfect, but then it turns out you didn't see that they really hated each other the whole time? People are just fooling themselves because maybe there's no such thing as real love."

"I know," I say in a voice I don't even recognize. My hands have gotten so sweaty I can barely hold the phone. "I've had the same thought. But I think you and I both need to maybe grab some courage. I do think there's such a thing as real love. I think it can work. I mean, I *know* it can work. We have to suspend our cynicism. Trust joy. I have a ninety-year-old friend and that's what he says: trust all joy."

Victor shoots a look at me and pumps his fist in the air. "Yes!" he whispers.

I scoot farther away from him and say to the caller, "We can't let our hearts grow too cold because of things other people did to us in the past. This guy—this guy who says he loves you—he's not the guy who left you years ago. He's a whole different person."

"Haha. That's what he says to me."

"So? Believe him. Go deep and talk to that part of you who thinks you don't deserve to be loved. Tell her to be brave. This is not the way you want to spend the rest of your life, is it?"

"No," she says in a quiet voice. "But what if I get hurt again? What if this is all a big lie, and I risk my whole heart and then it . . ."

"But what if it doesn't?" I say. "What if this is your chance for happiness that changes your life?"

"I don't know how to do it."

"Yes, you do. Look within. Tell the fear you've got this, and it can go away now." Mason's face looms up in front of me. Calvin and my granny seem like they're both in the car with me. I feel my voice getting stronger.

She laughs a little. "I think you might be a little bit wacky."

"Possibly," I say. "But you know what?" I can hear the wonderment in my own voice. I can't believe I'm saying this. "This is the same thing that's happening to me! I have a man who loves me, and I just keep pushing him away. It's all fear! Our fear tells us a big lie, that we're unlovable. But we're not, are we?"

Victor is smiling at me and nodding. "This is perfect, what you're saying," he says in a loud whisper. I bat him away.

"No," she says slowly.

"When we just guard against disappointment, all we're doing is hurting ourselves before someone else can hurt us. That's all this is. Let's make a pact not to do this anymore."

⌒᧬

By the time I get off the phone, there is absolutely no air left in the car. I look up and discover that Victor has pulled into a rest area, and he's smiling at me. I hadn't even noticed. I put my hand on the door handle. It's suddenly so clear that I need to call Mason. My heart feels like it's hammering away in my chest.

And Victor is melting down in front of me.

"Listen," he says. His eyes are moist. "We can make this work. I've never heard you talk that way. It's more than I hoped. You've been pushing me away, but now you see that I've changed. And we'll go forward—"

It hits me then. *Oh my God. He thinks I meant him.*

"No," I say. I push down on the door handle, but it doesn't budge. "No, Victor. It's not us. You did the best you could, but I can't. I don't love you. I'm sorry."

"No, wait. I could have done better maybe. Let's try again." His eyes look empty and frightened. "We didn't give this a fair chance."

"No, it's okay. Listen, I have to leave," I say. I push harder and the door opens. It's stopped raining. The pavement has puddles everywhere, and the sun is shining. There are cars and people everywhere. My head feels like it's spinning.

"You're leaving now? Right this minute?"

"Right now. I have to." My voice sounds very far away to my own ears.

Somehow, I get out of the car and go around to the back seat and get my suitcase out. I feel like my feet are moving without me giving them the proper instruction.

He gets out of the car and stands there, looking at me blankly, like he's in shock. His hand rests on the roof of the car. "What just happened? And how are you going to get around? This is nuts. Shouldn't we just finish our drive?"

"I think I'll call an Uber," I say. "And then I'm going to fly home."

He looks down and then squints, looks over at the traffic on the freeway. "Are you going back to that . . . that guy? *Mason?*"

"I expect so."

"Is it because he's going to help you be famous? Because all I want is for you to be happy, you know. That's what I've wanted since I came back . . ."

"I think it's because he loves me. He really loves me."

I plunk my suitcase on the ground.

"What about Louise?" he says. "She's going to be so disappointed that we're not together."

"She's fine," I say. "I can't live Louise's life for her. I've been doing that for too long and it hasn't worked for even one single second. She needs to see her mother living a full, regular life, with love and passion and all the rest of it."

"And what about me?" he says.

I turn and look at him. "Speaking as the Heartbreak Bunny, I'd like to offer you one piece of advice. You're grieving, Victor. Your wife just died, and you packed up your stuff and came running back to me. You're in no shape for love or moving on or anything else. You need to go write about a thousand poems and feel all your feelings."

"I think maybe you don't know what you're talking about," he says.

"Good-bye, Victor Steidley. I have to say it feels a little bit good to be leaving you before you got the urge to leave me again. Because this was always unsustainable."

"I wasn't going to leave this time," he says. "You're just getting revenge from when I left you before. Even though I've apologized for that and tried to make things right. Why are you being unforgiving now?"

"Bye," I say.

∽

The Uber driver comes long after Victor has gone.

By then I've called Mason. Calvin said to me once that love is like a blinding white light, a beacon that calls you forward. You almost don't have a choice but to feel its power. When you know, you know. It actually takes a monumental effort to push it away, he said.

I didn't know what he was talking about. That light was slow in coming for me, peeking around corners and getting in through the cracks while I closed my eyes to it. Funny how now all I can think about is Mason and all the moments we've had: when I first met him at Joey's house when I was doing the chant and opened my eyes to see him there; then Mason at the diner with his smooth talk and his kind eyes; Mason so friendly and competent at the television station—and then (I have to close my eyes for this) all the moments of him lying in bed next to me, tracing his fingers along my hip bone or kissing my eyelids. And then Mason in the sad, empty bedroom he'd shared with Tish, in tears and devastated by the fact that he was telling her good-bye once and for all.

I now know that's what healing looks like.

"Listen," I say when he answers, "please don't hang up. This is a woman who has been a big idiot, and I realize that you may not want to talk to me, but I have to tell you a big epiphany that I just had, which is that I love you."

I hear him take a sharp intake of breath, so I start talking faster.

"I'm not one for dramatic gestures of this nature—so please just listen and don't hang up. I miss you . . . and I don't know if you are in the mood to forgive me for everything, but if you would be willing to hear me out, I think I could show you where in my thinking I went wrong. And when I get back home to Connecticut, I can promise you some crab cakes. Ones that we would actually eat, and then maybe we could go get some coconut cream pie, and then go lie in a bed somewhere for about a week."

There is a silence, during which I gaze at all the people at the rest stop. They all seem so purposeful, determined, even if they're just hurrying to the restroom or standing in line to buy something from the vending machine. They all look like they know exactly what they're doing. But I've learned enough about people recently to realize that I can't be the only person in the whole place with a heart that's one big gooey mess.

"Are you still there?" I say. "Did we get disconnected?"

He laughs. Maybe it's the laugh that means *is this woman out of her mind?* or maybe it's the kind of laughter that appreciates the weirdness of life.

"Where the hell are you right now?" he says. "It sounds like you're in an airline terminal. Is this one of those airport epiphanies we see in the movies?"

"This is a rest area epiphany, outside Watsonville, California, and a whole bus just drove up and spilled out about a billion tourists who are all clamoring for restrooms and gum, and I'm alone here without even a car, but I'm going to get an Uber and go to the airport, and . . ."

"Wait. Where's Victor?"

"Oh, Mason, so much has changed. I kicked him out. It's such a long story and it's so ridiculous, even by the standards of somebody like me who makes her living listening to nutty epiphanies. A woman called the radio station, and then I saw things I hadn't seen before, and it's wonderful and terrible all at once. Something astrological or astronomical must be happening. We should probably read our horoscopes or look up the phase of the moon. Something in the universe has shifted, that's for sure. Louise has decided not to be with Leo anymore, even though he now wants them to live together again. She's going to live in a house with her friend Hildy, and they're going to raise their babies together. In chaos, I'm sure. We'll have to see how that works out for her, but what the hell? We all have to figure things out."

"Oh, Billie, you're talking way too fast. Come home."

"The thing is, I was wrong about so much."

"It's okay. Come home and we'll sort it out."

"Okay," I say. I close my eyes.

"And, Billie?" he says.

"What?"

"I love you so crazy much."

⌒

This is how I know it might be true: he meets me at the airport right in the baggage claim area. Only people who love someone would park and venture into the baggage claim area, and he has flowers and balloons. Which, it's funny, even as recently as two days ago, if I'd seen this at a baggage claim area, I would have described it as your basic, worst over-the-top love nightmare.

Trying too hard, I would have said.

Overcompensating for a lack of true feeling.

Showing off.

But here he is, and he comes over and kisses me, and then I grab him and kiss him back, and pretty soon we're in one of those ridiculous, showy, Hollywood kisses and people standing nearby applaud, and I don't even mind.

I'm fine with this.

"I have to warn you that I think I'm probably going to want to marry you," I say once we've got my bag and are headed to the parking lot. "I don't want to scare you or anything by proposing marriage to you right here in the airport. And I'm not a good risk, numbers-wise. This will be marriage number four for me. Two previous divorces and a death. Your friends will probably warn you against me. And—oh, Mason, I've got to give you fair warning: our house will have a lot of people in it, so I hope that's okay. Joey is welcome to be one of them—"

"No, God no."

"And maybe Louise, although I don't think so somehow. But Calvin has to come back. And we'll cook and have Martini Thursday, although it can really be on any night. I love music and making dinner together. And art projects. I might decoupage the cabinets one more time. I mean, unless you object."

"Tell me something," he says. He has stopped walking and is smiling into my eyes and holding on to me tightly.

"What?"

"Did they give you the high-octane coffee on the plane?"

He kisses me again, longer and softer this time.

No one applauds. I like this silent way better. This way I can hear the beating of my heart, and when I open my eyes, I see that the world seems to be throwing off little colored spangles of happiness. That's how it feels, like stars everywhere, on just an ordinary Tuesday afternoon.

I can breathe again, sinking against Mason as he opens the car door and helps me in.

When he slides into the driver's seat, I say, "I'm still the Heartbreak Bunny, you know. And I'm going to write a book. I'm the Heartbreak Bunny who now believes in love. We'll have to figure out how to explain that."

"I can explain it," he says.

EPILOGUE

So, I have to tell you what happened. It's a year later, and I'm thinking about Louise and me.

It's a funny thing about mothers and daughters.

All this time, I thought she and I were opposite.

I mean, I always thought I was constitutionally, temperamentally, even *clinically* unable to keep the house clean or to appreciate what she once called the "joy of all the labels facing front in a cabinet and all the forks nesting in the same direction in the drawer." I don't feel peace gazing at a room that's all beige and gray and white. I don't pine for silences and solitude and ironed shirts and square corners and pots and pans without a speck of baked-on stuff on them.

And she—almost since she was a baby, I saw how she craved not-talking above talking, and order above disorder. She has always had projects that she tackles head-on, with her head down and her lips pursed, and her jaw stuck in a position of determination. She has always liked lists. She likes folding things. I have seen the unadulterated joy on her face as she stacks paper bags in the pantry so that none of the edges stick out. She wanted one-on-one friendships while I craved a crowded table with everyone talking at once.

She liked spotless.

I loved chaos.

But something strange has happened in the past year.

First, me.

I'm getting married next weekend to Mason. Yeah, it turns out that you can be in love after sixty-one. And that there's such a thing as romance working out. Who knew? We're getting married in Edgerton Park, a low-key thing, unlike my other weddings, which were big and splashy, as though I was overcompensating for a lack of feeling. At least that's what the psychic I'm seeing thinks. She says Mason and I were connected over lifetimes—and that my granny was leading us to one another.

And okay, I'm writing a book about the whole thing and how you don't have to be miserable when love leaves you, and how you can learn to trust yourself . . . and I'm doing a blog about that as well. People write to the Heartbreak Bunny, and I answer them—long, slow, thoughtful answers that feel as though they've been dictated to me from somewhere else.

And maybe they have.

Kat moved to Florida, where she has a thriving Heartbreak Bunny business. Bob may decide to move there soon, too, she says, to be with her. But he's weighing his options. In the meantime, she's doing a lot of Heartbreak Bunny calls every week. Turns out a ton of Floridians have broken hearts and are holding on to items that make them sad.

Bernice went to live with her daughter in Ohio. She and Calvin talk on the phone every day.

Calvin lives with us and is still in charge of deciding on the menu and the cocktails for Martini Thursday, and we still dress up for the occasion. Sometimes Marisol comes over, too, with her guy 2M. Marisol's Man. And Edwin stops by; he sometimes brings a couple of his girlfriend's kids and one or two of their dogs. He says he sneezes sometimes, but I've never seen him look happier.

And Louise.

My Louise.

She's living in a tumbledown house just two miles from us, right across the street from the park. It's a lot like our house when she was a child, come to think of it, filled with love and chaos and friends. Hildy and Cyril live there, too, and so does Miranda and a baby named Raphael, whom she's the foster mom for and whom she is in the process of trying to adopt. Phoebe is pregnant—the natural way. She says her body just one day said, *Oh, wait. This is what you wanted me to do?* And it proceeded to start creating a baby. She and her husband are looking to buy the house next door just so they can share the backyard plastic pool and the kiddie slide, I think.

Louise's daughter, Melody, is six months old and has giant blue eyes like Louise's and blonde silky hair like Leo's. She babbles all the time and laughs out loud when I play peekaboo with her.

And the house—oh, that house! It's filled with noise and baby stuff everywhere. There are dolls and plastic blocks, magic sleep suits and wooden trains, rubber giraffes that squeak, board books, plastic spoons, sippy cups, windup music boxes, light-up plastic pianos, swirling color wheels, baby food grinders, dog-eared books about parenting, baby bottles of every size, sterilizers, bottle warmers, blow-up baby bathtubs, strollers and car seats and baby carriers, onesies, night-lights, video cameras that watch the baby sleep, baby seats that jiggle and play songs, and a rubber apparatus that covers the faucet in the bathtub to keep babies from bumping their heads.

You can't see the floor for all this paraphernalia, I tell you. But seeing the floor is overrated, according to Louise. She said I always told her that, and she didn't believe me. But now that she's a mother, she's done a big one-eighty on chaos. Or so she says. Sometimes I see her looking at the sticky fingerprints on the dishwasher, and I know she longs to wipe them clean.

So, here's a surprise: I do it for her. Having things straightened up around the house is my new skill.

And here's the thing that's the most surprising to me: Louise is doing a new blog and Instagram feed. It's called Babies Ate My Brain, and she writes and photographs it all. No holds barred. Authenticity shines through, in its bleary-eyed, puffy-faced, uncombed, unmade-up state.

Authentic as all get-out, as she puts it.

Leo stops by when he's in town. He's a photojournalist working overseas, so he's not around a whole lot. Hildy's ex comes by to see his son and to report on how unhappy he is with the neighbor he left Hildy for. It didn't work out so well after all.

That's the love business, though, isn't it? It ebbs and flows. The heart goes where it thinks it should go, and sometimes it has to beat a hasty retreat back to safety.

Victor lives in New York, but he comes often to visit Louise and Melody. You'd think he'd never seen a baby before, the way he loves this one. I still don't know if he's going to stick around for the long haul. He's a runner, as we know. And he gets bored by domestic life.

But for now, it's enough.

Oh, and Joey has a new love. He says he's going to be more careful with his heart this time, but I gave him my best piece of advice—in the immortal words of Calvin, sometimes you've just got to take a leap of faith.

That's what all fifty of the bunnies in the new national Heartbreak Bunny franchise will tell you.

You don't have to stay stuck. Throw out all the baggage you don't need. Never, I tell them, let a neon-green python-print bra steal your happiness.

ACKNOWLEDGMENTS

The day a sixty-year-old woman showed up in my head, claiming that she wanted to eliminate people's heartbreak by dressing up in a bunny costume and removing objects from their homes—well, let's just say it was a very strange day, indeed.

I FaceTimed my friend Beth Levine and told of her this alarming development. A character was harassing me with what could only be a story of such weirdness that no one would ever take it seriously. Why couldn't I be visited by a character with a little more . . . gravitas?

Fortunately, Beth did what she always does. She laughed and talked me into at least listening to whatever this character had to say. In the background, I could see Beth's husband, Bill Squier, hopping back and forth, with his hands folded, bunny-style, underneath his chin.

I wrote the first chapter that day, and Billie the Heartbreak Bunny was born.

My editor at Lake Union, Jodi Warshaw, instantly saw the possibilities and said she couldn't wait to read it.

Well! What was there to do but put aside my doubts and get to work?

Kerry Schafer, my friend and consultant in All Things Having to Do with Books (particularly quirky ones), read drafts again and again, even though she's got about a million other things to tend to, including writing her own brilliant books.

I also have to thank Kim Steffen and Nancy Antle for reading early versions. Kim did a vital copyedit when it needed it most. Leslie Connor listened to plot points over and over again. And members of my writing workshop—Thea Guidone, Mary Ann Emswiler, Marcia Winter, Grace Pauls-Ritchie, Sharon Wise, and Robin Favello—devoted hours of our workshop time into helping me bring the characters to life.

As always, I owe a debt of gratitude to Alice Mattison, my oldest friend in New Haven from back when we had toddlers together, and who talks plots with me over sushi once a month at our favorite Japanese place. And to Jennifer Smith Kleinsasser, the funniest of my relatives and who shares with me (and the Heartbreak Bunny) the idea that the world is a stranger and quirkier place than we ever suspected.

Thank you also to Deborah Hare and Linda Balestracci, who taught English to all three of my kids and became dear friends. Lots of love to Diane Cyr for forty years of friendship, during which we ran a weekly newspaper together, and to Marji Lipshez-Shapiro for lunches when we dissect human nature and come up with no conclusions whatsoever, except that we have to have more fun in life. Barbara Shulman outfits me with marvelous glass earrings with magical powers and accompanies me on walks that always turn out to be astonishingly productive. I run to my desk to write after talking to her!

I'm sending a big thank-you to Connie Combs Fitch, a producer at the local TV station, who helped me see a little bit more of what Mason Davis's job entailed. She's also been generous about inviting me to come on the noon show over the years and talk about writing.

There aren't enough thank-yous in the world for the team at Lake Union who help make my books come out into the world. Your attention to detail, your belief in me, your gentle guidance and careful editing make this such a fun process. Thank you to Jodi, who gave this book a thorough developmental edit, and to my new Lake Union editor, Alicia Clancy, who adopted this book far into the process and has helped make it her own baby, too. And as always, to my fellow authors who create such a fun community and are always ready to offer suggestions and help.

Nancy Yost, my agent, has been unfailingly generous and helpful over the years. She is always on my side, and holds my hand through all the phases of publishing a book.

Next, I couldn't do this work without the love and support of my family, particularly my husband, Jim Shelton, who has all too often been asked to act out scenes from my books while I'm writing them—and does it! My children, Ben, Allie, and Stephanie, give me happiness every single day, as do the partners they have wisely brought into our family: Amy, Mike, and Alex. There are no words for the joys of grand-parenting. Charlie, Josh, Miles, Emma, and Mila, you all have my heart.

And lastly, a huge thank-you to all the readers who have bought my books over the years and have sent me notes and reviews and told me how my words have touched you. You have meant the world to me.

ABOUT THE AUTHOR

Photo © 2018 Dan Mims

Maddie Dawson grew up in the South, born into a family of outrageous storytellers. Her various careers as a substitute English teacher, department-store clerk, medical-records typist, waitress, cat sitter, wedding-invitation-company receptionist, nanny, day care worker, electrocardiogram technician, and Taco Bell taco maker were made bearable by thinking up stories as she worked. Today Maddie lives in Guilford, Connecticut, with her husband. She's the bestselling author of eight previous novels: *The Magic of Found Objects, A Happy Catastrophe, Matchmaking for Beginners, The Survivor's Guide to Family Happiness, The Opposite of Maybe, The Stuff That Never Happened, Kissing Games of the World,* and *A Piece of Normal.* For more information visit www.maddiedawson.com.